MANNIGAN

MANNIGAN

A Speck of Light

L. Ross Coulter

Special thanks to:
Rory, my beautiful wife.
Sadb, my darling daughter.
Larry Contreau.
Prairie (the cat)
&
Ross Ake, AKA The Mix Curator
(youtube.com/@TheMixCurator)

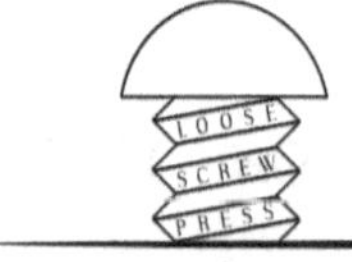

Published by Loose Screw Press, 2023
Mannigan - A Speck of Light
ISBN 978-1-7384407-0-2

Text © L. Ross Coulter
Cover design © Loose Screw Press
Illustrations © L. Ross Coulter & Loose Screw Press
All rights reserved.

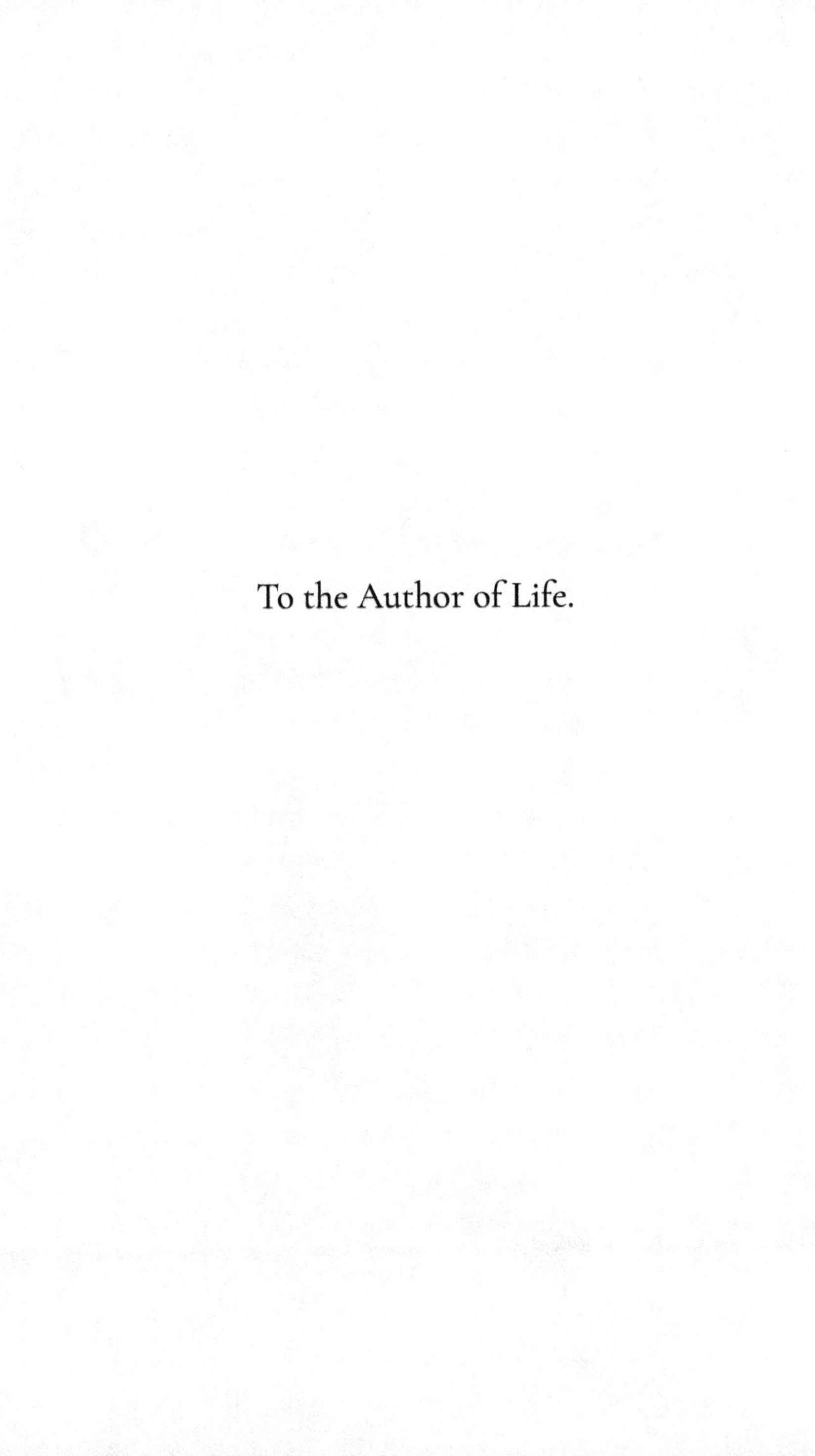

To the Author of Life.

CONTENTS

Maps. 2

Prologue – In The Beginning 7

Chapter 1 – Prisoner Number 52398. 11

Chapter 2 – A Bright White Room. 17

Chapter 3 – The Proselyte. 21

Chapter 4 – Toward The Ark. 41

Chapter 5 – His Name Is Mannigan. 57

Chapter 6 – The Gift. 69

Chapter 7 – Over The Wall. 77

Chapter 8 – The Sea Of Sand. .85

Chapter 9 – Desolation. 111

Chapter 10 – The Children Of Light. 131

Chapter 11 – Respite. 147

Chapter 12 – In The Hands Of Men. 167

Chapter 13 – The Palace Of Wish. 197

Chapter 14 – Katayoun. 221

Chapter 15 – Blood On The Sand. 237

Chapter 16 – The Weeping City Of Sorrow. 267

Chapter 17 – To The Ends Of The World. 297

Chapter 18 – The Valley Of Slaughter.. 307

Chapter 19 – Prepare For War. 325

Chapter 20 – Wrath. 333

Chapter 21 – A Place Of Darkness. 345

Chapter 22 – I Will Repay 353

Chapter 23 – A Speck Of Light 367

MAPS

Map of Greater Zeno
The Mountains of Mourn
The Sea of Sand
The
Confluence
Desolation City
Industrial Sector
Eden
ZENO CITY
Agricultural Corridor
Siege Wall
The River Jordan
Neourbia
Energy District
Libertaria
Siege Wall
Neourbia
Libertaria
The Praetorium
New Boston
Militarist Vanguard
Hetaeki
Citadel of Abundance
Ensenada
Northern Ribbon
The Epicurean Ocean

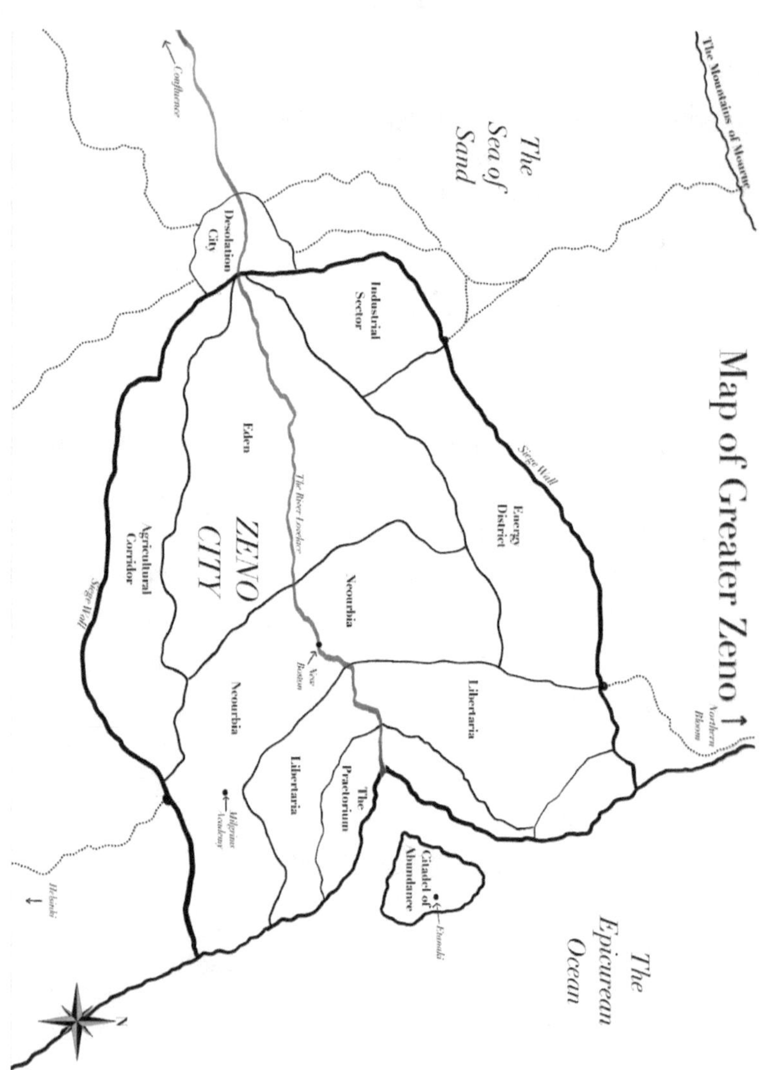

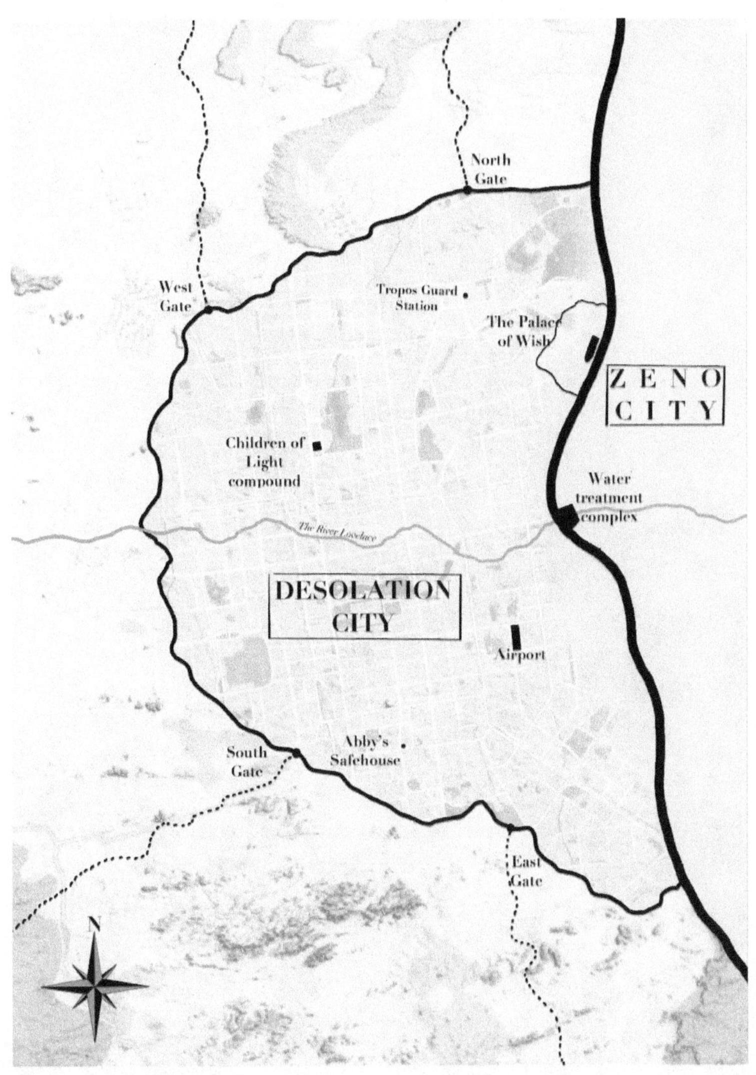

North
Gate
West
Gate
Tropos Guard
Station
The Palace
of Wish
ZENO
CITY
Children of
Light
compound
Water
treatment
complex
The River Lovelace
DESOLATION
CITY
Airport
Abby's
Safehouse
South
Gate
East
Gate
N

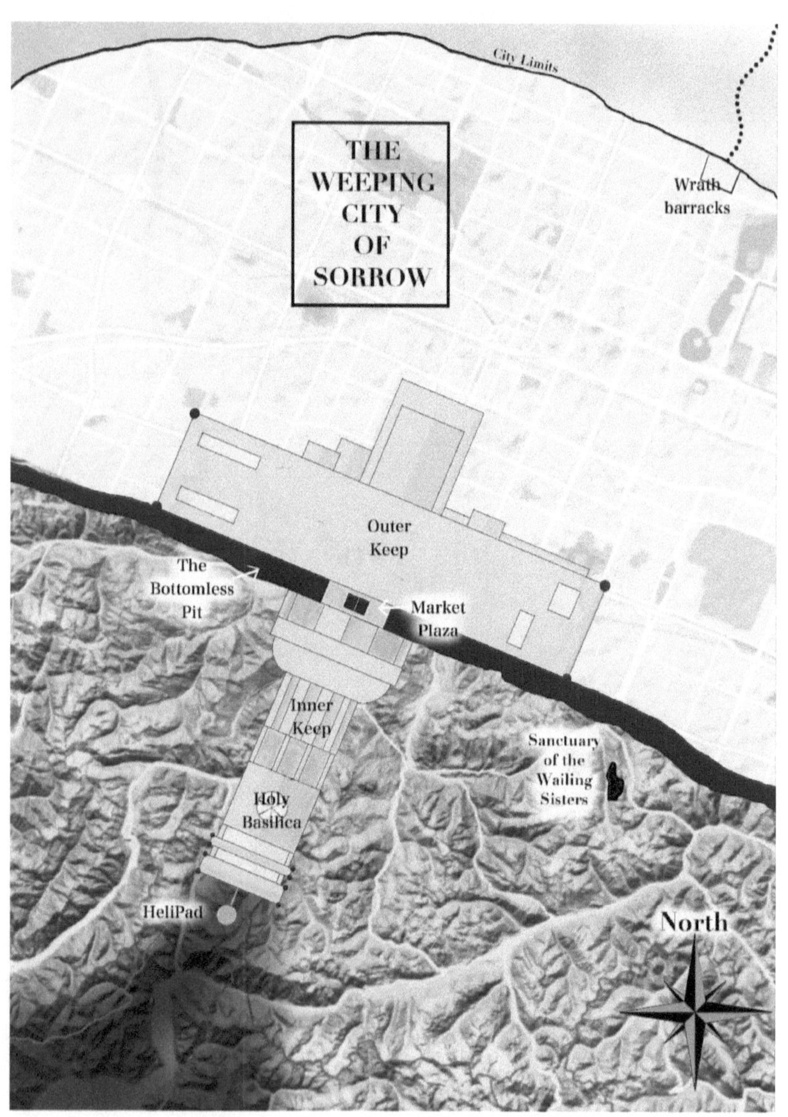

City Limits
THE
WEEPING
CITY
OF
SORROW
Wrath
barracks
Outer
Keep
The
Bottomless
Pit
Market
Plaza
Inner
Keep
Sanctuary
of the
Wailing
Sisters
Holy
Basilica
HeliPad
North

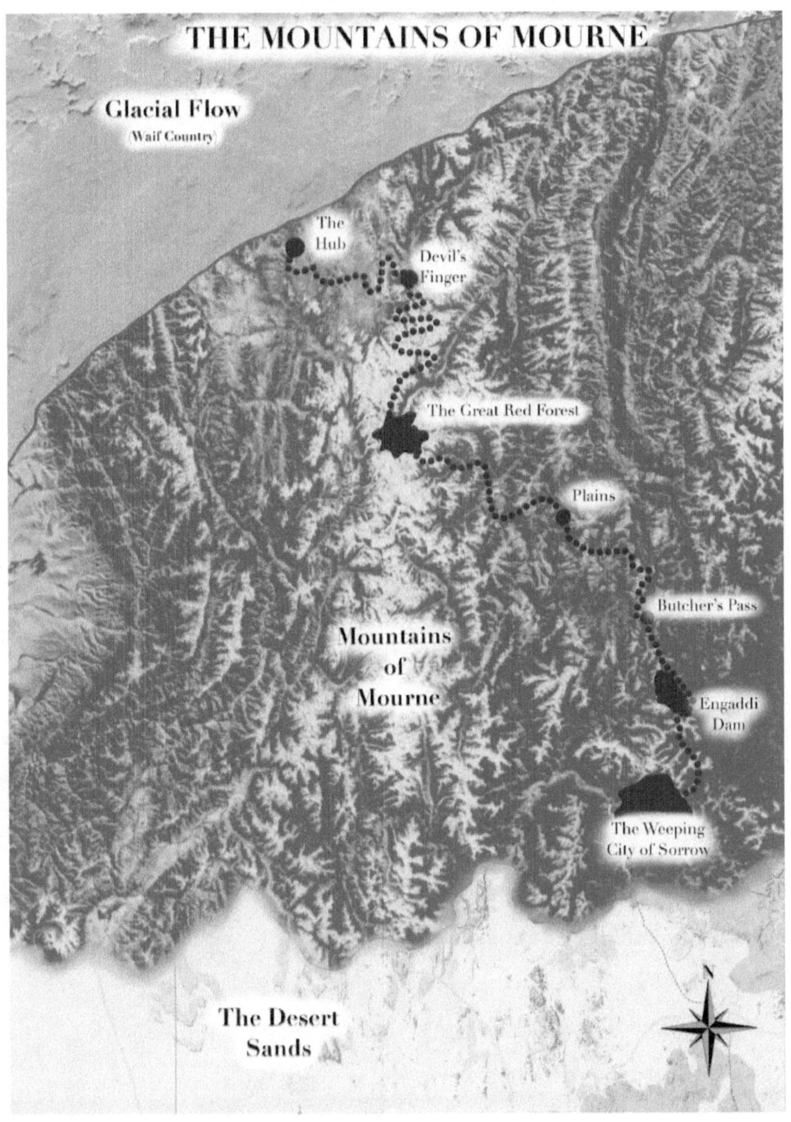

THE MOUNTAINS OF MOURNE
Glacial Flow
(Waif Country)
The Hub
Devil's Finger
The Great Red Forest
Plains
Mountains of Mourne
Butcher's Pass
Engaddi Dam
The Weeping City of Sorrow
The Desert Sands

Prologue

IN THE BEGINNING

When the first one struck the earth, it was already too late. For the fear unleashed by the news of their sighting unlocked the gates of war; and mankind loosed a hell of his own creation.

When the last one struck the earth and the seas subsided, flames calmed to embers and the ground shook no more. But fueled by an ocean of fire that spewed out from the depths, suffocating the shame of a trillion evil deeds done, an endless black cloud of dust encompassed the earth.

So as the grass withered, the flowers fell, and their beauty perished.

From what remained, survivors rose, and a new hope was born. A transcendent being. An enlightened mind. A man. Who, in great wisdom and boundless mercy, came so that he could give.

First, for the suffering of the earth, he gave the engines. Ten in all, each pierced a hole in the blackened sky, and where the earth again received day's light, life began to grow.

Then, for the suffering of the flesh, he gave the cities. Of these there were seven, one of each where life had been restored, and as his people grew beneath his wing, a hundred million sons and daughters were reborn.

Yet, still seeing much suffering in the depths of the mind, he wept, grieving their forms and how they had been made to be. So, as his final gift, he gave the Servant. Elegant and graceful, his greatest work, she was perfect; a sentience without measure. And draped like a web of white charmeuse across the cities, she gave her will to the salvation of man's torment.

"To you, O' mighty Vitruvius, architect of mankind; we give thanks."

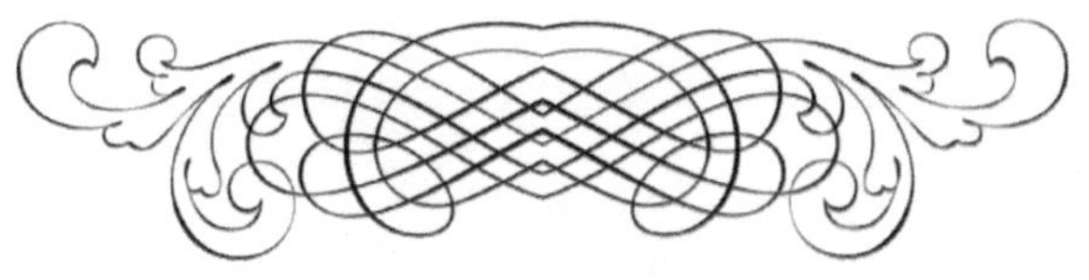

Feel the raindrops,
Dancing with grace.
Descending in final violence,
As they softly kiss your face.
Smell the fresh chaos,
Like you've smelled it before.
please let me in,
when I knock on your door.
Soon it is quiet,
Balance returned.
Order restored,
atonement confirmed.
You will let me in,
as I have been here before,
we wept together,
huddled on the kitchen floor.
Once I am in,
let us wipe clean the page,
I am your deafening silence.
I am your rage.

Chapter 1

PRISONER NUMBER 52398

Thick with the incessant crawl of a million mechanical motions, the air chatters with their sounds. It is hot. Humid. Legs and arms are outstretched, his ankles and wrists are held by cold metal braces. Not quite standing or being suspended, he is hanging somewhere between; not in pain, but not in comfort.

Ahead of him, a man is held the same way as he, and ahead of him again, another. And another and another. Each encompassed by a large metal band that tethers the extended limbs of their naked bodies.

Some burrowing beneath their skin, a twisted web of wires runs across their wretched forms, like starving serpents searching for a meal. And gazing down his own withered body past a band of tubes spewing from his nose and mouth, he sees their vicious tendrils wrapped around him.

He tries to scream, but through his stuffed throat and gaping jaws, nothing more than a shrill gurgle emanates. Eyes watering, he scans around in panic as his stomach knots in dread. Line after line, row after row, level after level; all he can see are splayed naked bodies, each captive within a metal band of their own, feeding and being fed. Endless aisles of perishable human product, stacked and preserved meticulously in a ghastly display of incomparable utility.

Connected by a labyrinth of glass walkways and elevators, hooded figures clothed in sterile white coveralls amble about their business. And as he stares at the huge letters sprawled across the concrete expanse that reads, 'STANFORD CORRECTIONS FACILITY' in faded yellow words, he knows it is not a dream.

He remembers, although not with clarity, the day his parents didn't come home. He stayed up late that night. Making an ungodly mess of the kitchen floor, he ate cereal from the bag, before washing it down with a mug of lumpy hot chocolate. Before, comforted by the faint odor of his mother's perfume from her soft sweater under his head, he held his teddy and fell asleep on the couch.

When morning came, he was woken by the doorbell ringing. Hoping to see their familiar faces, he rushed to the window and looked out through the curtains.

A thin couple stood on the porch, a man and a woman. And as the woman saw his movement at the window, she looked up smiling, and waved. Down the stairs, and stretching on his tippy toes to reach the latch, he opened the door to them.

"William, good morning!" the man said cheerily, adorned in a crisp pinstriped blue suit, with a matching tie and a white high-collared shirt.

Crouching down to him, and giving a friendly little wave, the woman smiled. "Hi there!" she said.

She was pretty, like his mom, with her golden hair loosely tied at the back and red lips that matched her long sleeved suit jacket and elegant slim formed dress. But her eyes were strange. Although in no way detracting from her beauty, they were different; one with tones of green and blue like a beautiful tropical fish, and the other, with a powdered gray pupil and an iris of midnight black.

"Hi," he replied, feeling a pang of caution and clutching his teddy tighter.

"My friend and I are with the Vitruvian social services," the woman spoke again. "And today, we have some good news for you!" Looking at Will with an air of expectation she paused, as if waiting for him to respond in excitement. "Don't you want to know what it is?"

He remembered hearing his parents talk about them and their strange eyes. About how glamorous and proper they were, and how kind they all seemed. He remembered too about how they weren't to be trusted. But they were not what he had imagined, certainly much nicer than he expected.

"Are you, Kol?" he asked.

"Well aren't you a funny one?!" she replied with a giggle. "Of course we are dear, how else would we know where to find you! But never mind that! Don't you want to know what the good news is? No?. . . Well, I'll tell you anyway! Yesterday your mommy and daddy were invited into beautiful Libertaria on official business. Nothing for you to worry about of course, boring grown up stuff mostly. But while you wait, it means that you get to go all the way to the other side of Neourbia and spend a few days in Boston! Isn't that wonderful! We have a special place there, just for kids just like you."

"Can't I stay here till they come back?"

"By yourself! Oh, no silly! Our job is to keep you safe. And we certainly can't do that here!" Wrinkling her nose in distaste, she glanced over his shoulder into the hall. "But don't worry, where we're taking you is a marvelous place – made by the great architect himself, bless his generous soul. You'll have so much fun and make lots of friends. And of course," she continues, gesturing to the stuffed teddy in his arms, "you can bring your friend Jeff there with you! Now, give me your hand and let's be off. The car is waiting."

With a gentle calmness in her eyes and a warm smile in the corner of her mouth, she offered her delicate hand, and grabbing it, he followed her down the steps toward a gleaming white vehicle parked on the street.

Curved and sleek with dark shaded windows, the rear door was already open, but approaching a row of stern Malleus soldiers that waited with their weapons raised at the house, he stopped in his tracks. On top of eight slender titanium legs with a metallic body littered by bulbous sensors, a spidered machine stood behind them. And as its mounted weapons and claws twitched and flickered in spasmodic bursts, it watched his every move.

"Oh don't worry about him!" the woman exclaimed, as she noticed his hesitation. "A silly old Arakhna like him is only interested in flies! You're not a fly are you?!

Will shook his head, and giving him a knowing grin as she pulled him along, they continued to the vehicle.

"Mind your head now," she said, as Will stepped in.

"Good morning William," an automated voice rang out. "Your destination today is the Milgram Academy. Please take a seat and choose what you would like for entertainment on your journey."

He remembered the softness of the plush fabric as he sat down and the bright and cheerful images dancing across the screens on the seat in front. But it was the sound he remembered the most. And as the door began to close and the harsh bark of the soldiers' commands cracked like whips in the air, he remembered the mechanical whir of robotic legs as men and machine stormed up the driveway and disappeared into the house.

*　　*　　*

With a shudder, the metallic band he is held within begins moving upward. But with a jolt, it turns sideways to slide parallel to the rows of the other captive bodies. Silently picking up speed, hollow faces flicker past in front of him, bloated and flared in the mechanical nest that coils around their shriveled anatomies. With eyes closed, they almost seem at peace. But then, as he sees terror and tears streaming down a sunken face, his heart sinks, as one, not sleeping like the rest, looks back.

A sudden bump rattles his body as his mechanized captor stops and changes direction. Upward now, propelled into the darkness above, he strains his neck to lift his head. And as the momentum of the machine slows he passes up into a room through the floor.

Rotated backward, blinded by a searing bright light, a hatch slides closed beneath his feet. Faced by a long strip of neon lights suspended from the ceiling, he flinches as a voice echoes in his ears.

"Manning — William," it announces. "Prisoner number 5-2-3-9-8, please confirm."

"Copy, 52398," a different voice resounds in response.

"Disconnect, scrub, and discharge. He's out of here."

"Copy that."

A masked face looms over him and a rubber gloved hand on his forehead stretches his eyelids back. Blinded, a burning sting of a bright red light flashes into his eyes. "Welcome back. 52398. You are not forgotten."

From behind, several metal arms extend around him with claw-like appendages on their ends. Hovering over his body in careful motion they examine him, first poking and prodding before, with a candid chirp, he is engulfed in a mist of frigid water. Shockwaves coursing through his bones, the sounds of motors and machines whine shrill in the air as the tubes in his skin are pulled free. With a wave of torment, pressure turns to pain, and ripping at his back and stomach with deliberate purpose the foreign bodies are wrenched from his flesh. Desperate gurgles and screams involuntarily spewing from his throat, every muscle and sinew spasms. And with each twitch and tremor, he drifts further away.

Chapter 2

A BRIGHT WHITE ROOM

As if glued shut, his eyes are heavy. Struggling to move, a hand holds him still on the bed.

"Call the doc and get him down here!"

A shimmer of light blinds him as faint outlines of figures move around a bright white room.

"Will? Can you hear me?" A woman's voice. "Try to stay still. You're going to be alright."

"Marissa," he forces the word out, but barely a noise emanates past his dry, cracked lips. His body aches as he tries to move.

"Don't talk. Just stay still. Please!"

"Marissa," he gasps, struggling to sit up. More hands grab him, firmer now, forcing him down.

"Please Will, just stay still! Where's the doc?!"

"I'm here, I'm here!" Another voice, a man's this time, slightly out of breath. Will can sense hurried movement around him.

"Will, can you hear me? I'm Doctor Barkoba. We need you to stay still! You're going to be alright but we need you to help us. Please Will! — Abby, 2mg of midazolam, quick as you can, he's going into shock — Breathe Will, it's going to be ok. We've got you."

The pinch of a needle biting into his arm, Will is engulfed in a tingling warmth. Releasing his arms and stepping back, the silhouetted figures of the doctor and the woman are faint, but as the light of the room becomes more bearable his mind slows.

Nineteen or twenty perhaps, in light blue scrubs, she is not much older than him, and with a strawberry blond ponytail, her forehead is wrinkled in concern and pale cheeks flushed. Next to her, with a crisp, white overcoat, a thin weathered man sporting a pair of neat round glasses studies him, before, taking a step closer, he sits down on the small bedside seat. "Abby, pass me the water," he says.

Feeling the end of a little plastic straw on his lips Will sips. It hurts. But cool on his swollen throat, it's a gentle relief as he swallows.

"Slowly now, too much will make you sick."

"Where am I?" The words quietly slip out of Will's mouth.

"You're in the Halfpenny rehabilitation center at Saint Juliana's," the doctor replies. "But don't worry, you're safe. We've had you for quite a while. You were sent to us from Stanford prison a few months back. You have been in a coma ever since."

As the words ring in Will's ears, it doesn't seem real.

"Marissa," he whispers with dread, as if the mere utterance of her name may make the answer shrouded by the haze of his foggy mind a sudden reality. "Please, where is she?"

"Marissa?" Glancing down at the screen in his hand, the doctor pauses for a moment before looking back up to Will's forlorn gaze with his kind dark eyes. "I'm sorry Will, I. . . I don't know how much you remember, but she's gone."

Will is cold. He can hear his heart racing in his ears. Flashes of borrowed moments flicker through his mind. The first moment their eyes met. Her smile and the feeling of her hand in his. When his world had burst into color and filled his head with simple dreams of a happy home filled with the pattering of little feet. Her long dark hair and then, the light blue headscarf she wore to cover its absence when she lost it. Her cold skin. Her casket. And the surge of summer rain that danced on its top as it was lowered into the earth. It was true, he could feel it, but as if a sullied dream, it felt as if it had never really happened. Yet suddenly washed by a flood of memory's pain, he sinks beneath a world torn apart.

"Breathe Will," the doctor continues, as a machine by the bed begins to beep in distress. "Just breathe. You're going to be alright."

His chest aches, his fingers are numb.

"Please Will!"

The machine's squealing rises.

"Dammit! He's going to hurt himself! Give him another dose. Put him under."

Flinching at another sting in his arm he is washed by a wave of sudden darkness. The shrill panic in his head slipping into dampened tremors, engulfed in silence he slumps back into the sheets.

But then he sees it. At the window, more specter than creature; the shadowed form of a black raven. Its wings spread open and head pointed to the early morning sky, its silken feathers glisten like oil under the golden gaze of the early morning sun. Thunder rumbling from the heavens, it leaps from the ledge, and as Will slips into the abyss, it rises into the new day.

Chapter 3

THE PROSELYTE

The sound of curtains being drawn wakes him as sunlight streaks into the sterile white room.

"Morning Will, how are you today?" Abby chirps. Pressing a button just out of sight, a motorized buzz beneath him raises the bed, leaving him propped as he groggily looks around.

"Sorry to wake you," she continues, "but Doctor Barkoba said he'd be down to see you, so I thought I'd get you up — Sit forward for a sec will you?"

Will obliges, and after taking the pillow from behind him, she switches it out with a new one she has on the bedside table.

"How are you feeling today?" she asks. Smiling at him with a hint of concern, she glimpses at the shadowed scars and dotted punctures that dash across his limbs and pallid face. "Do you think you're up to eating yet? I can bring you a light breakfast if you're ready?"

"Ok," he shrugs, his voice weak through his swollen throat. "I'll give it a try."

"Are you sure?"

"No," he gives her a pained smile. "But I've got to eventually, right?"

"That's the spirit," she grins. "Ok, give me a minute – I'll be right back."

Hurrying out of the room, Will is left alone with his thoughts. He liked her. It had only been a few days, but she had a way about her that somehow seemed to make things a little easier. His limp body ached with even the slightest movement and every draining motion seemed to deplete him further still. Yet whether giving a gentle hand as he winced to climb out of bed, or lending an arm as he hobbled to the bathroom at the end of the corridor, her presence always came with a patient smile. Time alone was agony. His mind was foggy but always returned to thoughts of Marissa and the things that would never be, so Abby's visits were a welcome reprieve. There was another nurse too, a large stern woman— 'Lillian Albut' by the title on her nametag—but coming in only to take blood samples and scan him, she hardly said a word.

"Here we are," Abby remarks, as she bustles in. Garnished with an assortment of breakfast items, she sets a metal tray down on a table in the corner of the room, before wheeling it over to the bed. "Just for tasting though. If you're hungry, we can get you more later. But for now, only a little. It's been a long time since you've had anything solid. You'll need to give your body time to adjust."

Despite the lingering odor of disinfectant, it smells amazing and realizing the call of hunger, Will straightens up as she swivels a section of the table around and parks the food over his lap.

Seeing his weak hands fumble with the packaged utensils, Abby takes them from him.

"Here, let me," she says, sitting down on the bed beside him before opening them and handing him a fork.

"Sorry. Thanks."

"No, not at all. You have healed amazingly, but you'll be pretty weak for some time."

"Yeah, I've been better," he replies, mustering a half-hearted smile. Pointing out the window to the courtyard below to where a group of uniformed teens are gathered, he continues, "I meant to ask — what's with all the students? Some kind of field trip?"

"Who? Them? Oh no. They're students here with Saint Juliana's."

"Saint Juliana's? The university?"

"Yeah, of course. Sorry, I thought you were from around here."

"I am," he replies. "I've spent my whole life in Boston—well, down close to the tenements—but I never knew this place was a hospital. Thought it was just a school."

"Oh, well it is a school. It was all a hospital at one point but was replaced by Galton General across town when they built it years ago. Halfpenny house here is the only medical part left. The rest became the school. It's a cool building actually, I can give you a tour when you're feeling up to it—in a chair, of course!"

"Sure, I've got nothing else on that I know of," he winces through a pained grin.

"You don't need to check your schedule?" she laughs. "I'll have to check with the doc first before we do anything, but it should be fine. I'm sure it would be nice to move around a bit. You've been cooped up for ages. Oh, and hey, before I forget, now that you're feeling a little better, is there someone we can contact for you? We tried looking through records when you got here first, but nothing seemed to come up."

"No," Will replies, giving a slight shake of his head as he puts the fork on the tray. "I'm ok. Thanks though."

"Well, no worries. If you change your mind of course, let me know, but the world outside isn't going anywhere anytime soon. We'll get you better first! Anyway, are you done with that?" she asks, glancing at his barely touched meal.

"Yeah, thanks. It's making me feel a bit funny."

"That's ok, you got more down than I expected. There's a whole lot of drugs in your system. If you can get it to stay there you're doing well."

Looking up as there is a knock on the open door, doctor Barkoba walks in carrying a clipboard in hand.

"Will, how are you," he asks, crossing over to the bedside. "I'm sorry I haven't been into you sooner. Your tests and paperwork took longer than I thought."

Pausing for a moment to sit on the edge of the bed, he takes a deep breath as he continues, "So, how are you? It's been a rocky road for you. But Abby's taking good care of you I assume. How are you feeling? You had a little breakfast?"

"Yeah," Will replies.

"Good. The food's not great I know, but it's not bad for a hospital. How about your pain? Are you comfortable?"

"I'm ok."

"Are you sure? And are you sleeping? We can adjust anything you need"

"No, really," Will shakes his head. "I'm fine. Thanks though."

"Well, that's good to hear. But do let me know if anything changes. And please, no thanks necessary. We're here to help."

"I will. Thanks."

Hesitating for a moment, the doctor looks over to Abby, "Abby, do you mind giving us a minute? I just want to run through a few things with Will."

With a knowing look Abby gives a little nod, and as she heads out the door, the doctor turns back to Will, "Look. I suppose helping you as best we can kind of leads me to the bigger issue I wanted to talk to you about. After what you have been through, for us to help you properly you need to make a decision about your next steps. And to do that, you need to know the truth."

"What do you mean?"

"About your time in Stanford, and your condition. . . I don't know the full details—we are not privy to that here—but based on the state of your body, I would say that after they put you in stasis you were likely sectioned under one of the common good laws. While you were in there. . ." Shuffling on the bed, he glances down at his hands. "They. . . They took nearly everything."

"I—I don't understand."

"Your organs. . . your parts. Most of what you have left are cheap biosynth replacements. Even your platelets and marrow have been harvested to almost nothing. And the toxicity report. . . You must have been part of at least a dozen pharmaceutical trials."

Will falls silent, his ears seem slightly hollow. "Why? What does that mean for me?"

"I don't know," he shakes his head. "I've been here for more than forty years and I have never seen so many procedures done on a single donor. What they've done to you, it's. . . It's a miracle you have survived so long. But realistically speaking, you're not going to live more than another four or five weeks."

"Weeks?" Will chokes out the words. "But I feel like I'm getting better?"

"I know, I know," Barkoba nods with a furrowed brow. "But that's just the drugs doing their job. It's not a treatment at all. If anything, at the doses you're on it's probably killing you faster. As your body deteriorates, the medication will become less effective. We can increase the dosage of course, but unfortunately, the higher the dose, the worse the side effects. I wish I had something better to tell you, but ultimately the choice for you—especially as you get closer to the end—is going to be between discomfort and consciousness."

Will listens to the words in silence.

"Will it hurt?" he whispers.

Barkoba sighs, "Well. . . that's the thing." Shifting in his seat as he lays his clipboard down on the bed. "If you don't want it to, it doesn't have to. We can, and will of course, keep you sedated as much as possible. But the pain you're feeling now is only going to get worse. And honestly, worse is an understatement." Reaching into his small chest pocket he pulls out a small white tablet between two fingers. "I won't pretend I understand what you've been through, or what you're going through, and I don't claim to have all the answers. But I have never believed in needless suffering or life without personal choice. So, however terrible it may be—and it is the last thing I ever wished to believe—but I believe that this is your choice." Placing the tablet gently on the bedside table, he gives Will a solemn glance. "And please, make no mistake, I am not saying that you should take it at all, I am simply offering you the choice. Do you understand?"

Will pauses to look at the little pill, so small it's almost invisible against its surroundings. "Is it painful?" he asks.

"No. Just like falling asleep."

"Can I think about it?"

"Of course. Take as long as you need. This is strictly between you and me. Whatever you decide it will stay that way. Alright? And Will, I know this is difficult, but just know that we are here to help you through this. You are not alone."

*　　*　　*

Will stares stunned out the window, as the room hangs in silence. Fleeting shadows of Marissa's whispered prayers haunt his mind. He had always wondered what the end would be like, but had never thought it would be like this. Wasting away to nothing in the company of strangers. What was the point? Where was the meaning?

Lost in his thoughts, he hardly notices as Abby returns and sits down beside him.

"Are you ok?" she says in a hush, resting her hand on his.

His words are just a whisper, "Did you know?"

"Yeah," she replies, "I'm sorry. I was not allowed to say anything until Barkoba had told you himself."

"It's fine. It's not your fault. I was just wondering."

Frozen for an awkward moment, she breaks the quiet, "Did you still want me to show you around?"

"Now?"

"Yeah. It might help take your mind off things. I can take you over to one of the campus buildings and maybe into the courtyard if it's not too cold. We could even go up to Barkoba's office. If it's clear enough, you can see the Etanaki out in the Citadel from up there. What do you think?"

"Ok," he answers with a defeated shrug, "Sure."

"That's the spirit. It'll make you feel better, I promise. Let me get your chair."

Rolling the wheelchair across the room and parking it beside the bed, she locks the wheels in place with the small foot lever. "You need a hand to get in?" she offers, as he slips his bony legs over the side of the bed.

"No thanks, I'll manage," he replies, mustering all his strength to slide off the sheets and lower himself into the chair.

"Hey Will?" She looks at him with kind eyes.

"Yeah?"

"I'm sorry for not telling you about. . ." she trails off and takes a breath. "If it was up to me, I'd have preferred to have been honest with you from the start, I would. This whole thing, it's . . . It's awful. I know you must feel—well, I mean— I can't imagine what you're going through, or what you've been through . . . but I'm so sorry."

Will could hear the sadness in her voice. She really cared.

"Thank you," he replies. "But it's fine, really. It was going to happen someday, right? Knowing the day doesn't change anything. Honestly, I don't know what I was living for anyway. Since my. . . Marissa—" he stops short, choking back the tears forming in his eyes as his voice trembles. "Life, for me, ended a long time ago."

For a moment Abby stares at his despondence, and as her eyes well up, she crouches down in front of him. "Look. I know we haven't known each other for long at all, and I can't imagine how you're feeling, but I believe everything happens for a reason—even this. And one reason I can see already is what you've given me. . . Even after all you've been put through, you're still a decent person. Most of the guys we get in here haven't been through half of what you have, and all they have left is anger and hate. But you—"

"You think my hate and anger is any less?!" he snaps, a sudden wave of anger exploding from the melancholic grip on his chest. "I have so much hate you couldn't know! You think I don't hate myself? For not doing more? Doing better? That I don't hate the people that could have helped, but didn't, because it was against the rules? The people that decide who's gonna live and who's gonna to die based on some arbitrary numbers in a program?! You think I'm better?! I'm not! I'm worse!—Far worse! I have so much anger and so much hate you have no idea! So much that it makes me sick! I feel I could burn the world to dust and let it swallow me whole and I wouldn't even care!!"

Without a word, Abby throws her arms around him and pulls him tight, pressing her soft warmth against his frail form. He resists at first, but as a deep pain within him releases, his body shudders as he sobs into her shoulder.

"I'm sorry," he sniffles, "I'm just tired."

"I know it mightn't feel like it," she says with a teary smile, pulling back from him and resting her hands on his, "but you're not alone in this."

"Thanks," he glances up at her as his shallow breaths return and his trembling shoulders settle. "For being so nice to me. I know you don't have to be." With a deep breath he steadies himself. "You couldn't be more different from the other nurse if you tried."

"Who? Lilian?" Abby says, looking at him, her cheeks rosy and eyes slightly red and watery. "Why? Did she do something?"

"Oh no, I'm sure she's nice. Just very serious, that's all."

"Well, with a name like 'All-butt', wouldn't you be a bit serious too?" she replies, a broken grin curving in the corner of her mouth.

"That's how you pronounce it?!" Will chokes out a laugh. "It is not?"

"It is," Abby nods, her face lighting up in a smile

"Seriously!? I've been calling her 'Lilian' just in case. But I didn't actually think. . . That's an unfortunate name to be carrying around!"

"And an unfortunate butt to be carrying around too!" she chuckles, relieved by the sudden change in mood as they both burst into laughter.

*　　*　　*

The building is quite modern, with traces of its real age only showing through in the figured craftsmanship of the heavy doors and ornate cornicing that encircles the perimeter of the ceilings. Clearly not the first tour she has given, as they meander down a series of corridors that lead away from the room, Abby pushes his wheelchair in a steady, practiced pace.

A rainbow-colored mosaic on the wall ahead indicates the entrance of a children's ward, and turning the corner, they are soon greeted by curious little faces. Some so preoccupied in games or books, do not seem to notice them as they pass, while others, with welcoming little grins, wave polite 'good mornings' before going about their business. One little girl, pulling a metal stand with a machine on top, stops her slow procession down the corridor to stick out her tongue as they pass. But as Abby gives a theatrical grimace of shock, the child's sullen air breaks into a big beaming smile.

Will smiles too, but in truth, it hurts to look at her. Although his perspective had changed since he met Marissa, he had often wondered if there was any wisdom in bringing new life into the world, knowing full well that it would be hammered to the point of destruction. The girl's pale skin and dark shadowed eyes are such a bleak contrast against the bright optimism brimming from her gentle spirit. Still suffering and hurting, but with such accepting grace. Not mired by bitterness or regret, just here, present . . . an angel on the earth if ever there was one.

At the end of the ward, a double door opens onto a large enclosed glass bridge. They are several floors up and the view of the enormous courtyard below is spectacular. Alive with a host of chirping birds oblivious to the world outside of their private paradise, it is dotted with large trees and decorative water features. Students, going about their day, sip coffee along lines of neat wooden benches, while others mill about laughing in jovial groups.

"So this takes us across from Halfpenny into Juliana's," Abby narrates. "There's another one on the west wing too. You can always cross through the courtyard below, but the bridges are handy when you're up here. If you look down there," she gestures to the courtyard's opposite end, "you can see the main gates. See there, just under that arch."

"Oh yeah," Will replies, straining to follow the direction of her pointing finger.

"The campus isn't much to look at I know, but there's a viewing point up above the gates that looks out over Halfpenny and the city—it's pretty epic."

Leaving the sterility of the wards behind, they cross the bridge into the gray, monolithic structure of the university that wraps around it. Despite its gloomy exterior, the hallways are bright and well kept. Lined with classroom doors, the studious mumble of lectures babbles out, and through the windows that line the other side, the true splendor of Halfpenny house is magnificent. Admiring the sharp contours of the grand romanesque architecture, they make their way down the long corridor, and rounding the corner at the end, they head down another sprawling hallway that stretches out in front of them.

"So this is the north wing we're in now," Abby continues. "You can still see Halfpenny on the left. But the viewpoint is just up ahead. We'll stop when we get there. You'll like it, I think. It's really cool."

Moments later, as the walkway opens up, the tiled flooring under them gives way to a thick glass platform. Solid glass windows on both sides stretch almost to the top of the building, with Halfpenny on one side and sprawling views of NewBoston on the other. Through the stack of glazed bridges on the floors below they can see the main campus entrance, bustling with people as they enter from the street. And just as Abby had promised, Halfpenny House is breathtaking.

At least a dozen stories high, its extensive stone cobbled towers and parapets stretch even higher, like some grand castle from a fairytale. It looms far taller than the university around it, with some stone sections and windowed rooms protruding as if by magic, over the distant courtyard below.

Will is taken aback. Except in pictures of the Citadel, he has never seen a building quite as magnificent or as strange.

"Cool, right?" Abby nods, pleased with his reaction. "We'll go up to Barkoba's office next," she says, pointing toward a long set of windows embedded in the tallest section of Halfpenny's steeply sloping roof. "Right up there."

"Will he mind?" Will asks, pulling his attention from the view to look at her.

"No. He won't even know, he's doing his rounds. And anyway, it's a total tragedy to have a view so beautiful and not share it!"

For a while longer they stay to admire the view before continuing on their way through to the adjacent side of the building and circling back to Halfpenny House. Crossing the connecting walkway, the hushed practicality and sharp odor of the hospital quickly replaces the youthful excitement of the campus corridors.

"This is us here," she says, as she rolls him through the waiting opening of a shiny elevator. "We're going right to the top."

*   *   *

As a chime rings, the lift car shudders to a stop, and stepping onto the detailed designs of the rich, thick carpet of the doctor's study, a musty draft of cool air blankets them. Quiet and dimly lit, giving an expansive view of the city and the rest of Neourbia beyond, full height windows run the length of the room. Large bookshelves and beautiful antique furnishings adorn every other square inch, and paintings of people and places from the old world hang proudly on the walls.

"This stuff must be worth a fortune," Will whispers in awe. "Where did he get it all? Is he loaded, or an art thief?"

"Barkoba?" Abby laughs, "No, nothing so exciting. I've known him since I was a child, I'm pretty sure he's just a regular old person. These have been here as long as I can remember."

"Who's that guy?" Will asks, as a huge gold-framed portrait in the center of the room catches his eye. The largest by far, it is of a pale slender man dressed in a pinstriped suit, with trailing tailcoats and a top hat sitting on his graying head. Marked by the shadow of an angry scar running down his left cheek, his thin face and hard, steely eyes mask a subtle yet discernible touch of sadness in his demeanor. With lips tense, as if just about to speak, he grips a cane tightly in one hand and the leash of a large, snarling dog, sitting at his feet, in the other.

"A bit ominous, I know," Abby replies, following Will's gaze. "Halfpenny's founder. Dagda Mannigan. Cool story, actually. You wanna hear?"

"Sure," he shrugs.

"I'll do my best," she smiles. "So apparently, way back in the earliest days of Zeno, he and his followers built Halfpenny and a town around it—right around the time when the second insurrection was squashed by the Malleus. I think the Citadel, the Praetorium, and some of Libertaria would have been populated to some extent, but out here and the rest of Neourbia would have still been a wasteland. Anyway, with survivors from the dustlands coming in from the west and people fleeing the insurrection in the east, this whole area became a refuge for anyone that needed help. Some time later, stories started coming out about high ranking Kol being assassinated in Libertaria and the Citadel, and it wasn't long until Malleus started trawling through Zeno looking for answers. When they came here, they came like they always do, and it was a bloodbath. Storming the place and wiping the town off the map, they slaughtered every man, woman and child they could get their hands on. Some people think that things were made up to justify another Malleus genocide—and the records from the time are a bit vague, so who knows what really happened—but the story is that the whole thing happened because it was the charitable mister Mannigan who was responsible for all the killings and the Kol were looking for revenge."

"Crazy," Will says, raising his eyebrows. "Was it true?"

"Who knows," she replies. "I'm no expert! But usually no smoke without fire, right? — Anyway, I didn't bring you up here for a history lesson. Come look out the window. It's got to be one of the best views of the city around."

The sun is setting on the horizon, and as its soft pink and orange luminescence lights the room casting thin black shadows, they are bathed in its gentle warmth. Wheeling himself over to the window, he stops beside her to gaze at the sprawling city stretched below quietly subdued by its glow.

Much like the rest of Boston, the tall, red-brick row houses are perfectly recreated in the classic colonial style to mirror how it would have looked in the old world. With the epic scale and magnificent detail bearing the unmistakable opulence of Vitruvian homage to the time before, it is nothing short of stunning.

Looking past the city limits and over the top of Neourbia's walls, the twinkling Libertarian skyscrapers towering beyond are engulfed in a cloud of transporters that swarm like drifting flies. Beyond them, the burning white beam of the Vitruvian Column blazes steadily up into the heavens. Following its brightness down to where it meets the earth, he can just make out the angular silhouette of the structure that it emanates from.

"Is that the . . ."

"Yeah," Abby replies, following his gaze. "The Etanaki. Cool, huh. Always reminds me how fragile everything is and how easily it could all be snuffed out—but in a nice way, you know—it's humbling."

Will gives her a skeptical glance, "Snuffed out? In a nice way?"

"Well, you know. I just mean. . . if that machine," she motions towards it, "or engine, or whatever you want to call it, ever stops, and the light of the Column goes out. It's goodbye sun and hello frozen wasteland. Except for maybe the Waif and whoever else is out there, I don't think the Darklands are survivable for anyone, especially people like us that are used to the comforts of the city. Most of us wouldn't last more than a few weeks—and the ones who did? They'd probably wish they were dead. But this isn't new. We all know it, and how everything hangs so delicately in the balance. But still, every morning when we wake up and every night when we go to sleep, we pretend it's not our reality. Like the end of us all isn't separated by the blink of an eye. I feel like we've been propped up by our own self-centered sense of righteousness for so long that we've forgotten that we share the very thing that permits us to exist. But if the Etanaki just stopped? All our bitterness and all our judgment would mean nothing. And in an instant, we'd all be the same. So, when I see the Column, it reminds me that it's only a matter of time until order is returned. You know what I mean?" Turning to him with her brow raised, she squints as the last of the sun's pink light glows in the strands of her hair.

"Yeah. Maybe." Will nods at her pensive expression. "We all stand on the scales of death in the end, right? Mind you, I'd be careful who you share that with. People have been branded as proselytes for less."

As the changing color of the setting sun sinks beneath the thin black band of the dust wall that hugs the horizon, they stay transfixed on the beautiful spectacle, occasionally pointing things out, but exchanging few words. Gentle clouds of angry oranges and reds reflect their color on the streets and proud buildings, engulfing them, almost as if the city itself has burst into flame. But as the last embers of the day disappears into a slit on the skyline, and their shadows crawl further and further across the carpeted floor under their feet, the sun's blaze subsides leaving only ashes, as the city descends into night once more.

*　　*　　*

Staring at the screen in the corner of the room from his bed, various segments enacting their self important tirade fizzle out with inconsequential meaning. Aches and pains racking through his body, the muted numbness of his misery bubbles up from the sullen beating of his grief that claws inside his chest.

Outside, the shrieking winds of a storm wage war on mankind, and listening helplessly as it sweeps by, it seems to shake the very foundations of the earth. He thinks of her — his Marissa, his joy. She is all he can think, yet he is numb. There are no tears to soak his pillow. Veiled shadows and distant laughter echoes, as memories of her gentle smile haunt the empty hollow of his heart. Until, as if silence itself whispers in his ear, his mind quiets and stills. Holding the little white pill in his clammy hand, a minute passes, then an hour. Heart racing, he moves it to his lips and swallows it.

'*Soon, my love. Soon.*'

It is hardly discernible, but there, like an orchestra tuning and preparing their instruments before a symphony, the cold needles of death slip up his body.

A gentle touch at first, each one a thought, a fear, a desire. But as they gather in strength, they sting, like a thousand strands of burning roots. Touch turning to pressure, they begin to squeeze and choke, as each pointed tip penetrates a hidden river of sadness. And submerging deep into pools of his tender misery, searing clouds of steam rise in screams from their place.

He sees her. There, in a fog on the edge of a precipice, washed in a warm haze of light. With long black hair flowing down the undulating bloom of her long red dress. Drifting like the single note of a song. But as she turns, a blinding white light speaks whispered words.

Quiet at first, it's like a soft summer breeze carried over still water. And then, rising, it crashes as if waves rushing up a stoney beach. Yet, as it grows in might and fury, and the heavens roar with the surge of all the oceans; he hears it.

'*Be still my child,*' it whispers, rumbling with gentle thunder in its presence. '*For neither life or death will separate you from my love.*'

Choking for air, his eyes flick open with a start and forcing his fingers down his throat, bile spews from his mouth and nose. He sees the little pill on the floor glimmer in the darkness and breathes, as the soft patter of rain from the passing storm outside soothes his senses.

Lying back, he rests his head, and for the first time in a long time, he is at peace.

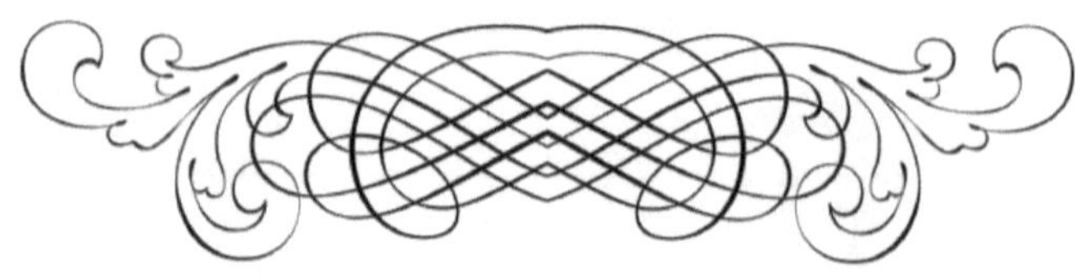

Peeled back my eyes into colorless sleep.
That speck of light.
Trapped, a heartfelt trek, I'm dust, yet unique.
That speck of light.
Controlled dementia drives me blind you see, or don't.
That speck of light.
Thoughts of things that I've left behind; of will, or won'ts.
That speck of light.
Of nights in fresh delight, my flesh delights.
Of self, enticing fight and flight.
Sweat drips, skin slips, the mirror rips, not quite.
Panic bottles in, dry throat itch,
one last kiss on lips, that's nice.
I softly close the door, as not to wake you;
my precious speck of light.

Chapter 4

TOWARD THE ARK

In delight of the storm's passing, warm rays of light stream through on Will as he stares out the window. Spellbound by the little white clouds that drift across the otherwise unblemished blue sky, he hardly notices as Barkoba enters the room and sits down on the bedside.

Still lingering in his trance, he looks at the doctor, unsure of what to say as he examines his expression. His voice is hollow and as he speaks, it is as if his words are coming from somewhere else.

"I tried," he says, in a defeated hush. "I couldn't do it."

"I know," Barkoba replies, with a sympathetic gesture towards the security camera in the corner of the room. "That is why I am here."

"Why?" Will sniffles. "You have another one for me?"

Barkoba pauses and takes a pensive breath before looking into Will's eyes. "I'm here because of you, Will. And everyone like you. Do you think what happened to you or Marissa was unique?"

Will's ears sting at the sound of her name and his face feels hot as he sullenly shakes his head.

"Can I show you something?" Taking a small touch screen from his pocket, the doctor places it on Will's lap. "Scroll down till you get to line 752."

Will complies, and scrolling down through the long list of names on its display, he stops as he comes to Marissa's.

"What is this?" he asks.

"Keep going to the bottom and take a look at how many more pages are after this one."

The list of names is several thousand long, and eventually reaching the bottom, he sees the page count:

11 of 324.

"Who are these people? What's it got to do with Marissa?"

"They are people like her, all deemed ineligible for resources for the good of collective sustainability. And that's just for this year in her age category. There's one for each sector of the industrial districts and one for prisoners and camp workers. I've even got one for minors in state care who will likely not make more than they take. Do you want to see them?"

"No!" Will replies, pushing the device across the sheets. "Why are you showing me this? Is this supposed to make me feel better?"

"Better? No. On the contrary Will. I'm afraid feeling better is a luxury afforded only to the blind. What has been done, and is being done, is a scar from which there is no healing. I came to ask you a question; If you could prevent what has happened to you from happening to someone else, would you?"

"What? Of course. Who wouldn't?"

"And why do you say that?"

"Because . . ." Will stops short and hesitates, taken aback by the question. "I don't know? No one should have the power to decide someone else's worth, right? It's not our place!"

"No, it isn't, is it," Barkoba replies, relaxing his tone. "I'll ask you this then; If someone had the power to stop all of this from happening to future generations and make the ones responsible pay for what they've done—should they use it?"

"Well sure. Yeah."

"So what if I told you that I had a way? Should I do it?"

"Look," Will interjects, irritated by the bizarre line of questioning. "If you had a way to stop the Kol, all I'd want to know is why you're here talking to me and not out there doing it. I'd love nothing more than to see them all burn, but it's going to take a lot more than a list of the dead to do it!"

As Barkoba watches him in silence, Will returns his attention to the clouds outside the window and clenches his jaw. Sliding the touch screen back into his pocket the doctor clasps his hands as he straightens up and continues.

"When I was young," he begins in a soft tone. "I met an old man who told me a story so strange, that I thought he must be ill. And yet, here I am, an old man about to tell the very same story. You are not the first to be hurt by the Vitruvian Empire, and you won't be the last. For as long as they have ruled the earth, people have stood against them, fighting and dying. But there are those who remain; waiting and planning until the time is right to strike so hard that Vitruvius himself will fall on his knees. So, as did the man who told me the story, I have waited and I have planned. And I am not alone."

Will gives him a dubious glance. "You really think anyone stands a chance against the Kol?"

"With the right means and the right method, yes. The Kol will fall, and balance will return to the world. But not, I'm afraid, without you."

"Me?" Will scoffs. "What possible use could you have for me? I don't know if you noticed, but I'm not exactly the picture of health."

"When the Empire was in its infancy, a man came here to Halfpenny and set about helping survivors and refugees rebuild civilization. He claimed to be part of an order that had been called to the safekeeping of an object of great power, that was said to hold both terrible change and perfect balance. An object that would free the one who held it from death itself. The history books will tell you that the man was a zealot and a fiend, seeking only to stoke the fires of rebellion; so when the Kol came and turned all that he'd built and all who he knew to ashes, justice had been done. But what they don't tell you, is that there were a few who remained, a few who remembered his order and its vision. A few who became many and who see—just as you do—the evil and injustice that cannot go unanswered! So in all the time that has passed since the beginning we have carefully curated the means to bring change. It too is a list, but not one of the dead. It is a list of the men and women of the Kol, whose power directs the madness that surrounds us. Men and women for whom without, the empire will descend into chaos. But you asked what use there is for you? Well, we have a problem. Our method is not quite complete. And until it is, the object of power will render no judgment."

Will raises his eyebrow. "You don't think—"

"Please," Barkoba cuts him short, raising his hand. "Let me finish. I know how this sounds, and I don't expect you to take my word that any of this is true. But I can show you. You can see everything with your own eyes and determine for yourself. And I assure you, that when we are done, you will see that everything—Legion, the list, the object—is every bit as real as I am."

The room falls silent as Will studies the doctor, perplexed. "Why are you telling me all this? What do you want from me?"

Barkoba lingers as he looks Will in the eye. "Whether by chance or by design, it would seem that the object is as unique as is the one whom it will allow to wield its power. And since the man who started it all, it has sat dormant. But in the generations that have passed, we have not been idle and have learned what makes it tick. From chemical and biological composition, to the psychological traits and quirks that form throughout our lives, it has the need for a very special person to suit its very special purpose. And with all that we know, we believe that person is you."

Will is quiet, half in the expectation of the doctor to say more and half in the expectation of waking from a dream. "But. . . Why did you give me that pill?"

"I know." Barkoba lowers his head. "And I am truly sorry. But you must be offered every choice before this one, including the choice to leave it all behind. The path I am offering you will make you well and extend your life, but you will not escape the suffering it brings, or the dark times that lie ahead. Through those times, if it is the path you choose, you must always know you were given a choice and that the choice was made alone by you."

Will stares blankly at the doctor as a sea of questions swirl in his head.

"Don't," Barkoba interrupts, as Will opens his mouth to speak. "You have done enough. No amount of my words or your answered questions will serve to help you know the truth. If you want to understand more, you must choose to see with your own eyes. So please, think about it, and make your choice. If you would like to look for yourself, just talk to Abby—she knows what to do. If not, it was a pleasure meeting you. But whatever you decide Will, thank you. You have given me hope for our future."

Standing to his feet, the Doctor gives him one last look, and turning on his heels he's gone.

*   *   *

"Is it ok if I come in?" Abby announces as she gives a gentle knock on the open door. "I came earlier, but you were asleep. How are you today?"

Coupled with painful exhaustion, the heat of burning thoughts hang like a thick fog over his head as she glides to the bedside. Vague memories of the Doctor's words solidify as he takes in the surroundings of his waking world. There's a tray of cold food on the table by the bed, and the voluminous billow of clouds thickening outside are stained purple in the evening sky.

"I'm ok," he mumbles through cracked lips.

"No, you're not," she replies with a sad smile as she lifts a cup of water to his lips. "Barkoba came to see you?"

Will nods.

"I'm so sorry for what you've been through Will—I really am," she says, glancing apologetically at the floor. "If there's anything I can do, just. . . I'm here for you, in whatever way you need, ok?"

"Ok," he replies. "Thanks."

He watches her as she moves around the room, first checking the equipment and clearing off the table, before leaving for a few moments to return with an assortment of light food. Waiting patiently as he slowly sits up, she lays the tray in front of him and takes a seat on the bed, before looking in polite silence out the window.

The pallid sight of the meal is unappealing, and as he picks over it, the pang of nausea tickles his throat.

"I don't know if I can eat," he says, pushing the tray away in disgust. "Sorry."

"That's ok," she replies, avoiding his gaze. "I'll take it away."

Reaching to pick up the tray, she stops as Will lays his limp hand on her wrist.

"He said you'd know what to do," he whispers. "If I wanted to know more."

Abby pauses as their eyes lock frozen on each others. "Yeah," she replies, with an earnest softness in her voice. "If it's what you want."

Will examines her sincere expression. "So you believe it? Everything he said? You could be locked up, or worse, even for talking about it."

Taking a slow breath she sits back down beside him. "When I was a kid, the Legion brought me here, from Stanford."

"Stanford?"

"Yeah," she says, lowering her head and pulling her hair to the side to show the faded pockmarks dotting up the back of her neck. "See, we match." Straightening up, she fixes her hair. "I don't remember much from before it, but my parents disappeared into the system protesting against religious abolition when it was introduced up north. I was too old for re-education, so they charged me as a probable seditionist and sent me away." Flashing a tight lipped smile, she shrugs. "I guess they weren't wrong."

"So you grew up here?"

"Mostly yeah. Or, not here exactly, but with Barkoba."

"I'm sorry. . . I—"

"Don't be," she replies with a dismissive shake of her head. "It made me who I am today, who I was meant to be. So do I believe? Yes, without a doubt. The Legion are my family, they're my life. And Barkoba is a good man—maybe a bit zealous for the cause sometimes—but he's only doing what needs to be done."

"But even against the Kol? The Malleus?"

Clenching her jaw she glances at him in sudden frustration. "If you knew what was going to happen to you before it did—Would you have done nothing but waited for it? We can't just sit back and let it happen. And what about the ones who are already gone? Don't they deserve retribution?"

As if he has truly seen her for the first time, Will's heart beats in unison with her anger, feeling the familiar weight of her sorrow as she stops and takes a shallow breath.

"I'm sorry," she whispers, falling quiet as gentleness fills her eyes again.

"Don't be," he replies. "So when do we go?"

*   *   *

Even though his end is only around the corner, Will still clings to his dignity. So rejecting Abby's gracious offer, he dresses himself, aching as he pulls the pants over his frail legs and slides his withered arms into his sweatshirt.

Returning with a wheelchair, she makes some adjustments to the hospital equipment around him before helping him shuffle off the side of the bed into it, and with a kind smile, she pushes him out into the narrow corridor.

Passing other ambling patients as they wander through the ward, Will examines each sickened body as they meet, mentally weighing the extent of their mortal woes. Some, frail and crippled, give a sullen glance as if to exchange their shared sorrow, while others seem no more than spectral husks. But although all are stung by their shattered forms, their greatest pain clings like shadowed cloaks as they drag behind them the burden of their heavy hearts.

At the end of a quiet hallway, they come to a halt in front of a large elevator and giving a happy chime, its silver doors slide open to greet them. Waiting as they close behind, Abby holds her hand up to the control panel as with a shudder the elevator begins its descent. Down the shaft, the dull pressure pops in Will's ears as he watches the neon numbers on the display count down. Until, the bold letter 'G' flickering off, the elevator stops with a jarring bump, and the doors open to reveal a gloomy passageway stretching ahead into the darkness.

The air is cold with damp, and judging by the musky scent, low ceiling and rubble walls, it is a place long forgotten by time.

"Where are we?" he asks, as the wheelchair rumbles over the cobbled surface of the claustrophobic hollow.

"Remember the story I told you about the guy who built Halfpenny?"

"Yeah."

"Well, while he was building in the world above, he and his followers were also down here looking for something that had been hidden for a very long time."

Emerging out of the darkness, a heavy steel door studded with rusted rivets blocks the passage ahead of them.

"They called themselves the Legion," Abby says, giving a wave up to a camera tucked in a natural crack between a protruding rock, prompting the steady mechanical clicking of gears to pull the door open. "And, as the ones before them, they believed they were the keepers of human equilibrium."

Glancing at Will, she follows his wide-eyed stare as together they gaze into the immense cavern carved into the solid bedrock that unfolds before them, its gaping vaulted ceiling glistening with the jagged tips of huge stalactites.

"And this," she continues, the vast emptiness swallowing up the sound of her voice, "is where it all began."

Several hundred feet high, it is easily as wide as a city block. Far above, as blades of daylight streak through the craggy roof, the air is filled with an ethereal mist that echoes with the playful percussion of falling water. Spanning the chasm's lower depths, a thin metal walkway dangles over the abyss. And as Will looks along its length, his astonished gape falls on a huge cubic structure hanging in the void.

Encased in glass and suspended as if by magic, the surrounding blackness irradiates with a gentle light glowing from inside its transparent sides. Stairs and platforms joining its host of levels, offices, laboratories, and sleeping quarters fill its form, dotted with furniture as if an elaborate doll's house.

"Well," Abby says with a smile. "What do you think?"

"It's . . ." Will whispers, lost for words as he gawks up at it.

"Come on, let me show you."

Trundling onto the narrow platform that terminates at a single door on the side of the gigantic glass cube, Will peers in wonder over the edge as they rattle across in the eerie silence. Nestled between jagged rocks that extend upward like sharpened teeth, he can just make out the faint outline of the ruins of ancient buildings.

"We don't know exactly how long the caves have been used," Abby says, as if she can hear his thoughts. "But from what we can tell from studying the ruins, people have used them to hide, and in some cases thrive, through some of the hardest moments in history. The Legion must have known that the fire and floods of the Tribulation were coming, as they hid everything down here that was needed to preserve their way of life. All that it needed was to be rediscovered. So while we do what we can to ease the suffering of the world up there, we wait and prepare."

Approaching the shimmering structure, Will looks up as a crowd of men and women gather at the windows above, pressing against the glass as they draw near.

"What are they looking at?" he asks with mild unease under their imposing gaze.

"Not what—who," Abby replies, as the glass slides open ahead of them. "Some of them have waited their whole lives for someone like you. So welcome."

The interior of the grand glazed structure is as impressive and surreal as the exterior. Littered with exquisite paintings and inspired sculptures from times long forgotten, every space available is adorned like the gallery of a fine museum floating in a case of ice. Stacked with what must be thousands of hand-bound books and manuscripts, tall ornate bookshelves garnish the glass floor of the long hallway ahead.

But its magnificence is quickly diminished by the unnerving stare of the people who line its walls in noiseless patience. And as Abby wheels him forward between their ranks, he is greeted by each with reverent bows of their heads.

"Don't worry," Abby says, leaning forward and lowering her voice. "We're just at the end here."

Reaching the end of the hall, they turn into a dim, wood paneled study encircled by cabinets displaying a further host of parchments and other peculiarities. Seated around a large walnut desk in the center, a handful of well-dressed men and women stop their chatter as they hear them enter, as Barkoba, sitting at their head, stands to his feet.

"Will," he exclaims. "I am so glad you decided to join us. Come," he ushers to the front of the desk, "join us."

"Thank you Abigail," he says, nodding to Abby as she brings Will's chair to a stop and turns to leave the room. "So, Will. What do you think of our home?"

"I don't know what to say," Will replies. "I've never seen anything like it."

"And I suspect you never will again. But this is only a prelude to the wonders that brought you here. Now, I will not inundate you with too much. But before they leave us in peace, can I introduce you to my colleagues; they have given their lives to the servitude of the cause and are excited to meet you."

With a proud motion to each, he introduces them. "Professor Menashe and Doctor Akiva are the heads of our research division." Glancing up at their expectant smiles Will mumbles his acknowledgment as Barkoba continues. "Logistics and special operations are spearheaded by Doctor Khita and Doctor Galgula, and, of course, Professor Eleazar who runs our eyes and ears in the cities." He stops and pauses to look at each one with gratitude. "Without them, this place, the list, and most importantly, you, Will, would not have been united at this moment in time. We owe them everything. But, as there is still much to do — ladies, gentlemen, if you could give us some privacy."

As his colleagues file out of the room with hushed obedience, Barkoba stands patiently, waiting until the door clicks shut, before walking around his desk and sitting in the large armchair.

"I will not bore you with talk," he starts after a thoughtful pause. "Look."

Gesturing towards a large screen embedded in the wall, live footage from inside a gloomy crypt flickers on, focused on a white marble pedestal standing in its center. Perched on its top, a black cube rests in place, not quite still, but shimmering, as it hovers over the smooth surface. No bigger than a closed fist, its faces glisten like sliding oil, bending and twisting the light around it, as if drawn to its peculiar form.

"We have had it for a very long time," Barkoba continues. "But in all our years, we have never understood it. It is, for lack of a better word, an object like no other, unbending to the laws of men and their universe. It cannot be touched or moved or measured, by any means of the earth. To even try comes with great risk – and believe me, we have tried. But, for the little we have learned, we have learned enough. We know it contains the power of great change and we know that the man who kept it through the Tribulation, had harnessed that power. We also know by the prophecy of the same man, that when the day came for its need, there would be another just like him, and great change would come again."

"And you think that's me?" Will asks.

"I do."

"And if it's not?"

Barkoba hesitates and looks up to the ceiling with a pained expression across his face. "With the exception of this room, this building is made almost entirely of glass. Clear, transparent—brittle. We strive to hide nothing from each other, and I will extend no less to you. If I am wrong, and you touch the object, I have no doubt that you will die. You are not the first to try."

Will's forehead wrinkles in a frown as he contemplates the doctor's words, "And if I don't die?"

"Your injuries and sickness will be no more. With its gift, you will be given power over death like men have never known. You, like those before you, will have the power to balance the scales of this broken world. To bring justice and vengeance to those who have made their gardens amongst the bones of the dead."

Barkoba pauses, tapping a button on his desk, as the image of the object goes dark.

"But it is, and always will be, your choice," he continues. "We can, if you wish, bring you back to your hospital bed and you can spend your last days there. Whatever this may be, it can only be, if it is what you choose."

"And if I choose to stay—and survive. . . what then? You'd have me what? Be your executioner?"

"Such an ugly word. . . but yes, by your hand, and others, it is judgment that this world needs. But you must understand; the ones marked for death are drenched in the blood of innocent lives. They are undoubtedly guilty. We have examined each and every one of them for years, and only by the most stringent standards of our morality and law have we listed their names. Without them, the Kol and the Vitruvian Empire will fall and this Godless swamp they force us to wade will cease to be! I wish it were not so, but think of Marissa, Will! Your parents! They weren't alone in their suffering! Think of the countless others. With every day that passes, more just like them are labeled and snuffed out by idle deliberators, walking carelessly about wherever they wish! As they trample the masses like delicate flowers beneath their feet, are we to do nothing?!!"

Drawing a long deep breath he slides open a drawer in his desk and produces a small gray case, unzipping the side to reveal a long steel syringe, and leaning forward over the desk, he places it in front of Will.

"If you are accepted and given the gift, then yes, the Legion would ask that you would bear the names of the guilty and carry out our works. But I hope that you understand. Our works are the works of good men, moral men. We are only trying to do what is right, and what needs to be done." Pausing, he gestures to the needle, "That is it. The list."

Will stays motionless, studying it carefully before tentatively picking it up to feel the cold weight of it in his hands as Barkoba carries on.

"It contains the biometric signatures of each and every one. In your bloodstream it will become an inseparable part of you. With it, and the right tech, there will be nowhere for them to hide."

"And if I said no?" Will's voice cracks as he asks the question, feeling the heavy hand of tiredness subdue his body.

Barkoba's tone softens. "The choice is always yours to make. We would not intervene."

They both sit silently, the ticking of the old grandfather clock on the wall filling the space between them. The mere mention of Marissa has thrown Will's mind into a spiral. His parents. . . His whole life feels like one long freefall, forever flailing and grasping desperately in the air for something to hold on to, always one thought from being able to elaborate on what is wrong, but distinctly aware that something is far from right.

"Ok," he says, casting a fatigued glance at Barkoba, ". . . I'll do it."

Prying loose the little cap uncovering the needled point of the syringe, he pushes the point into his arm and presses the button. Removing it slowly from his skin, he looks up at Barkoba, who is looking back at him with tear-filled eyes.

"Thank you Will," he whispers with a tremor in his voice. "You have made the right choice. Together, we will change the world."

Chapter 5

HIS NAME IS MANNIGAN

As the bedroom lights flick on, a strobing blue beacon on the bedroom roof flashes in unified rhythm with the monotone pulse of an alarm. Sitting up with a start, Will looks frantically around. But no sooner than his eyes have adjusted to the brightness, the door bursts open as Lillian rushes in.

"Sorry for the intrusion!" she yells over the racket. "There's a situation up top! We're going into lockdown!"

Grabbing his wheelchair she slams it into the bed.

"What happened?!" Will asks, wincing with each droning undulation.

"The Malterra came through the front of Juliana's about twenty minutes ago," she replies, throwing back his covers and ushering him towards her outstretched arm. "They may be looking for something else, but we can't take a chance. Here, put this on. The caves are cold."

Helping him shuffle into the chair, she wheels him out the door to the elevator at the end of the hall, mashing the buttons in impatient succession until the doors close. In keeping with the rest of the crystalline aesthetic, the sides of the elevator too are glass, and first dropping through the many floors of the Ark below, it pops out the lowest floor into the yawning blackness of the cavern. Held in a thin steel frame, it plummets into darkness, the huge glass cube growing distant above as they descend through the vastness of the cave. Until, reaching a host of bright white lights that illuminate the bottom, it opens onto a large concrete platform joined by several crude rubble trails.

Resounding with calls of urgency, the energy in the air is tense, as hauling equipment back and forth, a group of men and women load up a row of rugged vehicles parked in a line near the edge.

"Lillian!" the sound of Barkoba's voice calls out. Waving from the back of a large pickup truck, he shouts again, and as Lilian waves back, he grabs the side of the rusted roll cage and clambers down.

"Sorry about the early hour. You ok?" he asks as they approach. "Will, how are you? My apologies for getting you down here in such a hurry."

"Is everything ok?" Will asks.

"It will be, yes," he replies, "but we can't be sure. If by some miracle the Malleus find us, we could only hold them off for so long." He glances down the platform at a rumble from further down the chamber, before turning back to Will with a worried frown. "I know this is not exactly how we planned, but we are going to have to expedite our visit to the object. But it is still your choice. Are you sure this is what you want to do?"

Stifling the urge to acknowledge the simmering pangs of fear gripping his chest, Will nods, "Yeah."

About to speak, Barkoba stops short, as far above, a deep rumble reverberates through the cavern's gloomy depths. Listening, frozen, to its booming tremor, a shower of dust and pebbles rains around them.

Reaching for the side of a small device in his ear, Barkoba's face pales. "Jesse, what was that? Everything ok?" he says, listening intently to the response. "Ok, ok. It's ok. We've planned for this, remember? I know it's hard, but just let them do their thing—Do not engage!. . . I know, I know! But they're not our people, so just hang in there. If we have to, blow the tunnel. But until then, stay out of it! In the meantime, send the signal; full evac. Get everyone who's not needed out of here."

Finished speaking, he rubs his temple and takes a long breath, before turning his attention to Will and Lilian with fresh determination. "Ok, we've got to go . . . Lilly, Aaron has a spot for you up front," he gestures towards the line of waiting vehicles ahead, as their engines roar to life. "All going well, I'll see you in a few days, ok?" Opening his arms to her, she moves to him and they give each other a firm hug.

"Good luck," she says.

"You too. I'll see you soon."

Giving a half hearted smile, she turns to go, and joining a group tracking across the platform she heads towards the other vehicles.

"There's Abby now," Barkoba remarks, raising his hand as Abby approaches from one of the connecting trails, "Abby!!"

Dressed in tan coveralls arrayed with functional pockets and zips, she's followed by an Autocargo unit that rambles behind her on four large rubber wheels.

"Is everything alright up there?" she asks as she hurries over, gesturing to the thundering volume above. "Have they found us?"

Barkoba shakes his head, "We'll be fine. You got everything we need?"

"Yeah, it's all there," she says, motions to the Autocargo unit that has parked itself behind their truck to unload onto the flatbed.

"Good. Well come on then, no point hanging around – Will, let's get you up back," he says gesturing to the vehicle. "Abby, you're up front with me!" Climbing up onto the flatbed he reaches down to grab Will's hand. Pulling him up, he props him against the side. "It's a bit of a bumpy ride, but nothing to worry about. It's not too far."

The truck's sturdy engine starts up with a growl, and revving a few times, it idles into a smooth gurgle, sending plumes of black smoke billowing up into the upper expanses of the cavern. Probing into the blackness ahead, the array of headlights mounted on its front flick on, and with a jolt, they begin moving down a trail.

The deep thunder from the world above reverberating through the cavern like crashing waves, Will watches in silence as the Ark's glowing form grows steadily smaller behind them. And bumping and bouncing down the rocky trail, it is soon as if the darkness of the cave will swallow them whole.

To their sides, the faint outlines and looming shadows of crumbling buildings rise from the cavern floor, separated by narrow winding alleyways that disappear between them. He can almost see the ghostlike figures of laughing children as they play and the bartering chatter of traders in the market stalls that would have once lined the streets. But now, lost to time, this is all that remains; a city returned to stone, and a people returned to dust.

'Is this what is destined for us all? To be crushed under the relentless wheel of history. Formed in a shape and held in a time by a lifeless mechanical beat, only to be ground to ash and returned to nothing in a fleeting burst of hope?'

Rattled by a sharp turn in the road, the transporter's engine whines with the strain of the steep ascent as they climb rapidly up the curve of a long stone bridge. The carcass of the dead city dropping away behind them, the sounds of a river rushing below fills the cold damp air as they fly over the crest and rumble down the other side.

The trail leveling out, a cauldron of bats rises screeching into the darkness as they enter a narrow tunnel. Amplifying the blare of the engine to a howl, it is deafening. But with nothing to see but the hypnotic flickering of the light on the tunnel's walls that rush past, Will covers his ears and eases back to the soothing vibrations of the ground beneath the wheels.

*   *   *

Skidding on the loose dirt, the truck rolls to a stop. It is quiet, and as the engine shuts off, it is only the changes in the cavern's pressure that heave like a dragon's breath, and the occasional patter of unseen waters falling from high above that fills the silence.

"Well, what do you think?" Barkoba calls back to Will, as he and Abby step out and gaze up.

Bathed in the beams of the headlights, an enormous unblemished shard of rock stretches upward, protruding from the heart of the earth like the tip of a giant's sword.

"It's incredible," Will replies.

"It is, isn't it? It is the resting place of the object for as long as we have known it."

"Was it built by Legion?"

"We don't think so. We have studied it extensively. It predates any known records by thousands of years, and by some estimates even predates civilization. And it may not look like it, but from what we can tell it was formed naturally—or what we would consider natural at least. But come on, there is no time to lose."

Striding forward, he heads toward the single shadowed doorway at its base, as Abby climbs up into the back of the truck and helps Will shuffle down. With one arm held over her shoulder they hobble towards the structure's strangely smooth surface, until, stepping across the threshold, they are engulfed in total blackness.

"One second," Barkoba's voice rings out from the darkness. "There!"

With a thud and a click, an array of lights recessed into the stone floor illuminates, casting a warm glow into a vast hollow of the ceiling that slowly constricts into a conical point far above.

As if cut from the rock itself, the room is a perfect circle. Around its circumference, five ornate sarcophagi, each adorned with strange creatures and inscriptions, are centered around the white marble pedestal that stands proud host in the middle; And on it, the dark object, drifting motionless on top. It is smaller than it had looked on the screen, and the more Will stares at it, the more its shimmering black faces seem to move. Bending and flowing, it is almost as if it pulses or breathes, rippling with some unknown life. As if you could dip a finger into its surface and be left with a blackened stain, or perhaps, if you slipped, you could be consumed by it entirely.

"We call them the Judges," Barkoba remarks, ushering toward the tombs. "We believe each one wielded the gift in their time. And," he continues, following Will's unshaking gaze from the little black box, "if it accepts you, like it did them . . . you will be the next."

Will examines it. It is like nothing he has ever seen. Small, but somehow taking more space than it should, as in subtle distortion, the light and the space around it seem to draw toward it as if listening to its call.

"What do I do?" he asks in quiet fascination.

"Simply touch it," Barkoba replies.

With a hesitated thought and a resigned breath, Will slides his heavy arm off Abby's shoulder and takes a pained step forward.

"And Will," Barkoba continues with heartfelt sincerity, "whatever happens. Thank you."

Will nods in appreciation and looks back at Abby's pallid face. Her sorrow drifting like a summer wind, she gives a saddened smile as he turns to face the object again. And taking the last few strained steps toward it, he raises his trembling hand.

'Here at the beginning of the end, I will end as I began;
in the hand of mercy.'

A blinding flash pierces his skull and he is engulfed by a bitter cold.

Into darkness and the empty nothingness of chaos, he falls, soundlessly tumbling in a spiraled descent through an empty void.

In endless insignificance, a light is born. Only a speck. But one with such furious energy that it stings his eyes and warms his frozen skin; and as he gravitates towards it, it grows. A little at first. Then, a little more, as time adds days to weeks, and weeks to months. Further and further it expands, until, in terrifying speed, his body seizes and he braces for impact. And then — nothing . . .

*　　*　　*

A dull whining sounds shrill in his head. Opening his eyes, he squints in a daze at the vivid brightness of his surroundings, as nestled within a rich jungle of giant trees and vines, a disordered cluster of small huts made of clay and thatch form a primitive village.

The air, thick with smoke, is filled with anguished screams. Gunshots ringing out in the distance, he flinches. But hearing the frantic patter of feet splashing through the mud, he turns, as clutching an infant in her arms a woman in a torn dress runs past with terror in her eyes. Behind her as she flees, a dark-haired soldier raises the long barrel of his musket. And as his iron helmet and silver breastplate gleam with the burst of flame, he fires.

Will's fingers tingle, as the beat of his pounding heart drums in his head. Clinging to the still silence of her child, the woman's chest heaves with shallow breaths as the soldier walks over to her limp body. First prodding her back with the tip of his leather boot, he sets his musket down. Before, drawing his needled sword from its scabbard, he plunges it into her neck.

An agonized wail of anguish diverts Will's horror to the form of a bleeding man. Naked, but for a loincloth and painted streaks of vivid color, he thrashes as he is dragged from between the huts by three more of the armored brutes. Dropped to his knees before a large rock, they laugh with callous cheer as they hold his bare arms across it. And as their ax falls and his wrists divide, he looks to the sky and howls.

He is alone now. At the end of a bloodied trail in the mud where he crawled to his wife and child. Shuddering as he holds them in his handless arms. His eyes seem to shine; raw, exposed, and alive in a furious blaze. Burning, not in fear or pain or sadness, but with the heat of a blinding rage, and all the hate of hell's darkness.

In only the space between breaths, Will sees him again.

Now, as he kneels before a plinth of stone. His bandaged wrists held fast in prayer, he bows his head to the small black box that shimmers on top.

Another breath, as he reappears.

Now, in the stifling heat and fumes of a metallurgist's forge, his bristling shape illuminated by a burning glow. Birthed from his mutilated wrists, razored swords protrude, their bare handles driven by the blacksmith into each of his impotent stumps. But when his screaming stops and the blades ghastly beauty gleams gold in the flickering light, his laughter seems to shake the world.

Another breath.

A rain swept battlefield, bathed in the light of the moon. Fires burn and wind howls through the trees. Rivers of blood stream between piles of the dead and the dying. And there, him, the man with blades for hands, panting like a satiated beast among them, his body glistening crimson with the carnage.

Another breath, yet this one harder, as Will sees a beautiful Queen.

With rose red lips and long red curls, she's wrapped in tartan and robed in a royal blue cloak. But bound and gagged, tears stream down her face. Searching the sorrow in her eyes, he sees their reflection. And as the abhorrent sight of the cruelty that she is forced to witness soaks his soul, he mourns for her suffering.

Again, he sees her. Fallen before a shining altar. Reaching out, she trembles as she hums her broken heart and laying hands on the little black box, it gifts her its wisps of twisting shadows.

Chest tightening, as the amber hues of a rising sun kiss the rolling crest of a lush green hill, he fights for another breath.

Now in a crown of gold, she waits on a pale gray horse, and shrieking her terrible grief she raises her sword. With a roar, her army moves, sweeping like great waves over the encampment in the valley below. And as burning men and banners fall beneath her furious violence, the earth runs red with her song.

The faint clutches of unconsciousness reaching out, Will gasps for another fragile breath, now gazing on the crowded triage of a battered hospital.

Joining the anguished screams of patients, thunderous tremors of distant bombs blend in wretched ululation as a doctor hurries past. His pallid face and sallow skin are worn by the sins of war and his eyes echo a despondent heart. Yet he is no stranger. Will has seen him before. Not quite the same, this man still carries the marks of youth, but it is him.

And looking to the word stitched neatly beneath the Vitruvian seal on his stained white coat, he sees his name.

Mannigan.

It is dusk. High in a candle lit window, the man sits alone and weeps, as the city burns to dust on the horizon. Watching the relentless hells of war reduce it all to ash, walls rattle and the ground shudders beneath his feet.

First, just like a single droplet, Will feels the heat of his pain. Yet, as one drop turns to two, and two to three, the sky opens and it begins to rain. Light at first, dancing in delicate symphony, soon the full grandeur of his sadness comes alive. Roaring to crescendo, the heavens flood the earth as the man and his sorrow wash through him like a thousand jagged knives.

But then it stops.

In the sudden hush, Will's blood runs cold. His eyes blackened by a deathly gaze, the man lurches at him and stares straight into his face, plunging to the depths of his soul. Stripping it bare in an instant, he sees him. He sees all there is to be seen, he knows all there is to be known. And as fire and blood spew from his open mouth, he speaks with the bellowing voice of the tortured multitude, "RISE!!"

Chapter 6

THE GIFT

Vaguely aware of a speck of light faintly coming through what must be an opening at the furthermost tip of the concave roof above, it is quiet. Staring up at Barkoba and Abby leaning over him, he looks puzzled for a moment at their worried expressions.

"He's breathing. Will!" Barkoba yells, shining a light into Will's open eyes. "Are you with us? Talk to me?!"

"Stop," Will whispers through a dry throat, flinching at the blinding glare. "I'm ok."

"My God. . ." Through a nervous smile the doctor looks up at Abby's pale face. "He made it. What happened? How do you feel?"

Will's mind reels with what he has seen, and for a moment he lies in silence.

"Sore," he replies. Raising his hand to examine the black square burnt into his palm's flesh, he squints as little wisps of smoke trail from it.

"A souvenir," Barkoba remarks, peering at it. "Are you alright to get up? Here, let me help you." Putting an arm behind Will, he tries to help him sit. "Abby, come on girl. Give me a hand."

"I thought I was supposed to feel better?" Will winces from the pain as they pull him up and prop him against the marble plinth.

"Yes, well, you should. . ." Barkoba answers. "But give it time. We don't know exactly what to expect. For now we'll consider it a miracle that you are alive."

"But that means he has the gift though, right?" Abby asks. "Are we going ahead with the plan?"

"Yes, but—I don't know, I. . ." Trailing off, he glances at her with a look of concern. "I can't send you off until we are sure. It can't be for nothing. Hold on. I'll be right back." Getting up, flustered, he heads out the door towards the truck.

"I knew you'd make it," Abby smiles, turning to Will with a look of relief. "I knew it!"

"Well . . . 'ta-da!'," Will laughs weakly. "Now what?"

"I don't know. Barkoba, he'll. . ." She looks towards the doorway. "We've got to go to Desolation first and find Solomon. Once we've found him, everything can begin and then we can. . ."

Turning to the sound of hurried footsteps, she stops short as Barkoba rushes back through the doorway with a sunken expression on his face and gripping a snub nose shotgun by his side.

"Jesse just blew the tunnel!" he exclaims in a cracked voice. "I'm sorry Will, I really am — but there's no time!"

Lifting the gun as beads of perspiration form on his brow, he levels it directly at Will, "Put your hands up — Now!"

In slow perplexion, Will raises his hands. "What are you doing. . . Abby?"

"Bar!" Abby screams, scrambling to her feet. "What are you doing!! Stop!!!"

"I'm sorry, my girl. I can't send you out there until I'm sure."

"Sto—!!!"

With a deafening explosion, Will's arm explodes into vapor, sending a spray of bloodied mist into his face as the shockwave hits him. Slumping to his side, the sound of his scream is muffled by a shrill high-pitched squeal that permeates his head, as Abby shrieks with wild-eyed fury and tackles Barkoba to the ground.

In raw disbelief he lifts his arm, or what it used to be, and stares blankly at the mangled end of an elbow before him. It feels more numb than anything, and as he tries to wiggle his non-existent fingers, a tingle radiates up to his shoulder. Clutching the ragged limb to his chest, he recoils in sudden shock as fine tendrils like thousands of tiny hairs begin to grow from his bloodied stump, weaving and winding into each other. Pain rising in excruciating agony, they blend and multiply in a grotesque spectacle, stitching to one another to form intricate patterns of muscles and veins. In stupefied horror, he watches as the base of what appears to be a thumb forms on the head of his newly sprouted wrist. And as the mass blooms the roots of a hand, he yells over the howls of Abby's anger, "Stop!!"

Turning towards the sound of his voice, Abby and Barkoba freeze.

"Look!!" Holding up his extended arm, the fleshy fibers weave like breeding snakes as they form the tips of his fingers.

Abby scrambles over to him, stopping short to stare in horrified wonder at the sickening marvel.

"Thank God," Barkoba gasps.

"It's. . . It's you. . ." Abby whispers. Staring shaken, she glances back at Barkoba who is kneeling in silence. "The gift. . . He has it."

For a moment they are quiet, as the subdued resonance of the cavern's solitude soothes the adrenaline that courses through their bodies.

"I am truly sorry." Barkoba's hushed tone breaks the silence. "It was never my intention to cause you pain. I just couldn't. . ." Stumbling on his words, he shakes his head at his momentary madness. "I couldn't send her out there with you —I had to be sure. I'd never forgive myself if I was wrong."

"Couldn't you have done it another way?!" Abby snaps. "Like any other way?!"

"I know, I—"

"We could've. . . I don't know? Like, cut him or something! Did you have to shoot him?! What is wrong with you!!"

"I know!! I'm sorry!" Barkoba replies defensively. "I just couldn't. . . What if I'd made a mistake. Miscalculated or interpreted the texts to suit my own needs! I needed to know that he was what we thought he would be! If I'd led you all astray. . ." he lowers his head. "I'd never forgive myself. I couldn't send you out into the dustlands for nothing. I had to be sure."

"Don't you dare make it about me!!"

"No! I didn't m—"

"Can you two stop?!" Will cuts him short, as he pulls himself to his feet. "Please. It doesn't matter. What's done is done. If the Malleus are coming, what matters is getting out of here. Where are we supposed to be going?"

"So. . . you'll still help us?" Barkoba asks.

"Not you," he scowls, shaking his head. "My arm still hurts. But I'll help her." Turning from the doctor, he looks at Abby, "If it's still what you want?"

Studying the doctor's shaken form, Abby pauses, before turning her stern focus to Will. "Yeah. It is."

"Thank you," Barkoba says in a hushed voice.

Will inhales as he examines the doctor's earnest expression. "So what now?"

Clambering up from his knees, the doctor glimpses at Will in humbled remorse. "I have passage booked and a craft waiting to take you over the city walls to Desolation. Abby will fill you in on the way. If you would, Abby."

Her cheeks still flush with anger, Abby glares at him for a second before turning to Will. "Can I give you a hand getting to the truck?"

"No, I think I can manage," he replies.

"Well, come on then," she says, turning to the door. "Let's go."

His body still aches as he limps with Abby back to the truck, but a prickle of energy in his legs he has not felt for some time drives him forward. Grunting in discomfort, he hoists himself onto the truck's flatbed as Abby climbs in beside him.

"Here," Abby says, tossing a pair of coveralls from one of the cargo chests to Will as he sits down. "Put these on."

"Thanks," he replies. "So what's in Desolation?"

"There's a man there, Solomon. He has a way to help us find the people on the list."

"You don't know who you're looking for?"

"No—or well, we do. We just don't know exactly where. Most of these people are powerful Kol. They are not people that want to be found. But Solomon has a way. He used to be Kol – Malflatus if you can believe it."

"Really?" Will raises his eyebrows, "Jeez."

"Yeah, I know. Apparently he disconnected from the network in the Praetorium and fled to Desolation. Barkoba said he stayed hidden until the price on his head caught up with him. But when he was sent to the Queen for execution, she found out who he was and kept him for herself. So she faked his execution and kept him alive as leverage against the Kol."

"So where is he now?"

"Tucked away somewhere, apparently. We'll find out once we're there. Legion has contacts who are waiting for us, even one close to the Queen. We shouldn't be much longer than a few days."

Will studies the staunch determination in her expression. "Have you been out there? You know—out of Zeno?"

"No. . ." she replies. "You?"

He shakes his head.

*　　*　　*

Scuttling along the dirt trail that winds and twists through the darkness, Will and Abby sit in silence listening to the reverberations of the engine's low growl. Eventually passing under a stone archway into a narrow tunnel, they burst into an open clearing bathed in the light of the sun.

Spattered with tiny blue and pink flowers, and carpeted by a lush green grass that blankets the ground, it is quite beautiful, and as they squint up at the soft blue sky that radiates through a large opening in the cave roof, the truck skids to a halt.

"I don't see him?" Barkoba calls out, as he climbs out of the cab. "You see anything?"

"No, nothing," Abby replies.

"Not to worry, I'm sure he'll be here soon. Let's get loaded up anyway. We can wait inside."

With a swift stride to the center of the clearing, he stops short and crouches down, reaching ahead as if clutching for the breeze. Grabbing what appears to be the cavern floor itself, the air in front of him shimmers as he lifts it up and ducking under it he disappears.

"Did you. . . ?" Will starts. But interrupted by a muffled noise, a mass of fabric draped over a huge object appears in front of them.

The side of the material's edge lifting up, Barkoba peers out from under it.

"You two coming?!" he calls with a wave.

Hopping down from the truck and ducking under the edge of the fabric, Will stares up at the hulking form of a sleek black aircraft, taking a moment for his eyes to adjust to the dim light. As much an aircraft as it is a work of art; as if carved from a single piece of obsidian, the smooth lines of the magnificent machine's sharp geometry cut through each other in perfect elegance.

Will whistles through his teeth, "Must be worth a fortune!"

"It is," Barkoba replies, with a pleased grin. "Legion has a few wealthy benefactors and you'd be amazed what the

Trafaka can get their hands on if you pay them enough! It's a C–class Vitruvian Hawk. Go on in, take a look. Otto should be here soon but we might as well get some rest while we wait. I'm just going to help Abby load up."

The door on the side is open and as Will approaches, two simple steps protrude organically from the craft. Lined with rich ivory paneling it is detailed in a dark walnut trim, the cabin is luxurious and impeccably clean. Almost afraid to touch anything he moves cautiously inside. But as he slides into one of the plush leather seats, watching as the faint thud of the hatches closing outside shakes the little porthole windows, he exhales with a satisfied breath.

Chapter 7

OVER THE WALL

Wrapped in a red blanket embroidered with the Vitruvian seal, Abby, in the seat beside him, is still asleep. Donning a cushioned headset in the cockpit up front, the pilot is busy as joyful whirs and beeps sound out and the craft comes to life.

"Abby, wake up my girl," Barkoba says as the door slides open. "It's time to go."

"I'm up," she mutters, sitting up in a momentary daze. "I'm up."

Taking in her surroundings she pushes the blanket off. "Ok, I'm ready. Let's go."

As Barkoba's gaze lingers on hers, her expression softens in sudden comprehension of her words, and she grabs his hand. "Bar . . . I—"

"No," he interrupts, tears welling up in his eyes. "No goodbyes. . . please. I am so proud of you. I hope you know that. Now—go and do what needs to be done."

With a sudden howl, the aircraft's engine starts up, and as a blast of air rushes into the cabin, the doctor pulls away and steps out of the open door. Turning to face them, he shields his face from the whirlwind of dust and shouts over the noise, "Never forget! Vengeance is ours!! Let's make things right!"

Screaming with a deafening shriek, the floor shudders as the craft begins to rise. And as Will struggles to breathe against the crushing ascent, he watches as Barkoba, growing smaller below, waves goodbye.

It is over in a moment. Streaks of the morning sun blazing through the windows, the engine's roar dulls to a pleasant hum as they begin to hurtle forward through the sky.

Leaning around from his seat, the pilot smiles through a pair of big shaded sunglasses.

"I'm Otto, by the way!" he says, raising his voice over the chatter of the cockpit instruments. "Sorry about the rush! I was running late, so I thought it best just to get going and skip the small talk. Time is money and all that! Abby and Will, right?"

Giving a muted wave, Will smiles back, before glancing at Abby, who stares blankly as if she hadn't heard.

"Well it's very nice to meet you," Otto gives them a thumbs up. "We'll be a few hours over Zeno until we hit the dustlands, so get comfy. And providing I did the paperwork right," he adds with a chuckle, "I'm hoping the Malignus won't blow us out of the sky!"

*　*　*

As the city's expansive sprawl unfolds beneath and the mechanical thrum of the engine pulses through the cabin, Will is lost in thought.

The view is incredible. Although he has seen it in pictures and videos, he has never seen the city from the air with his own eyes. And having left Neourbia only a handful of times for brief holidays in Eden and the occasional work trip to Libertaria, he had never fully grasped Zeno's vast enormity until now.

They're just outside Libertaria by the look of it.

Peering past the shining spikes of Libertaria's skyscrapers, the fortified battlements of the Praetorium span the full length of the coast, accompanied by the monstrous shadows of the Malignus warships hovering above it. Past it, nestled in the sparkling waters of the bay, is the Island Citadel of Abundance, host to the needled flame of the Vitruvian column that spews skyward from the Etanaki's silhouetted form. And beyond that again, shimmering over the ocean, the rising sun creates a luminous halo that hugs the foreboding black wall of dust on the horizon.

Below, as the craft veers into a turn, he can make out the vast wall that separates it from Neourbia. Cutting the gray mass of the cityscape as it snakes its way through Libertaria to the sea, the winding banks of the River Lovelace come into view. And as he squints at the distant shape of its larger bridges straddling the water, he sees the familiar footprint of Boston, the place he had once called home. Further north of its urban sprawl, another city. D.C. perhaps. Or maybe Chicago. But blinded by the sun's rays bouncing off the plains of the energy district beyond, it's hard to tell.

Continuing their journey west, the white light of the column gleams like a silver pin behind as the sparkling sea fades out of view. Until, spotting the walls of the Neourbian city limits, they approach the lush green edges of Eden.

Supposedly the equivalent size of Neourbia and Libertaria combined, its natural splendor is vast. With rugged mountains, lakes and forests, it extends so far that it was not uncommon for its more adventurous visitors to vanish in its rugged grandeur, and as the thin gray line of the border passes under the craft, Will can see why. Endless shades of green, twist and bend through the ever changing natural landscape. Blending and mixing across windswept, grassy plains, epic yawns of rising cliffs and climbing peaks break the open mouths of dark ravines before spilling into lush valleys of evergreens, scarred by deep blue rivers.

On their trips there, he and Marissa had not seen much of it. More interested in each other's company and spending the rare cash that was so much effort to save, they had ventured out to camp a couple of times, but usually stayed in small towns, never fully delving into the real wilderness that Eden had to offer. It had always been a conversation they enjoyed, though. They had always talked about leasing a cottage on a bit of land and growing old there; learning how to farm and do things the old way, only venturing back to the city for their grandkid's birthdays or other big events.

"Come in DD-722." Crackling over the radio in the cockpit, a voice interrupts the silence. "This is Zeno border control, do you copy?"

"Loud and clear border control, this is DD-722," Otto responds. "What can I do for you today?"

With a rumble from outside, a fighter drone sweeps into view through the window. Arrayed with cameras and sensors that flicker in every direction, it levels off parallel to them as another one appears through the window on the opposite side.

"722," the voice on the radio calls again. "Please confirm your cargo and the purpose of your border crossing."

"Copy that. Cargo is 1 male, 1 female and medical supplies. Purpose of crossing is humanitarian aid training in Desolation City."

The radio hisses static as Will glances at Abby's nervous expression.

"Copy that 722. We detect weapons in your cargo bay. Please confirm."

Otto pauses, "My apologies border control. Weapons are small arms, self defense only—in case of emergency."

"Copy 722. They're not declared on your transport documents. Please transfer your weapons license."

"Yep, sure thing. . ." The tension in Otto's voice is palpable as he waves out to the drones. "Please stand by." With the touch of a few buttons, he clambers out of his seat and back into the cabin.

"Sit tight," he reassures them, lumbering down the aisle between their seats. "We'll be clear in a minute."

Opening a hatch behind them and rummaging around, he scans a small briefcase with a device from his jacket before shuffling back up to his seat.

"Come in, border control," he calls.

"Go ahead."

"Files transferred there now. Please advise." Another endless hush followed by a silence holds their breath as they wait.

"Come in 722."

"Yes, border control, go ahead."

"The fee for incorrect documentation has been deducted from your account. You are clear to exit Zeno. Have a nice day."

With a flash of their afterburners, the drones bank sideways in unison and disappear into the sky with a thunderous shake.

"Whoa, thank God for that!" Otto remarks with a sigh, taking off his headset and wiping sweat from his forehead with his sleeve. "All good back there?"

A comforting wave of relief washing over them, Will and Abby sigh as they relax in their seats, "Yeah, all good!"

"Good. Sorry about that. . . paperwork huh! I could've sworn I scanned those in—but anyway," he laughs, "we'll be over Zeno's outer walls shortly and from there, about an hour to Desolation."

*　　*　　*

The huge siege wall that separates Zeno from the harsh reality of the dustlands is somewhat surreal. But as they get closer to its monolithic form that rears from the earth like an ominous beast, it is its sheer scale that is most incredible. The towns of the industrial zone at its base are like dots compared to its majesty, and the putrid trails of smoke from their countless chimney stacks like fine wisps of hair. Yet breaking over the top of the wall's parapets, it suddenly seems small, as the blinding heat of the sun starched Dustlands stretches out before them. Like a lake of fire, it is seemingly endless, broken only by the great ice flows and the endless wall of dust beyond the reach of the Vitruvian column.

"And that's it folks," Otto calls back as some warnings flash on the control console. "We've just left Zeno airspace.

Welcome to the sea of sand." Gesturing out the windows, he rolls the craft rolls into a gentle pitch. "If you look north, you can see the Mountains of Mourne. See—up there, above the clouds."

Trailing his gaze upward, Will nods as he sees the snow capped peaks sticking up like jagged shards of glass into the heavens.

"There's a whole lot of strange going on out there though, I don't know if I'd want to visit, but it sure looks nice from here! And that," he adds, pointing along the line of the siege wall, "is where we're headed."

A plume of smog hugging the golden sand, the dark shape of the desolate city rises in the distance, and as its shape comes into view, the craft starts a slow descent. Speeding parallel to Zeno's monstrous outer wall that towers above them, Will and Abby are suddenly aware of the breakneck speed they are actually moving and the sheer size of the wall itself. Craning their necks as its top stretches out of sight, they stare in awe at the massive size of the looming structure.

"Well?" Otto asks with a grin. "What do you think?"

"What were they trying to keep out?" Abby asks.

"Seems a bit overkill, right! But hey, in all the war and weather, it's never been breached. So it has served its purpose —Sorry, one second." Pausing, the cockpit is filled with the shrill beeping of an alarm. "What the. . . ?"

Joined by a flurry of red and yellow that illuminate the console, the shrieking of a warning siren blares.

"Seatbelts!—Now!" Otto yells, "HOLD ON!!"

The craft pulling into a hard left turn, Will fumbles for his seatbelt as some bags slide across the floor. But no sooner than it clicks into place, the air is sucked from his lungs as a blinding explosion rips through the side of the craft. Straining against the force of every shudder, in panicked shock his fingers dig into his armrests. But with a sudden rattle, a barrage of bullets spray across the cabin. A ghastly hole steaming from the back of Otto's head, howling wind and smoke sting his eyes as the craft lurches into a nosedive. And as the ocean of desert sand rushes up to meet them, his eyes squeeze shut.

Chapter 8

THE SEA OF SAND

Sand, warm on his face, presses soft against his cheek as he opens his eyes to the searing rays of the sun. The calm whisper of the desert winds humbly sifting through the air, he squints around and moves his arms and legs. He's stiff—stuck, and looking down his chest, he sees what has him trapped. It's his seat, strapped to him just as tight as when he clipped himself in. Feeling his way down the straps, he finds the buckle and squeezes, and with instant relief from its restraint, he flops forward into the sand, inhaling some and instinctively coughing, before rolling over and propping himself up.

Blanketed by the shimmering haze of the reflected sun, sand stretches unobstructed in every direction interrupted only by the gargantuan mass of Zeno's wall.

Beside him, half buried, the remains of his seat rests on its side riddled with holes and missing large chunks. Clambering to his feet he brushes dirt off his face and examines the ghastly state of his coveralls in stunned silence.

Spattered with blood that spreads into large dark stains in the hot sand around him, they're shredded beyond repair. One sleeve is completely missing.

Shading his eyes with his arm as the distant popping of gunfire echoes out, a single line of smoke growing on the horizon.

'It had to be the craft—Abby.'

Already feeling his energy being sucked out of him by the oppressive weight of the sun's heat, he begins to walk. Hopefully she had a better landing than him. Whatever Barkoba and that thing had done, it must have done something, and by the looks of the grisly artwork he left painted thick on the sand behind him, it must have done it well .

'What happened? The pilot, Otto. . .' An image of the gaping hole in his skull flashes into his mind. *'Were we shot down? I thought we'd got the all clear?'*

The familiar rumble of engines interrupting his meandering thoughts, he peers into the setting sun as the shadowed glint of vehicles move through the shimmering heat. Two or three of them at least, they are odd looking machines, crudely modified to suit the unforgiving terrain of the desert. Lifted well above the sands reach they're perched on oversized tires, with lengths of fabric and animal skins secured over their rusted frames.

With a tentative wave Will raises his arms above his head, as shifting gears and veering toward him they kick up a cloud of sand.

From an opening in the roof of the first, the faint outline of a robed figure stares down the barrel of a mounted gun, as behind, equipped with self loading cranes, two smaller vehicles pull giant caged trailers piled with nondescript junk.

But as the convoy takes a slow turn and comes to a halt, Will's heart sinks. Protruding from the middle of the second trailer, scratched and blackened, the lettering DD-722 is written on the broken tail fin of a Vitruvian Hawk.

Standing frozen as the machines' deep grumble fills the uneasy silence, the desert breeze carries a choreographed swirl of dust through the air. He had heard stories of the Sea of Sand and its people. Stories of the survivors who had crossed it as they fled the Darklands and the sacrifices they had made. Stories of the heroes who fought and the angels who gave them shelter. And stories of those who gave in to the horror and embraced it; stories of raw hunger and sharpened teeth.

With a sharp creak, the back door of the first vehicle pops open and a ragged man clambers out, hopping down onto the sand with a long sledge hammer gripped in his dirty hands. The sweat on his bald head glistens in the light as he makes a few tentative steps toward Will with a toothless smile.

"Take it easy fella, nice and slow," he rasps, pointing up to the mounted gun leveled towards them. "Don't do nothin' stupid. He's jumpy on the trigger."

"Will!" Abby's desperate shout cuts through the tension.

Glancing to the sound, Will turns, but no sooner than he's moved a sudden burst of gunfire at his feet showers him with sand.

"I said slow!!" the man screams in a sudden rage. "Slow!!! You're no good if you're full of holes!" Gesturing toward one of the trailers where Abby is peering from behind the caged bars, he lowers his voice as he continues. "You want to go with the tasty lady, yes?"

His heart pounding in his chest Will pauses, "Yes," he stutters. "Yes—with the lady."

"Good. Go. Nice and slow."

Will's eyes fixing on Abby's, he takes careful steps to the caged section of the trailer as the man behind follows, poised ready to swing his hammer. On the back of the trailer, another robed figure pulls a thick rope hanging loose from the metal lattice, that with a creaky squeal, lifts open a small hatch in the side of the cage.

"Go!" the man behind him shouts, prodding Will hard in the back.

Climbing in amongst the piles of scrap metal and discarded mechanical junk, Will stumbles forward and scrambles over to Abby. Propped up against the side, her eyes are bloodshot and her sallow face drawn in anguish.

"I think it's broken," she mumbles, clutching her leg tight with a ripped length of cloth. "I can't stop the bleeding."

"Let me see," he asks, kneeling down beside her. But as she moves her hand, he recoils in surprise as a sudden rush of blood spurts through her fingers.

"I can't," she whimpers through the pain with fear in her voice. "It's not good. It's not good. I don't know how long I'll last like this."

Clambering to his feet, Will stands up and frantically looks around.

"Hey!" he yells at the robed figure sitting at the trailer's front. "Hey! We need help!"

Through the small slits in the fabric of his hood the man slowly turns to look.

"Hey! Please, she's hurt!" Will pleads, banging on the bars with open hands. "She needs help!"

With a shake of his head, the hooded man mutters under his breath and ambles over, stopping just out of arm's reach to examine Abby through the cage.

"Please," Will begs. "She's bleeding bad. If she doesn't get help she'll die!"

Turning his beady focus to Will, the robed figure lingers for a second, before turning and walking away.

"Hey!" Will screams after him. "You can't just leave her here!"

With a sudden rumble, the trailer shakes as the engines roar back to life and with a jolt, the vehicles begin to move. Settling down on the rusty trailer bed beside her, he pulls her unconscious head onto his shoulder.

"You're gonna be ok," he whispers under his breath. "You're gonna be ok."

*   *   *

Taking its cue from the light's retreat, the bitter cold of night consumes the scorching heat of the day as the convoy trundles through the desert.

A pit in his stomach, Will holds Abby closer as she shivers. Memories of Marissa's frail body come flooding back, poking and taunting his fragility with his uselessness.

'*Oh God, don't let her die. What are we even doing here?. . . If it wasn't for me. If I'd had any balls. . . I'd have accepted my fate instead of hiding from it.*'

A rumbling crack deep in the moonless sky above distracts him, as with a flash of white light, the vehicles speeding through the desert are illuminated as if by the light of day. Again, a crash like thunder, and as the first red wisps of dawn delicately crown the crests of blooming cumulus clouds on the horizon, another flash lights up the darkness. The vehicle ahead skidding to a stop in a wave of sand, Will holds on tight, as with another shuddering explosion bellowing out, their trailer rolls to a halt. leaping off the side as another shockwave trembles through the air, the robed figure up front is gone from his perch, running as he hits the sand. But flung viciously into the dirt with a screech, his shrouded head shatters like powdered glass. Then another blast, and another, the terrifying thump of its unseen force ripping through metal and bone. Screams filling the night, the rest of the vehicles grind to a stop, flames spewing out their windows as the passengers spill out. Yet as they scatter in all directions some fall through broken glass, wriggling in silent agony engulfed in the blaze.

Suddenly, Abby gasps as her eyes flick open. "Occuli!" she calls out terror.

No sooner than it is spoken, a pang of dread courses through Will's veins.

It is only one word, but it is enough. Occuli.

<hr>

High above the atmosphere, it hovers.

The three concentric rings of its massive shape slowing their orbit, its mechanical eyes and ears twitch as it absorbs the world below. Growling with the fusion hum of its Vitruvian drive, like the mighty scepter of a God, the long cold barrel of its terrible gun hangs still in its center. And as it decides the fate of all in its sight, it waits patiently for a command.

With a sharp crack of unparalleled energy, it moves how only it can. Dropping in terrifying descent, it falls like a comet, pirouetting its graceful weapon as it comes to a sudden stop and takes aim. Sounding the bells of death, it utters its thunderous verdict in a breath of white flame, before, choosing the next life to cease, it disappears with a shriek across the night sky.

"Hide!!" Abby yells with urgency, snapping Will out of his panicked trance. "We need to hide!"

Staying as low as he can, Will scans for cover as he scrambles between the piles of junk across the trailer. More shots burst from the sky, each one so loud he flinches as if he's been struck. *'There's got to be something! Anything!! There—a gap!'*

Unconscious again, Abby is limp as he scuttles back to her, so grabbing her arms and dragging her across the trailer floor, he shoves her between some heavy metal sheets before climbing in behind her. Heaving on her body in desperation as another two shots bellowing out in quick succession shower him with molten steel, the force of their impact is so close it shakes the ground. But before he has time to think, a hole in the sheet metal appears from nothing as the air is blown from his lungs.

Dazed, as a line of pale moonlight shines through its steaming edges, he stares down in disbelief at a circular cavity punched through the center of his chest. It's black and bloodless, and burning his fingers on its intense heat, his limbs seize up in shock as he flops to his side.

*   *   *

Cold and uncomfortable, he lies there. Paralyzed but not in pain, he's vaguely aware of the sporadic blinking of his gaping eyes, providing a soothing relief from their frigid stare. He can't inhale, and even though trying with all his might, his chest doesn't seem to move. The absence of its familiar feeling grows unbearable, an endless drowning, until all he wants to do is scream at its torturous suffocation. But he cannot, and other than his stifled thoughts, he lies still.

As the morning sun rises, the sound of death outside the dark nook dies away. Watching the faint movement of Abby's chest reacting to her struggling breaths, the slight pulsing of her heart registers faintly on the anterior of her neck as she lies curled beside him.

Carried through the hole in the metal a bitter wisp of smoke twists and curls as it drifts on the desert breeze. Followed by a twitch in his arm, his fingers move, and as sensation like a million tiny needles ripples down his spine, he gasps as he is freed from his agony. Feeling up along his body, a wave of nausea rolls over him as his cold fingers slip into a gaping cavity in his chest. working to close the wound, a grotesque ballet of weaving tendrils slide and slither as they close the hole. And as they relent, he gasps and draws a precious breath.

The hollow thud of a vehicle's door sounding through the eerie silence, Will cocks his head to listen as he hears the muffled sound of voices outside. Pulling himself onto his front, and climbing over Abby, he peers out from behind the metal panels. Forward to the edge of the trailer with his head low, he stops as the snarl of a dog's barking cuts through the air.

"Put your gun down and your hands up!!" a gruff voice shouts out.

Will freezes as the frantic yelps of the dog continues.

"Come out or we start shooting!!" the voice yells again. "You got ten seconds!"

Cursing under his breath he doesn't move, but as the double click of a gun cocking cuts through the panic of his mind, he throws his hands over his head and rises slowly to his feet. From behind the waiting barrel of a shotgun, a large stocky man glowers at him, straining as he pulls on the lead of the barking dog. Tall and heavily built, with a pair of worn blue jeans and a dark dusty t-shirt that fits tight over his thick arms, his mouth and nose are covered by a cloth tied around his head.

"Quiet boy!" he yells at the dog. "Sit!" Gesturing to the trailer with the shotgun, the whining dog sits behind him with its nervous tail patting in the sand, "Anyone else in there with you?!"

"My friend," Will replies. "Please, she's hurt!"

"We'll help in whatever way we can, but keep those hands up, ok?"

As he speaks, another two men come around the side of the trailer with their weapons drawn. First scanning inside, one climbs into the front as the other wraps around.

"Easy. . ." the big man with the shotgun says calmly, as Will turns to look. "Keep your eyes on me. I don't want to shoot you unless I have to."

"She's hurt bad," Will replies in desperation. "Please, I'll have to lift her out."

"Don't!" he snaps as Will turns. "Your job is to stay still. You're no good to her dead. . . Once we're clear, we'll get her out, ok?"

Will nods.

The screech of the trailer's hatch opening is followed by the scuttle of footsteps as the other two men rush across it.

"Clear!" the first yells.

"All clear!" the other responds. "I got one wounded! Get Elle over here!"

Will feels the prod of a gun against his spine as one them approaches from behind.

"Against the fence!" the man instructs with a shove. First patting him down, the tension in his voice relaxes as he lowers his weapon. "Ok, good. Turn around."

As Will turns to face him, a thin young girl with short cinnamon hair tied up loosely on her head clambers through the hatch behind him and rushes over to Abby's still form.

"Don't worry," the man continues, seeing the concern in Will's eyes as he tenses up. "Relax. She's a medic."

"Can you help her?" Will asks.

"I don't know," he replies. "But we'll do our best. Now, out!"

Ushered towards a dirty yellow bus by the big man with the dog, Will traipses across the golden sand to its open door, and up the three oversized steps, past the driver who nods from behind the steering wheel with a pistol held tight on his lap.

"Keep going," the large man directs Will down the aisle, past a row of men and women kneeling on their seats as they point their rifles out the windows. "There, sit. Put that on."

Nodding to a handcuff fastened to a chair down in an empty space, he waits as Will sits and snaps it around his wrist, he studies him with a somber glare. "You're gonna behave for me, yeah?" he asks.

"Yeah."

"Good. Otherwise I'll have to put you down in the luggage compartment. And believe me, you don't want that.

— Hey Pauly, scan this one, will you?" he calls out as he strides back down the aisle and off the bus.

"Yep, on it," a short stocky man with a sun-weathered face replies, as he slings his rifle over his shoulder and shuffles into the seat behind Will. With a dubious glance, he rummages through his backpack and produces a small electronic device.

Squinting at its display as sunlight streaks in, the double doors at the back of the bus burst open and as two men shove a crude stretcher onto the open floor with Abby laid out on top.

"Be careful with her!" Elle, the young girl yells, as she climbs in beside her and slams the doors closed. "Idiots!"

Frantically rummaging through the storage boxes secured to the walls, she pulls out a few small bottles and bandages, making a little pile with them beside Abby. "We need to get her back to Rachel!" she shouts up to the driver. "When can we go?!"

Three blasts of the bus's horn echo sharply into the air. A moment later the first of the group that Will encountered and the big man bounds up the steps, followed by the panting dog.

"What's the problem?! the big man calls up to her. "We got company?"

"She's bleeding out!!" she yells back. "We can't wait!"

"Who's left?" he addresses the driver with a sharp glance.

"Just Caleb and Mark."

"Hit the horn again!"

Again, the bus horn bellows out into the emptiness of the desert.

"Come on. . ." he mutters to himself, shading his eyes with his hand as he peers out the windows. "Where are they?"

From behind the wreckage of a smoldering vehicle, two silhouetted forms appear and dash over towards the bus. Rushing up the steps, the folding door closes behind them with a hiss and as the bus begins to lumber forward they stop to catch their breath. Both young, with dirty smiling faces, they're not much older than kids, if even that.

"You hear the horn, you leave!" the big man growls at them. "Next time we leave without you!"

"We know, we know," the older of the two replies. "Sorry Tom. We found a cash box bolted under the seat of the truck. We didn't want to leave it behind!"

"A cash box?! Come on boys, think! Have you learned nothing?! Your lives are a far more precious treasure than a damn cash box!"

"Yeah we know. Sorry Tom, but we figured—" He looks up at the man's stern scowl with an apprehensive smile on his face. "Well since Hannah said that we couldn't live on bread alone, we were going to use the money to buy everyone some extra food. Maybe even some chocolate!"

Tom is silent for a moment, his thick arms crossed and his face somber. But as the hint of a smile appears in the corner of his mouth, he grabs the scruff of the boy's shirt with his meaty hands and shakes him in feigned frustration.

"Pair of cheeky little bastards, aren't you!" he grins, making them both laugh. "Seriously though. Never do something like that again, ok? Stick to the rules, stay alive."

"I know, Tom. Sorry."

"It's ok. Lesson learned. Now, where were we."

As the boys find an empty seat he scans around the bus with a solemn gait, before sliding sideways in the row in front

Will's. His features show the slow burn of a lifetime of the beating desert sun and the weight of many hard times, but his eyes harbor a subtle kindness that is somewhat out of place in his intimidating presence.

"Well brother," he begins, as he looks Will in the eye. "If I take these off," he points at the handcuffs. "Are you gonna play nice?"

Will nods. And as the man produces a small key, he leans forward and unlocks them.

"So, you got a name?" he asks. "I'm Tom."

"Will," Will replies, distracted as he looks to where Abby and the girl helping her are huddled in the back of the bus. "Can you help her? Is she gonna be alright?"

"Elle," Tom calls to the back of the bus. "How you doing back there? Is she gonna make it?"

"I don't know. She's lost a lot of blood!" Elle calls out. "We just gotta get her back!"

Tom returns his sympathetic gaze to Will. "She's in God's hands. But you have my word. We'll do everything we can in our power. But she'll be alright. I've seen people pull through worse.

"Thanks," Will mutters.

The whining of the bus's engine lowering to a dull grumble as it levels out its speed, Tom looks him in the eyes. "That was quite the mess back there. How did you end up tangled with the Jackals?"

"The Jackals?" Will replies, staring at his shaking hands. "I—I don't know, we. . . We were shot down."

"Shot you down? From where?"

"We were coming in from Boston."

"In Zeno?! Jeez. No wonder you were shot down. What has you on this side of the wall? I don't know what you've heard but there's not much out here but sand and suffering. You in trouble with the Kol?"

"We were looking for. . ." Will motions back toward Abby. "I don't even know. She has some contacts in Desolation that were going to help us."

"So that Occuli wasn't looking for you then, no?"

"I don't know," Will pauses, "Maybe."

"Well you're lucky it showed up either way. We wouldn't have found you otherwise. The thing lit up the sky, led us right here."

Studying Will's pallid expression, Tom takes a deep breath before continuing.

"Well, with a little bit of luck, we'll get her fixed up and you'll be on your way, yeah? We should be there in a little over an hour."

"Where's there?"

"Desolation of course. There's nowhere else to go out here." Brushing some loose sand off his jeans he gets up from his seat. "Anyway, sit tight. If you need anything, just ask."

*　　*　　*

As the bus trundles through the desert, Will sits in silence. Bathed in a lazy yellow glow from the scorched world outside the dust covered windows, the form of distant dunes and large cracked canyons drift past the laboring machine.

Emerging from the edge of a boulder field, the grinding of gears sends a shudder through the floor, and shaken from his hazy trance, he looks ahead as the massive city looms on the horizon.

It has earned its name. A maze of ruin and decay fortified by a steel collage of thick metal panels, its vast

98

expanse of crumbling structures, shipping containers, tents and rusted corrugated shacks stretch far into the distance, stopping only where it meets the foot of Zeno's wall that towers above.

In quick succession, the horn beeps twice and then twice again as the dusty road ahead disappears through a large gate in the city's makeshift wall. Blocked by a long red barrier, the apathetic ends of field guns fixated on the desert behind protrude from a swath of camouflage netting on either side, and as they approach, a group of armed guards flag them down.

Hurrying from the shadows, a group of scrawny kids rush to scrub the dusty windows and as the bus comes to a stop and the doors open, two guards clamber up the steps. First scouring down the aisle in quick assessment, they amble down the back, pausing as they see Abby and Elle before turning and moving back toward the door.

"Just the two, yeah?" one of them asks, glancing at Tom as he passes. "You scanned 'em both I assume?"

"Yeah, of course," Tom replies. "Shut her's down. He was clean."

"Good stuff—you all enjoy your day now. Oh, and hey, Tom, send our thanks to the leading lady for the last shipment."

"I will do brother. Thanks."

The barrier blocking the road ahead swinging up, the kids outside squeal with delight as the driver tosses some coins out the window, and with a loud rev of the engine the bus lurches forward under the shaded canopy of ragged material over the street.

Some at least three stories high, the city's decrepit structures are no more than a spontaneous collage of platforms and bridges. Held together by an assembly of steel beams and plated sections interwoven with wooden sheets and fabric, they are dotted by the glimpse of the locals' sullen faces as they meander about rickety gangways and dingy alleyways.

It is not long before it all begins to look the same and staring listlessly at its unchanging specter, Will is lulled into a sullen stupor. But as a break in the buildings sends the sun streaming through the windows, he straightens up with a start as an opening in the claustrophobic sprawl gives way to the blue sky as it crowns the top of Zeno's wall in the distance. Steeply sloping into a massive basin cut into the desert floor, a sudden drop off at the edge of the road falls away, and following the line of the yawning chasm to its furthest corner where it meets the base of the wall, he sees the strangest thing.

Proudly perched in its waterless berth like the carcass of an enormous beached whale, it is a cruise ship. And as white as snow in the golden sand, it's magnificent, with black clouds of smoke billowing from its thick scarlet chimney stacks that protrude from its long deck. The trembling bellow of its horn reverberating through the air, he cranes his neck to get a better look, but as they sweep by a row of disheveled men lined up on the edge of the pit, the sight of bloodied ropes around their wrists distracts him from the wonder. Staring at their dejected faces, he flinches as the rippling crack of gunfire rings out and their bodies topple over the precipice with a sickening jolt. But before he has even a second to think, the bus turns down a side street and back into the complex jumble of the city's shanties and the ship and the horror are gone.

"The palace," Tom remarks over the noise of the engine, seeing Will's startled expression. "Where the Queen and her court play their games. Not a place you want to go. Nothing good has ever come from that place."

"But, did you see the. . ." Will whispers in stunned disbelief.

Tom pauses and looks at him with stern reflection. "It is their time. Keep your prayers for the living."

Through the labyrinth of dusty streets, the rest of the journey is in silence. Slowing only once to honk at a gang of dirty-faced children throwing stones, the bus rumbles along for what seems like hours until finally, just past some stalls selling hardware, they turn through a set of huge steel gates into a courtyard surrounded by tall, tightly packed apartments, fashioned in the same hodge podge manner as the rest of the city. And as the brakes squeal and emit an exhausted hiss of air, people emerge from the doorways at the bottom of the building and form a small crowd at the door.

"One of the ones we picked up is hurt pretty bad!" the driver yells out as the doors open, prompting a few from the crowd to rush around to the back. "We need to get her to medical!!"

Abby, still unconscious with skin as white as chalk, is lifted down on the stretcher, leaving a pool of dried blood behind on the floor. Getting up to follow, Will stops as he feels a heavy hand on his arm as Tom looks at him with a furrowed brow. "Not yet," he says with a calm shake of his head. "She'll be looked after, I promise. You stay with me."

As the other passengers disembark and are greeted with hugs and cheers, Tom keeps his hand firmly on Will's arm, sitting in silence until the bus is empty.

"Sorry to make you wait," he continues, once the crowd has almost cleared. "They deserve to enjoy their moment. We got lucky this time thank God, but not all of us are fond of the ones we save, especially if it costs us one of our own. Come on, let's go see Hannah. She wants to see you."

Walking down the steps, Will follows him across the yard through an open doorway. The bitter smell of decaying refuse mingled with the cooking of family meals hovers in the humid air and as he steps inside, it is almost completely dark, a stark contrast to the bright light of day. Up a narrow staircase and down a corridor, the metal floor clangs hollow under their feet. Until, reaching a heavy door at the end and announcing himself, Tom nods at the face that appears behind the sliding hatch, and with the bump of deadbolts, it swings open. Onto a rickety outdoor balcony that wraps in a loop a few floors above the courtyard below, a scruffy doorman slings his shotgun back over his shoulder, nodding at them as they continue on their way.

Past a few open doorways, the smiling faces of children glance up from their games as their mothers stand by pots steaming on the stove, as below in the courtyard, a group of kids kick a ball up against the side of the bus, shouting and laughing as they aim for the others sitting on its roof.

Stopping at a doorway with a faded blue curtain drawn over it, Tom knocks on the wall beside it. "Hello. . . Hannah? Can we come in?"

"Come in, come in!" A woman's voice emanates from inside.

Holding the curtain aside, Tom ushers Will in.

Sitting at a table, a small old woman with long silver hair beams at Will, adjusting the light fabric of her robe as she gets up. ""Welcome child!" she says, ambling over to them, her troubled movements and weathered face showing her age beneath her warm smile. "And Thomas my boy. You have done well. I hear there is another that didn't fare as well as this one?"

"Yeah," Tom replies as he places his large hand on her shoulder. "Just the two of them. There's a girl as well. She's in medical."

"Poor dear. Is she alright?"

"We don't know yet. She's alive, but hurt pretty bad. Nothing Rachel can't handle I'm sure."

"Oh my. . . It would be good to see how she's getting on," she mutters, glancing at Will as if she can feel his thoughts. "Philippa, dear?" Cocking her head she bends down, peering sideways under the table at three little children, two girls and a boy. Hunched together on the floor, they're almost invisible in their dimly lit surroundings. "Your turn little lamb. Go see Rachel and find out how our guest is getting on and then come back and tell me, ok?"

Without saying a word, the youngest clambers out, clutching a raggedy doll with straw hair, and pauses to examine Will with her big brown eyes. Lifting the bottom of her worn dress and scurrying out the door, the sound of her little footsteps trail off as she patters down the balcony.

"She won't be long," Hannah continues, giving a reassuring nod to Will. "Now then. Thomas — Could you give us a few minutes? I would like to have a quick word with our guest."

"Yeah. Of course," he replies. "I'll be right outside. Just holler when you need me."

Waiting until she and Will are alone, Hannah gestures to the empty seats at the table. "Please. Sit," she says, moving over to a dresser in the corner of the room and opening a cupboard. "Can I get you a drink?" she asks, glancing back at him. "You must be thirsty."

Taking out a bottle and a few glasses, she calmly pours two drinks and sets them down on the table, pushing one over to Will before taking a seat across from him.

"So, we could start with your name?" she asks, taking a sip from her glass.

"Will," he replies.

"Well it's very nice to meet you Will. I'm Hannah, as you might have gathered. Is that a hint of Zeno I hear in your accent?"

"Yeah," he nods. "Boston. In Neourbia."

"You are a long way from home."

Studying his face with a kind expression, she takes another slow sip of her drink. "Would you believe me if I told you that I dreamt of you, in the early hours of the morning?

"What do you mean?" Will replies, puzzled.

"Due north of the Desolate walls and east of Jackdaw canyon in your craft. I saw you fall from the sky. And when I woke, I sent Thomas out to look for you."

"I'm sorry," he scrunches his face. "I'm not sure I follow?"

"Don't be sorry, please. You would be forgiven for thinking me mad," she chuckles, straightening up in her chair. "But, on occasion, I am given sight of things I cannot conceivably see with my own eyes. And you, just last night, were one of those things. Now, I am not so naive to think that you will take my reality to be anything other than madness, but, whether you want to believe it or not, it is the thing that rescued you and your lady friend from the desert. And it is why you are here in this place, and in this moment. So whatever your thoughts are do not matter. It is the reason you are here."

Will pauses as he absorbs her strange words. "What, like some kind of fate?"

"Fate? No, hardly," she shakes her head. "I, or Tom, could have left you out there could we not? You are here because I heard and I obeyed. Why you are here however, is yours to succeed or fail at. But, if it is God's purpose that is to be fulfilled, if not by you, then by another — just in another moment in time."

Will smiles, bewildered but intrigued at the thoughtful philosophy of the little old woman. "So, kind of like, optional fate then?"

She laughs with a twinkle in her eyes. "Well yes, the option is always there. You'll never be forced which choice to take. But I like to think of it more as. . . optional participation; choosing to either walk our own way or to follow the path laid out for us by something greater than ourselves. . . Can I tell you a story?"

"Sure," he nods, quite curious as to what she will say next.

Taking another sip of her drink, she clears her throat. "When I was young and pretty—hard to believe looking at me now, I'm sure!" she laughs. "I had a vision, my first of many. But in my youth and arrogance, I ignored it—explaining it away as a bizarre coincidence triggered maybe by a chemical imbalance or psychological anomaly. Some years later, I had fallen into a dark place. My life and its hardships had confused me, tricked me, and worn me down. So clinging to the safety of bad men, I fell into a pit of despair. Cursing those that changed the things I could not control, and cursing myself for not changing the things that I could, I became so full of hate

—hate for the world and hate for what I had become. All I wanted was for it to be over. But how then, did such a sad character turn into such a magnetic, charming woman!" She grins. "Well, in my darkest hour, as I drew my last breath, naked and bleeding, discarded like a piece of trash and left for dead in the dustlands, I was found by a wanderer. And nursing my wounds, giving me food, and quenching my thirst, he—" Breathing in to stifle the tears in her eyes, her tone softens. "He showed me mercy I had never known. After some time, when I had regained my strength, I asked him why he had helped me. I had no way to repay him. I had nothing. All I was, was a poor and broken body. Yet when I said it to him, he stopped. And looking at me with such sorrow in his eyes like it was the saddest thing he'd ever heard, he said—and I'll never forget—he said; 'Oh my sweet child, do not be disheartened. For this is but a light and momentary affliction preparing you for an eternal weight of glory."

She pauses and inhales the deep comfort of her memories, before getting up and moving over to a large object shrouded by a long cloth, on the dresser in the corner. Pulling at the edge of the fabric, it slides off and reveals a large rectangular fish tank underneath, bubbling blue with clean water and an abundance of vividly colored little fish.

Will gasps, his earnest attention to her musings broken by the delightful display. "Are those real?!"

"Come, look," she beckons, producing a small paper packet of flakes from her pocket. "Here, help me feed them. See, like this. . . just a few little pinches at a time."

"They're beautiful!" he whispers in amazement. "The closest I've ever been to fish is in the Ether!"

Taking the packet from her, he squeezes a small amount of the pungent shavings between his index finger and thumb, in awe as the tiny flakes hit the surface of the water; sending the little fish darting with a flurry of delicate brilliance to where their food appears like magic in the skies of their world.

"Before he sent me on my way," she says, watching Will's fascinated face as he stares at the fish. "And once I was healed and refreshed. He gave me a gift. A book—not much bigger than my hand. He told me it contained the way to the greatest gift in creation. And all I had to do, was look." She puts her hand out, reaching for the packet of flakes and Will passes it back to her.

"So what then?" Will asks, breaking his attention away from the mesmerizing movements of the fish.

"Well, I looked, of course," she smiles at him kindly, "and then I heard. And this leads us to where we are now — still trying hard not to be distracted by all the little fishes." Watching his enamored gaze, she puts her frail hand on his arm. "So I extend to you the grace that was given to me. Our home is your home for as long as you want it to be, your friend too. And when you're ready to leave, you're free to take what you want to do what you need to do. We will give you all the help we can."

"Thank you, Hannah," he replies, taken aback by her kindness. "I don't know what to say?"

"Say nothing," she puts her hand on his shoulder. "Don't thank the pen for the writer's work. Eat, sleep, rest. Take care of your friend — Thomas?" she calls out.

"Yeah?" Tom replies a moment later, as his big figure fills the doorway.

"Did Philippa come back up yet?"

"What? Yeah, she's back under the table," he chuckles, pointing beneath the table to the little girl's cheerful face beaming back from between the other two smiling kids.

"How long have you been down there, you silly little lamb?" Hannah laughs. "Come here. What did Rachel say?"

She leans down as the little girl climbs out and whispers in her ear. "Oh thank God. Good girl, well done!" Pressing their foreheads together she speaks to her in an inaudible hush, closing her eyes before giving the little girl a kiss on the top of her head and sending her scurrying back to her spot.

"Well," Hannah continues as she turns to Will. "It may still take a while before she's up and about, but it sounds like your friend's going to be alright."

"Seriously? Oh that's amazing, thank you. Can I go see her?"

"Not just yet. Rachel is still finishing up with her. But as soon as she's conscious, we'll let you know. In the meantime," she looks over to Tom, "can you sort out a room and show him around? Some new clothes wouldn't hurt either if we have something that will fit. It looks like he's been playing with one of the queen's pets!"

Tom grins, looking at Will's ragged coveralls. "Sure thing," he beckons as he heads for the door. "Come on."

Leading the way up to the top floor of the stacked metal complex, Tom shows him to the room he's been allocated, and the very basic operation of the toilet closet that's emitting a nauseating odor from the end of the hall. Down on the floor below in the kitchen, he explains the rules around the big bath that's in the musty room behind it and how, for an hour after dinner, a time slot can be booked in to make use of any hot water leftover from the meal.

Will pays as much attention as he can about who to talk to if he's hungry and how they, as a group, take turns to do various chores; therefore maximizing social interaction and growing as a community. But, overwhelmed by the exhaustion of the day and the relief of hearing Abby is going to make it, he excuses himself to his room to rest.

It's basic, but has everything he needs. Two narrow beds and a chair. A single shelf with a horizontal pole connecting it to the wall—presumably for hanging or drying clothes—and a little curtainless window overlooking the rusted rooftops of the city's shanties below, interwoven by a mass of draping black cables that snake between them.

Trying a bit of the sweet bread from the plate Tom had prepared for him earlier, it is surprisingly good, despite its unusual appearance. But finding that he's not too hungry, he puts the remaining bit back before crawling under the thin bed sheet.

Chapter 9

DESOLATION

As streaks of morning light trails across the room, he stares in a peaceful trance at the cracks running across the ceiling and listens to his own quiet breaths, drowsy but refreshed. He hasn't slept so well in—he can't remember how long—maybe even before Marissa got sick. The usual aches from his nightmare's rigid angsts that torment him in the darkness are gone, and he lies still and calmed, free from the shadows of their twisting terrors and horrid screams.

Unsure of how long he has been awake, the indistinguishable chatter of the city's life hums outside the open window, occasionally broken by the honk of a horn or the thrum of a distant aircraft.

Fleeting glimpses of vivid memories wash over him. Some, bringing the warmth of a subdued smile to the corner of his mouth, and others, the searing sting of blame and regret, as history plays out its fixed diorama in an effort to entomb him in its perpetual present.

A knock on the door startles him.

"Yeah? Who is it?" he asks, sitting up in a hurried daze. "I'll—one sec!"

"No worries, take your time." It's Tom's voice. "I just came up to let you know your girl, Abby, is awake and talking. So whenever you're ready, I can take you down to see her, yeah?"

"Oh, that's great, yeah. Thanks. I'll—"

"I've got a change of clothes for you too. I'll leave them at the door. Come down to me when you're ready, I'll be in the kitchen."

"Perfect! I'll be right down."

Waiting until the footsteps have died away, he unlocks the door, and after glancing either way down the corridor, steps out and hustles to the end, inhaling deeply before braving the abomination that is the bathroom.

Sickened by the smell that seems to have permeated his head, he leaves in a hurry and grabs the little bundle of clothes from the floor outside his room. He laughs to himself as he reads the small note pinned to it. Scrawled in barely legible handwriting it reads, 'The new guy'.

The signs of heavy wear and repair are apparent, but definitely in better shape than his shredded jumpsuit from the day before, he pulls on the loose fitting cargo pants and t-shirt as he gazes out the window. He can just make out the faint outline of watchtowers along the unblemished face of Zeno's wall that mark the edge of Desolation's distant city limits; and what must be where the desert waters of the Lovelace flow under it into Zeno's filtration district. He had never fully grasped why the water treatment was discussed by the teachers at Milgram's with such importance when he was a kid. After all, how bad could glacier water be? But for some reason—obvious now of course that he's seeing it for himself

—the sheer size of Desolation and the extent of its impoverishment had eluded his understanding.

As the first pangs of hunger growl in his stomach, he takes one last look before heading out the door into the hallway and down the narrow stairs. Approaching the kitchen door, he can hear muffled voices and laughter inside and, as if a reminder of his defective social manner, his chest instinctively tenses up in anticipation. A handful of men and women are cheerfully sitting around a large table, helping themselves to a steaming pot of thick brown potage in the middle of it. Amongst an assortment of handmade wooden toys and soft animal skins, a few kids sit on the floor in a circle beside them, playing happily under the watchful eyes of their parents who occasionally interject from the table.

The conversation hushing, Tom gets up from his seat and beckons as he enters.

"Come in, come in! Everyone, this is Will," he announces with a warm grin. "Will, this is everyone!"

The group bursting into generous laughter, Will is welcomed with nods and smiles.

"Will is going to be staying with us for a while," Tom continues, "or at least until he's sick of us! So as per usual, play nice and be friendly!" He pulls up an empty chair to the table and beckons Will toward it. "Now brother, can I get you a bowl of Leah's famous breakfast soup?"

Beside him, a woman with a chubby baby propped up on her knee slaps his arm with a playful smile. "Oh, stop it Tom. I'd love to see you do better with what we had!"

He winks at her, sliding a bowl full of the brown mush in front of Will. "I know, I know. I'm only teasing. You're a miracle worker!—And hey," he lowers his voice as he leans forward to Will, "don't worry. We'll go down and see your girl in just a bit—she's doing fine. No point spending the day on an empty stomach."

As if in agreement the baby wildly flaps his arms. "Isn't that right mister!" Tom beams at him.

The soup is somewhat tasteless, but not unpleasant. And after the first few hesitant sips, Will devours the gloopy substance from his bowl, before, giving him a pleased grin, Leah fills it again.

Watching them laugh and talk with each other is quite mesmerizing. The meandering of their stories seamlessly bounces off one another's absorbing every different stream of each individual's consciousness so naturally. Even when in opposition with each other, it reveals nothing more than a mischievous spat in which they appear to delight in. On occasion, he catches a curious eye glancing at him, especially from the younger ones as they try to figure him out, and he— no doubt doing the exact same thing as them—glances quickly away pretending he wasn't looking either. But by the time they are all finished with their gracious introductions through a series of exuberant hand gestures and jokes—divulging who owns what child, their names, and who is married to whom— his mind is awash with so much new information that he retains very little.

As the food is finished and the baby starts to get restless and wriggle around Leah's lap, Tom slides his chair back and gets up, giving Will a nod. And with a thank you and a few 'nice to meet yous', they're off.

Out the door and through the corridors of the rusted steel structure, they wind down a rickety stairwell to the lower floors and into a bright but makeshift medical ward. Empty, except for one sleeping patient close to the end, whose rugged face is hidden under a tight bandage with spots of blood showing through the cloth, the worn beds are arranged in neat rows on either side. And passing between them to the door at the end, Tom gives a polite knock before walking through into a small room behind, filled floor to ceiling with shelves stocked with a variety of medical supplies.

Beside another door in the corner, the young medic from the day before is sitting at a cluttered desk, and as she looks up from a thick book, her face breaks into a smile.

"Oh, hi guys!" she says with enthusiasm, straightening the front of her light brown fringe and flicking her ponytail over her shoulder as she gets up. "I was wondering when you'd be down." Taking a few gangling steps toward them with her hand outstretched, she grasps Will's hand and gives it a light shake.

"I'm Elle," she says through a nervous smile. "I was with you earlier, or, well, yesterday. Don't know if you remember. I was with your friend, Abby—you know—in the bus?"

"Yeah, of course I remember. Thank you, Elle. So much. I don't know if she would have made it without you."

"Probably not," Elle replies, flashing a bashful little grin up at him and going quiet.

"Sorry for the interruption," Tom cuts through the awkward silence, raising his eyebrow at Elle as she vacantly beams at Will. "But maybe we can go and see her?"

"Of course, sorry yeah," she snaps out of her trance as her cheeks flush pink. "Yeah, no, it's no bother at all. I was just catching up on some homework Rachel gave me! I can do it any time." She gestures towards the desk. "We're doing the circulatory system, you know, like pumping blood and hearts and stuff?!"

"Elle. . . ?" Tom interjects, amused by her floundering.

"Yes, right, sorry! Come on through," she ushers toward the door beside the desk. "She's been awake for a few hours but is still real groggy. Rachel had to put her under to do her work and the stuff we use is—well," she laughs. "It does the job!"

Through another room, and into a storage area of some sort with a mass of bedding and clothes folded in well ordered piles stacked on shelves and racks, they emerge out the other end into a dim narrow hallway as Elle fills the silence with her energetic rambling, ". . .and some people even use it to fuel their transporters! Crazy right! Although, I don't actually know if it works or not, I mean like, I've never done it myself—oh, and sorry about that," she points up at the burnt out light hanging from the ceiling. "We haven't got round to fixing that yet, but like Rachel says; 'Calm yourself girl,'" she continues in a mocking voice, "we're provided for one day at a time!' So anyway. . ." she takes a big breath, "I guess there's no need to worry about it at the moment—it's only a lightbulb, right!? Anyway, just in here!"

Smiling back at them, she stops in front of a door and pauses, turning her head toward a muffled voice from inside the room across the hall.

"Actually, hold on a sec, will you? Let me just double check with Rachel if it's ok to go in."

Crossing the hall and opening the door, a woman inside glances up and gives an absentminded wave, before shooing them away as she points to the large satellite phone pressed up against her head.

"Sorry about that, yeah," the woman speaks into the phone with an air of exasperation in her voice. "Cephalex, doxy—it doesn't matter to be honest. I just need something, anything!"

"Well, never mind," Elle says, raising her eyebrows as she shuts the door, "I'm sure it's fine!"

*   *   *

"Abby!" Will calls out with a cry of relief as he sees her lying sideways on a bed, half covered by the ruffled sheets. Her face is a sallow shade of gray, but she smiles as she hears his voice. Rushing over, he crouches down beside the bed and looks into her weary eyes, as her voice cracks and she tries to speak.

"Take it easy, take it easy. You're fine," he interrupts her valiant efforts. Almost feeling her discomfort, he takes her soft clammy hand in his and strokes it with his thumb.

"Elle," Tom says, glancing at her with a nod toward the door. "Come on, let's give them a minute."

"Will, I—" Abby starts with a rasping voice as they are left alone.

"Shhh, there's no need to talk," he smiles at her. "There'll be plenty of time for that later. Just take it easy. You're alive, and you're safe."

"Where. . ." she mumbles, taking a slow breath through the sedated fog engulfing her mind. "Where are we?"

"I'm not too sure exactly, but we're in the city."

"Desolation?"

"Yeah, mission accomplished right!" he jokes. "Do you remember getting here?"

"No, not really. Just the crash, and then only little bits. . . Was there an Occuli?"

"Yeah, there was, I've never seen anything like it. It was. . . I don't know. Honestly, if it hadn't shown up, I don't know what would have happened."

"It wasn't supposed to be this way. I'm supposed to—" Wincing with pain she tries to get up.

"Just stay still, stay still! You won't be going anywhere for a while. We're alright for now, these people seem to want to help. Let's just sit tight for a while, ok? At least until you're a bit better." Distressed by her suffering, Will looks around. "Do you want me to get someone? I'm sure they could give you something for the pain?"

"No, you don't get it," she grabs his wrist. "Someone was supposed to meet us when we landed. Bar arranged everything! If we don't show up and they leave, I've got no idea how to find them again!"

"Can't we arrange another meet?"

"Maybe. But if they think the Kol got to us, they might just disappear—I know I would. Most of our sympathizers will help us, but they're not willing to go down with us, especially if they've got kids or families to look after."

"Can the Kol even get to us out here?"

"Not directly—not without an incident anyway. But make no mistake, for as far as the reach of the column's light, the Kol has influence. Every group and faction that is under their sight eat out of their hands, whether they like it or not. In their eyes, we're all Vitruvians. And sure, there are self proclaimed rebels and enemies of the empire. But at the end of the day, we're all eating out of the same big bowl—just different flavors to suit different tastes, that's all."

Straining to lift her head, she looks down at the contour of her injured leg under the sheet, before stifling a pained laugh, "But I dunno. I wouldn't go saying that around here! I don't imagine that's a popular sentiment. How long has it been since we crashed, anyway?"

"I dunno. Like, two days?"

"It's too long, they'll know something's up by now." She pauses in thought. "Do you think the people here would help us get in touch with Bar? I don't know what else to do?"

"Maybe. It's worth a try for sure. Do you have a contact or a number? I could ask Tom."

"Call this number—look, here," she shifts sideways and tilts her head, revealing part of a rose briar tattooed on her neck that winds down under her shirt. "See it?" she asks, as he squints at a series of numbers dotted out in a line just below one of the detailed petals. "Write it down. It will put you through to the hospital reception. When you get through, don't give your name or mention anything to do with Legion, just ask to speak to doctor Gamaliel."

"Gamaliel? Who's that?" he replies, grabbing a broken biro from the bedside table and scrawling the numbers on his wrist.

"I've no idea. But that's the name." Pointing to a small barb further down the tattoo to where the is name artfully scribed in decorative lettering, she carries on. "In an emergency that's who we're supposed to ask for. Oh, and another thing, I meant to ask, did they take yours?" Lifting her hand up with a furrowed brow, she shows him a small angry cut on the back of her hand, just between her thumb and index finger.

"What, your chip?"

"Yeah—or well, I'm not certain—but I can't feel it in there anymore. But if it is gone, we're completely stranded out here, all our emergency funds were on it. Did they say anything to you?"

"No, nothing. They scanned me when they first picked us up but that was it."

"Yeah, but when Bar. . . Are you still sure you even have yours?"

Feeling the absence of the familiar bump under his skin, Will falls quiet as he examines his hand.

"Well anyway, it doesn't matter. All I'm saying is we need to be careful. They may seem nice but we can't trust them, ok? We just need to get through to Bar."

A loud knock on the door startles them, and as it swings open, a woman in a worn lab coat bustles in.

"No need to get up, it's only me!" she chirps, as Will begins to stand. "You must be Will, right?" she asks, beaming at him with a warm smile that accentuates the wrinkled lines around her bright eyes. "And you, my lovely lady?" her voice softens with gentle concern. "I'm afraid I didn't get a name."

"Abby," Abby replies.

"Abby. How lovely! One of our little ones here is an Abigail too! She'll be delighted to hear that she shares a name with a woman from Zeno! Well, Abby, I'm very happy to see you awake. You were only a few steps from heaven's door yesterday!" Sliding one hand into her pocket, she rests the other on Will's shoulder before continuing. "Anyway, I don't know what Elle told you already, but my name's Rachel. I'm the in-house doctor, but if you need a surgeon or a pharmacist or a therapist, I'm your gal! Every day's a school day, right!" she chortles. "Unfortunately for now, I'm all we've got! But Elle's learning fast. Don't tell her though, I'd dare say she'll have me beat in a few years! Anyway, forgive my rambling," her tone shifts as she glances down at Abby's leg under the sheets. "The good news, young lady, is that your chapter is not over yet. I've taken everything I could find out of your leg and stitched you up. Some of the pieces were so close to your femoral they were actually resting on it, so consider it a miracle! But what you need now—and a lot of it —is rest, ok? I'm afraid Tom and his lot haven't been able to get any antibiotics for some time, so you need to give every bit of energy you have to your body to fight off infection. It is not a decision I want to make, and God willing, I won't have to—it's only minor at the moment. But if the infection spreads, we'll have to decide to wait and see or remove it. But not a worry for now, just plenty of rest. We're provided for one day at a time!"

"Remove it?" Abby asks, raising her eyebrows, as Elle comes in pushing a little metal cart with clean bandages and a bowl of steaming water sitting on top. "You mean my leg?"

"Like I said," Rachel continues, turning to take the cart and pull it close to the side of the bed, "it's not something we need to think about now, and we may never have to. So we'll be happy we have been provided for today! Tomorrow will worry about itself."

Behind her, Elle rolls her eyes as Will, seeing it, grins at her, which makes her blush.

"Now, if you would be a gentleman Will, and leave us girls be," Rachel continues. "We've got to change the dressing and clean the wound if we're going to have a chance, and this one needs her rest. You're more than welcome to come back this evening of course, I won't keep you two away from each other for too long." She gives Abby a cheeky wink.

"Oh, we're not. . ." Will starts, but trails off in shock as Rachel throws the bed sheets aside and exposes the battered shape of Abby's half naked body, marred with jagged cuts and sprawling black bruises. "Sorry, yeah, of course. I'll see you later."

* * *

Shaken by the sight of Abby's fragility, he wanders through the hallway to the storage room and back into the ward. Hearing the murmur of soft words from the corner, he sees Tom sitting beside the unconscious form of the bandaged man, whispering to him in a hushed voice as he holds his hand. Deathly pale and still, the man's skin is sickly sallow, and only the slow rattled wheezing of his breath and the almost imperceptible rise and fall of his scarred chest gives a clue to his place amongst the living.

Turning as he hears Will's footsteps, Tom wipes his eyes on the sleeve of his jacket, "Hey Will. You all done in there?"

"Yeah. Sorry Tom, I didn't. . . Do you want me to come back later?"

Tom sniffles and stands up, stretching his back, and puts his big heavy hand on the bedridden man's shoulder. "No, not at all," he continues. "I was just checking in on my friend here. Anyway, we got work to do today. I wouldn't be able to convince you to come along and help, would I? We could do with an extra body."

"Yeah, sure," Will replies, apprehensive of where his enthusiasm might lead, but eager to show his appreciation. "Anything."

"Well you don't have to, of course," Tom grins a little, seeing his expression as he glances at the injured man. "But it will save you being stuck here all day, and believe me, it's as boring as hell. By the looks of it it'll be an easy one too."

"Yeah, no, of course! What can I do?"

"Good man, thank you. Come on, I'll fill you in on the way. And hey, if it seems too much, you can always change your mind, yeah?"

Will nods in agreement as Tom gestures toward the door and leads him out of the ward.

"There was some kind of skirmish out at the airport a day or two ago," Tom begins, as he strides ahead. "We got word this morning that the queen's guard just left, so we're gonna try and get in there and see if there's anyone still alive that needs help before scavengers show up and clean the place out. Should be fairly straightforward. We're only gonna do a single sweep and then get out of there, so we should be in and out without any trouble."

"Any idea what happened?"

"No, not a clue. Your guess is as good as mine. It could have been official business, but who knows? Salome's lot are a law to themselves. Some of the time there's no reason other than them just flexing their muscles or trying to teach someone a lesson for looking at them the wrong way."

"Salome? The queen?"

"Yep, the one and only; the mad queen of Desolation — Just down these stairs here," Tom points to an open door on their right. "Yeah, she's quite a piece of work. Got a bit of a thing for removing people's heads too. You've heard about her I assume?" Tom looks across at Will with his eyebrow raised.

"No, not really."

"You heard how she got her name though, right?"

"No, never. Honestly, most people in Zeno don't know a whole lot about anything outside the city walls—or at least the people where I grew up. Most of everything we're taught is about the Empire. Anything outside of that is just folklore. Stories and stuff."

"So you Zenites don't even bother to learn about what goes on out here! And here was me thinking you guys looked down on us when you don't even look at all!" Tom scoffs with a hearty chuckle. "Well anyway, when she took power—and by took, I do mean took—she killed her father and had his head sent to her bed chambers cause, you know, why not," he rolls his eyes. "But anyway, some time after, she got it in her head that her handmaiden in the high court, who was also named Salome, was going to overthrow her. I guess she's not called the mad queen for nothing, so shortly after the execution she decreed that holding the name, her name, was punishable by death. And then. . ." Tom's face falls as his voice quietens, "she unleashed carnage on the city. Her men, her guards and their dogs, tore through everything. Hunted them all down, until she was the only one left."

Falling silent, the haunted look of a terrible memory plays across his face.

"You were there?" Will asks, as they reach the bottom of the stairs and pass the bus as they cross the courtyard.

"Yeah, it was a hard one to miss. . . They kicked in every door in the city—strung them all up, it was. . . Well, it doesn't matter now. It was a long time ago; a season for everything under the sun, right?" Glancing down he notices Will's expression. "Jeez, I'm sorry! I've gone and gotten all serious, haven't I," he laughs, motioning to a doorway at the end of the corridor. "Come on in here for a minute. I just wanna see how the rest are getting on. Hopefully we'll be ready to get out of here soon."

Entering a large musty room, Will looks around at an array of worn plastic tables. Organized with an assortment of various equipment, one has crowbars, bolt cutters and a rusted assortment of other hand tools, while another with dried food rations and another with a variety of faded medical kits. Recognizing a few from the day before, Will watches as a handful of somber men and women mill around and fill their backpacks. But so preoccupied with thoughts of the task ahead, they barely register his presence.

"Morning all! How're we getting on?!" Tom announces their arrival, receiving an unenthusiastic mumble in response. "This is Will, if you don't know already. He's going to be joining us this morning."

Will returns a subdued wave as a few glance up and acknowledge him with half smiles.

"Pete," Tom continues. "The medical bag is topped up, yeah? You done a double check?"

"Yep," a young athletic man with a rugged beard replies, giving a thumbs up from the back of the room. "All done and loaded up!"

"Good man. Do up an extra go-bag for Will as well, will you?"

"Sure thing Tommy."

"And hey, Pauly? When you're done here, can you go sort out some flare guns as well, one for each pair, yeah?"

Looking up from a table in the corner of the room Pauly nods with a grunt.

"Perfect. Everyone else ok?" Tom addresses the room. "Good. Ten more minutes. If you need anything, let me know. And remember, stick to the plan and we'll be back for dinner. We'll meet you guys there."

With a nod to the door he ushers for Will to follow and reaching a heavy steel mesh door at the end of the corridor, he jiggles a key in the lock. "You ever fired a gun?" he asks, looking back at Will.

"Yeah," Will replies. "But it's been a while."

"No worries, I'm sure it will all come back to you. Just don't shoot any of our guys, yeah!" He grins at Will as the door springs open with a long loud creak, and ducking his head under the low door frame, he steps into the room and flicks on a dim light.

Above a thin shelf covered in handguns, a multitude of rifles line the walls over meticulously arranged cubby holes of ammunition; each type identified by a picture of the corresponding weapon they are suitable for.

"Take what you want," Tom says. "But maybe something on the smaller end for now. Just till we see how that memory of yours is."

Picking up a matt black pistol that catches his eye Will balances it in his hand and holds its cold familiar weight. Distant thoughts of the frantic Boston summers stir in his mind. The shrill wail of passing sirens. The bitter scent of asphalt searing in the hot sun and the boisterous chatter of his friends. Marissa called them wasters, and maybe she was right. But they did know well how to pass a long day on a dusty street with nothing but the clothes on their backs.

"You happy enough?" Tom asks.

"Yeah, sorry," Will looks up as he loads a clip into the gun.

"We got nothing fancy unfortunately—just basic point and shoots—but Pauly does a good job keeping them clean and firing." He points down under the shelf, "ammo's down there. And hey, just before we go out to the others. I don't know what you were shooting before, I'll assume clay pigeons on an estate with some other Zeno pussy's," he teases. "But if you were ever using them for anything else—and I know it's not my business." His expression hardens. "But while you're with us you only shoot as an absolute last resort, ok? Never, ever, for any other reason, got it? We're here to save lives, not to take them."

"Ok, yeah, sure. Got it," Will replies, slightly confused by Tom's sudden intensity.

"Good. I'm not saying we'll even have to use them either, we rarely do. But if it comes to it, we play the defensive and get out of there as quick as possible."

He pauses, locking his gaze on Will's before softening his tone. "And hey—thanks for coming out with us. It means a lot."

"My pleasure," Will nods.

"Now, come on. Let's go. I don't wanna keep anyone waiting."

Locking the door behind, they march back down the corridor and out into the blinding light of the courtyard to the others who are kneeling in a loose circle beside the bus.

The balconies above hum with lively chatter, packed with what must be most of the building's residents. As, interspersed with the listless gaze of a weary few and the friendly little faces of children peeking out between the railings, cheerful friends and families talk and laugh. But with a long blast of the bus's horn reverberating through the air, the throng hushes to a deathly silence.

"Are we all ready?" Tom addresses the awaiting group. "Where's Elle?"

"I'm here!" Elle calls out, as she runs out the doorway behind them, skidding to a stop on her knees in the sand as she joins them. "Sorry I'm late," she smiles apologetically, before beaming at Will with a little wave.

"Come on girl, keep your voice down, everyone's waiting!" Tom scolds, giving her a stern look as he points subtly up.

Above, on an empty balcony, Hannah emerges. And as the crowd falls silent, the gentle calmness of her voice reverberates clear as all heads bow in silent prayer.

"Brothers and sisters," she begins. "Children of Light. . . As we are comforted, we will comfort. . . As we are sheltered, we will shelter. . . And as we are loved. We will love." She pauses and directs her focus to the group huddled by the bus. "If it is his will my friends, we soon will meet again. Take heart, and have no fear. For the world is in his hands, and he, has overcome it."

As a cool breeze whispers refreshing relief from the stagnant heat of the midday sun, a breath of peaceful tranquility hangs still in the air. Through the deafening silence, Will can almost hear his own heartbeat. But as the stifled whimper of a woman's tears suddenly shudders across the courtyard like soft rain, he watches as she buries her head into the shoulder of the old man beside her.

"Ok people," Tom's voice cuts through the silence. "Let's go. Pitter-patter!"

Without hesitation everyone in the circle around him opens their eyes and rises to their feet, grabbing the bags they have prepared and clambering up the big steps into the bus. Ripping through the air, the hearty diesel engine roars to life, and as it idles down to a steady shudder Will follows Tom onboard, nodding at the driver as they pass before taking a seat.

Throwing her backpack down in the spot in front of them Elle slides in after it.

"You guys mind if I sit here?" she asks, smiling at Will.

"You asking me?" Tom replies with an amused grin on his face.

"Well yeah, but—Will?"

Distracted as the bus rolls out of the compound and the tall metal gates creak closed behind them, Will glances up, "What, yeah, I mean no—of course I don't mind."

"Should I go ask Abby as well?" Tom winks at Elle with a stifled smile, who returns an intense glare. "Hey Pete," he continues, as Pete shuffles past them down the aisle. "Do you have that bag for Will?"

"Yep, one sec. I've got it down the back — Joe!" Pete shouts to the back of the bus. "Can you pass that backpack up? No, not that one. . . the one—yep that's it, cheers. And hey, Will right?" Pete looks over to Will with a hand extended. "Welcome aboard brother. Your help is very much appreciated."

A moment later, a gray backpack appears over Elle's shoulder and she grabs it and passes it up to Will.

"Thanks Elle," he says as he takes it.

She beams at him as she settles in her seat, "Of course, my pleasure!"

Unzipping the bag, Will looks at its well packed contents, doing his best not to pull anything out of place as he peers in.

"Don't worry about it too much," Tom mutters as he leans over. "You won't need any of it. It's basic stuff—you know; food, water, painkillers, a bit of cash, and all that kind of stuff, so don't leave the bus without it. But don't worry, it's just for emergencies. It's only if things go really sideways and you end up lost or left behind you'll be glad you have it. But you'll be fine," he adds, seeing Will's expression. "It hardly ever happens. Just stay close and there'll be no problem."

Chapter 10

THE CHILDREN OF LIGHT

Along the narrow dirt streets and through the never ending mass of decrepit improvisation that forms a sea of ramshackle homes, the dismal scenery of the city's shanty sprawl is bleak.

Past a large crowd of street traders and their patrons, the lingering wisp of fragrant spices and cooked meats fills the cabin, and as a curly haired toddler sitting on the handlebars of his mother's passing bicycle gives them a big wave, the bus returns a friendly honk. Spotting a tailor's stand, Elle leans back to point out the beautiful pelt of some gigantic animal displayed proudly in the center amongst colored cuts of flowing fabrics, until, as they leave it behind, they pick up speed and rumble further into the dusty slums.

The sun climbing higher in the sky, the clean continuous line of the river that cuts through the city comes into view, and as the congested traffic converges on a rusted metal bridge that spans it, they approach a chaotic bottleneck in the road.

"Dan loves this bit!" Elle chuckles, raising her eyebrows as the bus comes to a halt and the horn starts blaring.

"Who?" Will replies, as a gap opens up behind a battered little van, the bus lurches forward to begin its crossing.

"'Wheelman Dan!'" she giggles, gesturing up to the bus driver as the raging brown waters of the river becomes visible, thundering beneath them with an awesome rush. "But don't call him that. He hates it—he'd probably kill you!"

"He'd kill you first, Elle, for telling him!" Tom chimes in with a grin.

Will smiles, amused by their banter. "Duly noted. Is that the Lovelace?"

"Sure is. It's something else, right!" Elle replies. "Wouldn't want to get too close though. Imagine if you fell into that mess! Even if you made it out, you'd probably sprout an extra arm!"

Will laughs as he turns his attention to the murky filth barreling under them. It is hard to believe it is the same water that ran through Boston. The water that he and Marissa had spent many summer evenings beside, lost in jovial conversation without a worry in the world. Then, and there, with her—hidden from this—it seemed so clean and calm. But here, stripped bare? Somehow humble in what it is. Foul, but at least, honest.

"Is it sand that makes it like that, or what is it?" he asks, staring intently down at it.

"Yesss, sannnnd!" Elle chortles. "More like a whole heap of shit!"

"Elle!" Tom interrupts in a stern tone. "Guard your tongue, girl."

"Sorry!" she giggles, covering her mouth with her hands and blushing as Will smiles at her.

Leaving the bridge behind as they ramble east, the journey is uneventful, and except in parts where the shanty thins out and scrawny gaggles of barely clothed children swarm the bus with happy shrieks, it is quiet.

"Two minutes!" A shout from the driver stops the nervous chatter of conversation, and as the pitch of the engine lowers to a deep gurgle the bus slows to a crawl. Through the dusty windshield as small columns of smoke become visible from behind the surrounding buildings. Quickly checking their bags, the passengers move silently into position, kneeling on their seats and poking their guns out the windows, leaving only the grating crackle of the tires on the dirt road outside to fill the silence.

"See you guys soon," Elle says in a hushed tone as she slides out of her seat and shuffles down to the back of the bus. "Good luck!"

"Ok, everybody! You all know the drill!" Tom announces, as he gets to his feet and checks his rifle, clicking the safety off. "Stay in your pairs—don't take risks! If we can get even one back to Elle and out of here alive, we're doing good! Ten minutes in and out, and then we're gone – So keep your eyes on the time! Unless we gotta leave sooner, Dan will honk at eight. So when you hear it; you leave! No matter what! And as per usual, if anyone hears shots or sees anything suspicious, radio in and get back to the bus. If you're compromised and we need to come find you, shoot off a flare, but otherwise, let's keep it quiet. Any questions?" He pauses and scans around the attentive faces watching him. "Good. Let's go to work."

From the empty street outside, a bitter smell of burning wisps in through the open windows. Passing a sign peppered with bullet holes that reads 'Arrivals & Departures', Will flinches in horror at the grotesque gape of charred remains staring up at him from inside the husk of a smoldering car.

Quite small by Zeno standards, it is an airport like any other; cast concrete, with an array of antennae protruding from the control tower that rises from its roof. Behind it, a wide runway and four vertical landing pads are visible through the gaps in a tall metal security fence crowned with razor wire. At one time it probably looked quite nice, with the oddly sleek contours of the rounded pillars and large tinted glazing panels, a stark contrast to the rest of the impoverished city. And although the long cracks and crumbling corners of its weather stained facade clearly show the hallmarks of its age, it seems quite new against the backdrop of the city's ruination.

The reflection of the bus sliding past like a ghost in the tall windows beside them, they pull up in front of the large glass doors of the main entrance and with a long hiss, the bus comes to a slow stop. Flecks of blood dotting the walls, the signs of violence are all around, with rubble and shards of glass strewn across the pavement. But as the doors creak open, without a word, the passengers climb out of their seats and exit quickly down the steps.

Tom's voice is low as he taps Will on the shoulder, "Let's go lad," he says. "Stay close!"

Will's heart quickens in response, and swinging his backpack over his shoulders and squeezing his gun in his clammy hand, he follows Tom along the aisle and down the steps. Glancing either way down the path as his feet hit the dusty pavement, it is deathly calm, and other than the watchful gun barrels wavering out the bus's windows and the haunting swirls of dust that drift across the empty street, he sees no movement at all. Crossing into the cool shade of the terminal entrance, it is more silent still. The others have already spread out, each pair heading in different directions, and keeping his head low all he can seem to hear is the crunch of broken glass under his boots.

With an assembly of large bulbous lights forming large concentric patterns that stretch down the main atrium, it is a large, open space. Like a tomb. On the opposite wall, between the winding lines of bollards that lead to the baggage check-in booths, the side of a huge cargo plane parked on the runway is just visible through the long viewing windows. And as the eerie patter of their footsteps echoes as if stifled breaths, they sweep alongside a row of empty seats, toward a rigid mesh fence that separates the main terminal from the baggage carousels.

Instinctively swinging his gun up, Will freezes at the sight of the twisted body sprawled in a pool of dark blood.

"Keep moving," Tom barks back, hearing his hesitation. "He's a goner!"

Reaching a gate in the fence and rushing through it, a whistle from the other end of a carousel alerts them, as Pete and Pauly crouching behind it gesture towards something ahead. Glaring focused down the barrel of his gun, Tom sidles up to the edge of the conveyor, scanning for any signs of movement as Will crouches beside him and does the same. Motionless, they listen as a howl of desert wind whistles over the building, before without a word, they're on the move again, past another carousel and a few more rows of seats. From the corner of his eye, Will can see the other two following their lead, up out of their cover and dashing along the wall on the other side. Behind the next carousel and sliding to an abrupt stop, he ducks down again beside Tom, and taking a moment to catch their breath they watch ahead. Again, hearing the shuffle of the other's feet, they're up, darting past a handful of abandoned baggage carts. But just as the urgent growl of Tom's voice calls back to keep moving, the air thickens with a sickly stench.

Stunned by the nauseating odor and glancing to the side, Will's stomach turns at the carnage that decorates the white brick wall. Spattered in an organized line above the crumpled forms of bound men and women, scarlet bursts of blood sprayed in vivid display delicately trail to the floor. But they're moving so fast, in only a moment, it is gone.

The open stretch of the atrium coming to an end, they approach the bare face of a concrete wall embedded with two white doors, and reaching it with a few more hurried steps they press their backs against it and sidle sideways towards the closest opening.

"Has anyone found anything?" Tom whispers into his radio, panting as he tries to catch his breath. "We got a whole lot of nothing up this end."

Listening intently, he cocks his head as he waits for a response. Nothing. Silence. Then a click, followed by a hushed static fuzz.

A wave of agitated sickness washes over Will as he watches Tom's anxious expression, and swallowing as he tries to shake it off, he draws in a few staggered breaths.

"Yeah, we got two on our end—in pretty bad shape!" a sharp voice crackles from the radio. "Everything else down here's quiet. We're heading out!"

"Copy that, good work!" Tom mumbles, as he wipes his sweaty forehead with his sleeve. "Thank God! We won't be long. A few more rooms and I think we're done."

"Copy, copy—see you in a bit!"

With a muted flurry of footsteps from the other side of the atrium, Pauly and Pete emerge from between some carts and give a thumbs up as they reach the wall, as Tom waves at them and points towards the doors.

"Ok," he turns his attention to Will. "I need you to turn the handle and give it a gentle push. Then follow me in, ok?"

"Yeah, ok." Will replies, forcing a rigid grin through the uncomfortable tension in his body.

Taking a few steps sideways, Tom hugs the wall until he's right at the door frame, and closing his eyes in silent prayer, he holds his rifle tight to his chest. "Ok—you ready?" he whispers. "On three. . . One, two—" Before he's even said three, he spins around the doorway, raising his rifle as he moves, and as Will pushes the door open, he disappears inside.

As close as he dares, Will whips in behind him. With long windows that face out onto the deserted street, it is an open office of some sort lined by two tidy rows of desks. Glancing at the gaps between each one as they pass, they rush to the door at the far end marked with large red lettering, warning of the runway beyond. Reaching it and relaxing his tense expression, Tom looks back with a self assured nod.

"Ok, that's as far as we go," he whispers. "Let's get out of here!"

No sooner than the words are out of his mouth, Will's heart skips a beat as they are startled by a rustle from behind them. Snapping their weapons up towards the sound they freeze.

"Who's there?!" Tom calls out. "We're armed! But we're here to help if you need it. Otherwise just let us on our way and we'll leave you alone."

Inching forward with his weapon raised, he glances back at Will, pointing at a cluttered desk just ahead of him. Will nods and edges closer, parting his lips slightly to quiet his heavy breathing. But as a flicker of movement flutters from under a desk he jerks the barrel of his gun towards it.

"Don't move!" he shouts, as Tom whips his rifle to where he's aiming and hurries around to the other side.

"Come outta there!" Tom snarls. "Now!!"

Concealed by a stack of cardboard storage boxes, a small grubby hand reaches out from under the desk, followed by the terrified face of a young boy, no older than four or five, with dark hair and sad, wild eyes.

"It's just a kid!" Will says, stuffing his gun into the waist of his pants as he rushes forward and crouches down in front of the shaking child. "Hey, it's ok."

"S—Scabs," the boy's voice cracks as he points toward the door leading to the runway with fear in his eyes. "Scabs!"

"Scabs?!" Tom exclaims with dread, twisting toward the child's gesture and raising his gun. "Where?! — Now?!!" He fumbles for his radio and presses the button. "Everyone back to the bus now!! We got a kid here saying he's seen scabs! You copy? Let's go! We're leaving—Now!!"

"Copy that! — Loud and clear! — Copy, over!" The panicked chatter crackles in response as Tom releases the radio and glances at Will.

"Go time brother! Grab the kid, let's go!"

Seeing the urgency in his fearful expression, Will doesn't need any more. A surge of adrenaline tightening in his chest, he picks up the boy up off his feet and turns toward the door. Crossing back into the atrium with the boy's little arms wrapped around his neck like a small animal, he flinches as the crack of a single gunshot rings out through the crisp silence.

"Was that us?!" Pete shouts from across the open space, as he and Pauly dash from cover and begin to run. "Who's shooting?!!"

As a few more shots echo out, the blast of the horn from the bus rips through the air.

"Run!!" Tom screams, bursting out from the doorway, turning to unload a volley of shots through the opening before spinning round and breaking into a sprint. "They're on the runway!!"

"We got scabs on the street!!" a voice, accompanied by the crackle of gunfire yells from the radio. "Three or four at least! You guys nearly here?!!"

"Sixty seconds!!" Tom yells back.

Abandoning any notion of a clandestine end to the endeavor, the four men break into a sprint. Past the carousels and carts, more shots ring out and the sharp hiss of a single bullet whizzing by is followed by a maelstrom of flying lead. A spray of sparks showering them as bullets rattles across a conveyor, pulverized garments burst into the air as a line of suitcases explode. The little boy in his arms tightening his panicked grasp, Will strains to move as fast as his body can take him. With Tom's heavy footsteps close behind, he zips past a few more carts and through the huge mesh fence, past row after row of seats, as ahead, Pete and Pauly disappear out through the main doorway and up onto the bus. But before he makes the last few steps, like a sledgehammer, something slams into the back of his head as the boy flies from his arms and he tumbles to the ground.

Hot thick blood pouring down his arms, he clutches blindly at a gaping hole in his face and writhing and slipping in the intensity of a searing pain, he scans in a daze along the airport floor.

The boy, curled up in a ball with his arms over his ears, wails in terror at the violent cacophony of the gunfire, as Tom, shouting at the top of his voice, fires an unrelenting hail of bullets back at shadowed figures on the other side of the fence. But with a muffled pop, a bright cloud of red mist explodes from his back, and reeling sideways he hits the ground, clutching at a ragged hole in his shoulder. Deathly still for a moment, his face contorts with pain as the boy's frantic shrieks continue, until, rolling onto his front and shimmying across to him, he grabs him by his little shirt and drags him to cover behind a vending machine.

Will, stunned, fumbles, as he pulls his gun out of his waistband. The agony in his head burns like fire but as motion returns to his limbs and it subsides, he shuffles forward on his stomach and takes shelter behind a row of metal chairs.

With each bullet that hisses past, the boy's harrowing cries grow with terror. Shards of concrete and sparks shower into the air, and the sound of each desperate howl permeates further into Will's soul. And as he stares down at the royal red of his blood soaked shirt, he feels the first timbre of a tempestuous rage boiling in his belly.

Sticking his head out, he catches a glimpse of the shooters. Just beyond the fence, they're moving with the carts they're using for cover, and ducking back in, he glances over to Tom, who's staring back. Holding his shoulder as his blood pours from between his fingers, his anguish is mixed with perplexion and a look of fearful disbelief.

'Did he see?!' The thought rushes through Will's head as another hail of metal sizzles past them, blasting a cloud of debris into the air. *'It doesn't matter—not now! We've gotta get out of here or we're all dead! We gotta move, we gotta move—'*

"We gotta move!" he yells at Tom over the clamor.

'This is going to hurt!'

Bracing himself as he stands to his feet, a shard of shrapnel glances off his shoulder as he raises his pistol and fires as fast as he can. "Go!" he yells again.

With the whimpering kid in his arms, Tom scrambles for the door, and as their assailants scuttle for cover, Will yells again, firing sporadically as he walks backward. But as the thump of a bullet hitting his stomach knocks him sideways, and then another in his neck takes him to his knees, he screams as a deluge of blood laps over his hands. Pain blinds him as he hits the ground, but as anger rises deep within him, the gurgle of blood in his throat turns to a deep primal growl; and as his better sense begs him to stay down, an animalistic rage engulfs him. Standing to his feet in defiant fury he fires. Over and over, as bullets rip past him, and through him, until, with a hollow click, the report from his empty gun says no more. And turning on his heel, he runs out the door.

Out on the pavement, the air is alive with the sharp bullwhip cracks of gunfire. From the narrow openings in the bus's windows, puffs of smoke and fire spew into the street, and as Tom, ahead, scrambles up the stairs, Will bounds in behind him before crashing into his hunched back. Jerking forward with a loud roar of its engine, the bus begins to move.

The mayhem of the deafening noise and smoke almost unbearable, the crackling of munitions chatters all over the outer shell of the bus as they pick up speed. Grabbing the little wailing boy from the floor, Elle appears with a panicked stricken face and slides him into a foot space below the closest seat, before rushing forward to help Tom to his feet. Past the rows taken by the others firing furiously at the world outside, she pushes him sideways into a seat as a window explodes behind her.

"Keep pressure on it!" she screams through the deafening chaos. "I'll be right back!" Turning and flying back down the aisle to Will, she crashes down on her knees in front of him. "Where are you hit?! Where you hit!?" she yells, wide eyed, pawing frantically at the holes in his blood soaked clothes looking for an injury.

"I'm fine, I didn't get hit!" he shouts back. "Go back to the others!"

Her sickened panic turns to perplexion as she looks up into his eyes in doubtful confusion. "What?! You sure?! But the blood!!"

"It must be Tom's!" he cuts across her, seeing her horrified concern. "I'm fine — Go!"

"Ok, I'll. . ." She turns away and runs back over to Tom who's slumped backward onto the seat where she left him, pulling bandages out of her bag in a frenzy, before ripping the top of his shirt and packing a heavy padded gauze tightly against his gushing wound.

"Cease fire, cease fire!!" The desperate command cuts through the noise as Pete screams at the top of his voice. And as quickly as it had all started, it stops.

His ears ringing with a high pitch squeal, Will stares blankly through the cracked and dusty windows at the back of the bus. In the distance, growing smaller as the bus picks up speed, the outline of armed men lowering their weapons step out from behind a row of burnt out cars at the end of the street.

"Dan! Is she driving alright?!" Pete yells up to the driver, stepping back from the window and lowering his rifle to gaze around in the sudden quiet of the eerie disarray.

"Yeah! We're dinged up pretty bad but hummin'! She'll be fine!" Dan calls back shakily.

"Elle, how's Tommy?!"

"Bullet's in and out by the looks of it," she replies, through staggered breaths, preoccupied as she wraps his shoulder with a long bandage and pulls it around his bare torso. "But they got him good, he's bleeding bad! Is anyone else hit?"

"Everyone good?!" Pete shouts, scanning the drained faces of each passenger who respond with worn nods and feeble thumbs up.

"And the two down the back?" he asks, glancing over to the lifeless forms they picked up from the airport. "Elle?"

"What!!" she replies frustrated, as she tightens Tom's dressing, "I don't know! They're alive! We just got to get back! —Who's got the kid?!"

"What kid?!"

'*The kid!*' Will snaps out of his stunned trance and rushes over to the whimpering boy, hunched in a ball under the seat and hugging his grazed knees tight to his chest. Reaching out to him, Will slides his trembling form out, and as he picks him up, his skinny little arms wrap around Will's neck. Unsure if it's shock or just a wave of relief, flopping down in the closet seat, he's overwhelmed by a twisted jumble of emotion. Clammy and shaking, the fragile little fellow in his arms feels half dead, but as the subsiding adrenaline dissipates through his scrawny frame, his breaths slow and he rests his head on Will's shoulder.

The undulations of the tires rambling over the uneven dirt surface soothing his shattered nerves, a wearied shadow descends on him as the murmured whispers from the other passengers fades to silence. For a moment he closes his eyes, replaying the events over in his mind as niggling thoughts whisper in his ear, '*You should have got up sooner and fought back. . . If Tom dies it's your fault. You call yourself a man? And with this gift. . . What a waste.*'

"He ok?" Elle asks in a hushed tone, as she slips into the seat beside him.

"Yeah, well, in shock I'd say. But he's ok," he replies, glancing down at the boy's sleeping face. "You ok?"

"Oh yeah, I'll be fine. You know. . ." Forcing a blank smile she nods her head, as her eyes well up with tears, "Just tired is all."

*   *   *

The journey back through the dusty city and over the narrow bridge seems much shorter than on the way there. Under the tall metal gates of the compound the bus rolls to a stop and Elle, a little red faced to realize she slept with her head on Will's shoulder, gets up to help a barely conscious Tom down the aisle to a waiting stretcher. Greeted with warm smiles and gentle pats on the back as he steps off the bus, Will is surrounded by the somber crowd of friends and families of his fellow passengers. A kind, bright eyed woman with three small children at her heels extends her hands expectantly for the boy in his arms as he walks through them, and without exchanging a word, he gently passes him to her. Losing sight of the others as they're ushered inside he is suddenly overcome by a deep seated pang of loneliness in his heart, moved by their care but unsure if he should follow or just fall quietly behind.

"Fear not, child. A place has been prepared for you too." From behind, the sound of Hannah's voice comforts him, and gently taking his hand, she beams up at him through her wrinkled face. "Go, and rest. Clean clothes and a hot meal are set out in your room."

Taken aback by her warmth and her nurturing eyes, he looks at her, unsure of what to say. Pushing away the well of tears rising within him, he swallows the dry lump in his throat. "Thanks," he whispers. "Hey, is Abby—?"

"Sleeping. You can see her in the morning. But for now, rest. And besides," she points at his blood stained clothes with a soft chuckle. "I think you might do more harm than good if she sees you like that!"

*　　*　　*

As promised, a warm bowl of soup and half a loaf of thick hearty bread is waiting for him in his room. After wolfing it down, he strips down to his boxers and crumples exhausted onto the bed. And as the fading hues of the day's light radiates through the window and a cool refreshing breeze flutters peacefully on the tails of the worn curtains, he falls into a deep sleep.

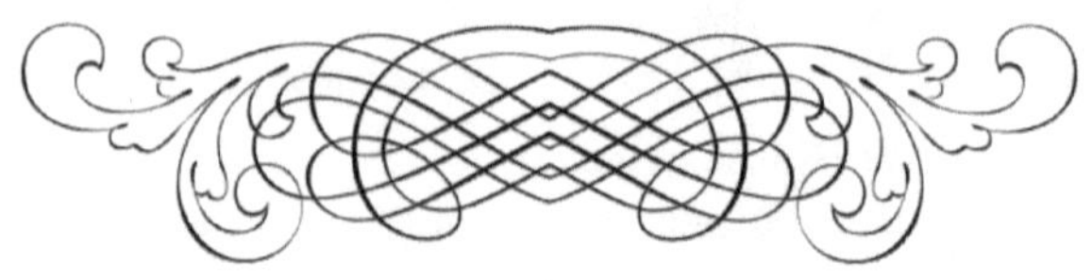

Come in my child and stay awhile,
take off your heavy load.
Prop it near the winding stair,
so tiring is the shepherd's road.
Come in my child and sit awhile,
and rest your aching bones,
Perch atop this ornate chair,
you see, it feels like home.
Come in my child and feast awhile,
and fill your deepest whim.
Sweet flesh and breads and hand pressed wines,
your needs are all within.

I ate my fill but hungered still,
and sat till legs were sore,
turning then to make my move,
I could not see the door.
Crying out into the dark,
I tried to look ahead,
and begging for the sight to see,
I heard a voice instead.

'Come here my lamb,' the shepherd spoke,
'and still your beating heart.'
'But where my lord, my eyes are blind?'
'Beside you, since the start.'

Chapter 11

RESPITE

"Breakfast's ready!"

Staring at the ceiling from the bed, a knock on the door startles Will with a jolt.

"Yep, ok," he replies. "I'll be right down."

In a drowsy haze, he slides his legs over the edge of the bed and rubs his face with his hands. Dressing in the set of clothes laid out for him on the chair beside the bed, he stops at the ghastly specter that they call the bathroom, before heading down the corridor to the kitchen. And pausing for a second outside the door in an effort to quiet his overwrought thoughts, he takes a deep breath before walking in.

"Good morning Will," Leah says, ushering him with a welcoming wave, as he nods to the friendly faces of the others gathered around it as they greet him. "Come, sit." With a warm smile, she gestures to the seat beside her. "Did you sleep alright?"

"Yeah, I did. Thanks—Leah." Will replies, unsure if he got her name right as he sits beside her. "Hey, have you heard from Tom yet?" He glances in concern at the empty seat beside her.

"Oh he'll be alright. . ." She nods to herself reassuringly as she smiles at the chubby baby boy on her lap, "he will be, won't he!" The infant gurgles in response to her playful affection. "It'll take a lot more than a silly old bullet to take daddy down, yes it will!!" Blowing raspberries on his round little tummy she laughs as he chortles with glee, before turning to Will, her expression softens. "I heard it was only by the hand of our maker that you came home to us yesterday?"

"Yeah," Will replies, as flashes of the chaos flicker in his mind. "It was."

"Well, thank you. For being there with him," she says, laying her hand on his arm. "I don't know what we'd do without him."

"So this little guy is Tom's?" Will asks, feeling uncomfortable in the silence.

"What. Yeah? Did he not tell you?!" she laughs, and rolls her eyes. "Typical!! Me and him are like – he's my husband! And yeah, this is our boy! Can't you tell? Look at the size of him!" she chortles, squeezing the baby's thick pudgy thighs as he squeals in delight with her affectionate tickling.

"I'm sorry, I didn't know. I should have guessed!" Will laughs embarrassed, grinning at the baby's exuberance.

"Oh no, not at all, don't be sorry! Honestly, it's classic Tom. Sure we wouldn't want him any other way!" She laughs again jovially, "he's not great with the details!"

Reaching to the middle of the table, she slides over a large loaf of bread on a board. "Here, help yourself. We had a good food run while you were gone, so there's more than enough for seconds, or even thirds if you want? There's more soup as well."

"You sure?"

"Absolutely, go ahead!"

Cutting two thick slices of the hard bread, Will examines some of the fixings on the table before taking a few thin pieces of white meat and piling it into a crude but hearty sandwich.

"So how long have you and Abby been a thing?" she asks.

"What? Oh no, we're not—we're just friends," he replies, taking a bite.

"Oh really? I'm sorry, Rachel said that—well, anyway, how'd you guys end up together? What's your story?"

"I. . . it's complicated. I—" Will stutters, taken off guard by the question, his face dropping as his mind becomes awash with painful memories.

"It's ok," she stops him. "I'm sorry. I shouldn't have asked."

Will looks down at his hands and fidgets with his fingers.

"Hey," she continues, lowering her voice as she looks him in the eyes. "If you ever need someone. We don't have much here, but as we have shared in suffering, we also share a wealth in comfort. You don't need to suffer alone."

"No, I'm ok," he replies. "Thanks though, I appreciate it."

"Sure, of course," she bows her head. "But the door is always open, ok?"

"Sure, thanks."

"Oh, I meant to ask," she says, her tone livening as she changes the subject. "You wouldn't have any interest in visiting Tom after breakfast, would you? He wanted to come and see you, but he's under Rachel's orders not to leave the bed for a day or two, so I said I'd send you down. Once you're ready anyway."

"Yeah, of course. I'd love to," he replies.

"You can go and see Abby while you're down there too of course. I'm sure she'll be happy to see you! Oh, and there's a bath ready for you once you've finished up here if you want to get freshened up." Pointing behind him to a curtained doorway in the back of the kitchen, she takes the final gulp of her near finished cup of tea. "That's not really a suggestion either." She grins as she glances at the dark black patch of dried blood on his neck under his collar line. "You're still a bit, icky."

The gift of Leah's personable demeanor and the delight of her and Tom's little boy, make the rest of the breakfast easy. Like old friends, words flow between them, with her giving agreeable little nods or looks to everything he says, instantly setting him at ease. When the food is finished, he stays at her request to help clear the table, bringing the dirty dishes over to the counter beside a big metal sink, before filling it with steaming water from buckets dropped off in the hall by a dusty old man.

Through the doorway in the back, she shows him to a damp, musty room with water stained floors and black blooms of mold forming in the corners. Pushed up against the window, a small white bath, half filled already, is waiting for him. So adding the leftover water from the dishes to it, he hurriedly strips down and gets in, scrubbing the dirt and flakes of dried blood off himself, while glancing over with mild consternation to the three quarter length curtain that covers the doorway.

*   *   *

Relieved to make it to the infirmary after taking a couple of wrong turns through the maze of narrow halls and stairwells, he finds Tom sitting up in the bed beside the injured soldier that lies as still and unresponsive as the day before.

"Will!" Tom grins as he sees him.

"Hey Tom," he replies, glad to see him in such an improved state. "How are you?"

"Ah, not too bad. All in a good day's work, huh!" he chuckles, wincing with the movement as Will sits down on the empty bed beside him. "We got those two out of there just in time apparently." He nods toward the drawn privacy curtains around the beds opposite them with a solemn glance. "They're in and out of it at the moment, but Rachel reckons a couple of weeks and they should be on the road to healing."

"What about the kid?" Will asks.

"What, the little fella? Right as rain—well—won't talk to anyone yet, but he's up with Hannah. She'll bring him around, always does. He's got you to thank for that. You should be proud of yourself."

"Me? No," Will replies, uncomfortable with the praise. "Anyone else would have done the same."

"Would they?" Tom's tone changes as he looks intently into Will's eyes. "Or should I say could they? Look, I know it's not my place. Whatever you are is between you and the Author. But what I saw was. . . I don't even know what I saw. When I looked at you, I'd swear, half your face was gone! But then it wasn't. And your eyes. . . they were as black as oil at midnight." Furrowing his brow he falls silent. "Do you mind if I ask? What did I see? You got some sort of tech?"

Will stares at his hands. "I—I don't even know. . ." he starts, glancing up at Tom. "It's a long story. I don't even know where to begin. I just wanted to try and change things and fix things in this hell hole. To stop the people—the monsters—that just get away with it. But tech? I don't know. I don't know what it is. I don't even know what I am. I—"

"It's alright," Tom interjects with a softness in his voice. "I shouldn't have pushed. You don't answer to me, or owe me an explanation. In this place, under the creator, we're all brothers and sisters. Whatever you've been through and whatever you've become is not without mercy or reason. Those two," he gestures over to the shrouded beds across the room, "and that kid you carried out yesterday. If the scabs had got to them they'd have been killed, sold or groomed up to scab for sure. And from what I've seen, the former would have been the kindest option. Your suffering is not fruitless. So, as long as you don't plan on going postal inside these walls, you're welcome to stay here as long as you want, ok?"

"Thanks," Will replies with a sullen nod.

Tom pauses and studies Will's joyless expression. "Hey, you want to know something?"

"What?"

"Would you believe that a long time ago, before I came to this place, I lived in a pristine, white, marble floored apartment in Caralis."

"Caralis?" Will asks, raising a doubtful brow. "In Libertaria?"

"Yep," Tom smiles with mild amusement at Will's surprise. "The very one. See this eye?" He points to his right eye. "Not mine — A welcome gift from Hannah when I got here"

"No way. Seriously?" Will starts, perplexed as he leans forward to examine Tom's eye, "You weren't a—?"

"Kol, yeah," he replies. "Born and bred."

Will laughs, "Get off it. You're messing right?"

"No," Tom shakes his head, taking a deep breath. "Not even a little bit. I'm full Chorion too, Zeno's finest!"

"Jeez. How on earth did you end up out here?"

"My parents were Kol, obviously, and their parents before that. Good people too, for the most part. Hard working, honest. Just doing what was required of them to save up and fit in you know. When I was younger, they would both take a month off work every summer so the three of us could spend a month together as a family. We had a ranch in Eden, real beautiful spot, lush and green on rolling hills—just out west of Sonoma if you know the area."

"No, not really."

"Well, anyway, one night I woke up and could hear voices downstairs, shouting in some language I'd never heard before. When I went down to see what was going on, I found three men with guns arguing, standing over my parents, who were on their knees with their hands tied behind their backs. When they saw me staring at them in my pajamas, they stopped, of course, but before I'd even realized what was going on, they'd grabbed me and dumped me beside them." Taking a breath, he glances up in recollection, "I remember. . . A strange thing about being Kol is, that whatever way the Vitruvian servant interacts with you, any normal emotions or impulses you have are overridden with, like a warm rush; a kind of peaceful contentment, it's the weirdest thing. So anyway, on my knees with them, my parents looked at me; and without a care in the world, they just smiled. . . still gives me nightmares. . . And then, as these brutes are waving their guns at them, my mom—in the calmest and most matter of fact way, no doubt knowing the Malflatus were watching it all through her eyes—tells them to surrender or die." He stops, momentarily lost in a faded memory. "They shot them both." Shaping his hand like a gun he presses his fingers to his temple. "Just like that – bang. And I didn't even care. I felt. . . nothing. Not sad, not scared. Nothing." He shakes his head as if to shake the thought from his mind. "Anyway, after that, they knocked me out, and when I woke up I was here; half dead and missing an eye!"

"What happened?" Will asks in amazement.

"I never found out. Hannah thinks I was taken for the Vitruvian tech in my head. But no one really knows. There's a lot of people, even the Queen, who will pay some seriously good coin to Trafaka or anyone else who can get it out of Zeno. But either way, after some shoot out with the locals down near third gate, Hannah and the Children picked me up and took me in. When she found out where I'd come from and what I was—or, what I used to be—she got me to swear that I'd never tell anyone. And a few months later, she got me this fellow. . ." He points to his eye, "Vitruvian biotech. Completely illegal out here and worth an absolute fortune but works just like the real thing. Better even!" He gives a hearty chuckle, "she doesn't look it, but I'll tell you; that woman is not one to be underestimated! I've never met anyone like her!"

With a fond grin, he turns his attention back to will. "So anyway. Now you know my secret, and I know yours. And apart from Hannah, how about we keep it that way? What do you think?"

"Thank you, Tom," Will replies. "That would be. . . I wasn't too sure what you were going to do."

"No thanks necessary. If anything, thank you. If it wasn't for you, I think that this," he glimpses at his bandaged shoulder, "would be the least of my worries."

"What's it like?" Will asks after a lingering silence. "You know, being Kol?"

Tom hesitates to think before he replies. "You ever woken up in the morning, completely comfortable? You know, not too hot and not too cold. Lying out on smooth crisp sheets with nowhere to be and nowhere to go, just relaxed. Like maybe you've died and are an angel floating on a cloud."

"Yeah, I suppose, once or twice maybe?"

"Well, that moment, as you're lying there and you haven't fully switched on yet. You know, you haven't thought about what time it is or what you have to do that day or any of that stuff, you're just there, suspended in the moment. That's what it's like."

"All the time?"

"Yeah, pretty much. As a kid, things were good. They were for everyone. We were happy. We never fought, never cried, nothing. My dad was a manager in a detainment facility in the Praetorium that held people until they got shipped out to Stanford, or Helsinki, or one of those places, and at dinner, he'd sometimes talk about stuff happening at work. He never described it in a harsh or graphic way, but looking back on it now, the things he said and in the place he was; he must have been part of some real horror. But back then? To him and to us, to everyone in our world, it wasn't right or wrong—it was just a job. Another day at the office. A world without cares."

"You ever miss it?"

"Ha—maybe. . . the idea of it anyway. A life without pain, regret. . ." He glances over at the lifeless soldier in the bed next to them. "It's easy for sure, comfortable. But it's not as simple as that. To be free from pain is to be free from compassion, and without that. . . I dunno," he shakes his head. "Sometimes a little bit of darkness can help us see the light. The Kol may have found comfort; but in doing so, they have become a slave to it and lost the thing that shapes them into what they were made to be." Trailing off in thought, he looks up with a start as he notices the silence. "I'm sorry, you should have stopped me, I'm rambling! So does your girl Abby know about your—condition—or whatever it is?"

"Yeah, she does," Will replies, "and she's not my—"

"Will!" Elle appears in the doorway grinning ear to ear and ambles over to them, leaning down and giving him a big hug. "How about that guy from Zeno huh?! He's not so— what was it you said Tom?—oh yeah, pampered!" Tom's face turns red as she chuckles. "Not so pampered after all, is he now! I'm only teasing though, Will. We all kinda thought that you'd be a soft touch to be honest. You know, being from Zeno and all. Except for me," she gives him a playful little smile. "I thought you—"

"Elle?!" Tom barks, trying to subdue the grin on his face. "Don't you have somewhere to be?"

Elle straightens up, her smile disappearing into an exaggerated, tight lipped seriousness. "Sorry Tom, yep, eh, I gotta go check out Judi's little one, she's got a rash or something!" Stifling a laugh she turns toward the door. "See you guys later!"

Tom sighs, raising his eyebrows as the door at the end of the ward slams closed. "No lack of energy with that one," he grins as he shakes his head in feigned exasperation. "Sorry about that. I think she might have a little crush on you."

"Yeah, I was starting to think that myself!" Will grins back as they chuckle.

"Anyway Will," Tom continues. "I imagine Abby is probably wondering where you are, so don't hang around on my account. I've got a long list of inventory to keep me busy." He gestures at the screen of a tablet on the bedside.

"Yeah of course," Will replies, getting up. "And hey, Tom, thanks for, you know. . ."

"Don't thank me lad, thank the one who made me, I'm only a messenger. We'll catch up later I'm sure."

*   *   *

Hearing the door opening, Abby looks up from the tattered book she's reading on her lap and her sallow complexion brightens into a smile. "I thought you might have forgotten about me!" she says.

"What, no, never! How's the leg?" he replies, moving over to her with a grin. "They swap it out for a droid one yet?"

She raises her eyebrows, in feigned shock at his comment. "A bit too soon for that one, no?!"

Will laughs and sits down in the seat beside her. "I know, I'm sorry. How are you anyway? You look so much better than yesterday."

"I feel better too. Whatever they gave me for the surgery must be mostly out of my system, my leg's killing me though. I heard you had quite the adventure yesterday. What happened?"

As best as he can, Will explains the events of the previous day, and although storytelling was never his strong suit, with a series of false starts and stutters he manages to get the gist of the trip through the city to the airport, and the war zone waiting for them at the other end.

"So wait, did anyone see?" Abby interrupts with a tone of concern.

"What?" he replies.

"You, your face! You got shot, no? And you healed!—Well, you must have, right?"

"Yeah, Tom did. But it's ok, I was with him this morning, just before I came here."

"What?" Her brow furrows as she straightens up in the bed. "What did he say?! Did anyone else?!!"

"No, no, just him. He said he'd keep it between him and Hannah."

"Hannah?! Who's Hannah, Will?" The frustration in Abby's voice rises. "We can't trust these people! They seem nice, yes! But we don't even really know who they are! What did you tell them?!"

"I know, I know! But what choice do we have? Last time I checked we were stranded in this place!"

"What did you tell them? Did you tell them about Legion, Barkoba?!"

"No, no! Nothing like that, no," Will replies defensively. "I didn't tell them anything—not really anyway—they didn't really ask!"

"Good. Well, at least that's something," she says, her irritation subsiding. "I'm sorry, I shouldn't have gotten so annoyed. I just—we had a plan, and now we're—it's just all gone wrong. Did you call the hospital?"

"No, I haven't had a chance. But I can go and ask now, I'm sure Tom will sort us out." he gestures toward the door. "There's a phone in the room across the hall I think. Or at least I saw that woman, Rachel, on one yesterday."

Abby stares at the floor in anxious thought as she chews the inside of her lip. "I dunno, if they say no, we're kind of screwed. Could we use it without asking? We can always just play dumb and say we're sorry if we're caught. What's the worst that could happen?"

"They could kick us out—kick you out," Will looks at her skeptically. "That would be a pretty bad 'worst'. You can't even stand up by yourself."

"But would they? Like you said, they seem pretty decent, right?"

"Yeah, but is it worth it? Can't Barkoba, and all this stuff not just wait until you're better? At least until you're moving around?!" he snaps back, irate at how pushy she's being.

"I dunno. . . maybe," she replies, deflated. "I'm just worried, that's all. Are we really safe here? Were we just unlucky to be shot down over the desert and then attacked by an Occuli? Or was it just a coincidence that the queen's guard raided the airport the same day someone was waiting for us to arrive? What if someone knew we were coming? Because if they did, they're not going to stop. And how long will it be before they track us here?" Hesitating, she looks pleadingly into his eyes, "Please Will, we've come this far. We have a duty. We have to at least try to make contact."

Will pauses and studies her in silence; she can be strangely compelling when she wants to be. "How would we even get it without Rachel or Elle catching us?" he asks.

"I dunno. I'm sure they'll be back later to change these bandages. Maybe while they're with me you could pop across the hall. I could keep them busy until you're back. I'll scream if I have to!" She gives him a sideways smile, "please?"

"I don't know—I just don't like it," he mutters. "But sure, we'll play it by ear and let's see what happens."

*　　*　　*

As morning turns to afternoon, they work their way through a few of the old fashioned and well worn board games left in an untidy pile in the corner of the room. Most are missing pieces or have instructions in a language they don't understand; but for a moment it's nice just to forget their unfamiliar surroundings, and the spiraling series of events that led them there.

A single loud knock interrupts them as Rachel walks in with a tray arranged with a simple but hearty breakfast.

"Don't mind me!" she chirps, as she gives the door a light kick closed behind her. "Just dropping off some dinner. How are you guys doing? Abby? How are you feeling?" she asks as she slides the tray onto the bedside table. "Quite an adventure you had yesterday I hear," she smiles at Will. "Do you always bring someone with a hole in them back from your trips?"

Will grins at her.

"I'm only playing with you!" she continues with a chuckle. "Now, I'm sorry I'm running a bit late! Normally Elle or one of the other girls does this for me, but they all seem to be caught in the perfect storm of busy today!"

"No, not at all! Thank you so much!" Abby praises her. "Will's been keeping me company anyway."

"Wonderful, that's good to hear. Real healing happens in the heart, doesn't it! Anyway, you'll have to excuse me, I've got to fly, there's a lot to do! But I'll be back in. . ." she checks a tattered plastic watch on her wrist, "well, hopefully within the hour. We'll give you another little clean and swap out the dressing, is that ok?" she asks, as she moves to the door. "Oh, and I meant to say, I managed to get a hold of some medicine to help with the infection as well, that should be in later today, so you won't need to worry about me practicing any more of my surgeon skills on you!"

"Perfect, thanks Rachel," Abby replies, laughing at her macabre humor.

As the door clicks shut, Abby winks at Will and gives him a playful pat. "See, there's nothing to worry about! There's no way we'll get kicked out! She's far too nice!"

Will helps Abby with her meal but after a feeble attempt she gives up, and they resume the game they were playing before the interruption.

An hour goes quickly by, and as promised, Rachel returns, popping backward through the door this time as she pulls a metal cart with clean strips of cloth and a warm soapy bowl of water on it. And as Will gets up to give her some room, she wheels it up to the side of the bed.

"Feel free to stay Will," she says, as she sits down on the bed. "If it's ok with Abby of course—I won't be too long." Pulling down the sheet covering Abby's bandaged leg, she examines the existing dressing.

"No, no. I'll give you guys some room," Will says, taking his cue to leave and moving to the door.

"You be back later?" Abby asks, raising an eyebrow.

"Yeah, yeah, of course. I probably just pop down to see Tom," he replies. "But I won't go far."

*   *   *

As the door clicks closed behind him, he takes a moment to breathe in the empty silence of the corridor, before, with a nervous tingle growing uneasy in his stomach, looking at the door across the hall.

161

'It would be a lot easier just to tell her you had a look but couldn't find it. She'd never know. And if you do go in, and get caught? What would you even say? After all these people have done to help, just to sneak behind their back?

You can't fault Abby's logic though; if someone is looking for us, and the queen follows us here? If the airport was anything to go by, God; a warning could save them all.'

For a second, he stays completely still and holds his breath as he listens. Nothing, but the quiet murmur from Abby's room. Two careful steps across the hall, wincing with each audible actuation, he gives the handle a gentle twist and slips inside. Scanning the windowless room for the phone he'd seen the day before, he moves past a filing cabinet and over to a heavy oak desk, set in front of a few tall storage cupboards against the wall. *Where is it?* The desktop is neat, with small stacks of paperwork meticulously arranged parallel with the edge, and several pens lined up in a row like soldiers ready for battle. Organized in a similar fashion, the drawers are much the same. In the bottom one is a clean snub nose revolver and a full box of ammunition, but still no phone. He turns and opens the metal door of the first cupboard; medicines, needles, bandages—*nothing.* Next one; lines and lines of colored folders, notepads—*there!* His heartbeat quickens as he grabs it, punching the buttons as he reads the faded numbers scrawled on his wrist. The device's little display lighting a luminous green, he presses the unit against his ear. A fuzz and a crackle and he takes another quick glance at the screen, to double check he's actually dialed—more static.

"Good morning!" The melodic tones of a woman's voice through the speaker makes him jump. "Halfpenny rehabilitation. June speaking, how may I help you?"

"Oh hi." He half expected it not to work, and freezes as his mind goes blank.

"Hello?"

"Oh, sorry, hi. . . I'm, eh, looking to speak to doctor Gamaliel?" he asks.

"Sorry who?"

"Doctor Gamaliel."

"I don't know if any of our. . . one second, hold please." There's a silence on the other end and he can hear faint talking and then her friendly voice again. "I'm sorry, we don't have anyone on our staff by that name. Are you sure you have the right place? Maybe he's over at Galton?"

"Emm, ok. Do you mind if I call you back?" he replies, flustered.

"No, not at all, anytime. I'm sorry I couldn't be of more help."

"Ok, well, thanks anyway. Bye."

The phone clicks and goes dead, and Will stares blankly at the screen. *'What was that? Did I get the name wrong?'* He checks the smudged ink on his clammy arm.

Putting it back on the shelf and closing the cupboard, he puts his ear to the door to check for sounds in the hall, before slipping back into the hall and taking a relieved breath.

A few minutes later, the door opens as Rachel bustles out, rolling her cart with her. "Sheesh, I'm not getting any younger!" she puffs with a grin. "Thanks for waiting. She's all yours!"

"Not at all, thanks Rachel!" Will replies, gratefully holding the door open for her while she passes and giving her a muted wave as she hurries down the hall.

Seeing her work for no other reason than to be kind, fills him with the nagging of remorse for being anything but honest. 'She would have probably helped if we'd asked.'

"Well?" Abby calls to him, breaking his distraction as he closes the door. "So? Did you do it? Did you get through?"

"Yeah, I did," he nods. "But the woman on the phone. . . She said there wasn't anyone there with that name—It was Gamliel, or Gamaliel, right?"

"Yeah, yeah," Abby replies, confused. "And it was the hospital you got through to? You sure you got the right number?"

"Yeah, of course!"

Abby pauses in thought and then puts a reassuring hand on his. "Well, I suppose it's all we can do for now. The Kol watch all communications on the network, especially coming in from outside the wall. So I'm sure there's a reason for the whole thing. Bar may be many things, but he's not stupid. So for now, we'll wait. And sure, if nothing comes of it, you can always try again in a few days?" She flashes him a cheeky grin.

He smiles at her cocky presumption. "You can do it yourself next time!"

*   *   *

With the sun retreating and a selection of new and pointless facts learned from several amusing rounds of Trivial Pursuit, Abby says goodnight as he carries out the tray of empty dishes, from their dinner that Rachel had dropped off a few hours before. Meandering past a snoring Tom, he makes his way up through the narrow corridors and eventually finds his bedroom; grateful for a mostly uneventful day.

Chapter 12

IN THE HANDS OF MEN

"Will, Will! Get up!"

Standing over him, the urgency of Pete's hushed voice cuts through the dark room as he shakes Will by the shoulder. "Come on, up! We need you downstairs!"

"What are you doing? What's going on?!" Will pushes his hand off him as he sits up and peers around in a daze. Illuminated by the moon's pale glow, Pete backs away from him, clutching the dark shadow of a pistol in his hand.

"There's a situation downstairs! Pauly's down there now! He told me to come and get you!!"

"Ok, ok. I'm coming," Will replies, unnerved by Pete's edgy movements. "Just give me a sec." His mind racing, he hurries to pull on his clothes as the icy night breeze from the sleeping desert drifts through the window.

Out into the hall, Pete leads the way, beckoning to another man waiting in the near darkness, before heading to the stairs. Down through the building and past the empty bus as they cross the open courtyard, they slink into another corridor and stop at a solid metal door at the end. Thumping on it a few times, there's a shuffle of feet on the other side and a loud clunk, as a heavy deadbolt slides open and the door creaks open. Ushered inside, Will squints around at the cracked tiled floors and tall lockers of a grubby changing room, illuminated by a line of bright fluorescent tubes hung on chains from the ceiling.

With two others standing ominously by his side wearing thick, dark boiler suits, Pauly in an agitated rage shouts from the end of the room, "Who'd you tell Will?!" he snarls. "Who'd you tell!!"

Between them, blindfolded with a grubby cloth and bound tightly to a chair, a man splutters through heavy breaths, as his crooked nose spews delicate trails of blood down his face an soak into the already saturated collar of his torn shirt.

Will stands frozen, perplexed at the horrifying scene before him.

"I won't ask again!!!" Pauly yells again. "Who'd you tell!!?!"

"What, I—what are you talking about?!" Will replies in shock.

"Don't play dumb! This guy!!"

Yelping in pain as Pauly grabs him by his ear and twists it, the man is forced to lift his head.

"Caught him trying to sneak in. And guess what Will, he says he's looking for you!—And your girl!" He glowers at Will. "So I'll ask you again; who'd you tell, and how'd this guy know you're here? He says he's a friend of yours, but seems to be a little foggy on the details. Ring any bells?!"

"I don't know, I don't know!" Will shouts back, his eyes darting around to the other men in the room. "I've never seen him before!"

"So you won't mind me knocking him about a bit more then?" Straightening his back, he grabs the whimpering man's sweaty hair with one hand before shaping his other stout hand into a fist, and bludgeoning it into the man's head who lets out an involuntary shriek.

"Stop! I don't know him! Stop!!" Will pleads, glancing to Pete who looks away with a sickened face. "Please, I . . .?! Just stop for a minute! I promise I don't know this guy!"

Pulling a handgun out from his belt, Pauly jams it into the man's knee, his face twisted in a malicious grimace. "You sure he's not your friend?! What do you think boys, think some speed holes will make this conversation go a bit—"

The sharp rattle of knocking on the door interrupts him, and as they watch in trepid silence, Pete turns and steps toward it. The deadbolt sliding across, the door is suddenly shoved open from the other side and the hulking frame of Tom stands in front of them with a blazing fury in his eyes.

"Gun down!" he growls, as Pauly, turning an ashen white shrinks back and stuffs his gun into the back of his belt. Silent for a moment, Tom's outraged stare probes them one at a time, before speaking in a low booming anger. "You dare to call yourselves Children of Light?! You have disgraced us beneath the eyes of our maker! Where is the light in this?! Is this how you treat your neighbor!? Your brother?! Dogs!! Have you learned nothing?! Where is your gentleness—your kindness!!!? Where is your faith!!!!?" The walls seem to shake with the reverberation of his wrath as he stops and takes a long deep breath, to collect himself before speaking in a calm, soft voice. "Go back to your duties. . . and beg the Author to show more mercy to you and your families than you've shown this man. I will deal with you all in the morning — Pete, you stay. You too Will."

In sullen obedience, Pete steps off to the side as the others pass and they file out the door, leaving the room tranquil except for the struggling wheeze of their confused and battered guest as he shivers in the chair.

"What happened? Who is this man?" Tom turns to Pete.

"The guys found him trying to get in. He says he knows him," he nods toward Will, "and the girl that came with him. He asked for them by name—knew they were from Zeno."

"I assume you scanned him? Was he chipped?"

"No, he's clean. We checked him twice."

Tom looks over at the bleeding man. "Is this true?" he calls out. "Do you know Will and Abby?"

"No. . ." the man sputters as a little more blood runs down his chin. "Or not exactly. I've never met them. I was sent to give them a message."

"Who sent you?"

"Please, I've got kids. I don't know his name, he just pays me – has been for years."

"So what's the message then?"

"I wrote it down. Here, in my jacket pocket—the left one," he motions to it with his head.

Stepping over to him to rifle through the man's pockets, Tom pulls out a small scrap of paper.

"'The Ark has fallen'," he reads it out loud. "'Queen's aid compromised. There is another. . .' Is this it?"

"That's all there was. Other than the names and where to find them, that's all I was given—I swear." the man replies. "I don't know anything else. That's all there was."

Will's heart sinks into his stomach and he feels like he's going to vomit as Tom turns to him with a stern furrow in his brow. "Does this mean something to you?"

Will's knees feel weak and his hands shake as Tom passes him the note and he reads the words;

The Ark has fallen.

Queen's aid compromised.

There is another way. Find it. The rebalancing is destined.

"Yeah, or, I don't know exactly—but Abby will. I'm sorry. I—I didn't know this would happen."

"God Will," Tom rubs his face in frustration. "What have you done?" He pauses for a moment, staring at the floor in thought before inhaling deeply and carrying on. "You," he addresses the man in the chair. "We are gonna keep you here with us until we have a chance to check into your story. You said you've got family?—I want names, where you live, their stories. You got a job?—I wanna know what you do and where you do it. I want your friends' names, the name of your dog—everything! And if it all checks out, and I do mean all of it, I give you my word you'll leave here unharmed. Understood?

"Yes," the man sobs. "Thank you. . ."

"But I've got to look after my own first so I'll only say this once; If you lie to me about anything. . . you will spend the rest of your days locked away, got it?!" The man nods in acceptance. "Good — Pete, have Rachel come look at this guy and then get him down to holding. And Will, I don't know what you've got us into here, but go down to Abby and wait there. I'll be down shortly."

Will can't bring himself to look at her as he slips through the door. The tightness in his chest seems to constrict so much it aches to breathe, and his mind races, overwhelmed by a deluge of thoughts.

"You ok? Is it morning?" Abby mumbles, waking from a restless sleep and peering disorientated at his shadowy form.

"Barkoba left a message," he replies, slumping down defeated in the chair beside her.

"What?!" she exclaims, sitting up and feeling around the bedside table for the switch on the scuffed lamp. Flicking it on, she looks at Will's pallid expression with concern in her eyes.

"What happened? Are you ok?"

"Yeah, I'm. . . Some guy showed up looking for us. He had a message. I'm assuming from Barkoba, but," he hesitates, recalling the man's savage beating and the look on Tom's face.

"Focus, Will! What was the message?!"

"The Ark. . . it's gone—fallen. And the queen's aid. . . Here, look," he passes her the torn scrap of paper. "Tom told me to come down here and wait."

Abby studies the note intently before turning it to check the other side.

"But it can't. . . Is that it?! There was nothing else?"

He shakes his head, crestfallen, and sits quiet. Dumbfounded, her shoulders drop as she slumps back into her propped up pillow, and stares in vacant disbelief as the words of the message sink in.

"I'm sorry Abby."

"So it's over," she whispers to herself.

*　　*　　*

Apart from her whimpers as she wipes away the bitter tears that tumble down her cheeks, they hardly make a sound in the seemingly timeless hours that pass and the first colors of the morning warm the room. Will can almost feel her fragile grief on his skin as it radiates into the stillness of the room, intermingled with an ocean of agonizing possibilities of what fates may have befallen the people she loved, and grew up with; and the only place she ever called home. And as Hannah and Tom enter the room with a solemn gait, she hardly registers their presence.

Gracefully sitting on the edge of the bed as Tom looms by the window, Hannah examines their sullen expressions, before resting her small frail hand onto Abby's.

"The message, child." Her voice is calm. "You have suffered a loss?"

Abby nods and sniffles, her head bowed.

"And have you—and your gift," Hannah turns her soft eyes to Will. "Put us in danger from the hands of blind men?"

"I—I don't know," Will answers. "If—"

"If we have, we are so sorry," Abby interjects. "We never planned for this."

"And who exactly is 'we'?"

For what seems like an eternity, Abby is silent under Hannah's unwavering gaze, but as if she can bear it no longer the whispered word slips from under her breath, "Legion."

A little smile breaks across Hannah's lips. "So, the stories are true," she replies.

"Legion?!" Tom snips from across the room. "What the hell is that?!"

Hannah raises a single finger to silence him, and he obediently looks away. "Please, continue."

"You know of us?" Abby looks up.

"I know enough. I know the force that drives you, and the hammer you were given to strike." Pausing for a moment, she glances at Will, "And I also know where it ends for all of you if you continue on this path. The Queen—what do you want with her? Is she one of the names on your list?"

"No," Abby replies. "I don't think so. But she has something—well, someone—who has a way to find them for us. Without him, we will struggle to get a hold of even one."

"So the Queen's aid in the note? Do you know who he is?"

"No. Someone was supposed to meet us when we arrived and arrange a meeting. I never knew any names. No one did except the elders."

"And the Ark?"

"It is. . . it was my home," Abby whispers.

"Well," Hannah sighs, "You're really in quite a mess, aren't you." Bobbing her head in thought, she stares at her clasped hands before continuing. "Here is what I think must happen. Once word gets out among our people—and it will—there will be some of us here that will think you've put our family in danger. If any of them give into their fear they—"

"If?!" Tom scoffs. "After what some of them have lost and what some of them stand to lose, we may have to fight off mutiny! And that's if no one actually comes looking for them! The Queen's guard! The Malleus! If they come we'll be cold alright, six feet under!"

"Your fear and your worry, my boy!" Hannah snaps, turning to face him. "Surrender it and be free lest it blind you!! Faith alone will light the way!"

Inhaling to reply, Tom stops short and falls quiet in a sudden loss for words.

"I know," Tom starts, "I just. . . I'm sorry. . ."

"It's ok," Hannah smiles, her voice softening again. "You carry the well being of this whole group on your shoulders. And you carry it well. But let us not forget that the future of all of us, friend and foe, lies in plain sight before the Author, and the outcome of each possible step has been examined. These two also are smiled upon," she gestures to Will and Abby. "And their paths have intersected with ours by no accident. So let's do the Author's will and show kindness and compassion. Judgment is not ours to give."

Turning her attention back to Will and Abby she continues. "Now, where was I? Oh yes. As much as I'd like to keep you here; as Tom mentioned, if the Queen or the Malleus comes looking for you, us and everyone in this place may cease to be. But we have been given hands to hold and feet to walk, have we not? So we must get you out of here."

As Will's face drops, she holds up her hand to interrupt his thought. "Wait, before you despair! You are not the first in need of refuge and we are not the sort to sit by while there is work to be done. We have many rooms hidden safely all around the city, and people there that will look after your needs. Can we offer one to you? You can stay as long as you like."

Will is silent and glances at Abby as she thinks it over through a furrowed frown.

"Thank you, Hannah," she sniffles. "That would be. . . It's more than we could ask for. Thank you."

"Tom?" Hannah looks to Tom. "Does that suit?"

"That'll do," he answers.

"Well it's sorted then," she exhales in satisfaction. "We'll go get things arranged now and we'll have you out of here in the next hour or two. Not a word to anyone, and if anyone asks, you're getting dropped off at the east gate with nothing but the clothes on your back. Ok?"

With a twinkle in her eyes, she gets up and beckons to Tom to follow her.

"Hey Tom?" Will calls out as Tom's closing the door.

"Yeah?"

"I'm sorry. . . for everything. I really am."

"Yeah. Me too brother," he replies. "Me too."

*　　*　　*

Stunned by the sting of sudden events and gnawed by the nervousness of the waiting departure that toys with them, Will and Abby are left sitting in an empty hush, dancing between grief and worry.

"You ok?" Will asks, looking at Abby's tear filled eyes as she stares numb at her hands.

She doesn't answer for a while, lost in a pool of dark thoughts. "They were my family," she whispers. "They're all I've ever known."

"I know, Abby. I'm so sorry."

"You think they're all dead?"

"They can't be, right? Barkoba at the very least. Otherwise we wouldn't have got their message? And I'm sure others must have escaped with him."

"He told me once that when the Malflatus get to their interrogations, they always get their way, always. He said that everybody breaks. What if some of them are with them right

176

now?!" she gasps, as the mere thought stifles her lungs with horror.

"Abby, don't. . . just don't. Don't even think that way. Barkoba got out, which means others got out too. Maybe it was just the Ark that got taken—everyone could have gotten out! We don't know anything, we just have to trust!"

"Trust!!" she hisses at him. "In what? Things have gone from bad to worse. I've spent my whole life planning for this. . . We were supposed to change the world! And now what? We're stuck in this place, completely at the mercy of strangers. I can't walk! We've got no money! No home to go back to, and no purpose!! You of all people—trust?!"

The all too familiar itch of helplessness ripples up Will's spine as her eyes blaze and her nostrils flare, and with each swell of anger that rolls over him, every muscle and sinew in his body twists until they burn.

"Will?" Abby gasps in sudden fear. "Your eyes!"

Shrinking away from her disgust, Will covers his face with his hands as his eyes become shrouded in the blackness of his fear. "I'm sorry," he whispers. "Were they. . .? I'm sorry. . . I. . . Tom said he saw the same thing when we were out at the airport."

"Are you alright?"

"Yeah," he replies, drawing in a long breath. "Sorry. . . Is it normal?"

"Well, hardly normal!" She lets out an uneasy laugh as a broad smile stretches across his face, a beautiful contrast against her blotchy, tear stained cheeks.

"Not like that!" he chuckles. "You know—I mean like— is it supposed to happen? As part of the thing, you know, the gift?"

"I don't know. Nothing seems normal anymore, so sure, why not—it's normal." She smiles at him and they look at each other silently for a moment.

"I'm sorry. . ." she says softly, glad at the respite from her sorrow. "I didn't mean to take it out on you. I've just no idea what we're supposed to do now."

The sound of someone coming down the hallway outside diverts their attention, and as they turn to look, Hannah breezes in, talking as she moves. "Sorry for barging in," she says, sitting down on the bed. "But I was just reminded of something that might be of interest to you. The message, the note, it said 'find another way', right? I had a thought. If you could ask the Queen directly, could she help you find the person you're looking for?"

"I suppose. . ." Abby replies, bewildered as to what Hannah is suggesting. "but. . . what do you mean?"

"It might be a long shot, but considering your. . . gift. Have you ever heard about the trials she holds in her palace?"

"Trials? No, nothing?"

"Well here, in Desolation, as part of the law; if you're accused of a crime, you are sent to be tried by the royal court in the palace. It was never a fair trial—more of a way to scare the populace as anything else—but since the queen took the throne, she's turned it from a private court into public entertainment, pitting the accused against each other or some other opponent. If the accused survives, they are set free, and if they don't—well—you understand. Anyway," she continues. "The queen's particular love for popularity has led her to make the trials more and more extravagant. So much so, that some years back she opened the trials up to the public, promising anyone free room and board in one of the palace cabins in exchange for participation. I'm sure you've seen by now that the people of Desolation live a hard life. Most struggle even for the basics, let alone being afforded with any kind of luxury. The palace on the other hand is, well, not lacking the ways of the world. So for some, a short life there compared to a longer life out here can be a tempting offer."

"So what would—"

"Patience child," she interrupts, with a kind smile. "At the end of each event, one survivor is declared champion. And as their prize, they are granted a single wish. . . Land, money, power—anything the flesh desires. As long as it props up her extravagant ego and thrills her hungry crowd, it's a wish that she dutifully grants."

"So we'd try and win an event?" Abby replies, with doubtful confusion written across her face. "I don't think that Will is—"

"How?" Will cuts across.

Hannah pauses and studies their expressions as she notices their tension, before looking at Will. "You just put your name down to take part."

"Just like that?"

She nods, "Just like that. Those willing to partake in the palace are never turned away."

"Will. . ." Abby starts, seeing the determined look in his eyes. "You can't. We've no idea of your limitations, or how much you can heal."

"I can heal just fine," he replies, shooting her a knowing glance. "And is this not what you want? Find Solomon, right?"

"I know, but. . ."

"Do you have a better idea? You want to hang around the desert until we get picked up by the Malleus or until I die of old age?"

"But what if we can get back to Bar? We could make a new plan."

"If the Malleus are looking. . . Even if we could get back into Zeno without getting caught, Barkoba's plan will almost certainly lead us right back here, will it not? And he said it himself, 'find another way'! This is another way! And besides, there's nothing for me in that place but painful memories. My life there ended a long time ago."

Abby lowers her head defeated, knowing that he's not wrong, but wishing so badly that he was.

"What do I need to do?" Will turns back to Hannah.

"I'll talk to Tom and see what can be done," she replies. "I'll be back shortly."

*   *   *

"I know, you're right." Abby says, disheartened as Hannah's footsteps disappear down the hall. "Are you sure you're ready?"

"No. . ." Will shakes his head, "not even a little bit. But if this is how we prevent more people from going through what—" He chokes on the thought of Marissa's name. "I don't know. My parents. . . yours? What happened to them in Stanford and all the other places like it? Maybe we can put an end to it, or at least slow it down. I can't just do nothing—not any more. What have we got to lose?"

"I know," she says, forcing a tight lipped smile across her despondent expression.

"Hey, so if I don't get killed on my first day. . ." he jokes, hating to see her sadness and flashing her a sympathetic grin. "What do I even say if I get a hold of Solomon? 'Oh hi

180

Solomon, I'm Will and I have a weird eye condition. Can you take a look at the biodata in my bloodstream?!"

"Who'd have thought Mannigan's successor would be such a tool?!" Abby chortles with a sniffle, playfully hitting his arm. "But seriously, no. If you, or when you find him; just tell him who you are, he'll know what to do. Bar said that there's few people that want to see the Kol suffer as much as he does."

"Knock knock!" They look up as Rachel's cheery voice rings out as she taps on the doorframe and bustles in, pushing a well weathered wheelchair. "I'm not interrupting am I? Do you mind if I come in?"

"No, not at all," Abby replies. "Come on in."

"So you two are going for a dramatic exit?!" she chuckles, resting her hand on Abby's shoulder. "Why am I not surprised! — Now, I hear that time is not our friend. So Abby, my dear girl, I have greatly enjoyed your company and would prefer to keep you here, but since I can't, I have packed you some medicine to help get you with your healing and tie you over until I see you next." She pats a hefty rucksack strapped to the back of the wheelchair. "It's all in here with clean bandages, clothes, food and some other things to keep you going. It will be several days before myself or someone else gets out to you, so I put a few paper books in there as well, to stave off the boredom. But aside from that I think we've got everything else covered, so try your best not to move around too much, ok?"

"Sure thing, I will. Thanks Rachel," Abby replies.

"Now Will, would you mind stepping out for just a minute while I get this lovely lady freshened up. Tom will be down in a bit to get you two out of here."

*　　*　　*

It is not long before Tom arrives to take them away, and after a heartfelt farewell to Rachel, he hurries them through the maze of the building's many hallways, pushing Abby ahead in the wheelchair.

"Pauly's gonna take you out to the safe house near Southgate," Tom leans forward to her as they reach the door to the courtyard. "And Pete's gonna take you out to the guard station up in Tropos," he adds, glancing at Will over his shoulder.

On the other side of the door, the rumble of engines starting sends a breeze of warm dusty air blowing in from under it.

"And Will," he says with a somber frown as they come to a stop. "Even with your talents. . . You are going to a very dark place. Your body may heal but. . . it won't be easy. And I know what you said before, but even there, you are not alone. If you call, he will answer."

Will pauses and looks into the kind eyes of Tom's stern face.

"Thanks Tom. For everything. And send my thanks to Leah will you? And the little man as well."

Tom nods and extends his hand. "Well, it's been a pleasure. I pray we meet again. You're one of the good ones."

Will grabs his hand and shakes it, humbled by the giant man and his gentleness.

"Now, Abby," Tom turns and looks down at her. "It will be a while before someone's out to you, but you won't be forgotten, I promise, so don't lose heart. We'll have someone out to you as soon as it's safe, ok?"

182

"Ok," Abby bobs her head with a weak but determined smile. "Thanks Tom."

As a horn honks from the courtyard, Tom opens the door and peering out into the blinding light of the day, the dry, hot air rumbles with the sound of the waiting vehicles. "Now, come on you two," he calls over the noise as he walks out. "There's a time and a season for all things under the heavens. And this one has come to an end!"

"Will?" Abby grabs Will's hand and looks up at him with tears in her eyes.

"Yeah?"

"I wanted to. . ." She stops as they stare at each other. "You were made for this, ok. Good luck."

"Thanks, I. . ." Will starts as he gazes at her pale resolution, taking a deep breath as he's suddenly overwhelmed by a rush of sadness. "I'll see you in a while, yeah. You can polish up my medals from the Queen for me!"

"Yeah. . . " she whispers, looking down into her lap.

The horn blares out again.

"Ok, come on Will!" Tom says, gesturing out the door towards Pete, who's sitting on a large gleaming motorbike with saddlebags draped over its sides. "We gotta go, Pete's getting impatient! Abby, you'll be over there in the buggy with Pauly! Where's he gone?—I'm sure he'll be right back. Come on, let's go!"

With a final glance at Abby, Will heads out, past a dune buggy with a sturdy steel roll cage to Pete, who's waving him over.

"You ready?!" Pete yells through the bandana that covers his mouth as he leans sideways and pats the leather seat on the back. Throwing his leg over the frame of the warbling machine, Will sits down, and after a few loud revs of the engine, Pete kicks the bike stand up off the ground. Rolling slowly under the huge frame of the courtyard's iron gates, Will casts a final glimpse back through the cloud of dust as Tom lifts Abby from her chair and helps her into the buggy.

As much as someone can practice or prepare the things they want to say when saying goodbye, it does not escape the inevitable fact that the act of saying them creates new things that need to be said which of course, by the nature of their creation, are impossible to realize until it's too late. So, as the motorbike picks up speed with a sudden roar and the compound disappears from sight behind them—it is too late. And as a pit in his stomach twists in a knot and a sickening sense of freefall grips around his chest, the realization of his control, or rather his lack of it, mutters its doubts in his head.

*　　*　　*

The baritone gurgle that emanates from the machine's throbbing engine draws all eyes on them as they rumble past the people of the dusty streets, bouncing on occasion as the wheels dip into a pothole or glances off a protruding rock. Eventually, as they turn down a narrow alleyway, they come to a stop and the hypnotic sound of the motor goes quiet, leaving their surroundings awash with an eerie silence in its absence.

"You ok back there?" Pete asks, pulling the bandana down around his neck.

"Yeah," Will replies.

"We'll walk the rest. I don't want this thing commandeered and sold for parts."

"What, the bike?"

"Yeah, the queen's guard has quite an eye for shiny things. They took a car on us last year for 'official reasons'," he gestures quotation marks with his fingers, "and left us to walk home. There's no saying no to them either once they've got their eye on something—I've seen 'em start their killings for less. Come on," he says as he begins to walk. "This way."

Leaving the motorbike behind and making their way to the end of the end alley, they turn onto a larger street lined with ramshackle two storey buildings. Most are abandoned or burnt out, but a few show signs of life, with some even embedded with small shop fronts that glow from the gloomy lights inside. As with a lot of the rest of the city that he'd seen so far, with the exception of the mayhem out near the bridge, vehicles seemed to be a rare commodity with only a handful parked off to the sides of the street. When one does pass, it does so with a subdued caution, careful not to enrage the ebb and flow of the meandering pedestrians that glower with blatant disdain at the mechanical intruder.

Up close, as they move through it, the poverty is painfully apparent. A group of scrawny kids hurling stones at a chalk circle on a wall stop to gawk as they pass. The sight of their protruding ribs that cast sunken shadows across their frail bodies is sickening, and as a mother smiles at Will through her cracked and blackened teeth, the wizened infant on her back stares up at the tuft of a passing cloud. After leaving Milgrams, most of the homes he'd stayed in had been in the poorest parts of Boston. He'd seen hardship and struggle. But this. . . this was not that. This was a tragedy, a grave for the living. Acceptance of the inevitable in plain sight on every hollow face.

"Is this your first time out in the city?" Pete asks, seeing his expression.

"Yeah," he replies. "Is it all like this?"

"No, not all of it. But most of it. I spent half my life out here. Would have died here too if the Children hadn't got me out."

"They find you on one of their runs?"

"Yeah. Picked me up after a cleanup."

"What's that?"

"What, a cleanup?" Pete glances at him with a raised eyebrow as they cross the street and turn a corner. "Oh. The guards do the rounds every now and then to clear out the dead and the dying to help stop the spread of disease. Obviously, dying or not, not everyone wants to be taken away, so sometimes things get a bit crazy. I was out running errands with my mom and we got caught up in the carnage. She hid me before getting hauled off. Pauly found me shortly after."

"Jeez, I'm sorry."

"Don't be. She might have made it a year or two more if things went well, but that would've been it. Believe it or not, the guards aren't the worst part of the city. It's everyone else you gotta watch out for."

"What do you mean?"

"Out here," he motions around them. "All citizens are free to choose their leaders, their laws and basically be who they want to be; totally free from the Queen's court or any rule of government. Trouble is, that when you leave people to their own devices with nothing to guide them but themselves, things get weird. When people find themselves free, like I mean totally free, to do what they want, well. . . this is what it looks like. The nature of man!"

"So why the guard then?"

"It was before my time, but from what I hear, things were worse than they are now, like a lot worse. And in all the madness, people went to the queen—or well, her dad or granddad or something—and begged for some sort of rule. So lo and behold, the guard was set up, in exchange for the peace tax of course. As you can see though, most of the citizens 'freedoms' are still in place; they only really step in for basic controls like cleanups, or sometimes if violence between gangs or the local warlords escalates; but it's better than nothing. I find it hard to imagine, but without them, I think this place might actually be worse."

"What a mess. . . Is that what happened at the airport? Gangs?" Will asks.

"God only knows what happened out there, but I suppose along with all the things going on in the city, the queen still has her own agenda and power plays; and she's not shy about carrying them out. She's up to her neck in it with every tribe and faction under the heat of the Vitruvian column, even the Kol—although I don't know who's playing who with that one. But for whatever reason it happened, I'm glad you were out there with us, otherwise we might have lost Tom. Not that we wouldn't stay the course, but it would have been a devastating blow to us all."

"Well thanks, but, I'm just returning the favor. If it wasn't for you guys I'd probably still be wandering around the desert."

"Oh, don't be so humble! Anyway, did we really do you a favor when we picked you up? I'm sure you have a plan and all, but you know where I'm taking you right?" He grins. "And besides, we only went out to get you because of Hannah."

"Yeah, maybe, but you didn't have to go. Why does everyone follow her so blindly anyway?" Will asks. "I mean don't get me wrong, and I'm not complaining. But do you always just get up and go out when she asks? Wouldn't it be safer to keep your heads down and just look after yourselves and your families? You seem to have enough going against you as it is."

Pete pauses for a moment, thinking before he replies. "We don't follow Hannah as such. . . I mean, we do listen to her and trust her to make the right decisions. But first and foremost, just like she does, we follow the Author of Life himself, each one of us as individuals. Her part, as is all of ours, is to simply help shine the way. And as far as blindly? We've seen farther with faith than we ever could with the limitations of our eyes. Same as looking after our families. Our blindness led us to believe that you were our brother, and that belief led us to take you in as one of our own. If that hadn't happened you wouldn't have been there with us in the airport, and. . . well, like I said, I'm glad you were. I'm pretty sure Leah is too."

The high pitched shriek of a turbine suddenly cuts through the sky, as an armed drifter bearing the queen's insignia on its wing rises into the air over the buildings in front of them blowing a cloud of hot dust down the street.

"Not far now," Pete says, squinting up, as it glides over their heads. "That's one of theirs. I'll take you as close as I can, and then you're on your own. Fingers crossed that no one shoots the place up while we're here, otherwise we'll have to do a runner and try again tomorrow."

An uneasy hush hangs heavy in the air as they move to the corner at the end of the deserted street. Pressing his back up against the wall, Pete takes a breath before leaning around the corner to scan the area ahead.

"Ok," he looks at Will with a stern expression. "You ready?"

Will nods.

"Once you're around that corner, put your hands in the air and just keep walking straight. It's about halfway down the block. Once you're in, just ask to volunteer and let them do their thing. They'll take care of the rest."

"How do I know which building it is?"

"Don't worry, you'll know," he grins. Grabbing Will's hand, he grips it tight. "It's been a pleasure. I hope the paths we've been put on cross again. Good luck."

"Thanks," Will replies.

Without another sound, Pete gives him a heavy pat on the shoulder and begins a brisk walk back the way they came.

"Hey Pete?" Will calls after him.

"Yeah?" Pete replies, turning around.

"You really believe in all that stuff?"

"Believe?" he laughs. "Do you believe the sun's gonna rise tomorrow?"

Turning again with a wave, he disappears into the distance, and once again Will is alone with his thoughts.

Staying close to the wall, he shuffles to the corner and pokes his head out to take a quick glimpse down the road he's heading. It's quiet and still, too still. With a deep breath, he raises his hands over his head and steps out.

Halfway down, the road gives way on one side to the stoic husk of a looming gray building. Heavily militarized and dotted with aerials and angled satellite dishes, long linear slits run horizontally along its scarred facade and an ominous hexagonal watchtower grows from its back. Surrounded by a razor wire fence that slopes outward at the top, it sits behind a flat concourse with rows of large cracked concrete barriers placed along its width. The distinct feeling of eyes watching his every move makes his skin crawl, and as he walks between them, he sees a single opening in the fence that leads to a rusted blue door perched at the top of a wide, monolithic flight of stairs.

Through the opening, a sudden shrill little sneeze reverberates through the silence and his heart skips a beat as, looking up, he sees the haggard shape of a young boy sitting on the top step. Filthy and wearing nothing but ragged shorts and a crude pair of sandals, he stares empty into the distance as he scratches the sore covered body of a sickly black cat purring on his knees.

Following a winding trail of dark dried blood that stains the concrete and ends in a congealed black spill at the top, Will continues forward up the steps, and as he reaches their spectral forms, he gives a muted smile. But so engrossed in their enchanted daydream, they don't even flinch, and he passes as if but a shadow.

On the landing at the top, he stops in front of the large blue door, taking a moment to examine the scuffed intercom box on the wall beside it before giving a hesitant push on the button in the center and a faint crackle sputters from it.

"Hello?" he calls into it. "I'm here for the trials."

With a click, it goes silent.

"Hello?" Puzzled, he scans around the ghostly plaza before reaching to press it again. But no sooner than he's stretched out his arm, he recoils with a start as the muffled bellow of a buzzer emanates from behind the door, and with the mechanical groan, it begins to open.

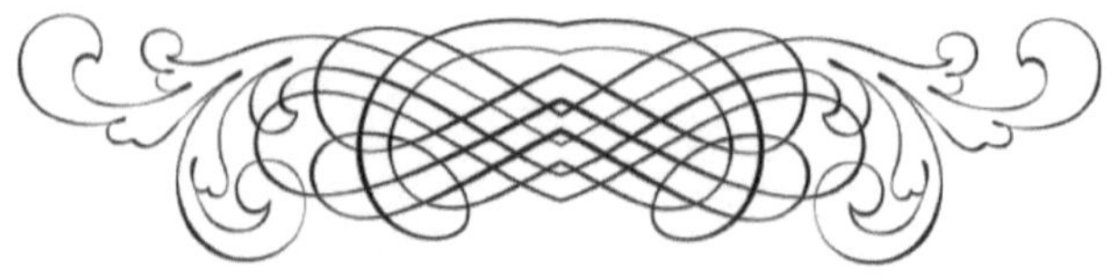

'Salvation is Repentance. Repentance is Sorrow'

Inlaid in a golden plaque, the letters of the words on the wall dance in the wavering glow of a thousand candles. The pain of yet another contraction searing through her back and down her legs, the women around her enveloped in lustrous, draping robes, chant mystery in the old tongue.

"Push my dear! You're doing wonderfully!" a veiled midwife exclaims from between her knees. "A beautiful healthy boy!"

The sound of the infant's cries flood into the high arched ceilings of the chamber.

"Almost there now, child. One more. . . nearly there!"

From a primal place slumbering in the depths of her being, the bellow of her anguish breaks free as she bears down again, gasping for life in the blackness of the night.

"Heaven be praised my sisters! Our tears have indeed been rewarded, another boy!"

Back and forth in unison, they sway until their chanting turns to tears. And shuddering in collective lamentation as they reverberate to a magnificent crescendo, their wails escape through the open tops of the tall pointed windows and are swallowed by the midnight sky.

*　　*　　*

Under the blood red roofs of its soaring towers and slender spires, proudly projecting from the back of the snow capped peaks, the grand halls and sweeping caverns of the Weeping City of Sorrow are a pallid place to live the happiest six years of her life.

Her boys, although still small, are already so smart and strong. At the hand of the sisters, they have been nurtured well and left wanting for nothing; fed the finest of foods, and dressed in the finest of garments.

But compared to the agony of letting them go, the pains of her labor are mild. So when the hand of the Wrath comes to bring them to their second birth and they kiss her goodbye, the primal anguish engulfs her once more.

*　　*　　*

Behind the stained glass windows that chatter in the whistling winter winds through, the warm chambers humming with the enchanting melodies from the chapel is an empty place to spend the worst six years of her life.

Except in the depths of prayer, her mind is never at peace and her thoughts run free with the possibilities of the many hardships her darlings are enduring in their training.

But in contrast to the torment of seeing them again, the pain of their departure is bland. The sweet boys that had once kissed her cheek had not come home. As their dark eyes and scarred bodies face each other with blades drawn, she is granted nothing but the stabbing validation of her sleepless nightmares. And when their steel flashes and her youngest falls, her heart turns to stone.

*　　*　　*

Surrounded by the vivid patterns of mosaicked floors, paintings and embroidered cloths, the ornate halls glistening with gemstones are a bitter place to exist for the last six years of her life.

All strength she has left is devoted to prayer. Prayer for her loves. For the peace of her youngest. And for forgiveness for the one who remains.

So when the day of his third birth arrives, she is at peace. And as he plunges his knife into her chest and lays her down to rest, she holds him in her warm embrace and fades away.

Without weakness.
Without fear.
Without doubt.
He is born a true believer. A warrior of the Wrath.

The Great Purification shows his worth. There, as the people of the Whispering Valley learn his name and the might of his pious hoard, the only whispers left are those of the converted.

The Conquest of the Western Plains show his wrath. There, as the unclean peoples of the sand groan. and the walls

194

of their stone city collapse, men fall from bone and all heads bow.

While away in the grand halls and sweeping caverns of the weeping city of Sorrow, under the blood red roofs of its soaring towers and slender spires, proudly projecting from the back of the snow capped mountains, a mother sings to her newborn babe;

Chapter 13

THE PALACE OF WISH

He has never seen such a strange sight. Cut deep in the desert floor, the cavernous basin yawns into the distance, stretching almost as far as he can see. And there it is, like an ode to the days when mankind ruled the seas in decadent comfort — the Palace of Wish. The crisp white lines of the gargantuan form gleaming like a shimmering pearl under the relentless blaze of the sun.

From bow to stern it must be at least the length of three city blocks, with its main deck and protruding red chimney stacks towering above, looming ten or twelve stories over the dark navy hull that disappears under the pale amber of the dusty desert floor. Propped up dutifully by the monotonous expanse of Zeno's ominous wall that runs behind it, it stands ready, proud; as if preparing to embark on a voyage through the sea of sand it calls its home.

"She's something else isn't she?" The short heavy set guard rests his hands casually on his belt as he stands beside

Will, staring up at the vessel with awe. "A real beauty. Probably the last thing most people ever want to see up close though—well, except for you volunteers."

Pulling his gaze away from the splendor of the palace, Will looks at him. A stocky man in scuffed tactical pants and body armor, his light blue formal shirt, barely visible under the mass of straps and pouches that litter his torso, sports a little white plastic name tag that simply says, 'Jim'.

"You bring many people out here?" Will asks.

"What voluntarily? Not really, one a week, if even. Nothing like the amount of people that are dragged out here to stand trial. I'll tell you," he chuckles to himself, "if I had a penny for every one!"

"Many people make it out?"

"Out of there?" he scoffs. "Well yeah, people make it out. We spend the best part of the day after bussing them back to town—'vindicated'. But in the shape that most of them are in I can't imagine that many last for too long after we've dropped them off. Anyway, come on," he continues, ushering to the Rover waiting in the sand behind them. "We should make it within the hour. Sorry about the stop. When you gotta go, you gotta go!"

Strapped back into the torn bucket seats, the engine roars to life as they speed across the upper lip of the precipice. First crossing onto the dusty trail that zig zags perilously down the cliff's sheer face, they bounce across the flat cracked surface of the basin floor as they hurtle toward the palace, leaving a thin plume of dust rising in their wake.

Cradled in its sandy berth in the opposite corner, its incredible size becomes even more apparent with every minute that passes. Each of the three intersecting circles of the Queen's royal insignia etched on its side as if small planets, and the enormous shadow it casts as if it has blotted out the sun. As on the myriad of balconies strewn across its side, a display of bright and fanciful garments swirl and ripple as scores of vibrant revelers sway and cheer to feverish music that blares out into the desert.

Moving parallel to the hull they pass into the cool shade of the ship's bow, and nearing an armored truck parked beside the base of a tall gangway that winds to the deck above they come to a stop, as three guards with rifles slung over their shoulders emerge and flag them down.

"Morning Jimmy!" the closest of the three calls out, as Will's escort shuts the engine down and waves.

"Long time no see pal! How are you?" Jim replies as he clambers out, and the two men shake hands. "Keeping out of trouble I hope? How's the family?"

"Ah, not too bad. You?"

"Same old, same old. You know yourself. Got my eldest into tech school finally! All going well, I'm hoping to get him out of this dump and into the energy fields in Zeno in the next few years."

"Can you imagine! Your kid out there! Sure, you could almost retire on what he'd be sending back to you and the missus!"

"I know right! Well, fingers crossed," he crosses his fingers. "Either way, the wife's well happy, so at least this waking nightmare isn't for nothing!" Pointing to the royal emblem on his shoulder he rolls his eyes as they both laugh.

"Anyway, I got a volunteer for you," Jim says with a gesture back toward Will. "Hey Will, come on up here. Meet my buddy, Callum!"

"So you're Will yeah?" Callum asks, examining Will with suspicion as he walks up to them. "So which are you, Will?

Are you brave, desperate, or stupid? Come here, let me get a look. . .”

Will stays quiet, uneasy at the man’s animated skepticism and unsure if he’s joking or serious.

“What do you say boys?” he calls back to the other two guards standing by the truck. “I’ll put a hundred on him making it through the first alive. Any takers?”

The other two guards sidle up and look him over. “Seriously?. . . Yeah sure, I’ll match you. No way he’s gonna make it. . . Loser pays out Monday?”

“Sounds good to me!” Callum replies, and as they shake hands he chuckles at Will with a haughty grin on his face. “Now, no pressure at all pal, but I’ve got money on you now, so don’t let me down! — You other fellas want in?!”

“No thanks, man,” Jim replies, shaking his head with a furrowed brow. “You know me. . . I’m not into that. It’s not right.”

“Oh! I forgot! Saint James!” he smirks and makes a face, chuckling with mild contempt as he looks to the other guard, “Billy boy?”

“No, I'm good. I don’t have the money.”

“Ok, suit yourselves.” he shrugs as he hands Will a thin metal bracelet. “Here, take this and stick it around your wrist —yeah, just give it a. . . yeah, push it till it clicks. Yeah that's it. I put your details on it this morning so once you’re up top just show it to them. They’ll take care of you from there, ok?”

“Ok,” Will replies following his gaze to the top of the steep gangway ascending up the side of the ship.

“Good. Now, as much as I like a good chat, it’s way cooler in the truck!” he beckons as he turns and walks towards the truck. “Come on boys — Oh, and hey Jimmy!” he calls back, raising his hand in a wave, "Good to see you man! Send my best to the missus and your kid. I hope it works out!"

*   *   *

The armored truck growing smaller in the distance, Will stands in silence, trailing his eyes along the winding gangway that hugs the side of the hull to where it stops far above.

"So you good," Jim's voice cuts through Will's distracted thoughts.

"What?. . . Oh. Yeah, thanks," Will replies, still gazing up.

"I'll leave you to it then. Good luck in there. And hey, Will?" he stops short as he turns to leave.

"Yeah?"

"For what it's worth. . . I dunno what got you to bring yourself to this place, and I know it's too late now. But we're not—us guards I mean—we're not all bad. Most of us are just trying to survive like everyone else." Reaching into his pocket he hands Will a piece of paper with an address scrawled on it. "My home, if you make it through your first trial and don't want to sign up for another. We can't offer much but we can sort you out with the basics. Enough to help you get back on your feet – if you want.

"Thanks, Jim. I. . ." Will looks at the note, humbled by the gesture. "It was nice to meet you."

"You too man," he replies, turning as he heads back to the Rover. "Maybe in another life we'd be friends."

*   *   *

As the sun makes its endless journey across the open sky scorching the earth with its steady gape, Will takes a one last look at the tranquil expanse of the empty desert basin, before taking the first step onto the gangway.

The faint sound of music and laughter from the gallery of balconies further down the ship's hull hovers in the air as he climbs the metal steps. Far above the hot sand, lines of round port windows give a flashing glimpse of carnal chaos inside as he climbs further still, until, after what seems like an eternity, the walkway ends, terminating at a single open doorway in the ship's steel face. He must be close to the top of the ship, as the feverous partying from above is so loud that with every pounding hammer of a drum and low rumble of bass beat, the platform under his feet tremors and vibrates. And peering through the shadowed opening into the cool darkness inside, he steps in.

It is a plain white room, with floor, walls and ceiling, indistinguishable in nearly every way. Interrupted only by a reception window and countertop and the penciled mark of a recessed door concealed in the wall beside it, its bland perfection is almost unbroken. Walking up to the partially perforated glass, he glances into the room beyond it. It's almost as sparse as the one he's in, with the exception of an unoccupied chair facing a small computer monitor set out before it.

"Hello?" he calls out, stopping short as he's startled by his voice's volume in the starkness of the space. Nothing, but silence and the dull throb of the music thrumming in from the world outside. "Hello?"

A small notice crudely taped onto the countertop next to a recessed black button reads; <u>Please knock for assistance.</u>

Puzzled by its words, he knocks, quietly at first and then a little louder, craning his neck as he tries to see as much of the room on the other side as possible.

"Anyone home?"

After trying the concealed door in the wall and returning to the counter, he tries again, harder this time. But as knocks turn to thumps and the glass shakes in its frame, he deliberates for a trepid moment, before reaching to it to give it a push.

No sooner than he's touched it, his finger recoils as the shrill tone of a buzzer pierces his ears.

"Who the hell pressed the button?!" an angry voice bellows out from somewhere inside, as with a shuffle and a few footsteps a tall woman in a prim skirt and pale cardigan struts out. "What is the meaning of this?!" she snaps at Will through tight white lips, glaring at him over a neat pair of round rimmed glasses.

"I. . . I'm here for the trials," Will stutters as he lifts his arm to show his shiny bracelet. "I'm a volunteer."

"Don't get smart!" she responds sharply. "I asked who pressed the button?!"

"I did?"

"What?! Why?! Who gave you permission?!! — Can't you read?!!!"

"Well no, I can but—"

"It is assistance you seek, isn't it?" she points to the sign.

"Well yeah, bu—"

"So in heaven's name!!" she cuts across him. "Why did you press the button? Too good to knock?!"

"I did knock!" Will replies exasperated.

"Don't interrupt a woman while she speaks!!" The woman's voice reaches a crescendo. "Rude and impatient?!!"

"I'm sorry. I didn't mean to. It's just that I was—"

"Ah, ah, ah. . ." she shushes him, before pausing to fan her face with her hand. "That's all I needed to hear. Why didn't you say sooner? An apology cools the blood like not much else, don't you think? Now. . . " she takes a long deep breath and closes her eyes for a second as if to compose her thoughts. "A volunteer you say? Where is the guard that gave you that?" She points to the cuff on his wrist. "I assume you didn't get here by yourself?"

"No, the guards outside. I was brought here from the city. They gave it to me and sent me up."

"Did they now," she sniffs with indignance. "Such little boys. Still hiding from the discomfort of responsibility behind their mother's skirt as they suckle her dry! No wonder her newborns wither from thirst! Well, I won't hide from my duties. Your arm please, put it up to the window."

Pulling a handheld device from a drawer in the desk, the computer signals its merry servitude as she points it at his cuff.

"Now, William. All done. Once you're in, if you need something or have any questions or just pick up one of the phones. They're all over so you'll never have to go far. Aside from that you're free to wander the palace and do what you like, but—" she continues, giving a displeased tap on the glass to the sign on the counter, "be very careful to stay within the limitations of the signs, and be sure to read them precisely. Their words are not to be bent or twisted to suit the reader. Each one has been meticulously placed as a guide to help you survive. And you'll see for yourself, survivability is not on the list of priorities in this place."

"I will do," Will stifles a smile as she glances up with a stern eyebrow.

"Now, go on through the door there and up the stairs to the deck. Triboulet will take it from there. He knows you're coming."

"Where do I find him?"

"Find him?" she smirks, pressing a button under the counter as the recessed door beside him as it shudders open. "Don't you worry. He'll find you. He'd never miss an opportunity to make a new acquaintance. "Good luck."

With a few more clicks on the keyboard she gets up from her computer, and without another word hurries back from wherever she came from.

Half wondering if she's coming back, Will stands for a moment looking into the empty office after her, before stepping over to the open doorway and walking through. In the landing of a narrow stairwell, two signs are displayed on the wall in front of him, with directional arrows pointing up and down the stairs; one reading 'The Entertainment' and the other 'The Accused'. Following the sound of the music he clambers up, and taking a deep breath as he reaches a heavy storm door at the top, the door pops open as he heaves on the latch.

*   *   *

A blanket of warmth and blinding sunlight envelopes him as he steps into a dense crowd on the top deck of the palace, deafened by the rhythm and blaring elations of lively people sprawled in every direction around him.

Above the throng of writhing bodies raised on an elevated stage, an unbridled gaggle of musicians unleash their melodic carnage, as to their sides suspended catwalks are packed with the gyrating forms of choreographed dancers.

Fused with the feral beating of drums, vivid, flashing lights strobe and pulse with the rapid euphoria of electric jazz swing. Thrilled whoops and screams fill the air as men dance and move in a frenzied fervor entangled with angelic women dressed in colored silks and flowing fabrics. Sweat and elixir flow as one, and as its raw perfume permeates the thick muggy air, it swells with the energy of the salacious ritual. Stunned by the cacophony, he watches the mass of moving bodies in awe, and marvels at its splendor.

A sudden bloom of beauty startles him as the form of a woman bursts from the crowd like a magician's bouquet. Her dark eyes locked on his, his heart skips a beat as she floats toward him, as taking one hand in hers, she pushes a large icy glass of a rainbow colored drink into his other. The heaving crowd parting instinctively in her presence, he follows her fluttering lashes and sultry smile as she leads him up a small flight of thin metal stairs and onto a crowded walkway. Stopping short as they are jostled by the swaying throng, their bodies collide, and as she turns surprised, his drink spills and drips down her front. Shocked, she looks down at the wet stain, but giving a cheeky smile, she flicks her soft eyes onto his and pushes the drink up to his lips, forcibly tipping it for him to gulp down.

He didn't realize how thirsty he was or how good the drink was going to be. Bitter, sweet, and everything in between. It's delightfully cold in contrast to the stifling heat, and so relieving as he feels it running inside his chest it settles like a cool oasis in his stomach. Her gentle warmth gripping tightly onto him swaying with the feverish beat, she grabs his hips and grinds into him as the rhythm of the blaring music changes tune.

"What are you. . . ?!" His words are lost in the volume of the band as he pulls away, but springing free from her grasp with such force, he bumps hard into the railings behind him and his empty glass flies out of his hand into the crowd beneath. The faint smash below confirming its landing, he lunges horrified over the edge as an anguished cry shrieks from the thunderous melody. Staring down on the mire his stomach knots as he sees a girl and hears her howls, and as the feverish rabble heaves around her a torrent of shimmering blood pours down her face.

Speechless, he stands frozen. But before he's even moved, he feels hands on his waist as the woman behind him grabs him again, pulling him eagerly away from the railings into the fray of surging dancers as she laughs at his sickened disbelief.

"Get off of me!" he yells, shoving her away as the simmering of anger heats in his belly. "Did you not see?! I've got to go help!!"

Stumbling backward, she stops, surprised as she's caught on either side by two burly men in crisp white trousers and matching maritime shirts who appear up the steps behind her. But as she turns to look, her sensual joy fades. With a sudden glimmer of recognition, her slender body goes limp, and as a black cloth bag is wrenched over her head and cinched tight on her delicate neck, she's dragged backward down the stairs. Seized by a surge of adrenaline, Will stands still as if spellbound by the multitude's gaping stare. Captured by the multitude of indifferent eyes as they dance, he's frozen. And as he watches her vanish into the sea of bodies, they continue the copulation of their primal frolic.

"Laaaaaaaaadies and Gentlemen!!" Interrupted by a booming announcement, the music stops as all eyes look to the stage. "It is time to break the enthrallment that immerses you to give a warm welcome to our generous host! The man who needs no introduction! The amuser! The charmer! The great distracter and the master of comfort and entertainment. It is the one! The only! The great Triboulet!!!!"

In whoops of joy at his name, the crowd erupts as it chants in bated anticipation, "Tri–bou–let! Tri–bou–let!!!" With heavy concurrence, the drums from the band join the hammering rhythm, filling the air until the sound roars like the ocean.

"Beautiful people of the world!" A shrill voice rips through the air from the speakers as the collective mantra comes to a sudden stop, and a deathly silence lingers in bated anticipation. "Good day to you all!!"

Exploding from the stage, a sharp blast rings out, ejecting a billowing cloud of white smoke, and within it, the silhouette of a tall and slender man held rigid in a theatrical pose. As the smoke clears, his long narrow form is revealed.

"It is I. . ." he continues in his piercing voice. "Your humble entertainer!"

His appearance is bizarre. Wrapped in a shiny black ensemble that stretches tight over his oddly long figure, a collar that continues up high under his chin cradles the back of his pale and hairless head. A thin crooked nose and a twisted smile bend across his emaciated complexion, and as he theatrically bows to the crowd, his dark beady eyes dart about like a ravenous bird's.

The crowd cheering, he raises his bony hands for silence.

"Shh, shh, shh. . . Calm yourselves my loves. . . Contain yourselves!" he quietens them in a dramatic whisper. "Now. You may, or may not, have noticed. . ." he says, fanning the remnants of the white smoke from the air with playful strokes. "But it would seem, that during the almighty blast that heralded my grand entrance in this snowy cloud. . ." With a sharp flick of his wrists, he points to the glaring baldness of an absent brow over his eye, that has added to the already strange features of his face. "One of my eyebrows has been blown clean off, and sent yonder, into your midst!" Waving his arm in a sweeping motion toward them, stifled laughs and hollow coughs run through the uncomfortable silence of the crowd. "So, as a gesture of good faith, and to save one of my most loveliest pairs of brows. Ten thousand pieces of silver, to the one who returns it!"

With a cheer the crowd shuffles with excitement as people begin to frantically look around their feet. Then a few muffled shouts from up front close to the stage, and then another, and then a scream as the sounds of arguing and fighting breaks out. Breaking free from the throng, a man with a bloodied nose rushes up the steps to the stage. But after only a few short steps he's leapt on by another, who hits him hard, repeatedly smashing his head off the metal railings before dropping him like a broken toy off the edge and onto the deck.

"Oooh a winner!" Triboulet exclaims as he claps his hands together in excitement as the man holds the eyebrow up proudly in his bloodstained hand. "Get it and clean it up! Go!!" he continues, flapping impatiently towards his aides waiting behind him before turning back to his audience. "And get this man his prize! Bravo!! Well done my friends!! — Now? Where was I? Oh yes. . . It is I! Triboulet!! Ladies and gentlemen! I trust you are all in pure comfort, good spirits and lacking nothing?!" Pausing, he waits as the crowd cheers in response to his words.

"Good, good! Well. Today I have for you, good news! The offering of a new volunteer!! Come up here and say hello to your fellow entertainers, my beautiful man!"

The crowd erupting into applause, Will winces and shades his eyes as he's blinded by the beaming glare of a spotlight. Bewildered by the proceedings and hustled to the stage by two more white uniformed men that appear in the crowd, he's stopped in front of a looming Triboulet.

"So, go on then lovely man," Triboulet asks, gazing at Will expectantly. "Tell the people your lovely name!"

Will hesitates, overwhelmed by a confusing mix of shock and stage fright, and looks up at the cadaverous giant's features. Whatever makeup was used to smooth over the imperfections of his skin has begun to mix and drip with his sweat under the heat of the desert sun, adding to his unsettling appearance.

"Will," Will replies, barely audible as the amplified echo squeals over the speakers.

"A quiet one," Triboulet remarks. "Well Will—ooooh, that's fun to say!—Well, Will. Well will. Wellwill, wellwll, wllwll,wlwl. . ." Mumbling to himself he trails off before snapping out of his self hypnotic trance and carrying on. "Oh boy, that's really something! Well—Will. . ." he grins and winks at Will. "Welcome! To the Palace, of Wish!" The crowd rolls with cheers again and the band breaks into music, accompanied by a lively drum beat as he continues. "So until you take the plunge over the edge to the arena—this Sunday morning at ten A.M. sharp," he exclaims exuberantly over the fervor, pointing to the shadowed chasm over the edge of the boat sandwiched between the port side and the towering wall of Zeno. "Your wishes, are our job! Good food, strong drink, heavy drugs! Good women, bad women, big women, dead women!" He grimaces comically and shrugs his shoulders, perplexed at where his rhyming led him. "And most of all, a non–stop–party! Whatever floats your boat! So strap yourself in, and above all else. . ." his voice rises to a shrill crescendo as the pounding of the drum beat barrels in unison as the crowd joins in; "Be free! Be happy! And be. . . Yourselllf!!!!!!" Fireworks shooting into the air above them as the acclamation explodes into its climax, the music strikes up with a renewed enthusiasm as the crowd resumes their wild dancing.

With a big grin, Triboulet leans down to Will and speaks with a hushed tone, "Now mister man, come with me and I'll set you up in a room!"

Putting his gigantic hand onto Will's back as they turn, he guides him off the stage though a curtain in the back, where they are joined by a small entourage of his white clad aides, and leaving the blaring music behind, they set off down a long hallway.

"Ok, well done everybody, seamless as always! Do we have a room for—what was it again? Will, right?" He glances down at Will, who nods in response.

"Yes sir," his head aide replies from up front of the troupe, handing a silver keycard back to Triboulet as the group struts purposefully down the corridor. "We got 12514 all ready to go."

Triboulet passes the keycard to Will, "So use this little fella to get stuff to work, and if it doesn't work on something, it means that something's not for you—make sense? Here, give it a try on the elevator." He gestures to the gold trimmed doors sliding open ahead of them and they enter it. "Just hold it close to the boxy thing there." A chime rings out as Will presses the card up against it. "See? Easy. You're deck twelve —first two numbers on your card there if you forget."

As the doors slide closed, a sudden flash of anger twists his features as he scowls down at his aides. "Who's got my eyebrow anyway?" he growls, "Is it gonna be ok?!"

"It's up in hair and makeup now sir," the head aide replies in a somber tone. "They've got their best guy on it."

"I never should have taken them off the mantle," he grumbles to himself. "Some things are just too special. . . I just knew it—Oh, and before I forget; the guy that does the booms and the bangs and so on, you know, the pyrowhatsits; Can you bring him to me for a little chin waggle?"

His aide pauses. "We threw him overboard sir, he tried to make a break for it right after the—"

"What?!" Triboulet shrieks. "Who told you to do that?!"

"You did sir."

"I did no such thing!"

"I'm sorry sir, but, after the a. . . eh, seat, of your pants gave way at the debutante ball—a few weeks back sir. You said not to wait for the order but to use our common sense — If such things were to happen again, Sir."

Triboulet inhales, about to snap back. But momentarily lost in thought, he rests his long bony fingers on his chin, before replying in a calmer manner. "Did you at least whip him, or burn him first, or something? You know, a little peepee smack? Cause if you didn't, maybe we could—like, I dunno—like, add that to our repertoire for next time? What do you think?"

"Absolutely sir, great idea!" the aide replies, in enthusiastic relief of the giant man's tempered response. "I'll draw up the paperwork and have it implemented throughout the palace right away."

Confronted by a bold black and white sign that simply reads; 'SMILE' as the elevator opens, they step out onto a patterned tile floor of a wide hallway lined with door after door of private cabins.

"You're just up here on the right," Triboulet says, glancing back to Will as he leads the way. "And some advice if I may—it's the decent thing to do anyway, I'm not just a pretty face!" He grimaces with an exaggerated grin and flutters his long eyelashes. "If you are to have any chance of making it during the trials, try not to get in a fight before it starts and be sure to follow any instructions on signs—two good ways to get yourself tossed overboard! And as the saying goes; it's better to have a human shield and not need one, than need one and not have one, so even if you don't like them—maybe even especially if you don't like them—making a friend before the big day can go a long way, and. . ." he looks to his aide in quizzical contemplation, "I think that's about it, right?"

The numbers 12514 carved delicately into its face in floral lettering, they stop in front of a cabin door.

"Well Will, this is you. It has been a pleasure. I'll see you on Sunday morning for the trials! I'll wave you from the booth! But in the meantime—feel free to feel free!" He winks to acknowledge his pun. "And if you need anything—and I do mean anything," he growls in a sudden whispered grin, lowering his face so close to Will's that his putrid breath thickens the air, before his tone snaps back to its usual melodic pitch, "just pick up a phone and someone will help! Ok?"

"Sure, thanks." Will replies, filled with unease at the sudden shift in the strange creature's manner.

"Great then!" he says, spinning on his heel and striding back down the hall with his aides in tow, who scramble to catch up from his sudden departure. "Ta-ta for now!!"

Watching him as he wiggles his fingers over his shoulder in farewell, Will listens until the sound of his nasal voice has disappeared before turning to the door. The device on the handle whirs as he brings his card to it, and pushing the handle down he enters the room. As the door swishes shut behind and he slides over the two brass deadbolts he takes a deep breath and savors the silence.

Well kept and tastefully furnished, the room's warm simple colors are softly lit by an array of ornate crystal fixtures suspended like teardrops from the high ceiling. Past the smooth layered mass of a plush king bed, a round oak table is surrounded by four matching chairs. And through the tall windows and beyond the balcony outside there's a soaring view of the expanse of Desolation's sprawl, stretching out beyond the upper edge of the massive depression in the sand where the palace is permanently anchored.

As the tension in his chest subsides and the semblance of security takes effect, he looks around the room's interior. Filled with an assorted mix of clothing and shoes, the enormous wardrobes seem to have something for everyone, from tuxedos to gym wear. And wandering past cupboards, a long leather couch and a dresser arranged with some light snacks, he sees, as advertised, a snappy red phone on the bedside. Finding a well hidden fridge tucked in the corner, he whistles through his teeth at the many cool glistening bottles of wine and beer and, taking a moment to deliberate, settles for two bottles of smooth hoppy ale before slumping comfortably onto the couch to drink them, and watch the setting sun fade to a scarlet red.

Subdued by the soothing hand of the nectar, he tries the shower. It works, such a miracle in itself, providing a simple but deeply satisfying comfort. The steady flow of clean warm water blankets him as the basin at his feet swirls brown with the stains of his toil.

'How long has it been since a brief respite from the ails of the earth? How long since I've been nestled by the solace of flowing water's delectable embrace, present and numb. If I could only stay in this moment forever.'

Deeply refreshed and drowsy, he sits on the side of the bed and bounces its softness under him a few times, relieved to be away from the buzzing of the world outside the door. He lies back, sinking into the many folds of the fabric, wondering if it's possibly the nicest bed he's ever laid down on. And as the fan purposefully thrums overhead, his mind drifts into vague memory and dream, as he succumbs to sleep.

*   *   *

In a cold sweat, he lies bathed in the pale blue light of a full moon that basks in the depths of the night sky outside the balcony window as the soothing whisper of a cool breeze ripples across the draping curtains.

Almost imperceptible, a soft knock on the door draws his attention. He stays motionless, it must have been another room in the hall. But then, three more knocks.

Rolling over, he sits up and fumbles for the switch on the bedside lamp, and flinches as its bright yellow light illuminates the room. First throwing on a t-shirt he ambles to the door, unlocking the latches and opening it, just enough just to peek out into the hall.

As it opens, a flash of soft brown eyes falls on his as the delicate features of a young woman gazes up.

"Good evening sir," she says, tucking a strand of her long black hair behind her ear. "My name is Katayoun." The vivid patterns of the gold and reds of her flowing dress shimmer as she gives a long curtsy and bows her head. "I am here as an offering from the great Triboulet. I'm so glad you're in—I thought I had the wrong room. Can I come in?"

Lowering her gaze to the floor, the light glints off scarlet crystals inset into a set of delicate gold bands that weave interconnected around her head.

"What?. . . no," Will replies, taken off guard and still half asleep. "I mean thanks, but no, I'm ok. I'm just trying to get some sleep."

As he closes the door, she reaches out and stops it with her hand.

"Please sir," she stares at him with a wistful smile. "You won't regret it. I promise." Sliding the trailing ends of her hair over her shoulder, she reveals even more of the plunging neckline of her dress, and seeing him diverting his lingering eyes, she arches her back, further accentuating the delicate curves of her collarbone.

"Seriously, no. Thanks," Will stutters, flustered as she smiles at him. "And it's not you, I'm just. . . I just want to be left alone, ok?"

Moving to shut the door again her protest is more forceful, and leaning hard, she attempts to wedge it past Will's foot that he's planted against it on the other side.

"I know sir, but please. . ." her voice trembles with an air of desperation as her smile suddenly breaks and tears well up in her eyes, her expression echoing the same knowing terror as the woman on the deck. "You don't understand!"

"Can't you just go find someone else?" he hisses at her in frustration, conscious of the commotion attracting any unwanted attention.

"Please! He'll kill me!" she pleads, keeping her voice low, "Please!" Squeezing her leg into the opening she shoves the door with both hands. "Even just for tonight! Please, I can't go back!!"

Will wrestles to close the door, but afraid to hurt her in the shrinking gap, he relents, and as it bursts open she flails past him and lands in a heap on the floor.

Glancing both ways down the empty corridor, he closes it and slides the locks shut, before turning and looking down on her, hot with anger as she huddles on the ground.

"Fine!" he snaps at her, "Stay! But first thing in the morning, you're gone! And you better not be some con artist! If you're looking for money, you came knocking on the wrong door!"

"I'm not, I promise! I'll be gone first thing!" she replies in a weakened whisper. "Thank you."

On her knees, she bows her head in defeated gratitude as she crumples in the center of the vivid billows of her colorful dress. And as a tear traces down her cheek, Will feels the sudden sting of sadness as the sight of her slight form hunched on the floor reveals the same frailty that consumed his bride; and another creature cursed into suffering.

"Hey. . . I'm sorry," he says, as remorse softens him and he crouches down beside her. "You ok?"

"Yeah. I'm fine," she sniffles, vacantly staring at the floor.

"Can I get you a drink or something? Here, let me help you up." Reaching to help her to her feet, he takes her hand, but no sooner than he's touched her she flinches and shrinks back. Surprised by her reaction, he raises his hands in submission, "I'm sorry. I didn't mean to. . ."

Unsure of what to say he backs away, and taking a floral bottle of white wine from the fridge, scrawled all over in some elegant language he's never seen before, he pours a big glass and brings it over to her, raising it in front of her despondent figure. "Couldn't hurt, could it? You look like you could use it."

The dark makeup around her sullen eyes is smudging, as without a word she takes it off him and lifts it to her red lips, chugging the entire glass down in one long gulp before handing it back.

"Thirsty then?" he teases with a sympathetic smile. "You want another?"

"Sure," she replies, being careful to avoid eye contact and pulling herself to her feet. "But give me a minute. I'll be right back."

Will watches her as she gets up, waiting till she's closed the bathroom door behind her before he goes back to the fridge to refill her glass and grab himself a beer. Setting the drinks on the table, he smooths out the ruffled bedsheets, and rifling through the cupboards for a pillow and a blanket, he arranges himself a makeshift bed on the couch. As he sits and waits, watching through the balcony doors, he gazes out at Desolation's shadowed silhouette in the distance as it rests under the watchful contemplation of the moon, its gleaming roofs like silver stones on a dark black beach. It is almost peaceful from this distance, strangely familiar in form like any other city. But it wasn't. So broken inside, with who knows what anguish being suffered on its hidden streets.

*　　*　　*

When she emerges it is as if she has conjured a hidden twin. Her hair reordered and makeup touched up, as she slinks towards him with a cheeky smile on the corner of her mouth she is quite beautiful.

"So you're some kind of nice guy, is that right?" she asks, stopping in front of him and gazing at him playfully. "Well, I'm anything you want me to be." Pushing the strap of her dress off her silken shoulder, she gives him a sultry smile. "So what will you have?"

Taken aback by the sudden softness of her body, in a seamless motion she steps forward and straddles him with the warmth of her inner thighs. Subdued by her captivating essence his chest tenses as the subtle notes of perfume and her sweet breath overwhelm his primal being. But with every awakening sense that engulfs him, memories rush in, and with a flicker and a flash, all he can see is her — Marissa.

'I'm yours,' her words breathe heavily in his ear as the flesh of her glistening body presses against his.

"Stop," he asks, as he tries to move out from under her. But with surprising strength she pushes him back. "Stop!" he calls out again, this time more aggressively, pushing away her advances as a burst of clarity shakes him from his physicality. "I said Stop!!"

A growl like a beast's emanates from his belly as his eyes blacken like slicks of oil, and faced with the creature she's unveiled, she lets out a scream of sheer terror. He grabs her arms as he stands and lifting her off her feet as he forces her back, he hurls her onto the bed. With a terrified shriek she bounces across the sheets and crashes into the headboard, and turning to face him as a wave of panic washes over her face, she pulls a long thin knife from her hair and lunges at him.

Landing on him like a wild animal she slashes and stabs as he grapples to pull her off. As rivers of blood spurt from his torn flesh, she squeals as he pries the blade from her fingers, and after tossing it across the room with a defiant scream he throws her back onto the bed. Bristling with rage, he looms over her defenseless form sprawled out beneath him, and as he reaches for her she raises her arms in an instinctive effort to survive.

But in that moment he hears it again. Again as before, it is only a whisper, and although indiscernible in its meaning, it is the whisper of a word. And as its resounding stillness rises like the roar of rushing waters, he is freed from the savage hunger of his rage.

Taking a stumbling step away from her whimpering form, he glimpses at himself in the mirror above the headboard. Horrified by the dark thing that is staring back, he shies away and covers his face with his hands.

"I'm sorry . . ." he whispers through a dry throat. "Are you ok?"

"Don't touch me!" she calls out in panic, scrambling across the sheets and curling into a quivering ball against the wall.

"It's ok, I won't hurt you, look!" As the last of the murk slides clear of his eyes in the mirror, he looks back to her shivering body.

"Don't!" she flinches away, as he goes to move. "Just leave me alone."

Speechless, he drops his head and slumps back onto the couch as a sudden surge of melancholy drapes over him. Twisting his heart and stifling his breath, his stomach knots and chest heaves as the poison of his grief wrenches his clouded mind.

Chapter 14

KATAYOUN

The clinking of cutlery being set out on the table and the intoxicating aroma of a full Epicurian breakfast fills his nostrils, as three dapper waiters lay down the last of a variety of dishes, before filing out the door.

"Sorry I woke you," Katayoun's soft voice calls out, as she gracefully leans against the glass frame of the open balcony door, with a long cigarette in her hand. "I thought you might be hungry?"

Adorned in an elegant flowing gown she's displayed like a postcard against the framed backdrop of the balcony windows, and as she gazes over her shoulder at him, he is unsure what to say. Compared to the terrified creature wrapped in her own slender limbs the night before, the indifference of her delicate demeanor gives nothing of her thoughts away.

"You stayed?" he remarks, puzzled, and second guessing his memory.

She examines him with her dark eyes before responding. "I don't know what you are," she replies, taking a drag of her cigarette. "But, for now, you are the lesser of two evils. You're a chatty sleeper too," she continues through a faint smile, blowing a slow plume of silver smoke out onto the balcony. "So who's Marissa?"

"She's. . . " Will stops himself, irritated by the invasive question. "Weren't you gonna leave?"

Flicking her cigarette off the balcony, she ambles over to the feast laid out on the table and sits down, pulling her chair in and before beginning to fill her empty plate. "So are you going to eat?"

Bothered, but intrigued, Will takes a seat opposite and does the same, adding some thick pieces of crispy bacon to the buttered toast on his plate.

"Tea?" she asks, poising the ornate teapot above his cup with a raised eyebrow.

"Sure," he replies. "Thanks."

The silence is uncomfortable as they eat, which, much to Will's dismay, highlights every unpleasant slurping and smacking of his brutish munching.

"So if you're here for the trials but not the entertainment," she says curiously, glancing up at him, "why did you come here? There are easier ways to die, you know."

"I'd bet there are," he smirks at her candor. "And I'd tell you, I would. But I don't know if there's any point. You wouldn't believe me. You, this place—all this," he motions to the breakfast feast and the surrounding cabin. "And all of whatever it is I've got myself into. I don't even know if I fully believe it myself."

"You could try me. I've seen my share of strange."

"Really?" He looks at her with mild amusement, doubtful that their interpretation of strange is aligned. "If you want. But I did warn you." Cautious not to divulge more than he has too, he takes a deep breath and begins, "Tomorrow, I'm going to try and win the trial and get declared the Champion. And then, when the Queen grants me my wish, I'm gonna ask for an audience with a guy that defected from the Malleus that she's been hiding. All going well, he's going to help me find some people I'm looking for. And when I find them I'm going to kill them."

As he finishes, Kata raises her eyebrow, "Seriously?"

Amused by her expression, he shrugs with a little smile.

Finishing their meals, they sit in silence for a minute, until Will looks up at her, "So I've told you mine. How did you end up here? What's your story?"

She doesn't answer immediately, but instead takes a few slow sips of her tea as she thinks about what to say.

"I made a mistake," she starts, her brow furrowing in contemplation. "My life, with my family—before here—was poor. Like, really poor. I lived out there," she gestures toward Desolation, spread out on the horizon beyond the balcony's glass doors. "I heard from friends that if I wanted money, like more than just the scraps we were used to, I could make it in the palace if I wanted to. My mom, of course, begged me to stay away. She said they were just stories and even if they were true it would not be worth the price. You know, that I was worth more than money and all that, and that things were worse here than in the city. . . But I did it anyway. And the day I left, I told her that she was just jealous, 'cause they weren't taking old washed up whores like her'. That was the last thing I said to her. . ." Her voice cracks as she smiles in disbelief at her cruel words. "She was right of course. This place. . ." A shadow of reminiscent dejection passes over her face. "You get paid alright, but not till you leave. And you can only leave if the Queen gives you a wish. So here I am, rich beyond my wildest dreams, but just a thing. Less than a thing. . . A slave to what I thought would save me. And if I don't perform, or there's a complaint. . . Triboulet, he's. . ." her face goes pale as she shakes her head. "When not masquerading as an angel of light, I think the devil makes his home in that man."

"That why you stayed?" Will asks.

Motioning down her body with her hand, she lets out a cynical laugh, "Who wouldn't want all this right?! Last time I went back early he nearly killed me. It was nearly three months before I could walk again. And now," she sighs, with a defeated smirk, "just when I thought it couldn't be worse. . . I'm pregnant. . . So what do you think? Does my story have yours beat?"

"I'm so sorry," Will replies as he leans back in his chair, stunned. "I don't know what to say. . . Is there anything I can do?"

"Can I stay with you?" she asks in a whisper, lowering her head as she swallows a stifled tear. "Just while you're here at least?

"Of course," Will replies.

"And, if anyone asks," she continues with her gaze fixed on the floor, "if you could just say that I, like, you know. . . rock your world. Please. Otherwise Trib—"

"Of course," he stops her. "Whatever you need."

Watching as she is choked by her sadness, he feels helpless, as the very air around her seems to drain of color.

"Consider me rocked Kata. . .yan? Kata—yenn?"

"Katayoun," she corrects him with a sniveled laugh. "But just call me Kata. And I'm sorry for last night. I just thought that you were. . . I'm sorry. I panicked. . ." The pain in her voice is clear as the day as she speaks. "So did it hurt? You know the—"

"What?" he interjects, twisting his face into jovial anguish as he mimes getting stabbed in the neck. "You mean the. . ."

Kata nods as a muted smile breaks across her face.

"If I said no, would you believe me?" he adds.

"No, not really," she replies, wiping the corner of her watery eyes with the back of her hand. "I'm sorry."

"Don't be sorry," he says with an empathetic grin, understanding, in part at least, what she has endured. "You didn't do anything wrong, just surviving. Sorry if I freaked you out."

A silence hangs in the air between them before Kata looks up at him, curious.

"So your—whatever it is. Is that how you're planning on becoming the champion?"

"Plan?. . . I don't really have one to be honest. I was just gonna see how far I could go." He pauses in thought. "I figure I'll either be the last man standing or dead."

"And can you. . .?"

"What?"

"You know, like, die?"

"I don't know. Not so far, anyway."

"But are you not afraid?" she asks, her tone softening, as if saying it too loud might wake it from its sleep.

"Yeah, I am. . ." he replies, bobbing his head as he attempts to form words from his feelings. "But I don't know what scares me the most. After I lost her—my Marissa. And the worst thing I could imagine had actually happened, the pain was so great I thought I would die. . . But I didn't. My blood kept flowing and my lungs kept breathing. And ever since, I've been trying to make sense of it. If I die; do I go to heaven and she'll be there waiting for me? Or is there nothing, and all that's left of her, in my memory, dies with me?"

"You loved her?" Kata asks, as he fidgets with his hands in agitation.

"Love?" he struggles to inhale as his eyes well up. "It's just a word. She was my world, my light in the darkness. . . So when I think of fear? Yeah, I'm afraid of pain and suffering, and everything that comes with it, of course. But when she was gone, I found a new fear, much worse than any I'd had before. What scares me now is where she went. Did her goodness, her light, everything that she was. . . simply get snuffed out? And if so, for what? What was the point of all of it?" His tone raises in anger. "I suppose, in a roundabout kind of way, that's why I'm here. If I can, if everything goes well—it will matter. I'll make it matter! The ones who hurt her will know her name, and it will be the last thing they hear as I squeeze the life out of their poisonous bodies." Releasing a hateful breath, he inhales and relaxes. "If I could save even one from going through what she did, she'd be proud."

"Well, whether you make it or not," Kata replies with a sympathetic smile. "Compared to the kind of man that I'm used to—believe me—she's already proud."

"Maybe," Will says as he looks up at her, grateful for her company. "I'm sorry, I shouldn't bore you with my ramblings. I'm sure you've got better things to do."

"What, no. Don't be silly. Anyway, did you plan on spending the day before your suicide mission sitting around reminiscing, or did you want to go do something?"

Will smiles at her tease, happy to have the subject changed. "Sure, yeah. Sounds good. Do you have something in mind?"

"We could go up to the sun deck for a bit of music and fresh air? It's usually fairly tame up there, during the day anyway. It would probably beat staying cooped up in here with a strange pregnant lady who forced her way in!"

After a quick call on the phone beside the bed, Kata steps out to the balcony for another cigarette as the waiters return and busy themselves clearing the abundant leftovers from the table.

The cabin empty again, Will emerges from the bathroom, wearing formal black suit trousers and a matching satin waistcoat, with a crisp white shirt underneath that he selected from one of the many options from the tall wardrobe in the corner. Giving his neat appearance an approving nod as he admires how well it fits, Kata slides her arm through his in a well practiced motion, and strolling out the door they leave the room behind.

*   *   *

The warm blue sky of a new day greets them, as with a musical chime they step out of the gleaming elevator onto a wide platform elevated above the splendors of the upper deck. The perimeter, wrapped by several tiers of lounge areas and bars, surrounds a large marine blue pool connected with a series of smaller ones filled with the excited yells and shouts of bikini clad women and boisterous men vying for each other's attention.

Perhaps sensing his apprehension as a whooping trio of girls that hurtle past in a water filled tube that twists around the deck makes him jump, Kata leads them to a jungle themed bar and orders two large luminous drinks before continuing the tour.

Across the white tiles of the poolside deck and under the canopy of the chiming casino's entryway, the delightful aroma of gourmet foods hangs sweet in the air as Kata jokes and laughs, pulling Will along with her.

In quiet admiration of her delightful manner as she effortlessly directs the conversation, Will finds himself at ease as they weave through the elated throng.

Eventually reaching a dining area suspended over the starboard hull, they sit down at a neat metal table with a sweeping view of the sea of sand below, and hailing a scantily clad waitress on roller skates they order some light food and another round of drinks. Motioning to Zeno's towering wall looming behind the other side of the ship, and the array of thick metal props that fastens to it, Kata launches into a humorous commentary on how maybe, just maybe, the Palace itself was just a child's toy left beside a garden wall from a lost history of giants; and how maybe the earth and its inhabitants were merely the forgotten remnant of a deity's amusing diorama.

As their drinks arrive and they order more, she recounts stories of members of the palace staff they see dotted about the open deck. Somehow managing to maintain a jovial tenor to the conversation, she describes tale after tale, of tragedy and broken circumstance that led them there, and the more Will hears the more each painted smile that drifts past seems to fade. Watching her as she chatters and moves, he is almost envious of her. Knowing the razor edge that her life is balanced, just sitting there—like a little song bird singing patiently in the eye of a hurricane—inexplicably alive in the moment.

Morning and afternoon roll together, and as the tangerine hues of the early evening irradiate the sky, the fervent pace of the bouncing music and the liquids and substances that fuel its accompanying human servants runs free. They chat and laugh, and for the first time in a long time, Will is barely conscious of the sting of his mind's throbbing wounds.

"Who are they?" Will asks, as a group of uniformed men arrive at the end of the bar with a dazzling escort of giggling young women.

"I don't know," Kata replies. "VIP's. Gotta be Kol, or Malleus, no? Who else dresses like that? The one at the back there is for sure, he's Mallagua. I spent a month with one last year – said he'd leave his wife for me and all! What's the matter?" Chuckling, she stops short, puzzled as Will looks down and covers his face with his hand. Her eyes widening, she lowers her voice. "Are they looking for you?!"

"I don't know," he says. "Maybe. I can't take any chances."

"Seriously, the Kol? The Malleus? What did you do? You're not trying to. . ." She leans back with a look of disbelief as she realizes his intentions. "I assumed there was more to your story, but wow! I thought I had problems!"

"What are they doing here?" Will asks, relaxing as the men are ushered away through the red door of a private lounge.

"I don't know, same as everyone else I suppose. Guys like that are here all the time," she replies. "They're good for business, I suppose. They're not short of cash."

"What do they do here though?"

"Do? What do you think? This is Desolation, the palace of wishes! You pay enough and there's nothing too twisted you can't have. No one on the other side of that wall has transcended anything—just learned to hide it better, that's all. It's not just Malleus or Kol either, or even just from Zeno. Seems to be from everywhere, inside and outside the Vitruvian reach. I've seen soldiers, priests, warlords. . . even had a king from the ice flows one time."

Sporting a bleach blond ponytail and a tight denim bodysuit, a waitress rolls sharply to a stop at their table, "Hey Kata? Do you have a minute?"

"Hey Leyth," Kata replies with a look of concern, sensing the urgency in the girl's voice. "You ok?"

With a cautious glance at Will, the waitress doesn't say another word but instead turns and heads over to the bar.

"Sorry, Will, do you mind?" Kata says, as she slides her seat back and gets up. "I'll be right back."

Watching as she follows the waitress over, Will tries not to be too obvious as he steals a glimpse of their tense exchange. Their conversation is heated and as it comes to an end, they affectionately hug before parting ways.

"What was that all about?" he asks as Kata comes back and sits down. "Everything alright?"

"Yeah," she replies, visibly shaken and rocking her head in nervous reassurance. "Can we go back to the room though?"

"Sure."

As before, she slides her arm through his again as they walk. But this time she holds it tighter, and without a single word between them, they cross back through the fray to the elevator and leave the thrumming of the deck top festivities reverberating above.

*　　*　　*

Heading straight for the fridge as the cabin door closes behind them, Kata pours herself a large glass of wine, downing it and pouring another to bring with her out to the balcony.

"You wanna talk about it?" Will asks as he joins her, glancing at her troubled expression as the last kiss of sunshine fade over the desert.

Silently musing on her glass until it's empty and lighting a cigarette, she barely registers his presence.

"I was. . ." she mumbles in a vacant whisper. "I was supposed to get out."

"What do you mean? Out of here? The Palace?"

"Hey you wanna get me another drink?" she says, ignoring his question as she frowns at her empty glass.

"Ok. Sure," he replies, puzzled by her curt response. Turning to head back inside, he stops short. "You sure it's a good idea, with, you know. . ." he gestures to her stomach.

"Have you not listened to anything I've said?!" she snaps in a sudden burst of anger. "A child, in this place?!! Have you any idea what they do to them? It would be a mercy to kill it!!"

"I—" Will starts, but she angrily cuts him short.

"You have no idea, do you!! Once they find out that I'm pregnant?!!!! I'll be the latest sideshow for all the freaks, and if I survive long enough to actually have it!?! The second it takes a breath, it will be taken away and. . ." she inhales and swallows her horror. "I just can't. . . Can't you just get me a drink?!"

*　　*　　*

Returning with a full glass in hand, Will hands it to her and leans on the railings beside her as she stares out over the open desert.

"I didn't mean to take it out on you," she whispers. "I'm sorry."

"Don't be," he replies, glancing at her furrowed brow. "You ok?"

Letting out a despondent sigh she continues as she rests her hand on the softness of her belly. "We were supposed to get out of here after the trials tomorrow. Both of us. But it's. . . I don't know what I expected. No one ever gets out."

"What happened?"

"I don't know," she shrugs. "My friend, Andre, one of the head chefs, he was going to get me out with some of the other girls too." she lets out a short reminiscent laugh. "Crazy fool. . . He lost his wife to this place last year and has been playing with fire every chance he's had. We reckon they'd have tossed him overboard ages ago if he wasn't such a good cook. Not the only one either, as you can probably imagine. There's enough people at the end of their rope that didn't need much convincing to help—even some of the guards. They were gonna get us out in one of the banquet supply trucks after the Trial. But apparently Andre was picked up by the Majordomo this afternoon. And if he talks. . . Taking the last gulp of her drink, she drops the empty glass over the balcony edge. "But either way—it's over. I think my little one is going to get back to heaven sooner than I'd hoped."

"I'm sorry," Will says, as she angrily brushes a tear from her cheek. "Is there any way I can help?"

"Help?!" Glaring at him in a sudden flash of fury, she hisses at him, "Even if there was! Would your grand plans to better the world take second place to helping me?! I mean, thanks for popping by and I wish you well; and I've no doubt whoever it is you're looking for has it coming! But why is it, that as soon as anyone gets even a shred of power—let alone whatever you have—that they want to change the world, and fix its problems, without even a semblance of effort to fix themselves?! Even if you and whoever convinced you to come here, by some miracle, manage to topple the Kol and become the new kings; are you really going to be any better than what you replaced, or just another vicious drumbeat to hammer on the back of the next generation? What makes you so different?! So thanks for the offer, but maybe reserve it for when it fits into your righteous mission! I'm pretty sure that saving one woman and her unborn child has never changed the world!"

"I'm sorry," he replies, deflated by her verbal assault. "I meant nothing by it."

Her voice calming, she looks at him with saddened eyes. "I know you mean well, I do. Just. . . You're not the first man with power to tell me about his righteous plans to change the world. I just don't know why it always seems to be some noble venture over the horizon. If humanity's grand designs were just replaced with an individual effort to really love each other, here and now, in the moment, one day at a time—I feel that real change would come about. I mean, when you look at me; am I more than what I am? Or am I nothing more than just a whore?" Her eyes lock on his with a determined gaze as she speaks, and as shame pulls his eyes from hers, she exhales and turns to stare silently out into the distance. "People like me or my baby don't fit into big plans. We'll always just be counted as nothing."

"I'm sorry," he says.

"No," she shakes her head," Don't be. I dunno, it's the way of the world I suppose. . . Anyway, I'm tired. I'm gonna go get some sleep. And thanks for the bed, but I'll take the couch."

"What? No," Will replies, "Please. Take the bed. I prefer the couch, the bed's too soft. I'll get a sore back if I'm on it."

"You sure?"

"Yeah, positive. Thanks though, I'm just gonna finish this and I'll probably do the same." He raises his half empty beer. "I've a feeling it's gonna be an interesting day tomorrow."

"Interesting?" she asks, glancing at him with an apologetic smile, happy to have the conversation lighten. "That's one way to put it." Turning to leave, she stops. "Oh, and hey, Will?"

"Yeah?"

"Thanks for today. It was the nicest one I've had in a long time, and sorry for my—you know. I didn't mean to take all my stuff out on you. I probably shouldn't have had that last drink." She pauses in an awkward silence. "Goodnight."

*   *   *

As the faint splash from the shower trickles out through the open balcony door, Will is left alone with his thoughts. And watching the fading outline of the city's shape in the distance glowing silver in the rising light of the moon, he leans a little heavier on the balcony and takes another swig from his bottle.

She's not wrong. He can't think of anything better than being away from this living nightmare, and getting on his way to wherever it is that he's going. Is it so wrong to want to change something that's in need of change though? Especially when it's for the greater good. Or was Hannah right in all her rambling; Maybe there is a path laid out for him? Maybe he is supposed to be here?

He smiles at the thoughts of the old woman rubbing off on him. Surely if he was supposed to be here in this strange hell, it would mean that this strange hell is supposed to be here as well? And if that was true, why would God, or the Author, or whatever they believe in, allow such a place to exist? Why permit the suffering? Where was the mercy in that? . . . Or is it that giving us true free will is more merciful? If the freedom to cause suffering was eliminated, would it come at the cost of free will? And if it did would we be much more than slaves?

The light from the bathroom stretches out across the wall, and then flicks off, as Kata emerges from the bathroom. Casting an inattentive glance over his shoulder into the darkened room, Will snaps his gaze quickly back to the view of the desert as he glimpses the delicate curves of her naked body.

For a moment he waits, wrestling with his basic self, before, unable to resist, he turns his head sideways, just enough for another stolen glimpse.

Covered only by her long black hair as she dries herself by the bed, the soft touch of the moon dances on her slender form, sending strokes of subtle shadows down her body. But pulling her hair over her shoulder, his heart runs suddenly cold as she exposes the bare skin of her back. Like a ghastly piece of abstract art, a vicious profusion of jagged scars run in every direction across her gentle shape, crisscrossed raw and deep with violent disdain.

Startled in horror, he feels numb as thoughts of what tortured terror must have ripped her apart wriggle into his head with their torment. Frightened screams and shrill laughter echoes in his ears as images of tearing flesh turn his stomach.

A shot of adrenaline coursing through him, he looks away horrified, overcome by a loathsome self disgust for being no different to what she had thought him to be.

Sickened by the thought of what was done to her, he finishes the foamy dregs of his beer as his shock turns to shame. And being careful not to make a sound, he slips under the blanket on the couch, to hate himself and the draw of his darkness.

Chapter 15

BLOOD ON THE SAND

His eyes forced open, Will gasps as bony fingers pinch his eyelids and pull the fleshy part painfully up, blinding him as the morning's light fills the room. Startled, he stares into the wild features of Triboulet, who's staring back with a broad grin stretched across his hollow face.

"Roooom service!!!" Triboulet calls out, as Will defensively pushes the ghastly man's frigid hands away from his face and sits up. "Sorry to wake you, but I had business with my lovely Kata-Yum, so I've had to sweep her away from you!" Straightening up, he rests both his hands on his hips. "And honestly, seeing you lying there. . . I couldn't help myself!! At first I was thinking; 'Oh come on Trib, don't be a scamp, leave the guy alone! He's just wading through some Z's, minding his own business—gonna need his rest for the big day ahead!' But then I was all like; 'But wait, no! How often do you get to say good morning aaaaand give someone a real good scare?!'" With a flamboyant cackle, he wags his long finger. "Not very often, that's how often! I'll say! Plus. . ." his expression changes to confusion as he raises his eyebrow, a different style from the day before, and points to the couch and the bed in quick succession. "I wanted to quiz the sleeping arrangement? What gives?! You guys get married, age fifty years, have an argument over who's turn it is to put out the trash, dredge up a lifetime's worth of resentment and then say things that couldn't be unsaid, leaving you on the couch?. . ." He inhales dramatically to catch his breath, "or what?"

"Where's Kata?" Will blurts out with obvious irritation, taken aback by the surprise awakening and the demented energy of the man in front of him.

"Oh my!" Triboulet gasps, putting his hand over his mouth. "How rude!! Not so much as a 'good morning!' What do you want with Katayoun? You know she is my Katayoun, yes? You can't keep her. She was only on loan mister, and don't you forget it! So you're welcome!" Letting out an indignant snort, he turns toward the door. "If you survive the day you can play with her again—or, well, maybe—we'll see how it goes. . . Anyway, your escort should be here pretty soon to get you ready—Come-come now!" he calls to his entourage of aides standing in the hallway as he walks out. "We've got work to do!"

Yawning as he rubs his eyes and puzzled by the bizarre interaction, Will jerks to attention as there is a knock on the doorframe.

"You're Will right? 12514?"

In a uniform similar to Triboulet's aides but with a dark gray with gold trim on the collar, a broad chested man with tight curls speaks to him from the open doorway.

"Yeah. That's me," Will answers, getting up from the couch.

"Hi, I'm Marcell, a deckhand for the Majordomo. Is it alright if I come in? I've been assigned to get you ready for the trial this morning."

"Oh, yeah. Sure," Will replies, gesturing to the chairs at the table and pulling one out for himself.

"Perfect, thanks." Marcell closes the door before striding over and sitting down opposite him. "You're not too hungover I hope?"

"No, not at all."

"Really? Good for you—that's half the battle. Most of you new guys go a bit hard the night before to settle the nerves and end up too ill to have a chance at a fair fight. Anyway, I'll cut to the chase. We're good for time, so eat, shower, get dressed—there's a decent selection of clothes that are easy to move around in, in the wardrobe there," he points behind Will. "Don't wear anything too restrictive—a dead man in skinny jeans is still a dead man. And has anyone walked you through the process yet?"

"For the Trial? No."

"No worries, it's all fairly simple. Once you're ready, we'll head topside to the ship's bow and get you registered into a group, then all you have to do is hang around and watch the show until it's game time. When you're called up, you and the rest of your group will be loaded into a drop box and craned down into the arena. And from there, you're on your own. Clear as mud?"

Will nods.

"Good. So anyway, between now and then," he continues. "Let's not make this whole thing any messier than it needs to be. My job is to get you there and keep you in line, in case you get cold feet. So please, don't do anything drastic like try and make a run for it, or jump off the balcony.

Understood?" Looking Will in the eye, he studies him as if trying to read his mind. "So, how are you feeling? Are you ok? You gonna do anything rash on me? You gonna do a runner?"

"No," Will replies with a dismissive shake of his head. "Nothing like that. You don't need to worry."

"Well, I'm glad to hear it, but I do worry. The mind is a changeable thing. So if you do start to feel funny you just do me a favor and let me know, ok? I'm here to help. I've got a bunch of things that can help take the edge off too. Uppers, downers and everything in between. I even make my own special cocktail if you want," he says with a wink. "It'll make you as strong as a bear and brave as a lion?!"

"No, I'm good," Will smiles. "Thanks though."

"Ok, fair enough; but like I said, the offer's open if you change your mind."

With a polite knock, a solemn procession of waitstaff file into the room, and in well practiced formation lay out a magnificent spread of fruits and ornamental pastries in front of them.

Lighting up at the sight of the food, Marcell reaches over to grab a mini chocolate tart. "Now Will, eat. Not too much or it'll slow you down, but don't skip it, you'll need the energy so" He pauses and takes a bite before continuing, "So you got a plan out there or friends for backup? Or were you just looking for a break from it all before you meet your maker?"

The thought of what he is about to do slowly twisting his gut, Will is not hungry, and feeling his tension rise with every word Marcell speaks he realizes there is no turning back. Drawing a deep breath he looks up from his hands, "How does someone get to be the champion? What do they have to do?"

Marcell erupts into laughter. "The champion??! Easy on, big fella! Are you serious?!" As he looks at Will's earnest expression, his laughter trails off. "Jeez, you are, aren't you? I don't know what you've heard, but if you even manage to survive the day you're doing well. Let alone become the champion. . . You'd have to take down Cain! And if I can give you any advice about anything, it's to stay as far away from him as possible."

"Who is he?"

"Cain? Look, your job, is to be as entertaining as possible without getting killed. That's it. If, by some miracle, you're still breathing when it's over, you'll have the option to go back to the city to recuperate or to stay here and enjoy this place until the next trial. I mean, I admire your ambition and all—it might even keep you alive—but forget Cain."

"Please, humor me."

Marcell scoffs. "Look, if you want to try your luck; you'll hear him when he's close and you'll know him when you see him. But seriously, if you want to see another day, keep your distance—from his friends too. They're the only group of fighters that have lasted long enough to get good at what they do, and that's only because of him."

Casting a concerned glance at Will as he gets up, he crosses the room to the balcony, before sliding closed the doors and locking them shut. "Hey, I know you said you weren't hungover, but you didn't take anything else last night, did you? I can give you something to level you out if you need?"

"No, I'm good."

"Ok. Suit yourself. Now, come on. Finish up, get clean and dressed, I'll be back in twenty to take you up top."

Not feeling hungry, the first tremors of adrenaline drip into Will's bloodstream. His mind races as he showers, and after sifting through a plethora of options, he throws on some casual cargo pants and a comfortable shirt, choosing familiarity over the practicality of some of the thicker, pocket laden outfits.

His heart skipping a beat as Marcell knocks on the door to collect him, together they walk along the hallway and down a floral carved stairway to a waiting elevator. With a resounding chime it powers them upward, opening onto the wide, sun soaked deck of the ship's proud bow.

All sporting the same gray garb as Marcell, the air is thick with the busy clamor and harsh commands of deckhands, as they herd chained lines of men and women to designated positions. And as a giant metal container cranes overhead washing them with its broad shadow, it disappears into the dark gap between the boat and the wall as it is lowered to the arena below.

"Don't mind them," Marcell remarks over the noise, seeing Will's horrified expression, as with the sharp crack of a whip, a chained man falls out of line with blood pouring from a wound on his face. "They're the accused. You won't get treated like that."

Staying close to Marcell as he heads towards the front of the bow, Will gazes around dumbstruck at the industrious spectacle. Screams and shouts fill the air, tainted with the bitter smell of dirt and sweat. Through the crowded chaos and up three small steps onto the green circle of a repurposed helipad, they approach a wooden writing desk set out on the sun bleached 'H' in the center. Busy writing in a leather bound book from his seat behind it, a tweedy, spectacled man peers up as they stop in front of him.

"Name and number?" he asks.

"Will. 12514," Marcell replies.

"Ah, yes," the man says, after rummaging through a messy stack of paper. "You'll be going down in number four —down there close to the end."

Following his finger as he points down the deck, a row of large shipping containers hangs above the edge of the port side railings, suspended by pulleys that were at one time used to drop life rafts into the sea. With huge bold numbers painted on their sides, the container's tops have been completely removed and the doors facing the ship have been welded open, leaving them a clear view of the sky above.

"Put your hand here please," the man instructs, as he retrieves a round stamp and an ink pad from a drawer beneath him and gestures toward the chalked outline of a hand drawn on the tabletop. After priming the stamp's head and grinding it into the back of Will's hand, the man pauses to inspect the imprinted number '4' that's left behind, before squinting up at him through weary eyes. "Go stand with the others, and good luck."

Across the deck to the first suspended container and past a line of fellow volunteers who are leering over the edge of the railings, Will follows Marcell as he strides down the deck. The bloodthirsty crowd roaring from the arena below, he can see madness in their faces. Some, hardly able to look, pull their sickened gaze away with pallid trauma while others in glee, hoot and cheer as they revel in the carnage.

Suddenly, with a shout from a deckhand, the piercing drone of a siren rings out as one breaks from the line and sprints through the crowd, pushing people to the ground as he bolts for the elevator.

Pulling Will down with him, Marcell drops to his knees as a volley of gunfire crackles out from the higher decks. And as if part of a dance recital, the entire crowd on the deck has followed suit. Hardly daring to breathe, Will stays still and waits, listening only to the deathly silence. But as a pained shriek cuts through the air he raises his head to look.

A deluge of blood trailing from a bullet wound in his leg, four red faced deckhands are dragging the man between them, each holding tight to one of his limbs. Reaching the railing's edge, he screams in panic as he's hoisted above their heads, his wretched form illuminated by the blinding beam of a spotlight. And as a fanfare of trumpets bellows out from below, he is gone.

With a wave of cheers rising from beneath, the shrill siren rings again, and as if nothing has happened, the crowd on the deck picks up where it left off.

Shaking his head as he gets up, Marcell offers Will a hand and pulls him to his feet. "God. . . this place," he mutters. "I guess this means I don't need to remind you not to try and make a run for it?" he glances at Will, looking a little shaken. "You ok?"

Will nods.

"Come on, we're just down here."

Reaching the container swaying off the edge with the number 4 crudely painted onto its face, he gestures at a gap in the line of onlookers.

"Just find yourself a spot and watch the show till you're called to the box, ok? Once you're in, there's a handful of weapons to choose from. Take what you can, but my advice— leave the guns for someone else; it usually just puts a target on your back. And hey—look at me," he adds, seeing Will's rising panic. "I know you're probably freaking out right now, but just remember; the only difference between today, and every other day since you were born, is that today you're not pretending. Death is inevitable my friend, always has been. Today is no different."

"That supposed to be comforting?!" Will forces a grin at his bleak words.

"I gotta try, no!?" he replies with a laugh as he turns to leave. "Anyway, best of luck! And you never know, maybe I'll see you later!"

*   *   *

Taking a moment to orient himself as he watches Marcell disappear into the crowd, Will scans around the busy deck before taking a place along the railing between two of his new teammates, as they look down at the arena nestled below at the base of the ship. Unlike the ship's hull on the sunny side that faces the city, this side is dark and cool and smells like death, with a series of large metal beams protruding from it to span the gap between it and Zeno's looming wall.

Leaning over the edge, Will can see everything that is happening below. Yet the exclamations of delight at the unfolding carnage from the mass of spectators, tells him more than his eyes ever could. Every balcony on every deck below, as far as he can see down the length of the ship, is packed with enthusiastic onlookers from every corner of the earth. Every shape and size and color, young and old. Dignified politicians and teachers of every flag and banner, united in their amusement. And as the sanguine bounty of the trial spills onto the desert floor beneath, with anguished cries and gurgled screams splashing and streaking delightful pinks and reds onto the thirsty sand, they cheer as one.

Shading his eyes as the blood curdling roar of an enraged animal echoes from above, a container with air holes in its sides sweeps overhead as it's craned to the edge. With an agitated growl trembling from within it, the chain it's connected to vibrates as it stops, dangling over the chasm, before, with a mechanical click, it begins its slow descent to the arena. The multitude below erupting in a wild crescendo of cheer launches into a chant as it drops, bellowing the frenzied chorus of, "Moi-rai! Moi-rai! Moi-rai!", until even the railings that Will is leaning on thrums with its enthusiasm.

"What are they saying?!" Will shouts to the man beside him over the deafening commotion.

"Moirai!—the queen's Panthera!" the man shouts back, engrossed by the spectacle, as with a deep thud the container hits the ground, kicking up a cloud of dust. "Look."

With a loud command from an armored guard at the arena's corner, a foreboding hush ripples across the gawking throng, leaving only the soothing whistle of the warm desert wind to fill the sudden peace. From beneath the ship, a solemn group of men and women robed in white emerge, traipsing with him across the sand, to where he arranges them in a semicircle around the container's bulking door. In inaudible words he addresses them, before bowing. And waving his hand in signal above his head, with a metallic grind, the container creaks open.

Will had heard of such things before, but only as myth and legend. Tales of places beyond the reach of the Kol were whispered in his childhood. Tales of the Waif in the wilds of the glacial plains, and their spectral ghouls, the Panthera.

He could see why stories were told of men dying of fright before even being struck. With an enraged wail reverberating out from the depths of its prison, the monstrous beast lunges out. Except for the vivid black stripes that scar across its muscular form, its thick fur is as white as the snow of heaven. And from the tips of its pointed ears to the end of its flicking tail, it is enormous, with each pointed tooth as long as a man's forearm and claws like razored rows of jagged knives.

In an instant it crushes two of the unfortunate souls beneath its massive paws, and as it pulls his head from his body in its powerful jaws, it tosses a third in the air like a paper doll. With a shriek of terror, a woman flees. But as a gunshot rings out and decorates the ground in a plume of her blood, she falls like a leaf in the sand. Satisfying its visceral desires, the beast roars over the agonized screams, shredding skin and breaking bone as it rips its way through the helpless group. But then, as if a fleeting nightmare, its judgment is done. As among the pile of mutilated bodies strewn about like the garnishing's of a butcher's table, it lies down to feast on its spoils.

Followed by whoops from the crowd as it erupts into a frenzy of applause, a cacophony of triumphant music flares from the orchestra as the few who remain alive fall to their knees and close their eyes in thankful prayer. And as fireworks burst from the lower decks in victory, they are humbly led away.

"Number Fours!!!! You're up! Let's go! Number fours!!!"

The grating announcement bellowing through the air, Will jumps as the machinery overhead springs to life and the colossal steel container marked with his number gradually lowers into position. With a resounding thud as its open side aligns perfectly with the deck, a vigilant deckhand raises a hinged section of the railing, providing access to its platform. Scanning the length of the deck as more containers descend into their designated spots, the panic rippling through the hordes of volunteers is palpable. Corralled into clusters, whips crack and harsh orders bark as they await the signal to proceed.

Pushed by the growing crowd behind, he moves forward towards the entrance as one by one, the men ahead step off the ship's deck and into the awaiting container. Then it's his turn, and catching a quick glimpse of the dizzying drop to the sand below, he's across the gap, following the lead of the others and shuffling over against the container's cold metal wall.

After the last volunteer is in, the deckhand follows behind them, crassly ordering a few of them out of his way before marching to a long panel door mounted on the side. Unlocking it with a bundle of keys chained to his waist, he slides it open to reveal a row of well worn weapons hanging on a rack.

"Wait!! Get back!" he yells, putting his hands out to stop them as the men surge toward him. "Get back!!" Resting his hand threateningly on the gun in his belt he waits until the men return to their spots against the wall. "Ok, thank you. That's better. . . right—listen up!! Look around you! If any of you want to survive, your best chance is to work as a team! Got it?—A team!" He looks around, dubious at the comprehension of the agitated expressions staring at him. "That means try not to kill each other! I mean, you can if you want to, but you don't have to! So try, if you can, to work together. You'll live longer. And it makes for a better show. When it's all over, it's a hundred pieces of silver if you make it. But if you make it as part of the largest team it's a thousand each, and if you need it you'll get medical here in the palace. Fair enough?! Good! And finally, and this is important; if you can help yourselves," he points to the weapons on the rack, "Do not take one until you're given the go ahead, ok?! There's a whole lotta riflemen watching you that won't hesitate for even a second if they think there's a threat to the queen, so don't give them an excuse!" He pauses and scans around before turning and stepping out of the container onto the deck. "Well then—Ladies, Gentlemen. Good luck!" With a wave farewell he mutters into the radio handset clipped to his collar, prompting the container to swing away from the ship, and as the palpable beat of the arena's symphony changes in preparation of their arrival, they begin to make their slow descent.

Will looks around at the others, most of which have their backs up against the metal walls as they feel the bitter frailty of their mortality. United under the blaze of the beating sun, some stare at the sky as they beg their maker for mercy, while others, gazing at their feet in a silent contemplation, resign to the seed they've sown and choke back the grip of their fear.

His chest tightens and his heart pounds slow and hard as they descend toward their uncertain fate, and the vibrations of the music and the crowd below grows louder. Crossing down into the cool shadow cast by the ship's mass and past the many stacks of bustling balconies, waves and applause greets them as colored confetti spews from the revelers and showers on their heads. But leaving it behind as they continue their descent, the bare face of the hull stretches out in front.

Making a slow controlled turn, the container gives view to a raised grandstand built up over the bloodied sand of the arena floor. Backed onto the base of Zeno's wall, a long curved canopy stretches over its top, shrouding a myriad of fanciful ladies and gentlemen that litter the rows of seats beneath, adorned in floral gowns, sharp suits and handsome uniforms.

With a sudden knock, the smooth motion of the container comes to a stop as they are dangled in line with an elevated booth protruding from the center. His ghoulish complexion exaggerated by the magnificence of his surroundings, Triboulet sits on the left and on the right the Majordomo, who stares at them through dead piercing eyes that gleam near as bright as his decorative steel armor. And there, perched on a slender black stone throne between them, draped in flowing purple and scarlet and adorned with a twinkling golden crown; Salome, the mad queen of Desolation.

She is truly beautiful. Parting her sweet pursed lips and turning ever so slightly to hear the whispers from her lady-in-waiting nestled behind the throne, her dark silken hair slides like honey to reveal the bare softness of her delicate shoulder. And as she raises her jeweled hand in the air, the crowd falls obediently under her spell. Standing from his seat, the Majordomo inhales deeply in the eerie calm as he prepares his thoughts.

"Some of you," his powerful growl crackles over the speakers, "may already know of the conspiracy uncovered in this great palace yesterday. But all of you all know what will happen next!! Treachery, betrayal and treason will not go unpunished!!" Pausing, he allows the words to reverberate as his piercing eyes probe the crowd. "But! When I kneeled before our great queen and begged to do what must be done, she, our gracious queen, in her wisdom, has instead asked for peace." Turning, he points to the top of the grandstand that becomes washed with the beams of spotlights that illuminate a row of battered and disheveled men and women standing chained in a line together.

"So behold," he continues. "The spirit of peace! To the leaders of this treachery, I say to you; You have till midnight to turn yourselves in, before these traitors—these pawns who you foolishly sought to steal away from our queen—will have their heads plucked from their shoulders!"

With a roar of enthusiastic ovation, the crowd stands to their feet as Will looks horrified down the ragged line of despondent individuals, dirty and bleeding and on the verge of collapse.

Kata!?! His heart sinks. Third from the end, with clothes torn and hair tangled, she stands in the shame of her torment, with her head bowed in sullen focus on her bare feet. His stomach turning in impotent dismay, the queen raises her hand for silence again.

"Brave fighters of the trial!" she speaks, with a stern gaze to Will and the other men held suspended before her. "You have chosen to face the inevitable. And for that—we salute you! Memento mori!!" she exclaims.

In unison, the crowd follows suit, "Memento mori!"

Echoing her cry, they raise their hands in salute, chanting in slow and rhythmic zeal as a restless drum beat fills the air with frantic intensity. With a sudden jerk, again, the containers begin to descend. The drum beat quickening as the sand grows closer beneath, Will struggles to take a breath through his tightening chest. But as the man beside him launches into a wild eyed ramble, Triboulet's sharp voice rips violently over the tumultuous noise.

"Ladies and gentlemen!" he blares as the crowd roars. "Boys and girls!! — The moment you've all been waiting for! With God as their witness and God as their judge! — Let the trial by combat, beginnnn!!!!!"

Will stands frozen, as all around him, the men rush toward the rack of weapons, pushing and shoving each other and grabbing at whatever they can. From the struggle an anguished scream rings out as a man staggers defensively away from another holding a bleeding wound in his chest.

Clutching for the sides, the container smashes into the ground with a grinding thud and he's knocked to his knees. Instinctively, as men spill past him onto the arena with their weapons raised, adrenaline forces him up, and scrambling across to the rack, he pulls a rusted dagger with a leather bound handle off it and follows behind them.

Off the edge of the container and into the hot sand, a scene of chaos greets him. Three or four of the other containers have already landed and the violent shrieks of the volunteers where they meet thickens the air as they tear each other apart. Mingling with the disorganized huddle of his group, a formidable man with curling tattoos on his bearded face yells to move forward, and as if lifted on the wind, they break into a charge. Ahead of them, a lone volunteer turns in a daze to the thunderous sound of their approach, before limply raising a handgun and opening fire. With blood curdling screams, men flail into the dirt, the sickening crunch of fallen bodies breaking as they are trampled. But without slowing, it is only a few short seconds before the shooter is engulfed by their frenzied blades. Panicked, Will pushes free from the throng's momentum.

Tumbling onto the dirt, a rallying cry sounds from behind a container to his left. His deluded notion of war is reduced to a dream, he can barely breathe. And as he snaps around to look, a handful of men and women, unarmed convicts of the trial, dash out in terror, their twisted faces contorted in fear. Behind them with bodies painted black, a savage horde of scarred men follow closely on their tails. Growling and yelping like mad dogs they gnash their teeth, swinging blades and hammers as Will watches in shock. Cut down as the gap between them is closed, the innocent and guilty alike shriek as the butchery befalls them. Until, as their anguished cries dwindle and the last gut wrenching hacks and vicious blows of the excessive overkill stops, the brutal assailants clamber satisfied off their prey. Standing to their feet and wiping the bloody streaks from their weapons, they turn their attention toward Will and his wavering group, transfixed by the carnage.

Overcome by a bristling silence, he can almost smell the dread as it seeps from the men around him, each hoping that they are not called upon to make the first move. But as they hold still, another warrior appears from where the wave of blackened fighters first came. Moving with powerful strides, the hulking form of his hairless head and herculean physicality is rendered in chalky white paint, that accentuates every jagged scar and shadowed sinew of his massive physique. As if crying tears of pure blood, red streaks stream from his deathly eyes down the cheeks of his hollow face. And as he stops still in his underling's midst, they shrink submissively in his wake.

A consuming whisper of silence lingering over the arena, he scans around his men, and then to Will and the trembling group around him. Before reaching over his head in slow deliberation, he draws out a razored sword and places its point firmly into the sand at his feet, clenching his meaty fists on the handle.

"Cain," the breathless mutters of what Will had assumed thickens the air. "It's Cain!"

"Well men?!" The quiet is shattered as the man with the tattooed face turns to Will and the other volunteers. "Are we going to die fighting or cowering?!" The determination in his voice cuts like a knife through the unease. "Cause I'm going out fighting!"

Letting out a warbling battle cry, he raises a curved ax above his head and after a hesitant few seconds, his cries are joined by the rest until they all are roaring. In gleeful acceptance of the challenge, Cain's men howl into the air in excitement as they wait eagerly on their master for a response, and then, with an approving bark of his command, they rush forward like a pack of hungry wolves.

The mass of bodies around Will bristles with defiant energy as they move, walking first, then faster until they are running, sprinting in a charge, with each foot landing hard in the coarse sand. With a sickening jolt, the two groups meet with defiant roars and screams as steel tears through flesh and the multitude of gawking spectators bursts into the frenzied cheer of bloodlust.

Moving with speed, a sharp pain explodes in the side of Will's head as he is struck with a heavy blow. Reeling from the impact, his knees weaken as he crashes under the feet of one of Cain's painted warriors, sending them both rolling in the dirt. The man is up almost instantly, and without hesitation swings his broad sword low, cutting through the legs of an incoming assailant that bounds past Will, a shriek of pain ripping through the sky as he falls.

Up, on his knees, Will is disoriented as he feels the thick flow of blood pouring down his head and neck. Instinctively as the blackened shape of the warrior lunges down on him, he raises his dagger as the head of the man's war hammer smashes into his face. Clutching the air as his vision blurs, he falls, pulling the man's sweating body on top of him as he hits the ground. The man growls in a rage as he pushes himself free and rises over Will, raising his hammer for another vicious attack, but all too late, as Will plunges his blade into the man's chest. Blood rushes over his hand, warm as it flows, and two thrusts turn to many. As if the blade is ravenous for the flesh it maims, lurching over and over into the man's collapsing torso, until, with a grotesque squeal he crashes onto him.

Pinned under the warrior's lifeless weight, Will opens his eyes as the last rattling breath escapes the man's flooded lungs, gasping with the stale stench of his bitter breath. Turning away in disgust, the crowd's elations begin to change. With a thunderous chant excitement turns to praise and looking along the blood soaked sand he sees Cain with his arms raised triumphantly to the heavens, surrounded by the remnants of his allegiant soldiers.

Pushing the perforated corpse off of him as it spills its wretched contents over him, the universe slows and Will feels different. He feels strong, hungry. Sounds of suffering tears and flickers of indifferent smiles rise from the depths of his memory, and from the volume of grief and laughter as it grows and multiplies; he feels the touch of a shadowed beast. The cold wrap of its needled fingers slide around his throat, twisting and squeezing, and desperately gasping for air his chest heaves as his mouth stretches open. But when he's released, it is not air he breathes, but the thick elixir of an intoxicating rage, poured like rich wine down his throat.

His eyes as black as the abyss, he stands to his feet as Cain's warriors look at him in apprehensive disbelief, tensing in instinctive preparation as a nervous hush delicately consumes the crowd's boorish fervor. Following the gaze of their collective fear, the atmosphere trembles as Cain stares at the blood drenched creature that is Will, standing amongst the butchered remains of the men and women that decorate the arena.

"He's mine," he snarls, raising his hand in command to his men as he glares at Will. "Come here to me so I can give your flesh to the birds and your bones to the beasts of the field!"

Will stands motionless, staring at him and holding his dagger loosely by his side. With a sudden dash, taking no more than three or four long footsteps to span the gap between them, Cain lunges, swinging his sword with fierce momentum, as Will falls to his knees.

A gaping gully of flesh carved from Will's shoulder to his waist, blinding pain sears from his open wound, as staggering to stand, the huge man's sword cleaves across him again. Gripped by agonizing shockwaves he reels back into the dirt. But as a soothing calm inside him quells the hurt, he takes another struggled footing and stands again.

Enraged, Cain leaps on him again, pounding, slashing and stabbing in a savage frenzy as he rains down a storm of hammering blows. Yet a small gap is all it takes.

Through the relentless brutality Will breaks his jagged knife free, driving it into Cain's side, again, and then again, each time penetrating his thick skin with more force and anger. A glimmer of fear resonating in the brute's eyes, with each act of violence he inflicts his rage becomes stronger, and with every wound he receives he returns in grisly kind.

Finally, a shriek; as half in pain and half in disbelief, Cain succumbs to the many mangled holes in his body. Falling back, he drops his sword, clutching his injuries and shocked at the deluge of blood that is soaking into the dirt around him.

"How do you stand?!!" his anguished cry echoes through the eerie silence of the awestruck crowd. "What are you?! Abomination. . . !! ABOMINATION!!!!"

Struggling to his feet as the pain subsides, Will reaches to the ground and picks up Cain's sword, feeling the weight of its bloodstained power before flicking his blackened gaze onto Cain. With a slow stride towards the crumpled form of his enemy, it screams for death, and as every sinew in his being tenses in consent to its call, he raises it above his head.

But as a cool wind sweeps across the arena, he stops as a sound swirls with the dust and sand in the air. As if the roar of a lion and the breath of a lamb it is both deafening and silent, and although a word does not form, he understands. Looking down at the crumpled form of Cain beneath him, he takes a deep breath, and as the fury that holds him dissipates, he throws the sword to the ground.

It is so quiet at first it is hardly audible, but like the first lonely raindrops of a thunderstorm, a pitter patter of applause reverberates from the grandstand, as Salome, the mad queen, claps her satin gloved hands.

"Ladies and gentlemen!!!. . ." Triboulet's sharp voice blares out over the speakers. "May I present to you!. . . The Abomination of Desolation!!!"

Like the thunder that follows the rain, the crowd erupts into applause. Joined by fireworks that burst in the sky, it grows louder and louder, until the acclamations seem to shake the ground itself. And as he's showered in vivid confetti, Will is stunned. Soon, the roar of engines joins the fervor, as motorbikes, dune buggies and trucks pour out onto the arena, honking their horns and kicking up large plumes of dust.

In a daze as he watches, Will's ears ring a high pitch squeal as trial attendants leap from the vehicles and get to work. The dead slung like slaughtered lambs into piles on the back of trucks, images of the slaughter carve themselves a deep home into his nauseated memory as the bleating calls of survivors seeking to claim their empty prize they howl as they're dragged by their feet across the sand.

From within the fog of chaos, a voice shakes him from his stupor. Soft, like a song carried on a fleeting wind, he turns his head to listen, and as it calls from the tempest, he hears his name.

"Will!" Flinching as a heavy hand lands on his shoulder, he spins around to see Marcell grinning at him from ear to ear. "Whoa! Easy on there big fella!" Marcell exclaims, taken aback by Will's vacant glare. "Sorry, I thought you heard me! Come on! The queen wants to see you!"

*　　*　　*

He remembers very little as Marcell, shouting in dramatic excitement over the engine of the motorized quad, takes him across the arena. Up a long ramp into an opening in the ship's hull they leave the clamor behind, and dismounting to enter an elevator that ascends to the highest part of the ship, they rise to the heights of the Queen's quarters, perched in the upper tower.

Shrouded in a white silk dress and a draping veil, as the doors slide open they are met by a voiceless girl, who, with a silent nod dismisses Marcell before taking Will by the hand, and leading him up a set of winding steps to a magnificent white stone bathroom at the top.

The ringing in his head fading as he showers under a crystal clear deluge of tempered water, tears flow freely down his face mixing sensuously with the stain of blood as he laments the sorrow that he's seen. And as he dries himself and wipes the steam from the mirror and puts on the regal clothing set out for him, an empty hollow twists in the pit of his stomach and his head begins to ache.

He barely registers the heavy knock on the door when it comes, and as two heavy set guards enter with hands resting on their holstered guns, he is silent as his wrists are cuffed and a collar linked to long chains is snapped around his neck.

Ushered out onto the landing, his mind wanders further into a dreamlike stupor as three tiny men, each no taller than his waist, march up the stairs towards him. Quite somber, and dressed in bright dapper uniforms that match the surreal surroundings, they give a nod to the guards, before taking the chains and pulling them tight. With a brief exchange of muttered words, two fall behind, and as the one up front gives a sharp yank, Will is taken across the landing and through another door, into the grand atrium of the royal quarters.

Down the gleaming steps of a gold spiral staircase and paraded along a plush scarlet carpet that runs like a bridge across the white marble floor, a towering window silhouettes a tall oak throne with strange images and fantastical creatures carved into its back. And leading him around it and shoving him to his knees, he gazes up at the Queen, as his shackles are fastened to metal rings in the floor.

Nestled in its soft lambskin seat under the radiance of a twinkling chandelier, she admires her sun kissed kingdom as her lady-in-waiting washes her naked feet in a silver bowl. Diverting the languid gaze of her beautiful green eyes, she twirls a long dark strand of her hair with her finger and examines him, sending a shiver down the silken folds of her cascading gown with every subtle movement she makes. With a dismissive twitch of her hand, the dwarfs scurry to her throne and vanish under the fabric of her blooming dress, leaving only the soothing sound of the warm water gently splashing onto her feet. Beneath her pensive contemplation, Will is quiet as the light sears its oppressive heat onto his back through the window behind him.

After a long pause, she speaks, her sultry voice pouring like honey, "Do you believe in power outside of the plain we inhabit?"

Will does not reply, but instead looks at her perfectly sculpted features and soft ruby lips, conflicted that such beauty could produce such suffering as a place like this.

"Many years ago," she continues, "I was sick. Very sick. My father tried everything he could, but nothing in this world would heal me. Even the medicine of Vitruvius himself was no match for my affliction. So in his final desperation, he sent an army of scouts to every corner of the earth looking for a cure. But of the few that returned from the far reaches of this inhospitable planet, none returned with any more than tales of terror. But one day, after all hope was gone; a man, rising like the morning star over the desolate horizon, presented himself at the palace, speaking of a gift of healing. And my father, in the depths of his despair, let him in. He spoke of magic, and miracles. . . and of a terrible price. 'An eye for an eye,' he said, 'blood for blood'. . . my father's life for mine. So, as I lay in the final throes of death, my father paid the price. And when his still, peaceful head was brought to my chambers, I kissed his cold, ashen lips and said farewell." She pauses with a wistful breath. "I walked that day, and ran the next. I had been healed! A new queen with a new life! Free to chase my passions and embrace all the splendors of the world. But sadly, time still blundered on, and again my body began to falter and wither under the weight of its relentless march. How he heard my cries? I do not know. But the man and his magic, soon returned. An eye for an eye. . ." she sighs in wonder. "Imagine all you could do, if age and sickness were no longer an obstacle; amassing knowledge and riches far beyond comprehension? You could change the world! The paltry worth of even one sacrifice would be so abundantly multiplied! And it was. With only a few, I had brought an end to the war with the Sorrow, and only a few more I'd orchestrated an alliance with the Kol! My people wanted peace, and I gave them peace. They wanted wealth, and I gave them wealth! They were so happy! Whatever they asked, I gave— even freedom from my own rule of law! They were free to choose their own path! And this place, the great city of Desolation; was transformed from pallid stagnation to an oasis of unbridled liberty!" In deep satisfaction, she inhales with a glint in her eyes.

"Once I saw the evidence of a power, beyond this plain, I began to see it in the fabric of everything. If it is true, what else is true? And if it is possible, what else is possible? What else am I not seeing—or maybe more correctly—being permitted to see?. . . So, when my chief steward, in his shameful suffering, finally bleated of his treason and started rambling about prophecies, I was keen to listen. And when I saw you today, and your beautiful black eyes; well—Son of Legion—I knew it was all true! The Legion and their list, the gift you play host to, and why you seek my Solomon. But hush!. . ." she raises her hand reassuringly, seeing Will's demeanor tense at the revelation of her knowledge. "I mean you no harm. On the contrary in fact! Although I share a bed with the Kol and their Vitruvian God, it is by necessity, not by desire. I am simply submitting to a brute standing over me as his hands are around my neck. I would gladly see them taken to their knees, and will gladly help you do it! I have arranged an audience for you with Solomon at his refuge in the hermit kingdom, and when you return, I will get you passage on one of the Kol transits back into Zeno—if it is your wish, of course! I will warn you though, my belief in prophecy and the power of the unseen is far from unique. After your performance in the arena it won't be long before the Kol and others—foe and friend—will come to seek you for your power. So if we are to succeed, we must make haste! What say you?"

Will hesitates and looks to the floor as his mind's a flood with flailing thoughts and questions.

'It's what I want. It's what Abby wants.'

Deep scars streaking across soft skin, flicker through his consciousness.

'With all the pain she's fostered in her hellish paradise, this woman can't be trusted. She's no better than the Kol! At least they hide their depravity!'

'But it's why we're here. Find a way, right? This is a way!'

Sad eyes haunting a gentle smile, patter across his mind.

'We can't shake hands with the devil and walk away unscathed? Is this not how all plans of noble intention seed their destruction?'

'But we need allies. Those who share our goals and serve our end. Surely the stain of it would be forgivable with all the good we'll do?'

'Maybe. . . but is forgivable the aspiration of how we are meant to be?'

The warm touch of a kind hand holding his, stills his heart.

With a deep breath he gazes up to the expectant eyes of the Queen.

"Kata." The word drifts from his mouth like a cool, sweet scented breeze on a stifling summer's day, and as he hears its fleeting whisper tremble through the hollow void of the room, it reverberates harmoniously in his soul.

The queen raises a thin eyebrow.

"The slave girl?" she says, sitting up straight. "What about her? What is she to Legion?"

"Nothing," Will's voice cracks as he speaks. "But it is my wish. And my wish is for her freedom."

"You'd throw away your gift?!" the Queen hisses in a sudden rage. "Your destiny!?! The power to change the world, for a used up whore?!! Who do you think you are!!"

Her outrage washing over him, Will stares down at the chains around his wrists, grappling to understand what had compelled him to blurt out Kata's name.

"If you truly believe in the unseen," he says as he looks up. "Is it possible my being here, in chains before you now, is exactly where I am supposed to be?"

The queen glares at him, but is silent as he continues. "If there is a chance I am supposed to be here, I cannot trade what I know is the right thing today, for my wishful perception of the future. Only the unseen knows what tomorrow will bring."

An eerie silence hovers between them as the sound of his words fades to nothing.

"You remind me of someone," she says with a low breath, examining Will in deep contemplation, as the anger in her demeanor fades away. "So be it. I will grant you your wish. . . But, on one condition."

"Name it," Will replies.

"You can take the whore. But only if you continue your mission to Solomon. My curiosity may be my undoing, but I am interested to see how much truth is in your prophecy. Besides, she will be safer with you in Sorrow. Triboulet is. . . well, some would prefer to see a little bird crushed than to be freed from a cage."

Will is hesitant, almost expecting her to burst into laughter and announce her offer is nothing but a cruel joke.

"Well?" she says, mildly irritated at his hesitation to her gracious offer.

"Yes," Will replies. "That would be. . . thank you."

"My pleasure. . ." she says with a little smile, as she lowers her head in a self appreciating bow. "Then let it be so — Children!!!" she shouts, prompting the three little men waiting patiently in the billowing ruffles of her gown to clamber out from their hiding spot and hurry into a row in front of her with their hands clasped behind their backs.

"Paxton," she looks to the first. "Release this man from his chains and send for the Osprey!"

"Yes, my queen!" he replies with a nod, fumbling through his pockets for the keys to the shackles.

"Harold."

"Yes, my queen?"

"Find the slave girl and have her brought up to the flight deck."

"Right away, my queen!"

Waiting for him to scuttle off, the queen turns her eyes on the last little man and beckons to him.

"And Marley," she continues, reaching a hand toward him. "Dear sweet Marley. Come here my child, look at me."

With his head bowed, Marley takes small steps to her, and placing her delicate fingers under his chin, she raises his somber face to hers. "I need you to go play with Triboulet until this man has left the palace."

Marley nods, as his face falls in despair.

"Shhh. It's ok," she speaks to him in a gentle tone. "I know his games can be a bit rough, but I need him distracted till the girl is gone. And you'll be doing it for me—you'll do it for me, won't you? It'll make me so very happy, and you do want me to be happy, don't you?"

"Yes, my queen."

*   *   *

As the heavy pulsing of a helicopter outside reverberates through the atrium, Will feels a wave of relief as he stands to his feet. But as he glances up at the Queen's imposing magnificence, he knows, deep down, that the terrifying beauty on the throne before him will bring nothing but death.

"And just like that, Will of Legion. It is done," she addresses him, extending her pale, upturned palms as if the performer of a great magic trick.

Almost as if tasting his thoughts, her enchanting eyes flick up and lock onto his.

"Trust me, child," she says, flashing him a coy little smile. "Together, we will change the world.

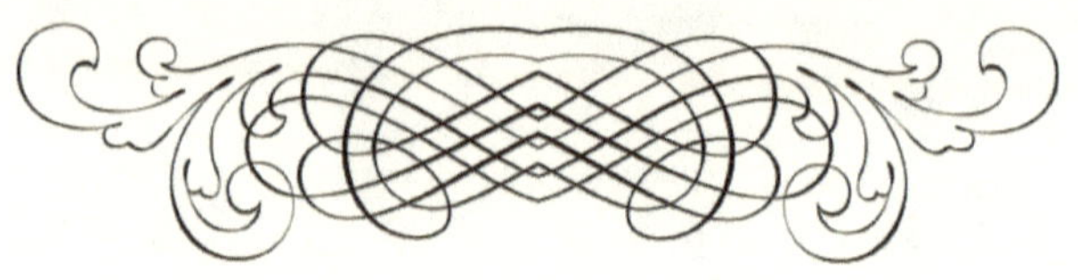

My wounds are too great, I cannot go on.
I've succumbed to the darkness, I'm a bird without song.

Leave you to sleep? And let you alone?
I have purpose for you, it's not time to come home.

Leave me to suffer, my last struggled breath,
All that I see is shadow and death.

But the shadows you cast are while you walk away.
For you cast them yourself, in front, there to stay.
So reach out, take my hand, and turn to my light.

But my eyes cannot see it! It's absent from sight!

Oh' your eyes and your ears, and your keen sense of smell,
hold you quite captive in the realm that you dwell.
Is my light not apparent by the shadow you see,
as it lays there doubting what permits it to be?

So reaching out desperate for the light as it spoke,
I felt its warm hand, and from shadow, I broke.
Then turning around and facing light's blaze,
I fell to my knees, beneath its kind gaze.
And as shadow retreated to hide far behind,
I'd been freed from its specter, and loosed from its bind.

So next time, consumed by the shadow you cast,
filled with your torment and wounds from the past.
Look not at the absence of light in your form,
but instead past its edges, to where hope is reborn.

Chapter 16

THE WEEPING CITY OF SORROW

The snow crested valleys and icy canyons pulse with the constant thrum of the whirling rotors on each of the bulky aircraft's thick wingtips, sending birds fleeing into the skies, and a herd of hoofed creatures sprinting up a craggy incline. As the blades tilt on their axis and the craft prepares to make its descent, they begin to slow, clearing the glistening side of a sheer rock face, before approaching the circular platform of a landing pad, perched high above the yawning chasm. From its edge, a thin walkway spans the void below, and reaching the far side, it meets the grand parapeted walls of the Weeping City of Sorrow.

Rising from the mountains like a frozen beast, it is truly magnificent, with tall, fairytale towers extending high into the crisp blue skies. Crowned by vivid crimson slate roofs and embellished with narrow stained glass windows, its majestic arches and imposing fortifications are only bested by the sheer splendor of the snow capped peaks that surround it.

A violent cloud of powdered snow twisting beneath it as the hovering machine drops to land, an ordered assembly of somber men waiting below shield themselves from its wake. And as little white wisps spin across the cobbled surface, the heavy rubber tires meet the ground.

The shrill whining of the engine ramping down as the cargo hold shudders and the lights flicker on, Will feels Kata stir. She fell asleep almost the instant the Osprey lifted off from the palace deck, and wrapping her in a blanket while trying not to linger too long on the sight of her swollen red eye or the deep gash in her nose and lip, he had gently pulled her sideways and laid her head on a folded jacket on his lap.

Startled by a howl of crisp frigid air, his breath is cut short as the ramp at the craft's tail lowers, giving view of a line of ceremonial Sorwian soldiers standing beneath the banner of the Crimson Tear. Clad in shimmering scale armor and brandishing broad swords and long shields, they stand like iron statues, as the head of their ranks, a man in a heavy fur trim cloak that drapes over his long tunic, gives a sweeping wave.

With a reassuring nod, Will helps Kata to her feet, and they walk across the steel fuselage and down the incline of the steel ramp. Clutching his cloak and shielding his face as the Osprey lifts off with a deafening roar, the man advances toward them

"Here," he yells over the noise as they reach him, handing them a flowing gray cloak. "Her head must be covered in the kingdom!"

Waiting for her as she puts it on and pulls up its drooping hood, he gazes after the Osprey as it rumbles down the valley and the tranquil stillness of the mountains returns.

"That's better," he continues, with a sigh of relief. "I am Mathius. Aide to the kings. Welcome to the Kingdom of Sorrow. You are not too shaken after your journey I hope? The weather up here can be hard on the machines, not everyone can keep their previous meal in its place."

"No, we're fine thanks, just glad to have made it," Will replies. "I'm Will and this is—"

"No need for introductions," he interrupts. "We've been expecting you. Come, I have been sent to bring you to the Basilica. If you would be so kind as to follow me," he motions behind him towards the looming battlements of the city walls. "The kings are eager to meet you."

Ushering them toward the narrow bridge that trails off the edge of the helipad, the line of soldiers parts their ranks as they pass through their middle, before turning on their heels to follow in an ordered line.

On to the open platform, Will takes a nervous breath as they cross. Barely wide enough for two people to pass, it sits precariously on spindly gray piers that vanish into the gloom below. Baffled by a frigid breeze, he gazes up in awe at the sheer enormity of the citadel's stone fortifications. A true behemoth, how a creation of such magnitude ever got built was a marvel, but how it was done in such an inhospitable place as this was nothing short of a miracle.

Through the gateway in the base of its looming wall, they march under the steel pointed portcullis and into a long tunnel, lit by flaming torches mounted on the walls. The heavy footsteps of the soldiers echoing ahead of them as they reach the end, tall steel studded doors creak open, leading into an open cobbled courtyard encircled by tall granite columns that support the towering structure above. Passing beyond the huge iron doors on the other side, Will's eyes widen in astonishment as they file onto the mirrored stone floors of the Basilica's vast golden atrium.

Greeted by the stoic gaze of majestic statues and vivid brilliance of detailed tapestries, long streaks of warm sunlight fall like warm rivers over them from the windows high above. Staring up at the vaulted dome ceiling sitting proud on top of an exquisite array of columns, he is lost for words. But as Kata holds his arm a little tighter, he looks to her humbled face, bathed in the bright glow of royal yellows, purples and reds.

Brought to an abrupt halt as the soldiers form a semicircle behind them and drop to one knee, the purposeful melody of a trumpet bellows out as they reach a raised marble platform. Along its length, atop three wide steps, twelve noblemen sit, six on each side, adorned in fanciful regalia that drapes over their long tunics with their distinct family insignias emblazoned on their chests. And in their center, on three exquisitely embellished thrones, the Kings of the city in somber repose.

"Welcome honored guests!" the nasal exclamation of the marshal's voice echoes from the edge of the group. "To the Weeping City of Sorrow!"

With a knowing glance from Mathius, Will and Kata follow his lead and take a knee beside him, as a volley of trumpet calls commend the marshal's statement.

"Your names, if you would!" the marshal asks, puffing his chest out in self importance.

"Will. . . Will Manning," Will replies, his voice seeming to get lost in the vastness of the massive chamber. "And Kata.

Katayoun," he adds, glancing at the blank stare of Kata's ashen face.

"William of Legion and Katayoun of the Desolate City!" the marshall declares. "May I introduce to you, the wisest of us all! — The Kings of men!!!"

Another volley of trumpet calls cutting through the air, he gives a low bow towards the imposing figures of the three throned men.

"May I introduce," he bellows, gesturing to the first king, a stern heavyset man with a gleaming broadsword resting on his lap and plated armor that spreads across his broad torso and arms, "the hand of the Wrath of Sorrow; General Balthasar!"

Motioning to the second, a well kept, pompous man with slight features, wearing a beautiful ruby surcoat and a thin silver crown that decorates his luxurious velvet hair, he continues, "The head of the Sigh of Sorrow; Lord Gaspar! And. . ." With a dramatic wave as he presents the third king, an old, somber with a clean white beard and a jeweled mantle of pure gold draped over his black satin robes, his monologue reaches its climax, "the most esteemed, and wise. . . The voice of the Tears of Sorrow; Melichior the High Priest!!"

The fanfare's trumpeting acclamation of their introduction growing to a grandiose crescendo, it abruptly stops, leaving an eerie, hollow silence as every eye in the room waits for their words.

"You come from Desolation, yes?" the high priest asks with a booming voice, gripping a golden staff in his wizened hand by his side.

"Yes," Will answers.

"But you, at least—you are not a Desolate?" He casts a dismissive glimpse at Kata, before looking back to Will. "Where are you from?"

"Zeno," Will replies hesitantly, unsure where the question is leading. "New Boston."

"Vitruvian then. . . And you were sent by Legion?"

"Yes."

"Hmm. I have long heard stories of them and the prophecies of their warrior. I heard too of your victory against Cain." Glancing up with a subdued smile, he pauses in contemplation. "The mad queen, Salome; She has requested that you be given an audience with a man we have in our care on her behalf. He is to help you garner information to use against Vitruvius?"

"Yes."

With a solemn nod, the priest falls silent and slowly strokes his beard.

"Gaspar, Balthasar—what say you?" he asks, looking to his sides.

Taking a deep breath, Lord Gaspar straightens up in his throne. "While there is much value in keeping our relationship with the Queen courteous," he begins. "Our deal with the Kol is already fragile and the income we gain from the mines is almost incalculable. Are we willing to take a chance at losing it all, for this man and his Legion's goals?"

"Their goals are our goals, are they not?" General Balthasar interjects with an air of disdain in his voice. "Does your trade deal overshadow the past?!"

"Don't be so dramatic, General," Gaspar scoffs. "I am merely suggesting that we do not cross a line that could cost us our wealth unless we are sure of the outcome. Aligning with this 'Legion' carries risk. And the best interest of the people needs to be kept first and foremost!"

"Risk!!? The risk to the people is the deal with the Kol that you are so keen to grow! You may have been too young to remember, but I was not. I remember when the mountains ran red with rivers of blood! I remember when our women and children were rounded up like cattle to slave in their farms and factories? Are they to be weighed against the gold in our pocket?!"

"That is not what I am saying!" Gaspar replies defensively. "I'm only saying tha—"

"Stop," the high priest barks. "This is not the place for your quarreling!!! Gaspar! Will you grant this man from Legion his request or not?"

"I. . . I'm just— Fine, yes!!" Gaspar responds with a red face and slumps infuriated into his throne.

"Balthasar," the high priest continues with a deep breath. "Do you have anything else to add?"

"Yes, thank you your eminence; If I may." The General looks with a stern brow at Will. "I must ask. How are your people aligned with the mad Queen? She is no less the devil than Vitruvius himself. Is her way of life more pleasing than his? What is she to you?"

"No. She's nothing. A means to an end. We've got no allegiance to her at all," Will replies. "I didn't have any other choice. She was my only way to find Solomon. . . Honestly," he glances down at Kata, her battered face barely visible hidden under the thick fabric of her hood. "If I had my way, I would as soon see her killed as anyone."

"And your Legion? What is it that they want? What is it that you want?"

"I. . ." Will stumbles on his words under the General's steely gaze. "No more than I deserve—no more than we deserve. We want an answer. Justice. And a reckoning for all the harm that's been done. Maybe one day we'll get a new start, and freedom from the hand of the Kol."

"A mission of man's virtue. This pleases me to hear," Balthasar glances sourly at Gaspar. "And Solomon? What is it that Legion wants from him?"

"I have been told Solomon has a history with the Kol, and that he has a way to help us find some people we are looking for."

"What people?"

"Not people—Kol. Kol who are vital to the operation of the Vitruvian machine. Legion have given me a list, they've stamped it in my bloodstream, and if we can just—"

"So you look to take the head off the snake?"

Will falters, as the three kings glare at him in silence. "Look, I understand that you don't trust our intentions— honestly it would be strange if you did. But for what it's worth, I've no intention of staying longer than I have to. Legion has no interest in this place. Once I've got what I need, you'll never hear from me again."

"It is not your intention I question," the General continues, examining him in careful deliberation. "It is your motivation. I have seen men's justice before. However, If you aim to fulfill what your prophecy claims you will, I will not stand in your way. Maybe we'll meet on the same side of a battlefield one day."

"Very well then," the high priest speaks. "It is decided— we will play our part. Mathius, take them to Solomon and make sure they get everything they need."

"Yes, my King," Matthias answers, lowering his head in respectful acceptance.

With a sharp blare of a trumpet, the assembly concludes, and as the noblemen begin to mutter amongst themselves, Mathius gives a gentle nod to Will and Kata as he stands to his feet. The company of soldiers filing into formation behind them, they march in a line across the other side of the immense atrium and into the confines of a tall, pointed vestibule. Guarding its heavy doors, two humorless soldiers snap to attention and swing them open as they approach, and as a frigid wind howls in, speckles of snowflakes dance across the floor.

Out in the crisp alpine air, they cross onto a long covered walkway that runs between two rows of smooth stone pillars. Through the openings on either side, a wide strip of snow kissed grass spans the gap of an inner courtyard, lined with ornate benches and delicate winter flowers that surround the frozen surface of a long rectangular pond.

"Good afternoon, Captain," Mathius calls out, as they approach an ordered group of soldiers waiting at the end of the walkway.

Distinguishable by his more decorative armor and the purple plume on his helmet, the Captain steps forward. "Mathius, how are you?" he says, shaking Mathius's hand. "So this is them?"

"Yes. Will, Katayoun — This is Captain Ascha of the Sting. He'll look after you from here." With a nod, Will and Kata greet him as he returns the gesture. "You have been given instructions of where to bring them?" Mathius continues.

"The Wrath barracks at Engeddi gate, yes?"

"Yes. They're to meet with Lord Solomon. Just show them to his quarters. I believe he's in Faeirfeld at the moment, but has been requested to return. The Wrath have been notified also."

"Not a problem. I will have them there by evening."

"Excellent. Thank you Captain," Mathius replies, before looking back to Will. "Now, if there is anything you need while you are here," he glances at Kata. "A physician perhaps? Well. Just ask when you arrive and I will have it arranged. And the Captain and the Sting will protect you of course, but I will remind you to keep her head covered at all times. There is no need for an incident if it can be avoided."

Will acknowledges him with a slight bob of his head.

"Good. Well, I will leave you to it. I wish you luck."

"Thanks."

"Well then — Captain, M'lady," he says as he gives a courteous bow. "I will leave you to it."

As he turns and heads back towards the Basilica, the soldiers split into a double line with Will and Kata in the middle of their ranks. And with a gruff command from the Captain, the procession begins its march along the hand cut stone floors and under the high vaulted ceilings of the castle's inner keep.

The gleaming light of the Basilica's grandeur dissipates as they continue, and albeit not as bright, its decadent opulence is on such a scale that much of it must only be enjoyed by the birds who can roam its magnificent heights. Trekking between the monolithic features of wide outer courtyards, they gaze up at the flying buttresses connecting its edge, before retreating into yet another beautiful arched hallway covered by an ornate rib vaulted ceiling.

Although the depictions are sometimes unsettling, everywhere they look seems to be detailed with fine stained glass images and intricate carvings, and littered by statues of stoic men and mythical creatures. Spellbound by the unearthly surroundings, at one point, crossing out to a walkway that wraps the very outer wall of the upper battlements, it gives way to an icy precipice beneath, that screams and whistles with the black mountain winds. But returning inside, and meandering through more winds and bends for what seems like hours, the lifeless quiet of the inner keep comes to an end.

Turning onto a large concourse, they pass a lone man mumbling to himself, and then a lively group of hooded women carrying baskets. Busier and busier, the crowd grows. From ten to hundreds, and soon they are plowing through a noisy surge of bustling citizens from every walk of life, like a ship on the open sea. Until, reaching two huge gates that yawn open in the stonewall at the end and pushing through the masses, they emerge onto the market plaza.

Suspended above a deep black canyon that divides the towering faces of the outer and inner castle wall, the expansive cobbled surface that joins one side to the other is brimming with exquisite smells and the energetic hustle of trade. A bright patchwork of color, the entire space between the parapet walls on its farthest edges is lined with row after row of market vendors' booths, forming narrow corridors for the jostling hive of their enthusiastic patrons.

Marching into the fray, the delightful scent of spices and simmering cuisines fills their nostrils as they are wrapped in thick clouds of aromatic steam that billows up into the crisp mountain sky. All manner of trade occupies the host of counters; from the fine cuts of tailor's cloth to the practical mastery of the blacksmith's forge. Artists, jewelers, and artisans alike, all feverishly peddling their wares—let alone the sheer quantity of meat, produce and culinary delight that seamlessly intersperses throughout the many marvels.

"Can you see them?" Kata shouts over the clamor as she grips Will's arm.

"No," he shouts back, scouring the crowd for a sign of the soldiers with a nervous smile. "We must have got separated. This place is crazy! Let's just keep moving!"

Swept past many more dazzling trinkets and yelling salesmen, a break in the throng appears ahead of them as they approach a heavy steel railing that wraps around the dizzying edge of a gaping hole in the center of the plaza's surface. The yawning opening to the chasm beneath is spanned by a delicate arched bridge with an ensemble of musicians strumming a jovial melody from its highest point.

A faint smile runs across Kata's lips as Will looks at her, entertained by the merriment, as she watches them send their sounds reverberating into the hollow abyss below. Stopping for a moment as they reach the railings to peer cautiously over the precipice, he scans around to get his bearings before, giving a gentle nudge to get her attention, he nods to keep moving along the edge. With a round of applause, the song ends and the musicians unceremoniously dive into the throes of a whimsical ballad, the upbeat tempo drawing in some of the passing revelers to spontaneously break into dance.

Still searching for a fleeting glimmer of a soldier's armor as they approach a gang of scruffy kids hooting and laughing, his body tenses, aghast, as he sees the object of their entertainment. Crouched at their feet, half naked and chained to the railings, the huddled form of a bleeding and battered man lies on the ground, mercilessly waiting for their next blow.

"Hey!" Will yells in outrage as a stocky young teen lunges at the man with a vicious kick, and, urged on by his attack, a little boy no older than six or seven, throws a stone at him causing the whole brood to squeal in delight.

"Hey! Stop!" Will shouts again as he breaks away from Kata to get closer. "What do you think you're doing?!"

Pushing his way into the rabble, he grabs a brutish child's arm as he raises a heavy rock above his head and squeezes so tight that the boy shrieks and looks up at him with a frightened face.

"All of you stop it! Now!!" He's angry now, as he steps between the violent assault and the captive man. But as a stone flies through the air and hits him in the face, the gang boos him and begins scrambling for more things to throw. A handful of the older ones approaching with fists clenched, Will knocks the first to the ground. Ready to lash out again, he braces as three more get close, but suddenly they stop in their tracks as the heavy footfall of soldiers rushing in behind them rings out.

"Let them go!" Captain Ascha bellows, striding into the middle of the fray as the kids flee in terrified panic at their sudden arrival.

Relieved that the situation's diffused, Will turns and crouches down by the chained man. "Hey, are you ok?" he asks, putting his hand on the man's cold shoulder.

"What are you doing?!" the Captain yells. "Stop!" Glowering, he points to the chained shackle on the man's leg. "Leave him be! Do not interfere with God's work!"

Alarmed, Will rises to his feet, "What? Why?"

"He has been sentenced to death and all the suffering that comes with it! To comfort the judged is an act of treason!"

"But look at him—he's defenseless! You can't just leave him!"

"You dare challenge my authority?! The authority of the High Priest!!?" the Captain growls drawing his sword, as Will, feeling every fiber of his being tense and the embers of anger ignite, glares at him with a glimmer of rage in his eyes.

"Will," Kata whispers to him as he feels her gentle hand on his arm. "Don't."

As the rest of the soldiers draw their blades, the sound of sliding steel cuts through the tense silence that's descended on the gawking crowd.

"I was only. . ." Will starts, looking at the burning scowl of the Captain surrounded by the stern faces of his men.

"No explanation necessary!!" a loud voice rings out, as a rugged, bearded man pushes out from the crowd behind them and approaches them confidently. "You were only doing what you thought was right." Raising his hands, he stops between the aggravated men. "Please Captain, lower your weapon. The man didn't know any better, he doesn't know our ways!" He looks at the Captain sternly, "Besides, is he not under your care?"

The Captain pauses for a moment, before stepping back and sheathing his blade. "Forgive me, my Lord."

"It is alright, there is no harm done." Turning to Will, a friendly smile breaks across the man's face as he extends his hand, "I have to say, I never thought the day would actually come. It is very nice to meet you. I am Solomon. You will forgive the Captain, yes? He is simply following the letter of the law."

"Yes, of course. I'm sorry, Captain." Will gives an apologetic nod at the Captain. "I was not trying to question your authority."

Motioning to the captive man hunched on the ground, Will turns back to Solomon, "What did he do anyway, to deserve such punishment?"

"I have no idea," Solomon looks at the prisoner. "Convict—what evil have you done? What is your charge?"

Pained, the man pushes himself up into a sitting position and leans with his back against the railings, before looking up at them with kind eyes. "Thank you for your mercy brother," he says to Will. "My charge is for trying to bring mercy too. The mercy of the God these people claim to worship, but do not know."

Shocked whispers ripple through the throng of onlookers, as the man takes a deep breath and begins to speak.

"People of Sorrow!" he cries out. "The holy men you follow have long since forgotten who was leading them. And now, in their wandering pursuit of earthly whims, they have taken away the key of knowledge. They have blinded you from the truth itself. They feed you with words from the holy book that are twisted and skewed to suit their gain. A retelling of a retelling, that leaves you empty vessels; nothing but a shadowed outline of the author's true words. Can you feel the warmth of the sun, or hear the notes of a symphony, from a man's account?! If you could only see them for yourself, and listen — You would hear. Yet, I weep for your souls. It is not I who is the prisoner here."

The collective outrage rippling through the crowd, Will's stomach knots as the hiss of angry words spewing into the air with hateful malice.

"Blasphemy!"

A sharp stone flying from the throng, the air becomes thick with boos and vitriolic screams as a bystander lunges out of the fray and kicks the prisoner hard in the side of his head.

"Heretic!!"

With a unified heave, the crowd surges forward, overcome by their poison toward the prisoner as they try to get their hands on him.

"Captain!!" Solomon shouts at Ascha as he motions to Will. "We'll all be thrown in the rift if we lose our guests to this rabble!"

With a commanding shout, the Captain and his men assemble into a new formation, packing defensively around Will and Kata and interlocking their shields. The thundering of heavy blows raining down on the armored wall, screams of pain rip through the sky as bodies are skewered by the soldiers' blades. And as men and women fall to the ground, they're crushed under the heaving weight of the masses feet.

With a booming gong, the ringing of a church bell pierces through the open air, and as if a spell has been cast, the madness stops.

Disorientated from the chaos, Will watches in disbelief as in almost perfect unison, the entirety of the plaza's congregation falls to their knees and bow their heads in solemn prayer.

With another deafening gong, the bell rings again, this time bringing the crowd out of their trance and back to their feet. A few disgusted glares are cast at the lifeless prisoner, but perhaps by the handful of perforated corpses at the soldier's feet, the bloodlust is gone, and the throng returns to whatever business had brought them there.

The Captain looks back at Will and Kata with concern, "are you hurt?"

"No, we're fine," they reply, shaken.

"Thank God," he says with a sigh of relief, before scanning around and seeing Solomon shaking his head in disbelief, clearly unsettled by the sudden turn of events. "My Lord, are you hurt?"

"No, no. Thank you Captain, I'm fine. If you could get them out of here and bring them to my quarters I would be grateful," he replies. "I'll meet you there. I have some business to attend to first."

"Yes my Lord, of course," the Captain replies, as with a hand gesture, the soldiers form a line to his sides and prepare to move.

"And hey," Solomon grins at Will. "Welcome to Sorrow."

*   *   *

Much like the inner keep of the castle citadel, the outer keep is a labyrinth of stone hallways and grand courtyards, but noticeably more dreary, lacking the fine artistry and ornate luxury. But its deficiency is more than compensated for by the abundance of life.

Lined by a seemingly endless number of little doors that lead to the modest accommodations inside, the thronging corridors, interspersed with discrete chapels, long food halls and bustling common areas, are filled with the happy screams of energetic youth and warm, friendly banter. With the mechanical stomp of their escort's advance dampening as they clear the echoing passageways, the armed procession finally exits through the massive steel gates of the looming exterior wall, and Will finds himself outside once again.

Looking down from the busy thoroughfare sloping away from the citadel's entrance, the comforting odor of burning firewood lingers in the air. Massed with crude stone homes and buildings they sprawl in every direction, thin spires of black smoke trail from the chimneys. And as he stares out over the sprawl of winding cobbled roads and muddy side streets that dash in illogical disarray between the city structures, the procession of soldiers stops as they approach a row of saddled horses, tied and waiting patiently for their riders' return.

First flipping a silver coin to the attendant who's leaning on the long hitching post, Captain Ascha gives a sharp whistle as his men disperse towards their respective mounts.

"M'lady," he calls out to Kata. "You ride with me. And Will," he continues, directing Will to a horse mounted soldier ahead, "go with Nathaniel."

Leaving Kata with the Captain, Will walks up to the soldier who greets him with a nod, and after clambering up behind him, they're off.

The journey through the grimy city sprawl is uneventful, and as they trot past endless little houses and taverns, Will is grateful for the horses; as much for the welcome break from the long walk as for the escape from the stinking filth that runs raw across the streets.

Close to the city's edge as the buildings thin, they cross a narrow cobble bridge into the wide open courtyard of a huge cavalry barracks. Alive with the clamor of enormous horses and the attentive activity of stable hands rushing about their business, the convoy comes to an abrupt halt as the Captain's command reverberates on the surrounding stalls and outbuildings.

An excited shout ringing out, a young boy comes bounding down a set of steps with a big grin on his face, "I'll take them from here!" he says.

"You Solomon's boy?" the Captain asks in his serious manner.

"Yes sir," he replies as he jogs up to them. "My father said you'd be coming."

"We will part ways here then m'lady," the Captain calls over his shoulder, as Will, listening from up ahead, slides off the back of the soldier's horse and walks over.

"Thank you, Captain," he says, as Kata drops onto the ground beside him.

With a grunt, the Captain bows his head in acceptance before swiftly turning his horse, and with the clatter of hooves, he and the soldiers clear the courtyard and race back over the bridge into the city.

Beaming up in delight, the boy looks up at Kata with big eyes. "Are you one of them?" he asks "From the city in the desert?"

With a little nod, her sullen gaze softens and breaks into a smile. "What is your name?" she asks.

"Elik," he replies.

"Well Elik," she says, amused by his honest little expression and tousled hair, "did your father say what to do with us once we arrived?"

"Oh, yes. Of course. I forgot," he chortles and beckons to them as he turns on his heels. "Come right this way."

Up a narrow set of stone steps to the living quarters built over the stable stalls below, he scampers into a large rustic kitchen with an open fire crackling at the end. Pulling out one of the empty chairs from around a stout oak table set in the middle, he grins at them as they do the same and sit down.

"I'm glad you're real," Elik blurts out, unable to contain his enthusiasm. "Father said he wasn't too sure! But he's told me all the stories a thousand times! Did you know he used to be in the Malflatus!? You're so lucky—all I've got is this boring place! He says if I work as hard as him, I can make a life just as dull as his!" He rolls his eyes and laughs. "I bet your life's not boring. . . What happened to your face?!" he says, pointing at the discolored gashes on Kata's face who smiles back, charmed by the unfiltered babble of his curious demeanor.

"Oh, nothing. . ." she lets out a playful laugh. "You should have seen the other guy! You wanna see?"
With a bob of his head, he cautiously plods across the room to examine her injuries.

"That's cool. . . does it hurt?" He reaches to touch them, with mild concern on his furrowed brow.

"No, not really," she reassures him. "You know, you remind me of my little brother when I was growing up. He was never lost for words. I'd say he's much older than you now though."

"Well," he says, reaching to touch her hair as she lowers her shawl onto her shoulders. "You remind me of Bella. . ."

"Who's Bella?"

"Oh, we walked past her on our way up. She's the dark one in the stall beside the steps with the white dot on her nose."

"A horse!" Kata chuckles and tickles him as he laughs, letting out little snorts.

*   *   *

In the hours that pass before Solomon returns, Will is relieved. Tired, but content in the unsophisticated comfort of the home, the boy and Kata are sprawled out on the floor in front of the fire with a deck of cards. And as they talk about nothing in particular, the presence of their playful laughter is like a refreshing breeze. After all she'd experienced, and survived; that she could still laugh was a miracle in itself. In a strange way, it made his suffering, and even Marissa's, seem somehow compassionate.

In those times, when he was swallowed by despair itself and the depths of his grief stung with such malice that he thought he would die; had his prayers been heard? Was he so blinded by the confines of his existence that he had missed the hand of mercy when it reached out? Is there someone out there who Kata would look at—just like he's looking at her now—and begrudgingly contemplate thankfulness? Are the limits of suffering boundless? Or is death simply a measure of grace?

"Don't get up!" Solomon exclaims as he strolls into the room some hours later, setting down a tray piled with bread and meat carefully on the table. "I see you've met Elik — You behaving yourself boy? Taking good care of our guests?" He looks over at the pair with a bemused grin before sitting down. "Good. Come, eat. Your game can wait!" Beckoning for them to help themselves, he fills his plate, before taking a bite and watching them curiously as he chews.

"It's a fire lily," he says, following Will's gaze to the searing scarlet petals of a delicate flower, displayed in a vase over the fire. "A cyrtanthus ventricosus to be exact."

"It's beautiful," Will replies.

"It is. It was my wife's favorite. I get one for her every year after the fires on the highlands burn out. I was actually on my way back when you arrived, otherwise I would have come and met you."

Pausing for a moment, a twinkling grin breaks on the corner of his mouth, "So, I was told you'd be a catalyst for an uprising, but no one ever said you'd be so effective! Do you start riots everywhere you go?"

"I—" Will starts defensively, but stops, seeing Kata's stifled smile as she takes a sip of water.

Chuckling at her expression, Solomon looks back to Will, "Oh I'm only teasing! Seriously, don't worry about it. It's not the first time the Children of Light has caused trouble, and I don't imagine it'll be the last either. I'm glad I showed up when I did though. You getting locked up would have really slowed things down."

"He was one of them?" Will asks, his heart sinking at the thought of Tom or Leah suffering the same way.

"The Children? Yeah, he was. You've heard of them? I thought the Vitruvians had stamped them out from the cities?"

"If it wasn't for them, I'd never have made it here. They helped me in Desolation."

"Oh yeah? I think they hate them down there as much as they do here." He glances at Kata, "Queens got a thing for them, right?"

"Yeah," Kata replies with a sullen nod. "She likes to feed them to her creatures."

"Sheesh! That's harsh. At least we only throw them into the Rift! Not that it makes a difference — For every one of them that goes in, another three seem to spring up. But anyway—" Solomon lightens his tone and smiles, noticing

Elik's worried little frown, "it's nothing for us to worry about. We have other business to attend to. So Kish has agreed to take us out to the Hub in the morning. It is a long trek out there, so once we've finished up here, I think a good night's sleep will be in order. It may be a while until we get another!"

"The Hub?"

"Legion is still looking to cull the herd, isn't it?"

"Yeah?" Will replies.

"Well the Hub is where we need to go. The equipment I need to use the biodata they stamped you with is far beyond the means of this place. They did give it to you, didn't they?"

"Of course, yeah. But what is it?"

"Oh, It's a Subdomino of the Vitruvian Servant. You know, like a network terminal if you know your tech, modified and encrypted of course," Solomon continues as he peels an apple with a small knife. "With it, we can take a look through every eye on the Vitruvian network to find who you're looking for. I'm sorry. I assumed you knew. Barkoba didn't tell you?"

"No," Will shakes his head.

"Oh, that's how I got wrapped up in all of this. When I arrived in Sorrow first from Desolation, I was supposed to be sent to the prison beneath the mines of Mourne. But with a lifetime of knowledge about their enemy in my head, the Wrath General thought it was a total waste, and offered, with a bit of a fight, to give me freedom in exchange for information. I don't know what Barkoba told you about me, but I've got no love for the Kol, so I gave them one better and offered to build them the Hub—under their ever watchful eye, of course. Legion must have spies in every corner of the earth to have known where I was, let alone what I had been enlisted to build! But it was shortly after I started building that they contacted me. I half thought you guys were probably just crazy, but with a chance to help with something that could truly hurt the Kol, I didn't need much convincing. And here we are."

He pauses and puts the knife on the table. "Honestly, I'd almost forgotten. It's been over thirty years now. I don't know if I ever really believed someone from your prophecy would show up! But when I was told that the mad queen was sending a man from Legion to see me, who, depending on whose story you listen to, is potentially unkillable?!!—Ha! I nearly fell off my horse!" He laughs to himself and absentmindedly pops another chunk of his apple into his mouth. "I will ask you though, on a more serious note; Keep your party trick to yourself, ok? I seriously doubt anyone will believe the rumors, but if it comes up, just deny it. Put it down to training from Legion, or even luck—it really doesn't matter. But if you haven't figured it out already, these people are deeply religious. And if they find out about you, my guess is that they'll think you're an angel, a demon or something in between, but either way it will likely mean blood on the streets."

"Sure," Will replies, before stopping, puzzled. "So Barkoba knew you were up here?"

Solomon raises his eyebrow, "I take it he didn't tell you that either then?"

Will shakes his head, "No, he didn't."

"Well, I wouldn't take it personally. I'm sure he had his reasons." Taking a long swig from his mug of ale and swirling the bottom of it, he looks over to Kata who's helping Elik with his food. "You're good with him. You have children of your own?"

"Me? No," she replies. "Someday maybe."

"Well, plenty of time. You're only young. . ." he pauses thinking. "Hey. . . I don't know what your plans are, and I don't mean to presume, but you wouldn't want to stay here tomorrow instead of coming out to the Hub, would you? Obviously if you're set on it I would love your company, but it's a good ten day ride there and back, so unless you enjoy saddle sores it would probably be easier. And you'd be doing me a favor—and him," he gestures to Elik. "He's not really had a gentle hand since his mother passed. It's real nice to see you with him, you're a natural. What do you think, boy? Would you like to spend a few days with the lady?"

Elik grins, and gives a hurried little bob of his head.

"I. . ." Kata starts, unsure of what to say.

"No, no, don't answer now! Sleep on it and see how you feel in the morning! But I assure you this place is comfortable and safe. . . and in the kindest way possible, it looks like you could do with a few days' rest." He stands to his feet and stretches his arms. "Anyway, like I said, sleep on it. You must be tired, I know I am. Either way, we leave at sunrise, but I will leave you with that thought. The bedroom and washroom down the end of the hall is yours — Elik, come on boy, let's go, bed!" He claps as the boy clambers up off the floor and follows him.

*　　*　　*

It is still dark as Will slips out of bed. First stopping by the bathroom sink to splash water on his face, he wanders into the dim light of the kitchen. Where, sitting down on the thick sheepskins laid out on the hearth, he is warmed by the dying embers of the fire.

'Marissa'.

If I had said something different, pushed harder, fought harder? Would I still be with her now? They reduced her to nothing but a number and defined her as a mere investment. They quantified the totality of her metrics, her prospects and her worth, projecting her value like a thing to be used for the sustainability of the common good. It was them who did that. . . But did I do enough?

And it's not that they were so wrong, they were just so empty of the truth! Her radiant laughter and her love for music, and how she delicately glimmered when she danced. Where was the measure of that? They knew nothing of who you really were.

In you was a goodness I had never seen. A beauty. More sunsets and shooting stars than I had ever thought there could be. And now . . . it was all dust.

You deserved more. I should have done more.

When the letter with its Vitruvian seal came through the door and gave the verdict of your worth, forming your name and 'no longer eligible' in a twisted sentence of death, I tried everything. Through the sleek private offices and magnificent federal buildings of Libertaria, I argued. I fought! I questioned them, grilled them—for weeks! But they were so pleasant and so well-dressed and so well spoken. The Kol managers and supervisors had an endless sea of rules and regulations. Their words of counsel seemed so wise and their directions so helpful. But all it did was send me to more counsel and further direction. My words were like they had no meaning at all. I got confused. I got tired. *I'm sorry*.

Despising his weakness and his selfish cowardice as he stares into the fire, he is sickened by every revelation of things he should have done differently. Every stray eye. Every day wasted. Every time they'd fought. He could be so cruel when he was angry.

'Why did I do that?. . .Why was I like that?'

The echoes of the dark days that followed, drift in his memory like a blackened fog of despair. The Trafaka and their trade . . . and the Ether they sold. The relief it gave from the realities of his new living hell. How quickly it became the only thing that he lived for. Needing it, and consumed by it; shackled to the comfort of its fleeting respite. And finally, as the drone of the Malterran cruisers hovering over the apartment block brought the Malleus kicking through his front door — it all came to an end.

'Forgive me my love. You deserved better.'

The soft sound of footsteps breaks his attention, as Kata emerges from the bedroom with a blanket wrapped around her shoulders.

"You're not cold?" she asks, sitting down beside him after throwing on a few split logs from the basket.

"No, I'm alright. You sleep ok?"

"No, not really." She gives a subdued shake of her head. "I can't stop thinking. I have dreamt of being free for so long, but all I see when I close my eyes is everyone I've left behind." With a saddened sigh, she turns and looks up at Will. "What are we doing here, Will?"

"I was wondering the same thing myself."

"No, I mean us," she rests her hand on her stomach. "I can't just up and leave like you. I can't go home. If I go anywhere near Desolation or my family. . . Trib will—" she inhales sharply with the thought, ". . . I can't even. . . I hate him! I hate all of them so much! Can't you add them to your Legion's list?! What makes them more deserving of life than the Kol?"

"I don't know," Will answers, feeling the anger that simmers in her eyes. "They're no better. . . Maybe even worse. But I don't know. When this whole thing started, I never actually thought it was gonna play out. I just wanted to make someone pay—make someone suffer. And in a weird way, it all made sense. But now. . . All I see is shades of gray, trapped within other shades of itself. All blended and muddled in such a mess that it's impossible to see where one starts and the other begins. And with every day that I move forward and this waking dream seems to become more of a reality, I can't help but wonder if more carnage—even if it is well deserved—is going to change anything for the better?"

Kata shrugs as she stares back into the fire. "I don't know. . . maybe not. But it'd sure make me feel better."

In silence, they sit for a while, as flickering shadows dance across the room and the crackling fire radiates its glowing heat.

"Did you decide if you're gonna come out tomorrow?" Will asks.

"I don't know," she replies. "I was thinking of taking Solomon up on his offer. Being thrown around on the back of a horse for two weeks isn't exactly conducive to the healing process—can't be good for the baby either. But I don't know. After what we saw yesterday too, this place is a bit. . . I mean a step up from the palace for sure, how could it not be? But, and it probably sounds crazy, at least there I knew the rules."

"Yeah, I know what you mean," he replies. "They're a different breed under a different banner, but they've got the same hungry belly as the rest of them. We'll get in trouble if we're not careful. But Solomon seems ok. And besides, Barkoba vouched for him—well, not that I trust Barkoba," he chuckles with a deflated smile. "But I feel like I don't really have much of a choice. Either way, I have to try and get Abby back to Zeno, I owe her that. I can't leave her stranded out here. The queen said she could get me on one of the shuttles over the wall, so if I can at least get her that far, it's not completely impossible."

"The queen!?!" Kata exclaims, trying to keep her voice down. "You're not thinking of going back are you?! Jeez Will! I get that you want to help your friend, but whatever the queen is offering is only to help herself! She'll have you served up on a silver platter if she finds something better!!"

"I know, but what other choice do I have?! I can't just do nothing!"

"No, I'm just. . . I'm sorry. Just be careful, that's all," she trails off, staring at her clasped hands. "And hey, I meant to say. . . thank you. . ." She pauses and looks at him. "I don't know what you said to get them to let me go, but thank you. I thought I was. . ." She puts her hand on her stomach, and glances down at it. "I'd given up."

"Don't thank me. Really. If it wasn't for the words a wise old woman put in my head, I'd have probably left you there."

"Well, words or not. You didn't have to act on them, but you did. So thank you."

As the loud gong of a bell in the distance rings out, it is joined by the startled whinnies of the horses in the courtyard below.

"I should probably get going," Will says, looking at the clock on the wall as he gets up. "See you in a couple of weeks, yeah?"

"Yeah, of course. Go. And good luck."

"Thanks," he replies, with a little nod. "You too."

Without another word he gives a muted smile as she nods back, and turning and leaving the heat of the fire behind, he heads out the door.

TO THE ENDS OF THE WORLD

As the clatter of hooves on the cobblestones fills the air, Will walks past an assembly of two dozen Wrath soldiers, solemnly preparing their sturdy horses. Compared to the clean shaven polish of the Sting, the Wrath are a foreboding presence. With powerful size, rugged beards and oily hair, their formidable forms are shrouded under long black cloaks and thick furs that are drawn over the heavy scales of their armor. But it is their eyes that are the most remarkable, and as Will feels their haunting gaze burning from their weathered faces, they seem closer to animals than men.

"William, good morning!" Solomon calls out, tightening the leather straps of the saddlebags hanging from the side of a magnificent black horse. "Arcane — meet Will!" he says to the horse and grins at Will. As if saying hello, the huge creature lets out a long snort, sending a cloud of his breath into the cold air, before turning to look at Will with his dark brown eyes. "You're going to take care of him aren't you boy!"

Solomon continues, rubbing the side of the creature's neck as he winks at Will. "You'll be in good hands with this one—foaled him myself. He's getting on in years, but his age has made him patient and gentle, so he won't be any trouble to you—or you to him, for that matter. Come on, hop up!"

With a bit of effort, Will is up and sitting on the horse's saddled back, and gripping the reins, he slips his feet into the stirrups.

"Easy on!" Solomon talks to the horse as it takes a few nervous steps. "Relax Will, loosen up. Talk to him, give him a good rub. . . There you go, and don't worry. In a day or so, it will be second nature to you and you will be the best of friends!"

*   *   *

As Will and his new companion grow acquainted with one another, Solomon returns on a large brown horse of his own. "Ready to go?!" he asks.

Will nods, and as Solomon clicks twice with his tongue, both horses move side by side, in well practiced unison toward a large metal clad gate on the far end of the yard. With sleek black rifles slung across their backs, the horse mounted Wrath have formed into two somber rows, and moving beside their waiting ranks, dark eyes and courteous nods greet them as they make their way to the front.

"Good morning Major," Solomon calls out, as they reach the head of the column of cavalry. "Apologies for the delay."

No less formidable than the rest of his men, with a long beard, short unkempt hair and a brutish physique, the Major flashes them a welcoming smile as they approach, "Not necessary, my friend," he replies, turning to them with a welcoming smile as they approach. "Your lack of discipline was anticipated."

Solomon chortles, grinning at Will as he continues. "Will, this is Major Kishnach of the Wrath of Sorrow. My closest friend. . . and my babysitter — Major, this is William Manning."

"Yes! Of Legion!" the Major adds, his sharp gaze meeting Will's. "I have heard all about you. Solomon has told me many wild stories over the years, but until a few days ago I had just assumed he was a babbling fool," he glances at Solomon with a teasing grin. "And please, don't mind the formalities—call me Kish."

Releasing Will's grasp from his firm handshake, the Major lets out a shrill whistle, and with the mechanized grinding of gears, the gates ahead begin to open. From an outhouse to their side, three slender watchmen drones snake silently out of their charging bays with a hiss, and vanish into the sky. With another command, the column of cavalry begins to move, through the gate and under the arch.

Beyond the stoney gray of the city's outer wall dotted with tall round towers, the landscape ahead opens up with sprawling beauty, plunging down into a sweeping valley lush with grasslands. And as they trundle towards the twinkling river nestled winding through the valley floor, the fresh scents of untouched wilderness fills their nostrils.

*   *   *

"Major!!" a voice cuts through the air, and looking back, they see a lone rider galloping past the soldiers towards them.

As the Major raises his hand, the column of cavalry comes to an obedient halt.

"Major!" the fresh faced rider says as he reaches them in a cloud of dust, pulling on the reins to calm his excited horse. "I apologize for the intrusion, I have a message for you." Reaching inside his vest, he produces a letter and passes it to the Major. Who, breaking the seal from the front of the envelope, reads it carefully before responding.

"No need to worry lad. Tell the Captain we'll make camp and wait on the plains of the valley floor, beside the river just north of here. They can catch up with us there."

With an understanding bow, the messenger disappears back the way he came, and with another command from the Major, the procession continues on its way.

"What was that all about?" Solomon asks.

"Oh, nothing," the Major mutters, deep in thought. "Odd, that's all."

"What?"

"It was an order from Lord Gaspar. Captain Ascha of the Sting and a company of his men are to join us on our trip to the hub."

"Lord Gaspar? Since when does he have the authority to make such decisions?"

"I don't know," the Major shakes his head. "I have little interest in getting caught up in politics though, so we'll entertain the request. A company of Sting won't slow us down that much, they're swift riders. And anyway, they'll absorb some of the fire if the natives try to take any potshots at us." He gives a cheeky grin. "Come. We forge on."

With an abrupt command, they pick up pace, trotting in a lively clip down the roughly laid surface of the roadway cut into the side of the steep valley.

"So I hear you defeated one of ours in trial by combat?" The Major looks at Will inquisitively. "A Wrathian by the name of Cain?"

"Maybe," Will replies. "But it wasn't like that. It was him or me."

The Major lets out a hearty chuckle, "Isn't that always the way? And don't be so humble. The man that you fought was not only one of the Wrath, he was once one of the Weeping City's best. In fact, the only reason that he is not on Balthasar's throne is that he couldn't put his sword down. For all the love of power and money in the world, nothing compared to that man's love for war. At the end of the war, when we finally brokered peace with the Kol and started to rebuild, he declared us all cowards. And then he denounced our Kings and our God, and defected to the Queen's palace. Cut through near ten of the basilica guard on his way out, and two dozen of the Sting. So don't be so humble. Hundreds, if not thousands, have fought him and failed."

"I'd no idea."

"See those men behind you?" he motions back to his soldiers. "Many of them believed he couldn't be defeated. Some even thought he had made a deal with the devil. Because of him, many have questioned our ways—and our God. So today, they're here as much under my command as they are out of respect for you."

"You didn't think the High Priest let you come out here because he was feeling friendly did you?" Solomon quips. "Despite his sunny exterior, believe me, he's not always so accommodating. Queen aside—saying no to the man who felled Cain would have made him very unpopular, and he knows well how to keep things sweet with the people."

"So is it true?" the Major adds, glancing at Will with a raised brow. "You can't be killed?"

Solomon scoffs, "You don't actually believe that, do you?!"

"I'm just asking!" the Major laughs.

"No it's fine," Will replies, with a grin. "But sorry to disappoint—I still get hurt like everyone else. If anything, I've been injured more in the past few weeks than I ever was in Zeno!"

"Well. I'm impressed either way. Getting one up on Cain? I think we could stand to learn a thing or two from you and your Legion. I thought the Wrath had the best training in the world. Maybe we could trade secrets some time?"

"Sure," Will replies. "It would be my pleasure."

After the roadway veers sharply north, the procession crosses onto a dirt trail that leads further down the valley, into the crook of the steep mountain ridges on either side. It is truly magnificent, and growing wider as they continue their descent, it opens up onto rich plains of farmland, filled with vivid patches of healthy crops.

Sporadic bits of casual chatter fill the next few hours, but mostly they ride in silence, and as the last rays of sunlight disappear over the tips of the mountaintops, they reach the wide grassy bank of the river. Leading the horses to the edge of the crisp, dark water, they stand guard as the animals drink their fill. Before marching them up to the rich greenery and forming a circle, they make camp for the night.

*   *   *

Illuminated by the early morning light, the valley is bathed pink from the glowing clouds that drift above. But as the playful babbling of the river is interrupted by the deep blare of a watchman drone's horn high on the slopes above, Will awakes with a start. Around him, the soldiers of the Wrath are stirring from their sleep and as they quickly prepare themselves, the alarmed whinnies of the horses reiterate their urgency.

As Arcane nuzzles him a gentle good morning, he follows their lead. Packing away the light material he'd used for bedding before giving the huge animal a few long strokes of his coarse hair, he climbs onto his saddle. And as a faint rumble reverberates in the air, he scans up the valley trail as a full company of Sting cavalry wind towards them.

"Hang back with me," Solomon calls to him from on top of his mount as he trots up to him. "Leave this to Kish."

Easily outnumbering them five to one, the massive company of the Sting's horses thunders in front of them in a billowing blanket of dust, coming to a standstill as Captain Ascha, riding at their head, shouts a command.

Major Kish, standing next to two of his own, waits, as Ascha rides forward to him and dismounts. Before, shaking hands, the two men exchange murmured words.

"They don't like each other, or what's the deal?" Will asks, leaning over to Solomon.

"No, nothing like that," Solomon replies, watching intently. "They're all on the same side. But to the Wrath, the Sting are like, I dunno, there's rivalry there, maybe even a bit of resentment. The Sting will show them up when they get a chance and are always vying for their position."

"What's the difference?"

"What? Between them? I'll assume you mean besides the obvious?" Solomon laughs. "No, I'm joking. The Sting are maybe not as tough as the Wrath, and a little shinier, but they're still soldiers—and good ones too. But the biggest difference? I don't know. I suppose it's a job for them. The Wrath, on the other hand, are born and bred for war. They don't know anything else. From the time they're little, their lives are nothing but training and conditioning—physical, psychological, even chemical. It's both an art and a way of life. By the time they're done, every one of them is required to be a master of the Sorwian way of war. So even if there is only one left to fight, every Sorwian tactic, technique and technology will survive."

"Seems a bit excessive?" Will says.

"Maybe," he shrugs. "They're not exactly people-people. But it's effective. If it wasn't for the Wrath; this place, Sorrow, and its citizens would have been wiped out a long time ago. But I'm always amazed at people's capacity to forget the hard times. At one time, Sorrow's borders extended from here, all the way to the edge of the ice flow. But they spent so much money fighting the Kol, that they lost most of it to the local warlords and tribes — day by day and piece by piece. One of the conditions of the armistice when the war ended was that for thirty years, the production of the Wrath had to be stopped. So when the Kol warships left, to fill the deficit of fighting men needed for policing and guarding the city walls, the kings created the Sting. Some of the Sorwian even saw it as a kind of veiled compliment, you know, that their warriors of the Wrath were so tough that even the Kol were afraid of them. But looking at it now? I see a certain genius to it. I'm not saying they are saints, but what used to protect the Sorwian was an army of husbands and fathers, paid in duty and honor. But now, with the Sting, it's bought and paid for like everything else—a commodity. So, these days, depending on who's lining the coffers, the control and enforcement of our very ideas are at the mercy of whatever men hold the purse strings. . . It's like the old Vitruvian proverb; 'A dog honored with meat belongs to his grumbling belly, but a dog honored with love will die happy, starving by his master's side.' The likes of Lord Gaspar and the other noblemen see the Wrath as immovable idealists of a dead era, who won't comply with the new order of things. But my fear is that when push comes to shove, the Sting won't weather the storm, and will instead choose themselves over the people of Sorrow."

Finished with their exchange, the Major and the Captain give respectful half bows to each other, before turning and mounting their horses. Returning to his men, the Major gives an order, taking his place at the head of the column as they assemble into formation with practiced ease.

"Here," Solomon motions toward an opening in the Wrath's ranks, a few rows back from the Major. "We'll stay back here until Kish calls us up."

With a few whistles and clicks ringing from their ranks, the long company of the Sting soldiers follows suit. Falling into position behind the Wrath they form into line. Before, with a bark from the Major, the serenity is drowned by the thunder of its enormous clatter. And as the gentle song of the river and the morning birds are consumed by the noise, the procession begins to move.

Chapter 18

THE VALLEY OF SLAUGHTER

The next few days pass as if in a vivid dream. Breaks to stop and eat are always short, and apart from the stolen moments to refresh the horses, the only respite from the relentless march is at night to sleep. Even then, after assembling into a tight outward facing triangle and sending watchmen buzzing out into the surrounding hills, they are only allowed a few precious hours.

Climbing up the valley, they cross the crest of an abandoned dam from the old world, that holds back the blackened waters of Engeddi lake beyond. Leaving the trembling roar of the deluge that spews from its sprawling face behind, they wrap around the winding trail that hugs the lake's edge, before making the steep ascent up the adjacent hills. Where, reaching the top and into the cold, narrow gorge of Butcher's Pass that cuts through the towering mountains above, they emerge onto the soft rolling slopes of the pasturelands.

The crimson cradle of the Great Red Forest glows like embers in the valley below, and as they enter the cool fluttering whispers of its canopy to the welcome shade of the sun's stinging rays, the sounds of the horse's hooves fall mute on the thick bed of leaves that blankets the trail. Descending into focused silence as they enter a picturesque glade, rifles are drawn and formation staggers as a scout's horn bellows out, sending a frightened family of deer scampering away through the trees. As there, in the underbrush, some highlighted by streaks of dancing light or tantalizing smatterings of colorful butterflies that hover close, twisted bodies of the dead, striped with fresh and bloodied wounds, are already attracting the angry buzz of hungry flies.

They ride late that night, till the confines of the forest is far behind them, and reaching the base of the rocky climb of the Devil's Finger that protrudes from the snow capped mountains towering above, they stop and make camp.

*　　*　　*

As dawn breaks, Solomon beckons to Will, and after checking their packs and sharing a solemn farewell with the Major, the two men leave the mass of soldiers far behind to continue up the winding trail alone.

The bitter whistle of the frozen air stinging their eyes as the crumbling path levels out, they carefully trot along narrow cliff edges, holding their breath as they stare off the precipice. Until, as they begin the trek down the mountain's far sides to the lower slopes of the monstrous peaks, they whisper a silent sigh of relief.

"That's the northeastern glacier—Waif country," Solomon calls back, as they break over the ridgeline of yet another craggy slope and stare in awe at the glistening wall of sapphire ice that fills the horizon ahead. "And that. . ." he continues, pointing up the pencil line of a jagged path rising high in the distance, to a shining building perched on top, "is the Hub. We'll be there by nightfall."

Squinting up at the mere speck of a shape Solomon is pointing at, dwarfed by the domineering scale of the glacier's frozen blue expanse, Will is stunned by the sheer grandeur of the icy spectacle.

"It's amazing," he gasps. "I've never seen such a thing. So that's the extent of the Vitruvian Column's reach?"

"Yep. Beyond that, the Etanaki has no power—well, Zeno's one at least. It's something else isn't it?! Can't melt it all!"

"Why did you have to build it so far out here?"

"Not practical I know," Solomon replies. "But if the Kol ever got wind that Sorrow was building a hub, it could trigger another war. That's why we left Kish and the soldiers back at Devil's finger. There's only a handful of people who know that it exists and even less of us that know how to get here. Besides," he chuckles, "I think the kings of Sorrow preaching their anti-tech stuff to the masses and then building this thing was a bit too hypocritical, even for them!"

"What's the deal with that anyway? I mean I get that they might be skeptical about some things, but there's probably a lot of good they're missing out on too, no?"

"Undoubtedly, yeah. But anything seen to be outside of the natural order of things, is deemed a sin by the priests of the Tear. The people have learned to do what they're told. You've seen it yourself, they're none too soft on sinners."

"Yeah, but is executing people not a sin in itself? Who are they to judge?"

"I'm only the messenger!" Solomon grins, jovially putting his hands up. "Once you're in charge you can decide what's a sin for yourself!"

Will laughs, "I'm sorry, I'm just curious. I take it that it's not all off the table though? Some of the stuff the soldiers have seems really advanced — can't be far off Vitruvian. Like those guns the Wrath have, they look pretty fancy."

"Their rifles? Yeah. They are. Optically linked 'fire and forgets'—a nice bit of kit. Fortunately for them, the Sorrow war machine got a free pass with some of the rules in their struggle against the Kol. They've taken every liberty with it they can, too. They've got artillery, anti-aircraft, mechs, drones —even warships. But it's all kept out of sight under the city. It's something else really. Kish took me a few years ago. There's got to be hundreds, maybe even thousands of people, just churning these things out, twenty-four seven. It's like a different planet compared to the backward museum they keep up top. Only time I've ever seen anything even remotely similar was when I was Malflatus." Stopping his thought as they reach the start of the steep climb to the building at the top, he tousles his horse's mane. "Won't be long now!" he adds, making a few encouraging clicks with his mouth.

"So you were one of them?" Will asks, his curiosity getting the better of him.

"The Malflatus?" Solomon scoffs. "Yeah. In a different life."

"What was it like? You know, being one of them?"

"That's a. . . That's a tough question. Not human anyway. . . It was like flying, or floating. Drifting. Kind of awake, but not. And you can move—man can you move. The speed is. . . When I was in the network, I was like an eagle, but faster even, and I could see everything. One minute, I could be watching a burning river of lava ten miles wide outside the siege walls of Epicuria through an Occuli on patrol. And the next, looking at a Kol child being sung to sleep through the eyes of their mother."

"It sounds amazing."

"It was. . . Until it wasn't." He pauses and his gaze hardens. "I must have done it a thousand times before—and I don't really know what made this one different—but I was doing a 'monitor and control' out in the industrial district, during the scheduled termination of an unproductive section of workers. Mostly just checking the supervising Kols' mood and stress, adjusting any of their levels that were drifting outside of the parameters and things like that. And this one Kol, a woman, she'd just given the order for the doors on the mess hall to be locked and thermo dropped through the windows. But as the screaming started from inside, her stress spiked. Normally it might do a little blip, but this was different. I'd never seen anything like it. She was feeling it all. And no matter how much I pushed her dose, it wouldn't go down! She was happy and smiling like the rest of them one minute, and the next she was on her knees wailing like a baby. I didn't quite know what it was at first. You gotta remember too that I'd never felt anything before; no real feelings, no emotions, nothing. But then, like a hammer, I felt it. . . I felt her — A wave of everything she was feeling. Pure horror and fear and. . . and the shame. . . man, it was terrifying. I still feel it now sometimes."

"So what happened?" Will asks after a silence, seeing the drain it's having on Solomon just to think about it.

"I put her out. . ." he exhales, in a whisper. "Fried her brain — Couldn't have an anomaly like that walking around. . . But after it was done, whatever had happened to her had done something to me, broken something, like the facade had cracked. And as the months went on, I began to feel them all, each pinprick of pain. Until one day I saw myself for who I was. There was no greater good, no justification or moral superiority, nothing. . . I was a darkness who'd been convinced he was a light. . ." Trailing off into dark reminiscence, he inhales sharply and his crestfallen demeanor breaks into a smile. "Anyway, it's my burden to bear — All I can do is try and make amends, right?" He motions ahead to the concrete form of the Hub looming up ahead of them, adorned with tall antennae and shining dishes littering its roof, connected by a multitude of thick black cables and pipes running neatly down its sides. "That's kind of why I jumped at the chance to build her. She'll give a serious advantage against those bastards if we ever end up in a war with them. Given enough time, and if I know where to look, I can see through the eyes of most of the Kol and their machines on the network without them even knowing. That's where the biosignatures on your list will go a long way. Looking for one person out of billions is, obviously, like trying to find a needle in a haystack—especially if they don't want to be found. But once that data's in and under the eye of the servant, it's only a matter of time before they start popping up. Any idea who they are?"

"No, not a clue." Will replies, shaking his head.

"And are you ready?" Solomon glances at him with a sudden air of seriousness in his tone. "You know—when the time comes to do what you have to?"

"I don't know," Will shrugs. "I'd like to think so. I guess I'll find out when it's time."

Solomon nods, "Well. So long as you know that they deserve every bit of what's coming to them."

"Whoa there, boy!" Solomon calls out, as they reach the rocky outcrop at the top of the incline. Drawing alongside the ominous concrete structure, more of a bunker than a building, he stops beside the cap of a water cistern that's protruding from the earth, as he dismounts and stretches his legs. "Come on, you can tie him up here."

Sliding off Arcane's strong back, Will fills a bucket full of ice cold water from a tap and sets it in front of the hardworking animal, before following Solomon to a thick steel door embedded in the side of the Hub's drab wall. With silent deliberation it slides slowly open, and as they step inside a small airlock they're met by a warm rush of sterile air.

Through the inner door that swishes open ahead of them, the relentless whine of machinery permeates their ears as they cross onto a slender metallic walkway. Suspended from the ceiling on either side, rows of long cylindrical chambers containing thousands of golden tubes and wires hang like alien jewels, humming with energy and almost bursting with thick bundles of wires that snake above into an industrialized blackness. Deafened by their volume as they pass between them, they arrive at a glass walled room in the building's center, situated at the end of six other rows all identical to theirs. Pristine, and illuminated bright like a laboratory, banks of elegant monitors and sophisticated hardware line its interior, and as they step across the threshold and the soundproof door cuts the shrill noise of the servers to a distant murmur.

"It's louder than I remember!" Solomon remarks, rubbing his ears as he looks around with satisfaction. "So? What do you think? Beautiful, isn't it?"

"I don't know what to think," Will replies. "It's amazing. I've never seen anything like it. I'm assuming you didn't do this by yourself?"

"No, not at all. It took greater minds than mine to put all this together. A small team of us lived up here for nearly ten years before we even fired it up, and it took another two to fine tune it. Kish sent up a dropship every other month with food and materials and such, but other than that we pretty much worked non stop. Here, sit down." Gesturing to one of several seats tucked under the elaborate console that encircles the room, he walks across and sits down beneath a massive set of curved screens. With a familiar reach, he opens a drawer in the cabinet beneath to reveal a row of thin gray cylinders neatly arranged inside, taking one out as he continues. "We'll spend the night here and head back to Kish in the morning. But before we do anything, we'll get your biodata first loaded up. Once the machines are rolling, we can relax while they do their thing."

"Sure, sounds good. What do I do?"

"Just give me your hand," he replies, reaching out and taking Will's hand as it's offered. Making an adjustment on the cylinder, and resting the tip on Will's wrist, the device clicks as a sharp sting radiates up Will's arm.

"You gonna be ok, big guy?"

"I hope so," Will replies with a grin, looking up from the tiny red indentation on his skin.

Chuckling as he turns back to the desk, Solomon inserts the cylinder into a metallic receptacle, which beeps as it closes over it. Followed by a rising computerized whir as the surrounding equipment springs to life, information begins to dart across the screens. And as his fingers run with familiar ease over the assembly of keys on the table's surface, with a final tap, the lights in the room dim and he swivels around on his chair.

In the room's center, a small conical device fixed to the ceiling starts spinning, and with a sudden flash a large, vivid hologram of the blackened planet appears in front of them, rotating in slow orbit. Beside it, as Will watches its mesmerizing motion, a broad tombstone shaped object rises from the floor, morphing as a set of panels extend out of its sleek face, to form a strange, forward leaning seat.

Without a word, Solomon begins to strip off his several layers of shirts, until, pulling the last layer over his head, he walks over to it bare chested and sits down. Leaning forward and pushing a button, as he rests his face and arms on the corresponding pads, small dots of light shining from the ceiling flick on. Locking onto a line of dark pock marked scars running down Solomon's spine, Will's wonder turns to horror, as with a soft hiss an array of thin metallic tentacles slide out from under the seat. Grumbling under his breath, Solomon's arms tense, as upward like needled fingers they grow around him. With an abrupt cessation of their sound, their ends curl back on themselves to face him with their pointed tips. As in vicious unison, his body jerks with the impact as they submerge themselves into his body.

The skin around each fleshy piercing welling with a thin rim of blood, Will looks away in disgust. But as a trembling flicker ripples across the surface of the holographic planet, objects and landmarks appear.

The Vitruvian Columns of the cities appear first, like blazing needles dotting the blackness of the dying planet's suffocating dust, and then, in the places where the dust has been displaced by the ravages of a weather system, the sharp whites of glaciers and ruby flames of lava flows peek through.

Details pouring onto it as the planet revolves, oceans and deserts take shape, their forms materializing beneath the toxic clouds.

With a sudden shudder, the image shifts from its distant overview, suddenly falling at breakneck speed in a nosedive towards Zeno. The city's massive outer walls coming into view as it rushes underneath, they hurtle over Eden and Neourbia, and then to Libertaria and out toward the open ocean. Clearing the shoreline and reaching the Citadel of Abundance, they rip past the Vitruvian Column that blazes from the Etanaki, and as it vanishes behind, Will can make out a fleet of Malignus warships in the distance hovering above the waves. But before he has time to stare, they're gone, as the speeding image takes a sharp turn and streaks along the coast, past the Praetorium and into the southern desert. West along the line of the city wall to Desolation, it whips beneath them, and as the majestic peaks of the Mountains of Mourne expand from the horizon, they descend upon Sorrow's pious towers and elegant battlements.

Then, without warning, the hologram goes black and disappears.

Will squints as the room brightens, and as the machine's luminous needles release their grip on Solomon's body, he begins to stir. Inhaling sharply, he sits up with a jolt, and looking around in a daze, he gasps.

"Are you alright?" Will asks, rushing to him to help as he tries to stand. "What happened?"

"I—I'll be fine," he replies, wincing through a furrowed frown. "Give me a hand. Help me up. Something's not right." Using Will's arm as a crutch, he hobbles over to the counter and slumps into the seat. "I. . . Just hold on for a minute."

For a few moments, he's silent, strumming his fingers across the keypad as maps and images flicker rapidly across the screens.

"There," he continues, hitting a key and turning on his seat as the hologram behind bursts to life. "Look!"

The orb, responding as he makes motions in the air, rotates and expands until the unmistakable form of Sorrow is in clear view, and zooming in closer still, he stops its movements as the city's inner keep dominates their view.

"That," he says, frozen as he points to a little red dot blinking steadily in the center. "That's from your list," he whispers through a pallid stare. "That's one of them."

"What?" Will replies, as the realization of Solomon's words grip tense in his chest. "In Sorrow?"

"I'd need more time to be sure, but I'm fairly certain. I gotta talk to Kish. Go out to my horse and grab the radio will you? It's in a saddle bag right up the front."

*　　*　　*

Will's mind races as he hustles down the walkway and out through the airlock.

Rummaging through the saddlebags, he glances up to the sharp cry of a raven, as it soars from beyond the top of the majestic glacier, before gliding downward and disappearing into a ravine.

With the radio in hand, he heads back inside, returning to Solomon who's still sifting through a sea of data on the screens.

"Come in Major?" Solomon says, taking it without looking up. ". . . Major, come in?"

The radio returns nothing but a faint static. "Come on, Kish," he mutters to himself. "Come in Major!" His voice rises in frustration. "Kish, do you copy?"

"Where have you been?!" The Major's irritated voice crackles over it. "I've been trying to call for ages! Where are you?"

"We're at the Hub. Sorry, I left the radio with the horses. Hey, have you heard from the city since we left? I think we might have a problem."

"That's why I was calling!" the Major replies. "All our comms went down a little while ago. Even the satlink. Something's not right, we gotta get back. What did you find out? What's the problem?"

"I can't—" Stopping short, he pauses in thought. "I can't explain over the radio. Go ahead without us, we'll catch up. We're leaving now."

The radio clicks as Solomon puts it down, before looking up at Will with pale distress in his eyes. "I'm sorry Will. I don't know what's going on. But if there's something happening in the city, I have to go. It might be nothing, but I can't leave Elik. Once I know he's safe, I'll find them all for you and Legion, I promise. I'll live up here if I have to, but I can't leave him."

"No, of course," Will replies. "Come on, let's go."

Turning to leave, Will stops short as Solomon exhales a pained breath and flops back into his seat. "You need a hand?" he asks as Solomon hesitates, before responding with a limp nod.

After a slow shuffle past the banks of computer servers and out to the waiting horses and the crisp mountain air, Will pushes Solomon up onto his mount.

"You gonna be alright to make it back?" Will calls out as they make their way down the steep incline in a cautious trot.

"It'll pass," Solomon calls back, already getting a bit more color in his cheeks. "If we ride through the night, we should catch up to them about midday tomorrow."

*   *   *

Holding any kind of consistent speed is difficult on the rocky terrain, and as the shadows grow longer and the rays of the setting sun reflect a final hurrah of white light on the looming glacial face behind them, the cool blackness of night falls. Aided only by the faint light of the moon, they ride for hours, until the soft pinks and tangerines of dawn paint the sky. Reaching the bony prong of the Devil's Finger that looks down on the lush valley below, they set down briefly to attend to the horses, before making the rocky descent down into the foothills.

"Not far now," Solomon says, pointing to the fresh tracks in the mud ahead as they splash across a small stream that runs across the trail.

Sure enough, as they reach the valley floor and ride through a tree covered glade, the horn of a watchman bellows from the mountainside. Passing a handful of the Sting standing guard by the trail who salute as they pass, it isn't long before they emerge out into a wide open plain and gallop toward the main body of the soldier's triangular formation, camped in an open field on the edge of the Red Forest. Dismounting as they approach the outer line of the Sting and their resting horses, they pass through their ranks and make their way to the huddle of Wrath warriors in the center.

"I'm glad you made it," Kish greets them, standing as he sees them approach.

"Me too," Solomon replies, glancing up at the forest behind as a gust of wind ripples through the sea of its broad red leaves. "I wasn't keen on going through there by ourselves. Any word from the city?"

"No, nothing, everything's still down, and two of our watchmen have gone dark. Last transmission we got from near the city showed smoke trails from inside the walls and—" Seeing Solomon's despondent expression he stops. "Hey. . . your boy will be fine. You've taught him well for times like these, have you not?"

"Yeah," Solomon nods, reassuring himself.

"So what happened up there at the Hub?" the Major continues.

Solomon hesitates, scrunching his face as he looks up. "Look, I hope I'm wrong, but, one of the Kol on Legion's list. . . It looks like they are in the city."

"In the city? In Sorrow?!" the Major exclaims as his face goes pale. "It would explain why our comms are down. Are you sure?"

"I don't know, they may not even be Kol. But it's enough to make me worry."

"Without a doubt. If the Malleus somehow got past our guns. . ." Pausing, he rubs his face as he takes a deep breath, "Anyway, it is tomorrow's worry. One thing at a time. Did you get what you needed?"

Solomon shakes his head, "No. I need more time. As soon as I saw that the Kol might be up here with us, I dropped out of symbio. But there's gotta be a few dozen at least—spread all over." He looks at Will. "You'll have your work cut out for you."

"Well, I suppose on the bright side" the Major adds, with a somber look. "If this is the Kol and we survive, at least you'll have Sorrow on your side. I just hope it's not too late. We never should have stopped fighting them. Anyway, you'll forgive me," he excuses himself. "I need to talk to my men about what we could be up against. We ride first thing."

*   *   *

Lying beside the sleeping form of Arcane's large warm body, Will struggles to sleep, plagued by anxious thoughts of what lies ahead and all that's left behind. Drifting between vivid manifestations of his fear and the gentle pain of the life with her that seems so far away, he questions if it ever really existed. Perhaps it is all the fabrication of an apathetic omnipotence designed to sustain him just enough to avoid his soul collapsing beneath the true acceptance of what man's depravity would bring?

Her face, her smile. . .

Would it have been better to have never known her and be free of the empty pain and the gnawing anger? Or is the real beauty of creation the graceful bloom of life in a place of darkness, renewed in a baptism of fire from the charred remains of a scorched and blackened earth?

An anguished scream in the darkness and as his eyes flick open, a heavy hand is over his mouth as a searing pain tears across his throat. A cascade of warm sticky blood spilling through his fingers and rushing down his front, he lurches backwards clutching an open chasm ripped in his neck. His lungs gurgling; sputtering bubbles froth in his hands as he falls onto his side. And as the moonlit figure of a soldier of the Sting above him turns and slips away, the air becomes thick with screams of violence, and the sharp crackle of gunshots echoing into the night sky.

His energy waning with every weakening pulse, Will's mind screams as he struggles to stay awake. But as the dreary stroke of unconsciousness draws his eyes closed, a burst of defiance sparks to flame. Within the raw mutilation that is his throat, the slither of angry tendrils sprouting between his fingers writhe as they grow, and choking a staggered breath he tastes the freshness of the early morning air.

Scrambling to his feet he scans frantically around, as with a cacophony of raging roars and anguished squeals, scores of the Sting clash with the furious might of the Wrath. The ground strewn thick with bodies, men separate men from bone, but overwhelmed by sheer numbers, the Wrath begin to fall as they're pierced on all sides by their brethrens' blades.

In rigid anticipation of agony, his body locks up as a glimpse of a Sting's sword flashes from behind before plunging into his body. But instead of pain, something else sends chilling tingles down his spine. He feels the blade through his skin, wrenches in its torture, yet it is numb, as hissing with burning hatred, the growing flames of anger in his belly burst into a blinding rage. From deep within his soul, a low growl emanates from his body. Grabbing the hands of his attacker's on the hilt of the sword buried in his chest, he heaves it out of his torso. The snapping of the man's splintering fingers ringing out like fireworks under his grip, he squeezes with all his might, until with one last jerk, the blade is free. Swinging the tip upward between their bodies, a childlike fear registers in the soldier's wide eyes, as with a burst of energy, the blade shoots vertically into the softness under the man's chin. With terrifying ease, its point explodes out the top of his head. And lifting him clean off his feet, high on the end of his sword, a torrent of rich blood streams down his arms.

The next few moments are a blur. Time seems to slow as bodies drop left and right at the end of his flailing weapon. Bullets puncturing his flesh, lumps of muscle and tissue spray around him in a carnal mist. But with each savage wound, the slender interlacing tentacles left behind writhe in delight, as they fill the dark gouges that remain. Intoxicated by the spell of a hunger he has never known, the soldiers scatter like paper dolls under his fury. He feels nothing, thinks nothing. He doesn't tire, or even seem to breathe. Just living from one savage blow to the next, in a rage so pure it almost feels good. Like drowning naked in a silky black oil that pulses with pure vitality.

"Will!!" the scream of Solomon's terror fills Will's head, "Will!!! Stopppp!!!!

In front of him, his face aghast in fear, with hands raised in resignation to the pending ferocity, Solomon cowers before him. Stopping still, Will looks around in a daze, and seeing the blood soaked weapon poised over his head ready to strike, he lowers the blade.

The world rushing to a standstill, the stagnant hush of fresh death lingers in the morning air. Gazing up at the sky as the warm tones of soft light washes the ragged remains of the dead, he sees the first splendor of the day breaking on the horizon. In the distance, the last of the Sting flee into the safety of the forest. And as the disheveled handful of the surviving Wrath sheath their weapons, they stare in disbelief at the surrounding carnage.

"They died well!" the Major's voice booms out as he gazes at the twisted corpses of his fallen men. "But we are still here. Today is not our day. Wrath! We have work to do!

Gather what you can, and quickly! If the Sting have done this here, who knows what they have done in Sorrow!"

Turning to examine Will, he hesitates as his men hurry in unquestioning obedience. Smeared dark in the blood of the dead and still clutching his trembling sword, a specter of death, and as the two men's eyes meet, they stand in silence.

"So this is the soldier of Legion. . ." the Major starts. "Are you angel or demon?"

With nothing to say Will lowers his gaze and looks away.

"Well, no matter," the Major continues. "For whomever you speak. I believe we owe you our lives."

Chapter 19

PREPARE FOR WAR

As the Wrath round up the frightened horses and rummage through the mass of scourged bodies that are spread across the field, Will wanders across the battle stained grass to Arcane, who's waiting, right where he left him. Snorting nervously through flared nostrils, the horse braces his neck upwards in protest as Will grabs the reins. But after a few hushed words and a gentle stroke down his long neck, he stills and relents to his master.

Mounted, he checks his pack and joins Solomon and the Major, as the Wrath that remain, assemble into a line behind them. Before, with a loud bellow, the procession canters down the trail toward the shaded canopy of the Red Forest.

Under the cover of the noble trees, words are only whispered and they slow to a gentle trot, but clearing its shroud as night falls, they ride as hard as their stoic mounts can bear. Hiding in the undergrowth off the trail, they stop only once to sleep for a few precious hours before, as night gives way to another day, they continue their vigorous pace, trailing across the lush pastures towards Butcher's Pass.

*   *   *

"Major!" the shout of a Wrath calls out from the back of the group, as he gallops up to the front. Raising his hand to halt the march and muttering to the rider as he reaches him, the Major ushers his men to gather round.

"The watchman just picked up a column of riders coming out of the Red Forest," he addresses the group as they form a huddle in front of him. "It looks like it's Captain Ascha and his men—thirty or so in all. I do not know how you feel about it, and it would mean delaying our trip back to Sorrow, but if we could take Ascha or one of his lieutenants alive, we may be able to find out more about what we're going up against." He looks around at the stony faces of his warriors. "I do not imagine a touch of retribution for our fallen brothers would hurt either. What say the Wrath?"

"Till the end," one of his men utters, with a respectful bob of his head, followed by the stoic reiteration of his words by the rest.

"Till the end!!"

"Solomon? William? What say you?"

"Just tell me what to do," Will replies, with a despondent shake of his head. "This. . . mess. None of you would be in it if it wasn't for me."

"My thanks for your sword, but this is no mess," the Major corrects him. "It is a chance to die well. How many men have that gift? — Solomon, brother. What say you? Are you with us?"

Solomon lifts his pensive gaze from the ground and takes a deep breath before replying. "I don't know," he shakes his head in thought. "If the Kol have taken the city and turned the Sting against us. . . What if they're looking for me? How long is it going to be before they find my boy and start. . ." Falling into unspeakable memories of Kol persuasion, he trails off.

"I don't claim to understand your fear," the Major contemplates Solomon's slumped form with pity. "But you are no good to your son if you are dead. If we can learn anything from our enemy—especially if it is the Kol—I believe we will have a better chance at survival."

"I know, I know. I'm just. . ." Solomon hangs his head in defeat. "I don't know. It doesn't matter. I am with you, of course."

"Very well." The Major clicks at his horse and it whinnies as it turns. "We will ride to the dam at Engeddi and prepare their graves for them there."

*　　*　　*

The rumble of the horses' hooves echo up the sheer stone face of the pass as they gallop through its cold, narrow corridor. And as they emerge out the other side on the upper foothills, they can see the black waters of Engeddi Lake, nestled in the basin below. As night falls, they set down for a few hours of uneasy rest under a thicket of broadleaved trees clustered close to its shore, and before the sun has even risen, they continue to ride along its banks.

Ahead of them, breaking the crest of the lake's mirrored surface, the long curve of the dam's parapet wall comes into view, stretching across its width between the looming stone towers that stand solemn on either end. Perched on the line of supporting piers and arches that straddle the thundering spillways below, they cross onto the flat surface of the dam's concrete walkway. And under the arch of the first tower, relieved by the shade and feeling the cool haze of water on their frothing mouths, the exhausted horses slow their pace.

From the top of Arcane's strong back, Will gazes over the edge at the rushing white water as it hurtles down the spillway into the billowing torrent of turbulent energy below. Until, passing to the other side and under the second tower, they trek onto the trail on the other side. Leading the horses down the steep embankment to graze by the river's churning waters, they hike back up to the top, and as the men gather on the dam's crest using their heavy packs as seats, the Major gathers them around with a whistle.

"Well Wrath," he addresses their surly glares. "As every day that came before, today might be our last. We are outnumbered and outgunned. But let us not forget, the Captain and his Sting are only men. We, are the Wrath. So let us do what we were born to do. We fight till we win, or fight till we die!"

"Till the end!!" the growling shout of the Wrath mirror his defiance.

"But," he continues. "Let us not die in vain. With a bit of luck, and the help of Legion's fury, we will all see the sunset." Looking over each of his men who nod to him in respect, he turns to Solomon.

"You're familiar with the Carver aren't you?"

"I wouldn't say familiar," Solomon replies. "I've only ever fired it on the range. But I can make it work."

"Good enough. Go back down to the horses and set it up just off the trail. If anyone makes it across the dam that isn't Wrath, cut them in half, ok?"

Solomon gives a stern nod as the Major continues, "Will — Go with him and help him get it set up, that thing is as heavy as hell. But once you're done, come back up here and wait in the second tower until the Sting arrive. I have no doubt that they will send scouts ahead before crossing, so I want to use you to lure them across. After seeing what you can do, I suspect the prospect of capturing you will intrigue the Captain. A gift like yours could demand quite the price. So put on a show and let them believe they will take you."

"And Wrath," he says, taking a long breath as he points towards the first tower at the far end of the dam. "We will climb the parapet and hide in the spillways beneath until they pass. And once we're behind them, we'll do what we do best. Understood?"

"Aye Major," the soldiers concur with a muttered chorus.

"Good. Come on then, let us prepare the way for death."

*　　*　　*

As the soldiers busy themselves rigging bolts and cabling into the outer face of the parapet and practice swinging up over the edge, Will and Solomon, having loaded their packs with some essential supplies and small arms, set off down the path. Reaching the horses by the river, and relieving one from the weight of the long, padded carrier containing the Carver, they trudge back up through the meadow to the bottom of the trail, before traipsing into a thick patch of underbrush with a good view of the path. Relieved to put it down as they find a small clearing, Solomon flops down on the ground and begins to unpack it.

"Thanks for your help," he says, catching his breath. "There's no way I could have got that up here by myself. Thing seemed to get heavier by the minute."

"Yeah I know, right," Will replies, with a sweaty grin. "Do you need a hand or should I head off?"

"No I'm good from here, do your thing. And hey. . ." Hesitating with a stern gaze he looks Will in the eyes. "Can I ask you something?"

"Sure. Anything."

"If for some reason I don't make it out of this. Can you find my boy and make sure he's ok?"

"Don't talk like that," Will dismisses. "You're getting back. Anyway, you have that thing to keep you company." He gestures to the grim cobalt barrel of the Carver poking from the bag. "You'll be fine."

"I know. . . but if. . . Just please Will, promise me—he's all I've got." An air of urgent desperation rings hollow in his voice as he looks up with pleading eyes.

Will pauses, taken aback by the man's sudden weakness, and feels the stinging reflection of his own. "Sure," he replies. "Of course."

*   *   *

Alone with his thoughts and the chirping of crickets that sounds through the cascading rumble of the river, there's a soothing peace in the air as Will walks back up the steep path to the top of the dam. His legs don't ache like they probably should. If anything, he feels like he could go on forever. But as contorted images of the Sting warriors' agonized faces flicker in his head, he can see the telltale signs of their lives before their bloody end.

A well groomed beard. A tattoo. . . A ring on a finger. His stomach knots.

'They deserved it though, didn't they? . . . You were asleep! What kind of coward attacks someone in their sleep? If it was anything, it was justice.'

'Maybe. . . But it didn't feel right. It felt right—powerful. . . Satisfying even. Where is the good in that?'

As he reaches the top of the dam and looks along the empty stretch of walkway, the Wrath are already in hiding. Into the musty interior of the tower, he shimmies up onto the stone windowsill that overlooks the river far below. And stuffing his backpack behind him like a pillow, he runs his thumb over the razored edge of his sword as he gazes down the valley and waits.

Chapter 20

WRATH

In near silence it speeds, hovering over the trail. With every slight change in elevation and mild breath of wind that drifts across the lake, it adapts and corrects its movements as it hisses away from the lumbering column of Sting and toward the dam.

The heat signature of a small fawn and its mother in a distant clump of sycamores is logged and categorized. And as the earthen trail transitions to the flat concrete surface of the dam's walkway, for a second it hangs still as it scans the heavy oak door of the first tower.

Banking sideways, it darts in through the broken window beside it, emerging only a moment later, quite satisfied that there is nothing to note. With a high pitch buzz, it ascends sharply, before dipping sideways and dropping over the edge of the parapet wall, and into the billowing cloud of tumultuous mist emanating from the cascade of water churning violently below. Cautiously altering its speed as it moves through the moisture laden fog, it flies parallel to the slipway, scrutinizing every detail within its view until it reaches the base of the tower at the other end, and ducking through the arch of the spillway, it moves up and along the lakeside and inspects the same, before zipping up to the dam's top surface and back to where it began.

*   *   *

Will has been watching for so long he wonders if they had found another way around. But when he hears the faint whine of the little black drone at the dam's far end as it darts over the edge, his heart quickens its steady drum in anticipation of the coming carnage.

After what seems like an eternity, he sees it again, this time as it pops back up from the other side. Down the long curve of the dam's crest, it calmly drifts toward him, and closing his eyes and inhaling deeply, he stands up and steps out the door, shading his eyes from the sun.

For a moment, it stops as it registers his presence, before continuing on its mission past him, to explore the tower he had spent the night in. Satisfied that it is empty, it emerges and crosses off the end of the dam to scan the surrounding trees, and content that its mission is complete, it ascends vertically and hangs still, to keep a watchful eye on the trail below.

Then silence.

At first, the faint whinny of a horse and the clatter of hooves reverberating across the water breaks the calm. Then, a shadow of movement, and as Will peers into the distance, the mass of Sting riders loom into view as they leave the trail on the far side and lumber onto the dam's crest. More than he expected, impossible to count at this distance as they pass under the first tower, but forty at least, and as he feels their heavy steps tremor through the ground, he squeezes the hilt of his weapon tight with a shaking hand and draws his sword.

But then it stops.

Raising his hand at the head of their ranks, the procession comes to a standstill as Captain Ascha orders them to halt.

"Come on. . ." Will mutters to himself through a clenched jaw. "Just a little further."

Time seems to stop, as the stillness fills with trepid silence. Gaze held by gaze, stern and steady, masked by the thunder of the dam's rushing water. But as Will stifles a bated breath, and the Captain's sharp voice echoes through the air a shot rings out.

With a shriek, Will drops to his knees in agonizing pain as a bullet rips a hole in his stomach. Faltering for a moment as blood streams down his leg, he puts his hands on the ground to steady himself, and glimpsing the wound's grotesque healing, he staggers back to his feet. Grunting as the pain subsides, he straightens up, and as a hatred for his attackers simmers in his chest, he breathes deep and slow in wait for their next move.

In quick succession, two more shots ring out, sending him stumbling back. Then another and another, each exploding in puffs of fine, red mist as the bullets pierce his flesh. Falling sideways, he drops his sword, as blood and anger mix. He tries to move, but as another volley plows into him and he hits the ground again, a shrill bellow of a war horn surges into the heavens.

Unleashing a hail of lead as they ride, the ground beneath him rumbles as the full weight of the Sting breaks into a furious gallop. Every movement he makes, every motion, is met by another piercing hammer blow. Blinded by the stinging punishment of each bullet, he twists and writhes on his face as the column's rapid approach grows to a crescendo.

But just as he braces for the onslaught, as if the earth itself is falling apart, a terrifying explosion ripples through the dam. Wrath grenades erupting beneath their feet, screams of men and beast wail in bloodied carnage as a fleshy swath of the Sting's flank is projected high into the air. Horses shriek and Sting's anguished cries fill the sky as they crumple with ruptured organs and splintered bone. As from the smoke, the men of Wrath appear over the wall.

Like enraged serpents, the barrels of their weapons bellow blazing fire, felling screeching men in every direction. And then, too close for guns, they reach for their hungry swords and let them eat their fill.

Their powerful blades feast with blinding speed. Hacking and tearing, bodies fall in grisly horror, maimed and twisted as they soak the stone black with their blood.

As the Captain, staring in dread at the unbridled violence is flung his rearing horse, Will watches as a soldier, consumed in a blanket of fire, staggers from the flailing throng. But as the man screams in silent agony among the slaughter of his friends, and falls contorted in the mound of writhing butchery, Will feels nothing. No sympathy, no sorrow. Only rage. And as something dark inside of him revels in the man's sickly expression and the high pitch whine that floods his ears is replaced by the sound of the frightened dying, the sickening tangle fills his senses. Until, as the chaos that inhabits his heart reigns supreme, he raises his sword and runs.

His blade gouging a deep chasm across a fleshy back, the first man he reaches drops like hung meat, and before he's even fallen, he plunges it through a second with such force that the hilt sinks into his soft belly and the blade bursts out the other side. Abandoning the weapon, he jumps onto the back of another, raining vicious blows as the man paws desperately for freedom. But as his shrieks rise in panicked terror, Will takes his head between his hands and squeezes with all his might, savoring the dread in his bulging eyes.

'Will.'

A voice.

The whisper of a warm breath trembling in his ear, Will's world is filled with a deafening silence. Frozen in fear, and glaring in hate at the man locked in the grip of his savage hands, he stops; as without word and without sound, the man speaks. And, as he asks not for peace and pleads not for mercy, Will's blood runs cold—as he begs for forgiveness.

Shocked, Will releases him, staring in a haze at the broken form of his gasping victim.

Draped in a soldier's cloth and plated in the steels of war, he wears the form of a man, but his eyes, as confused and fearful as when he huddled in his mother's bosom—are the eyes of a child.

Clambering to his feet, Will gets up and starts to speak. But before he's said a single word, a sudden pop rings out and he's sprayed with blood, as the Major striding towards him fires a single shot into the man's head.

Stunned, Will gazes up at him, his ears ringing shrill, almost as if in a dream. But giving him a pleased smile, the Major puts his heavy hands on his trembling shoulder.

"In time, they will write stories about you," he says. "I have never seen anyone survive such an onslaught. And yet, here you are, standing without so much as a scratch!"

Motioning to the ragged battleground behind littered with the dead, stifled screams dot the eerie silence as the Wrath execute survivors and strip them of their worth. "We have won a great victory today thanks to you," he continues. "Come, let's see what the Captain has to say for himself."

Dirty and bruised, with hands bound behind his back, Captain Ascha kneels in front of a handful of the Wrath, as they stand over him with their swords drawn.

"His feet," the Major orders his men as he approaches, "bind them."

Glaring down at the humbled Captain, he pauses in thought before speaking in a low growl. "I already know you will talk, Ascha. But I am curious how you will die. What way do you want it? With honor at the end of Wrathian steel, or blubbering like an infant?"

Shaken, but with a silent stare of defiance, the Captain glares at him.

"Very well," the Major shrugs and makes a casual motion toward the thundering precipice beyond the dam's edge. "Have it your way."

First connecting his feet to a length of thick rope and tying the other end to the railing, the Wrath soldiers grab the Captain under his arms and hoist him up onto the parapet wall, and with a vicious shove, he falls backward off the edge. The rope's slack vanishing rapidly behind him, he drops. Until, with a loud snap, it goes taut; and as he slams hard into the side of the spillway, it tremors like a fisherman's line as the merciless weight of the rushing water batters his defenseless body.

After a long calm breath, the Major motions to his men, who begin pulling on the rope and hauling the Captain back to safety.

Soaked and bleeding in a limp, shaking heap, he splutters and gasps for air as he's returned, but with another callous nod from the Major, he's dragged to his feet and perched back on the edge.

"W. . . Wai—!"

Desperately struggling for air, the Captain begins to speak, but is cut short, as again, he's tipped off the edge, slapping the face of the spillway's thunderous current seconds later and vanishing below its surface.

Pulled up again and returned to the walkway, he lies huddled in a dripping pile at their feet, retching in reflexive response as water spews from his nose and mouth.

"Gaspar," he sputters. "Gaspar!"

"I had no doubt it was that snake!" the Major snarls, as he crouches down beside him. "Tell me something I don't know! What did he do!?! What's going on in the city?!!" He grabs the Captain's pale face in his hands and lifts it to his own, slamming into the Captain's nose with his fist. "Why are comms down?!! Speak!!!!!!"

Will has never heard of a Carver before, let alone what one sounds like. But as the electric crackle rippling up from the valley below sends the Wrath dashing for cover, he knows it's something to be feared.

Its burning white beam bursting from the undergrowth by the trail, the Major pulls him to the ground as the air pulsates with its howling energy. And ripping across the valley floor, it leaves long black scars in the earth behind its blazing touch. Following the light of its razored beam, Will's heart sinks, as with the unmistakable elegance of Malleus design, two armored aircraft skim low over the river towards them.

The resounding electrical warble blaring out again, another ripple of energy from the Carver scorches a line along the river bank. As with a blinding flash and a shockwave that thunders through the air, the first aircraft erupts in a ball of fire. Narrowly avoiding it, as shards of smoldering debris fly in every direction, the second craft pulls up sharply, simultaneously letting loose a barrage of missiles that purposefully turn toward Solomon's position. And as they disappear into the trees that flicker with pockets of light, a sea of flame engulfs the riverbank and the woods beyond it, roaring with searing fury over the trail as it swallows everything in its path.

"Burner incoming!" The Major yells over the fray as the delayed rumble of the blast shakes the ground. "Take cover!!"

Freed from the frozen awe of the spectacle, the Wrath warriors burst into action, scrambling for cover and firing, as with a deafening roar the craft clears the top of the dam and ascends swiftly into the air above them. Falling from its rear, six spherical objects like black eggs silently drop from the sky and land hard along the dam as cries of 'Arakhna!' ripple through the air. Stationary for a moment, their form convulses as metallic legs emerge from their sides, revolving and cycling their appendages through a startup sequence, before, with mechanized deliberation, the cruel machines stand to attention and turn their deathly focus to the Wrath.

"Charge!!!" the Major bellows his command, as the Arakhna lurch into a spasmodic sprint towards them. Gunfire erupting in all directions, Metallic legs tear off and sensors explode in flames and sparks as the Wrath's weapons unleash.

Will is suspended in time. He cannot move. He cannot breathe. But as he listens to the fragrant melody of hate born fury pouring from the hearts of the Wrath as they charge, the dark thing that resides within him growls with delight. One foot in front of the other, he runs. Faster and faster with them. Following their lead. Over piles of butchered men and slaughtered horses as flurried bursts of return fire hisses past their frantic stampede. In an instant, they are on top of the machines, and the machines are on top of them. Furious sounds of steel and bone and rivet ringing out as Wrath and Arakhna fall.

Strength and pain mixing and swirling as he strikes and is struck, orchestral screams and slashing blows burst and explode in magnificent fervor. But as he looks up in shock to a sudden shrieking howl from the sky, the sunlight is blacked out as an inferno of heat entombs him in a blanket of fire.

Flat on his back, dazed, he watches as a delicate trail of vapor slips from the cooling barrels of the Malleus aircraft above, as all around, burning as they blindly swing their swords, the Wrath scream and collapse into charred, smoldering heaps.

Marred by black soot, the weight of an Arakhna's heavy legs lands on his chest, and as he struggles, another one, and then another. In a mechanical frenzy of their callous limbs, they crush and squeeze, tightening down with every exhalation he makes, and as the pressure becomes unbearable, he feels he might just simply burst. In their lifeless lenses, he fights as the reflection of his own haggard face looks back at him. But as a slender mechanized lanyard descends towards them, from the armored belly of the Malleus craft above, he has nothing left. Reaching the top of his Arakhna captor, it connects with a click, and succumbing to their strength he lies helpless. As cocooned in its grasp as it retracts, he is drawn into the air.

*　*　*

Libertas — Aequitas — Venustas.

Etched in the craft's steel hull, the words of the Vitruvian adage scars the wall.

"Ascha you dog! What have you done!!" the Major's anger bellows out from further down the row of cramped cages.

Hearing murmured words as he peers through the narrow steel mesh into the dim interior of the Burner's dank holding pens, Will can just make out the Captain, standing beside the shadowed form of another man, barely visible in the lusterless glow.

"You don't need to die with the old ways, Major," Captain Ascha replies. "We can build a new world—Sorwian and Kol together! United under the Vitruvian banner we can flourish!"

An eerie silence lingers for a moment, filled only with the deep hum of the craft's engines.

"What is it that you lack?" the Major asks. "What is it that Sorrow did not provide?"

"Comfort, Major," he replies, after a pensive hesitation. "Real comfort. Why do we deny it to ourselves? Why do we deny it to our people? We could be so much more than we are, so much happier. Think about it! Is there nothing they can offer that you would not want? When my wife passed I thought she was gone forever. But they brought her back!"

"Do you really believe that?" the Major scoffs.

"I know it is hard to imagine, and I didn't until I saw it! But she was real—as real as you are now! Drifting like an angel through the Parisian streets of the Ether. . . We danced and drank wine, late into the night, just like we did when we were young. Is there no one you would like to hold again?"

With a long sigh, the Major responds in a saddened hush. "Of course I would Captain. And I am sorry for your pain. But what you saw was no more your wife than an elaborate drawing on a wall. She is not real. Vitruvius cannot give what he does not have."

"How can you say that? You weren't there, you didn't see her! She was everything I remember—every look and every word. My joy, my comfort. And it can be shared with all of Sorrow! Is that so wrong?"

"The thing you call comfort is but a Vitruvian chain that holds your head from looking up to the light. If you see your Charlotte again Captain—and I pray that you do—it will not be in this short walk of life."

"Listen to yourself!" the Captain snaps. "How can you be so sure that your reality isn't the fantasy?! I do not know what else to say to you Major and I am truly sorry it had to be this way. But I hope you know that everything I did, I did for the greater good."

The sound of footsteps ringing out on the metal deck, the droning hum of the Burner's engines fill the calm as they fade away. As, holding his knees in the corner of his cage, Will is left in silence.

Chapter 21

A PLACE OF DARKNESS

Head first into the confines of a small stone cell, the door slams shut and the deadbolt clunks into place. It is dark —void of all light. And slipping in a thick pool of slimy filth that covers the floor, Will scrambles to his hands and knees. There are no windows in this sunless abode, and feeling around in the blackness, he sits on a rough block that protrudes from the mire.

An anguished shriek or a rattle of a door sometimes echoes through the musty tunnels of the prison, but otherwise it's a quiet place, touched only by brief whispers of madness that slither from undefined places. Occasionally, the dank air is penetrated by putrid odors as the stomach contents of the condemned is disturbed where it putrefies on the squalid floor. And as the metronomic notes of dripping murk, and the uneasy scuttle of tiny feet scratching for a paltry meal forms a soothing rhythm, he drifts off into a troubled sleep. But it does not bring rest. Instead, it brings confusion; as time loses aim and wanders with the sound and the stench that waivers through the air.

A bowl of apparent sustenance with a spoon sticking out of it falls through a grate in the door and lands, upended, in the scum on the floor. Keeping to the walls, careful to avoid the deeper pools in the middle of the room, Will picks it up before recoiling in disgust and dropping it, as a centipede crawls from its middle. Back on his stoop, he puts his weary head in his hands, and as if sensing his despondent heart, the foul creatures that feed off fear awaken in his mind, to prod and poke every facet of his soul.

*　　*　　*

A faint sound—a scraping, reverberates from somewhere in the darkness. . .

There it is again.

Scraping, scratching. . . Dry, itchy skin.

A whisper.

Getting up, he inches along the face of the wall and freezes, alert, as he turns his head to pinpoint its source. Feeling a slight draught of air coming from a small gap in the stone face, he presses his ear to it and listens intently, hearing it again.

It's faint, but unmistakable.

"Is there someone there?" he calls out, pausing to listen again. "Hello?"

"Yes. . ." a hoarse voice responds from the other side of the hole, followed by the shuffle of feet. "Yes, hello? Yes, I can hear you" The latent odor of a man's stale breath drifts with it. "Who's there?"

"Will. . ." Will replies, surprised for a moment by the volume of his own voice. "My name is Will."

"Well, I. . . It is nice to meet you Will. For a moment I thought you were just a voice in my. . . My name is Amos. My apologies, I did not know I had company. If I had I would have cleaned up a little better!" Giving a raspy laugh, the man splutters as he breaks into a grating cough. "Forgive me. What is it that has you down here?"

"Down where? Where are we?"

"We're in the bowels of the city. Last stop before the Rift."

"The city? Sorrow you mean?"

"Yes, yes. The very one. Where men come to weep their sins away. You are not Sorwian I take it?"

"No, Zenite. From Boston."

"Ah, I see. I couldn't place your accent. Have you been here for long?"

"A few days I think," Will replies with slight uncertainty. "You?"

"Longer. Months maybe. Or even more, it's. . . it can be hard to tell, you know?"

Will nods in agreement, vaguely aware that the man can't see him. "Why are you here?"

"Ha," Amos chuckles to himself. "I'm still not sure of that myself. I was, in the beginning. But in recent days, doubt has creeped up on me, and now I wonder. . . Maybe I went down my own path and not the one set before me. How can God's purpose possibly be fulfilled in a place like this?"

"What happened?"

"I asked a man to question himself. But. . . I don't know. It's a long story." His voice trailing off into hollow nothingness, the creeping quiet slides back through Will's cell.

"Honestly," Will breaks the silence. "If you'd care to tell, I'd love to listen. It's nice to hear something in here other than the rats."

"It is, I suppose. . ." he mumbles to himself. "Well if you want. . . Where to begin. . . Have you heard much about our Holy book?"

"Not much. Little bits and pieces from stories I've heard. But not a whole lot."

The man's voice goes quiet in the blackness. "I suppose I should start with my family then." Clearing his throat, he inhales slowly as he begins. "At the founding of Sorrow, my bloodline was ordained to protect and conserve the sacred book. So when I was young, as all the firstborn males before me, I was sent from my mother to indentured servitude with the priests of the Tear, where I learned how to live by the many divine laws set by the Order. When my head was suitably full of knowledge, they released me to the Chapel Vault to train under my father. And there, until the day of his passing, he taught me everything there is to know about how to protect the book. How to keep it and clean it and care for it —even how to control the environment around it. You'd be amazed how quickly a change in temperature or moisture in the air can damage something so fragile. Even our presence in the room as we went about our duties would send moisture levels skyward, so we would breathe and move just so, carefully and cautiously, so as not to raise our heart rate or break a sweat."

"You liked it then? Taking care of the book?"

"Liked it? Oh yes! Spending my days in the presence of the word of God! What greater honor is there than that?!! The book is what started it all!!!. . . Forgive my excitement. It has been a while since I have had such bright thoughts." Stopping, he inhales deeply before he continues. "From the ashes of the Tribulation to the mountains of Mourne, the founding fathers of Sorrow rose. And with them, they carried the book. From every corner of the blackness, survivors crawled to hear its words and crossing the ice and sand they came to find the way to salvation. So as the people grew great in number, the weeping city grew and the book's message spread far and wide. It wasn't called Sorrow back then of course. In those days, there was much joy and laughter. But, it was not to last. With their marvels and machines, and words as smooth as butter, the Kol came, speaking of peace and light. But when bombs fell and men began to die, we were lost, and our hearts turned to fear. So looking for a place to keep the book safe, the elders of the time built the great Chapel Vault. And you should see it! What a wonder!! Grand obsidian columns and tall vaulted ceilings, crisscrossed with huge oak trusses sitting like a crown over ornate rows of pews. And gold everywhere, lining every surface—it's magnificent! At the front, there's a towering arch of stained glass, so when you walk up the aisle, your body glows in all the colors of heaven, and when you reach the top and climb the white marble steps of the pulpit —the sacred book! And compared to its splendor, the room seems pale." Sighing, he pauses in fond revelry. "I wish you could see it. I have spent most of my waking life in the chapel, and it was no less marvelous on the last day as it was on the first. . ." The echo of his voice trails off. "But I'm rambling— where was I?. . . oh yes. As the whispers of sedition and sabotage wove into webs and the hand of fear took hold of Sorrow, the Chapel Vault was closed to the public. It was temporary at first, but weeks turned to months, and before long the elders and noblemen were deemed untrustworthy too. By the time my great grandfather began his training, with the exception of the humble caretaker and high priest himself, the Chapel, and the Holy writings in it, had been locked to every citizen of the nation."

"What happened? Did you let someone in?"

"No, no. No such thing. But I broke my vow. . . Conservators are sworn to protect the book at all costs. The contents of the book, however, are prohibited. After all, ordinary men could not possibly be trusted to understand the word of God by themselves. Holy words are for holy men. So to protect it from us, and us from it, we wore a black veil through which we could not see. . . That, is why I am here."

"You looked?"

"Yes. . ." he whispers.

"And?"

". . . and I heard . . ." Filled with sadness, his tone shifts. "We had got it all wrong. So, so wrong. The book. Yes, it was magnificently crafted with detailed lettering and intricate, majestic illustrations. But it was just a book—ink and paper. But it's words. . . As I read them, my world—the very universe held to my eyes, began to fall away. And for the first time I saw beyond its limitations. As I read, the dead ink came to life and my eyes opened. I saw color where it was not before and heard music that broke my heart. And as I learned; my soul, like a seed with water, began to burst with life. It was then that I realized. . . We, the Sorrow. . . We had lost our way. We had entombed something living, in dust and in darkness. . . No wonder we did not grow." He pauses and takes a deep breath. "I did not know how—nor am I a brave man—but I suddenly knew that I was to share my epiphany and that it would change the world. So first with my dearest friend, and then with some of the brothers of the Tear, I shared and they listened. And as lamentation for our failure passed, together we rejoiced for our chance at absolution. When we requested an audience with Melichior and the crowned heads of Sorrow, we thought it was the best way. After all, who would understand better than the high priest and his wise men? No one was closer to God than them! So, kneeling at their feet as they sat in quiet rumination, we poured out our revelation, and when we had finished, we bowed our heads and prayed as they muttered amongst themselves. But when he asked who we were to know the will of God and the soldiers bound our hands and read us our charge, we knew our fate. Blasphemy, dissent, desecration. . . So, here I am."

"Do you regret it?" Will asks, as a silence lingers in the surrounding darkness.

He hesitates before replying with subdued resolve. "The road to salvation is in the words of that book. If only men would read it for themselves with open eyes and listen! The great city of Sorrow is built on the very back of its wisdom. Yet away from its words, we have slowly forgotten to listen for the voice of its author. And now, in our pious arrogance, we live by a twisted version of we created by ourselves, to suit our selfish hearts and justify our foolish deeds. So, do I feel regret? No. I am no soldier, no hero. I am no more than a single note of a beautiful song. But no more than a note regrets its sound as it sails from the mouth of its creator, do I regret what I was made to do."

For a while it is silent and neither man speaks. Until, as the musty quiet is broken by the hollow echo of footsteps and muffled voices growing louder outside their cells, Amos takes a contented breath. "It is time for me to go," he whispers.

"Go?" Will asks. "Where?"

"A place prepared," he replies as the sound of keys in a door rings out through the pallid air. "They come for me. . ."

Will's stomach knots as the sharp bark of cruel voices echoes through the hole in the wall.

"And Will?"

"Yeah?"

"Remember my chains. For without them, a door to you would remain shut."

*   *   *

The muted sounds of aggression subsiding into silence from the hole in the wall, Will returns to the cold block in the corner as a feeling of desolate emptiness washes over him. Acutely aware of his discomfort and his vile surroundings, he drifts in and out of the plains of slumber as tears roll down his cheeks, and sorrow gently strokes his head until he is subdued.

Chapter 22

I WILL REPAY

As the door opens, Will is limp as he is rained with blows and shackled. Offering no resistance, he is dragged down the corridor. Cattle prods burning into his sides, he makes no sound as he is crammed into a small steel cage. And loaded onto a small wooden cart and rolled through a winding maze to the world above, he curls up and rests his weary head on his knees, defeated by the earth.

* * *

Caught by the crisp winds of the mountain air, the heavy timber doors swing open and slam into the adjacent wall as the cart passes through, shaking as it rumbles over the cobblestone path.

The grubby jailers grunting as they pull it ahead, Will shades his eyes as welcome rays of light flicker through the holes in his cage. Peering out, a horde of disheveled men and women line the narrow, muddy streets, their gaunt and sickly eyes staring as the cart rattles past. But as their diverse amalgamation of heartfelt looks and angry screams holler as one, he's showered with scorn and hateful spittle, as waste rains down from the open windows above.

Through the filth of the outer keep's tangled laneways and under a grand archway, the sprawl of the outer keep is left behind as they trail onto the wide expanse of the market plaza. From every caste of Sorwian society, its length and breadth is filled with a jeering crowd, and as Will is carted through their sullen mass, they whisper and mutter in fretful dread.

Approaching the railings at the chasm's edge, a clearing of wounded prisoners is surrounded by a neat line of Sting soldiers, and ushered through a gap in their ranks, Will is brought to a halt beside them. The uneasy scent of fear wavering in the air is palpable, and swallowing the lump in his throat, he gazes across the yawning depths of the Rift to the long arched bridge spanning across. It's empty, but as he scans upward to its crest, his eyes fall on a small platform that protrudes from its side and hangs bare over the open abyss.

"It will be an honor to die by your side."

Will turns his head as he hears the familiar voice of the Major from the ground beside his cart. With clothes torn and patterned with dark bloodstains, his face is so badly battered that only one eye remains open.

"Is it that bad?" he says, wincing with the movement as he laughs at Will's horrified expression. "Save your concern. All men of the sword die by its blade. It is the way."

"What happened?" Will asks, perturbed by the Major's disfigured complexion.

"I don't know. But Sorrow has fallen. Gaspar, and the Sting—they lowered the city's guns and betrayed us all."

"How?" Will replies, "I—"

A fanfare of trumpets and the chorus of marching boots grows loud in the air as a column of Sting foot soldiers punches an opening through the crowd at the foot of the bridge. Parting a wide gap in the throng to create a clear path, they line themselves along its sides as more soldiers approach from the other end and do the same. A clear path through the crowd now joining the gates of the inner and outer keep across the arch of the bridge, a handful of workers rush along it, rolling out lengths of smooth crimson carpet as they go.

The crowd falling silent, four Arakhna drones prowl from the inner keep, followed by a short fat man strutting ceremoniously behind them in loose brown robes. And as the machines stop on either end and scan the crowd with stuttered outbursts of erratic movement, the man continues past them, up the bridge to its highest point, and clears his throat.

"My fellow citizens of Sorrow!" he bellows, his voice reverberating clearly on the stone surfaces of the castle walls that tower above. "It is with great honor that I introduce the most esteemed and wise; The head of the Sigh of Sorrow — Lord Gaspar!!"

A roar of cheers erupting from the crowd, Lord Gaspar ambles along the scarlet carpet and up the bridge, waving to the masses. Behind him, Captain Ascha follows, accompanied by a stern, solid man in a sharp black suit, wrapped in the rich comfort of a thick fur coat that runs down past his knees. But as they reach the top and take their place beside Gaspar, Will's heart sinks. Between them, barely taller than the railings, with puffy red eyes and tear stained cheeks, stands the sad little figure of Elik.

With a smug grin, Gaspar slowly examines his subjects before raising his hands for silence. "Today!" he begins, "is a new day! Men and women of Sorrow. Lords and ladies of the royal houses. Physicians, engineers and people of science. Tradesmen, artisans and farmers. Mothers, fathers, children—citizens all!! To you, this great city is forever indebted!"

The crowd roaring in a barrage of praise, he waits for it to dissipate before continuing.

"As you know, there has been much friction in the past few weeks in our struggle for a better future. There are those who wished only to subvert peace and freedom and to bring us back into the arms of war. So, although today is a day of celebration and new beginnings—it is also a day of sadness. I say this with nothing but a heavy heart. . . For those that sought to harm us were not some foreign force or distant threat, but our friends and our brothers. So in sadness we will bid them farewell. . ." With a sober stare at his feet, he pauses for a moment's silence before resuming his speech. "But! We must begin our new journey. So before we do our duty, I must introduce two men for whom without, we would surely be in the throes of chaos, and for whom with, we will march together as one people into a better tomorrow!! Without further adieu, may I give to you — the hand of the Sting of Sorrow — General Ascha!!"

With hand clasped behind his back as the crowd's elations rise, Captain Ascha takes a pompous step forward to give an acknowledging nod.

"And," Gaspar resumes the introduction, ushering to the fur clad man behind him. "The Vitruvian Legate of Sorrow, Praetor Galen!!!"

As if absent, or under a spell, the man doesn't move or even flinch as the hoots and whistles of crowd's acclamations rise in his honor, but instead stands motionless, with his expression fixed in an empty stare. His formidable presence is almost admirable as the surging flattery of the masses fills the plaza. But calm and collected, as if a man adored by ants – his contempt for their praise shines through.

As Will watches, his chest tightens as a malignant flicker of hatred stirs and whispers its want.

'Dead eyed thing. If I could feel you writhe as I squeeze your life from your worthless neck, I would surely die happy.'

A commotion at the bottom of the bridge draws his attention, as a procession of the Sting emerges from the inner keep and makes a slow march up the red carpet. Behind them, stumbling as they are dragged by their chained wrists, Melichior the High Priest and General Balthasar follow with pained defeat in their eyes.

Reaching the protruding platform that hangs over the chasm below, the men's short haggard steps are stopped. And as the General is shoved through the gap in the railings, Gaspar glowers at him as he speaks, "Balthasar of the Wrath!" he growls. "You and your fanatics stand guilty of conspiracy and treason against the Lords of Sorrow! What do you say to your charge?!"

In trepid silence, the crowd hushes as the General examines the dark abyss below. His large chest rising as he draws a long breath and turns, he locks his somber eyes on Gaspar who seems to shrink beneath his defiant blaze. But then, without a word, he steps backward off the ledge and disappears into the gaping blackness below.

A hushed murmur runs through the crowd, as Gaspar lurches forward and peers in over the railing after him.

"Traitor!!" he exclaims, shocked and straightening up in red cheeked outrage. "Make no mistake! That was an admission by any other name!! Bring the priest!"

With an impatient flap to the soldiers, he beckons for Melichior to be brought forward.

"And you, High Priest!" he growls, as the old priest is nudged whimpering onto the platform. "Will you do the same? Do you feel guilt?! For centuries you and the priesthood of the Tear have held the citizens of this great city by the neck. For centuries you have done nothing but stifle our desire to grow! But no more! No more will we be restrained by antiquity! No more, will we be subdued by the words of old men! And no more will the proud men and women who built this great empire with their sweat and blood be held back from embracing their destiny!"

Melichior is silent as he stares into the blackness beneath. But with a commanding flick of a wrist from Gaspar, the enthusiastic delight of the masses explodes, as a sword is plunged into his back.

Aghast at the spectacle as the priest shrieks and stumbles sideways off the platform, Will flinches, as with a sudden jolt and a rattle of his cage, he starts to move. The cobbles rumbling under the wheels as he is rolled around the edge of the pit, his chest grips his pounding heart as he's taken up the incline of the bridge's arch. In full display of the swarming plaza and deafened by their thundering sound, he flounders against the sea of fear that rings throbbing in his head. Staring down, as the Major and the other disheveled prisoners are goaded onto their feet and lined up with brutish force against the railings, panic blooms to terror. And as the cart jerks to a halt at the open railing at the bridge's top, he freezes as he looks straight into the cruel gaze of the Praetor.

With sunken face, sallow and lifeless, the man's watchful gape seems to seep into his soul. The venomous hiss of the crowd grows strangely dim, an icy wetness trickles up his spine, until all that he thought he was, is smothered by fear.

Through the haze of dread and Gaspar's droning voice, a terrible scream shrieks through the air from below, as with a flurried slash of the Sting's swords, the first prisoner drops to his knees in a squealing heap. With the roars of the crowd rising in waves, the soldiers hoist the man's butchered carcass over the railings and move onto the next. Scream after scream howling out in anguish as they hack their way along the line towards the Major, Will watches in helpless horror at the methodical carnage, as another man falls and then another. Each tossed like waste over the edge.

"People of Sorrow!!" Gaspar's proclamation cuts through the nightmare. "For those of you who do not believe in the need for unity — May I present to you — William of Legion!"

As Gaspar motions towards Will's cage for his captivated audience, the sound of Will's name seems to silence the very universe as it is uttered.

"General Ascha!" Gaspar says. "Show them!"

Turning to Will's cage with a grin, Ascha pulls his sword from its sheath, and with gleeful energy, he plunges it in a frenzied blaze through the gaps in the bars.

Shrieking, Will's hands and arms are shredded to the bone as he tries in vain to stop its vicious edge. He can't move. He can't breathe. But before he has even felt the full force of the pain, Ascha stops. And yanking his bloodied sword from Will's flesh with a growl, he pulls a pistol from his belt and fires. Over and over with deafening force, ragged holes spray from Will's back as lead rips into his defenseless body, until, with the hollow click of an empty magazine, the brutal savagery is finished.

As silence hovers over Will's haggard corpse, his restless limbs begin to stir, and as the first whispers of unease resonate through the plaza, the thing that dwells within him whispers its discontent. As it awakens, his agony succumbs to fury, and as he pulls himself up against the cold metal sides of his prison, he glares through blackened eyes at the gawking throng with utter hatred.

Gaspar breaks his disturbed fixation from Will and pauses, before turning his attention back to the wide eyed shock of the mob.

"As you can see from this abomination," his tone trembles as he resumes his denunciation. "The nights are getting longer. And with it—it's shadows. Yes, we are a brave people, and yes, we are a strong people. But we are alone. So I ask you this! What do you want for your children? To survive against the darkness to come? Or to thrive, with all the might and wisdom of the human race? Alone, we are kings. But together, my friends, under one banner — We will be gods!!"

He bows his head as a surge of solemn applause washes over him, before raising his hands for quiet and turning to Will.

"And so, as our first act of unity — Creature, in the name of the Vitruvian Empire, I condemn you to an eternity in the bottomless pit. If death does not come for you, you will wish it did!"

With a courteous nod to the Praetor, the soldiers push Will's cage forward onto the platform as the masses erupt in venomous acclamation.

As the horror of his fate unfolds in his consciousness, Will scrambles against the bars, thrashing and pounding on the steel with his fists in an agitated fury. And as the agonizing shriek of another prisoner rings out as he is hurled over the edge, the cage darkens as the shadow of the Praetor looms up to the bars.

"Do you think Abigail will scream like that when I find her?" he says.

Will's stomach turns at the sound of her name.

"And I *will* find her," the Praetor sneers, with a smirk on his face. "Poor girl can't go too far on such a bad leg."

In a rage, Will screams in frustration. Pummeling frantically against the cage, the flesh on his knuckles tears off and bloodies the bars. But no sooner than it rips off, it has healed, and as the front wheels of the cart drop off the edge of the platform, he is thrown forward as it hangs over the emptiness below.

Suddenly, a burst of gunfire cracks the sky with a deafening blare. Elation turning to terror, a wail of chaos ripples through the onlookers. Scanning the panicked crowd, people scatter in all directions. But as her hood falls to her shoulders, he sees her. Kata.

Firing rapid bursts from the rifle pressed tight against her shoulder, metal shreds bodies as soldiers fall like cut weeds. Transfixed by the fury of her wrath, he watches as behind her, the disfigured form of a man steps out, and raises the ominous barrel of a Carver from under his robes. In an instant, it is over. Without so much as a word, the barrel of the weapon is aimed directly at Will. And before he can utter even a scream, with a blinding flash, it unleashes its unfettered violence.

*   *   *

Light and heat and pain.

Then silence.

All is calm as Will opens his eyes.

The hard surface of the bridge is cold under his back and as the taint of burning flesh penetrates his senses, muffled screams of gunfire and violence drift on the breeze. Trailing his fingers across the searing crust of his disfigured face, he raises the charred hunks of blackened meat that were once his hands. Strangely absent of sensation, he turns his dreamlike gape to the vivid blue sky beyond, as the dark silhouette of a mourning raven high above catches his eye. Almost motionless as it rides the unseen waves of an updraft into the heavens, it is quite beautiful as it watches for its hapless prey. But with the sudden force of a hammer, the air splits with a thunderous roar. Seized by a sickening terror, he reels beneath the deafening call. And as a burst of white light blinds him, he gazes into eyes; bright like the fire of the sun.

The great howling of a tempest as a word like a multitude of waters rushes into his ears.

A name.

His name.

'Will.'

Reaching out, as he tries to speak, a shallow dry rasp scratches from the seared depths of his lungs. But there are no words there. And in that moment—as all is stripped away —he knows.

He knows he is known.

He knows he is seen.

He was not alone when he screamed into the storm. He was not abandoned when he clung to a rock and was chewed and thrashed by the raging sea. And when he was spat onto a desolate beach, broken, with nothing but darkness in his veins and hate in his heart; he was not forsaken. So as the raven dives with a shrieking cry, he wells with joy and sorrow as tears stream down his cheeks.

Peace rushes in as breath rushes out.

Like a soft summer breeze sweeping gently over still waters, life slows and time comes to a standstill as he is washed by the sound of the wind.

'Wake, from your colorless sleep,' it whispers. *'I will give you rest.'*

Exhaling, he succumbs to its warm embrace and closes his eyes.

But he is not ready yet.

Clean, crisp air rushing into his body, the raven speeds towards the earth.

Curling its wings behind and holding them tight, gunfire and clashing steel mingles with screams of agony and terror, as the howl of warring men rips through the air. With frantic speed, as blood spills like water on the ground, it vibrates through the relentless forces of the stratosphere's howling winds. Yielding to what it has been committed, the very air reverberates with chaos. And breathing it in as hate satiates his pain, Will stands to his feet.

It is carnage. The anguished wails of the dying floating on the breeze, blackened scorch marks that streak across the walls of the castle keep hiss as they burn. His dark red blood spilling through her fingers, Kata kneels in a pallid daze beside Solomon where he has fallen, as Wrath and Sting alike lie still; like paper dolls scattered by the wages of their earthly woes.

The sound of Elik's stifled whimpers from the far end of the trembling bridge jar his senses. Turning his blackened eyes towards the inferno that engulfs the other end, he can feel their fear, as Gaspar, Ascha and the Praetor, stand trapped between him and a wall of the fire's consuming heat. And bristling, he glares at the Praetor who's holding tight onto Elik's quivering little hand. "Let him go," he growls.

With a sullen smile from his dead eyes, the Praetor cocks his head as the shadow of a Malleus burner overhead arrives at his cerebral behest. "Who are you to make demands of me?" he smirks.

With a squeal of warping metal, the bridge twists, and with a sudden shudder, a portion of railing breaks free and falls spiraling into the darkness of the Rift.

"General!" Gaspar calls out, glancing back at the blazing fire behind them. "Do something!!"

"You'll kill us all, you fool!!" Ascha yells, drawing his sword and stepping forward, as the roar of the flames intensifies. "Let us pass!!"

Clenching his teeth, he snarls, and in a sudden flurry of movement he bursts into a charge. In an instant, the space between them is gone, and dipping with a masterful lunge, he plunges his sword through Will's chest with a defiant scream of rage.

Together they stand embraced with eyes locked, as Will adjusts to the searing discomfort of his impalement. But as his fury bubbles with bitter vitriol, he raises his arms and places his hands around the soft warmth of Ascha's throat. Feeling the pulse of panic quickening in his grip, he begins to squeeze, pulling their heads so close that their foreheads touch and he can hear the desperate rattle of stolen breaths.

Ascha gasps, thrashing in desperation. Releasing the sword that's trapped between them, he fumbles for his daggers, and pulling them free, he wildly thrust the blades over and over into Will's chest. But no more than drops of rain on a hot summer's day do they have an effect. And as his veins swell and his eyes bulge, Will stares at him; immovable. Watching, waiting, until, as the wretched bones in his throat collapse with a sickening wheeze, his heartbeat stops.

Above, as the Burner descends with a deep rumble, Arakhna spill from its opening belly onto the plaza and begin whirring to life. Dropping the lifeless husk of Ascha to the ground, Will drags the sword from his chest and glares across the bridge, as it shakes with another deafening creak.

"For God's sake! Let us pass!! We'll all die together?!!" Gaspar screams in desperation. "What do you want?! We can give you the world! You could be a king!!"

Will stays silent, fixed and unwavering, locked in a death stare with the Praetor as the Arakhna swarming at the base of the bridge behind him prepares to protect their master. And as they rush, he holds steady with tranquil resolve.

Like a pack of ravenous insects, they're on him, hacking as they pin him beneath their impaling limbs. Crushing, as they wrap their frigid legs around his torso, the jarring screech of the bridge's twisting metal cries for mercy under the extra weight as he struggles and snarls. But in an instant it's over, and he's held still.

As the machines scuttle away, the Praetor takes a cautious step forward. First examining the one locked around Will, before approaching with Elik by his side.

"Like I told you, Gaspar," he calls behind him. "Legion's prophecy is no more than a hopeful wish. Come. Let us go from here."

With a satisfied breath and a final look of disdain he moves to step past, but puzzled he glances down as Will grabs his ankle. "Really?" he smirks, reaching for his sword with a muted grin, "I do admire your determination, but do you really need me to cut it off?"

Will can hardly move, and the agony of the machine breaking more of his bones with every passing second blinds his thoughts.

"Elik," his voice crackles as the soulful eyes of the boy turn on him. ". . . Run."

Mustering the last of his waning energy, he pushes his other hand free, and with it, the gray orb of the fusion grenade he had pulled from Ascha's corpse.

In wide eyed terror, the Praetor shrieks as it rolls to the ground, drawing his sword with an infuriated roar and thrashing to break free from Will's grasp. But as he frantically brings his blade down in savage succession and the sounds of Elik's little footsteps patter away, a shockwave rips through the plaza.

With a deafening burst of light and fire, the ground shudders as an enormous ball of white fire blooms into the sky. Expanding into the open belly of the Malleus warship above, engines whine and sirens blare as it keels sideways, before pounding into the huge city walls with a thunderous roar. And as the visceral hues of a furious heat engulf the twisting steel, the bridge plunges into the darkness of the Rift.

Chapter 23

A SPECK OF LIGHT

Spiraling down in a frenzied blaze, steel and fire falls as Will falls with it.

In these depths, light and heat is a stranger. But as the radiant carnage plummets through it, it illuminates, and warms.

Deeper still, the dancing immolation descends. Past the jagged rocks and black waters, that dark things call their home. For an instant, they see what they have never seen, they know what they have never known. A glimpse of the impossible. And although for just for a moment, for the first time they see each other, and themselves. Shadowless and naked, bathed in humility and washed by the warmth of the light's humbling touch.

* * *

The fire of the twisted bridge dwindling, his enemies' broken corpses fade. And as time comes to a standstill Will is entombed by an endless night.

Like cruel laughter dancing through the hollow chambers, he cries until there are no tears left. Till there is only silence. Darkness and decay.

His eyes are of no use here. Sight is constrained to the gropings of his skin. Damp earth and black water. Time leads to more time, and empty dream to empty dream. As thought and word babble indistinguishable from his lips, he wanders blind in the endless night.

With clicks and chatters, invertebrates call from the gloom, and dragging his long beard and matted hair through the mire, he crawls on his face, as hunger and thirst torment him with their endless plague. Yet indentured to his immortal gift, the absolution of death does not come.

What is this absence in which I lie?

Here, beyond man's paragon of time; is this what I am to be? Absent of perception. Doomed. A wandering star, adrift in eternal darkness.

His heart leaps as the ground beneath him gives way, and flailing with the crumbling earth, he tumbles further into the void.

Motionless again, both awake and asleep, the agony of despair returns.

Cursing his affliction, bone heals and flesh forms like new as he cries in fevered misery. And as the earth hears his call and answers with a mighty tremor, rock and stone rains from above.

Crushed under its weight, he's trapped. Held in rigid stasis in a stillness he has never known. A living statue in a torture of no end. Every fiber and sinew of his being screams as he begs for change. But when at last it comes, the sound of rushing water brings a new tomb of dread. Sound turning to sensation he screams as he's slowly submerged, and as sensation turns to horror, his lungs fill with icy blackness.

Yet, he is not forsaken.

Lost to death in the cold caverns of the eternal void, a rumble stirs him from his timeless torment. A violent lurch, he's moving, carried by a sudden surge.

He floats. Drifting between wake and sleep. But in that place of silence, his grief is not unheard. In the oozing bile of the planet's bowels the waters still as his chest rises in celebration. A breath of life.

With a reflexive spasm of victory, air rushes in.

'Will.'

A whisper in the silence as a fleeting bubble rises from its tomb.

'Will.'

A softly spoken call as a rhythmic trickle dances down a rock.

"Will."

At first, it is just a flicker. So small he is hardly sure it is there at all.

But there, again. Just a speck. So beautiful. Light. Brighter and more vivid than he has ever remembered. And then a sound. A song. As, hope rising in his heart, the joyful melody of a desert sparrow sings its thanks for a new day. His arms and legs thrashing, he stands to his feet. Louder still it calls, beckoning towards the blinding radiance.

Walking, running now, he gulps a sweet breath of fresh air that drifts in through the hollow. Then heat, and blinding light as he stumbles from the mouth of a black stone cave.

And as he stands in the babbling waters of a glistening stream,
he falls to his knees, cradled by the warmth of the rising sun.

THE END